THE QUEEN AND THE GYPSY

By Constance Heaven

Constance Heaven

The Queen
and the Gypsy

Coward, McCann & Geoghegan, Inc. New York

First American Edition 1977

SBN: 698-10794-2

Library of Congress Cataloging in Publication Data

Heaven, Constance.
   The queen and the gypsy.

   1. Dudley, Amy Robsart, Lady, 1532?-1560—Fiction. 2. Leicester, Robert Dudley, Earl of, 1532?-
1588—Fiction. 3. Elizabeth, Queen of England,
1533-1603—Fiction. I. Title.
PZ4.H4418Qe3   [PR6058.E23]   823'.9'14
                                    76-44004

Printed in the United States of America

'Beware of the gypsy. He will be too hard for you all;
you know not the beast so well as I do.'

> Dying words of Thomas Ratcliffe, Earl of Sussex,
> concerning Robert Dudley

The Queen and the Gypsy

Kew, Monday evening, 9 September 1560

It was several hours since the news of his wife's death had reached him and it still seemed unbelievable, it still had power to shock. How many times over the last two years had he had cause to wish her dead, had even sometimes hoped for it and then thrust the thought away, loathing himself for it. But now it had happened. They had found her lying at the foot of a flight of stairs, her head a little twisted to one side, her neck broken, still and quiet with her skirts spread out around her, the hood on the bright hair undisturbed . . . accident? Suicide? Murder? Which?

For months scandalous rumours had been rife about him . . . on New Year's Night he had slept with his new love, she was with child by him, he was planning to rid himself of his wife, to divorce her, poison her . . . no punishment, however savage, had stopped the lies flying from mouth to mouth. And now she was dead, every finger would be pointed at him from the highest to the lowest. Was ever a man caught up in such a cruel web of circumstances? He was too much in the public eye. Whatever step he took, whatever move he made, could have a sinister interpretation. His wife dead might prove a far more effective obstacle to his love and his ambition than ever she had been alive, and yet he was innocent. That was the damnable part of it! Absolutely innocent. He had never lifted a finger to harm her, and even tried impatiently, clumsily, irritably, to show concern for her . . . If idle thoughts, if deep buried desires, never expressed, proved a man guilty, then we should all be condemned a dozen times a day!

He tried to steady himself. He looked down at a letter he had begun to write . . . 'Methinks I am here all the while as it were in a dream . . .'

That was true enough. It *was* like a dream, a hideous nightmare out of which there was no awakening. He shivered and then

1

pulled himself together. If he went on like this, he would work himself into a fever and that would help no one, least of all himself. He was behaving like a fool. It was this damned place. It was cold and damp, too near the river for comfort. Where the devil were the servants? He opened the door and shouted angrily, forgetting that when he had ridden in a few hours before, guards in front and behind, the blank astonished faces staring up at him had so enraged him that he had strode through them and up the stairs, slamming the door against them.

They had been waiting outside in the passage, afraid to knock, and now they came running, still half scared. Their lord was usually of so sweet and even a temper that his rage and the rumours of his disgrace that had come with him, and grown in the telling, had filled them with alarm. Now they set to work in earnest, building the fire, lighting the candles, bringing sweet-scented linen for the great bed, spreading fur rugs on the bare floor. He stood at the window with his back to them, his fingers drumming on the small panes of the lattice, until his steward nervously plucked at his sleeve.

'I am sorry, my lord, to be so unprepared. We have done what we could, but we did not expect . . . we had no word of your coming . . .'

'I know, I know.' He was brusque. 'It is no matter. Bring me some food, whatever you have . . . and wine . . .'

'Yes, my lord, at once. It is already being prepared.'

He turned when they had gone. Already the room looked more welcoming, the logs beginning to blaze, the chill fled before the golden light of the candles. When the food came, he ate little but drank deep of the wine. That at least was good. He had sent several barrels here in the spring. It was barely a year since Elizabeth had given him this little manor of Kew, and he had been so occupied he had not yet had time to furnish it to his taste. They called it the Dairy House, and it was a pleasant enough place when it had been set to rights. He had liked the thought of it, set in gardens on the banks of the river and only a stone's throw from her favourite palace of Richmond.

'We can be alone there for an hour, or maybe two . . . I'll row you there myself.'

She had looked up at him with her unfathomable eyes that were sometimes green, sometimes golden.

'When is a Queen ever allowed to be alone, Robin?'

'Whenever she chooses if that Queen is you,' he had murmured, kissing her, lip against lip, his blood leaping to meet hers.

But now it was finished. Christ, it couldn't be! If he lost her now, he'd run mad. He poured more wine and swallowed it quickly, his nerves taut as lute-strings. God damn the bitch! Why did she have to die now of all times . . . and in such a way . . . instead of decently in a bed, of a sickness that no one could question, so that no one could whisper that foul word, murder.

He got up and began to pace up and down the room, trying to think clearly. Why had Elizabeth acted so savagely? What else could he have done? Where had he gone wrong?

The message had come in the morning, shortly after noon. They had just come in from riding in Windsor Park, Elizabeth in the highest of spirits. The new geldings he had ordered from Ireland had more than fulfilled their promise. How she adored to ride fast, and how he loved to find better and better horses for her. They had far outdistanced their retinue and she laughed with pleasure as he lifted her from Grey Sparrow's saddle, letting his lips brush against hers. She slapped his cheek lightly with her embroidered glove and they went into the hall of the castle side by side, his hand protectively at her elbow, his enemies biting their lips at his easy familiarity.

Then that fool Bowes had to come stumbling into the royal presence. Where the hell were the servants to permit him to come through, white with dust from hard riding, sweating and breathless, crying out in a voice for everyone to hear, 'My lord, my lord, it is your lady wife . . .'

He had seen the look on her face before, somehow, he had got the fellow away to his own apartments and he had come stammering out with his story.

'Your lady . . . she is dead, my lord.'

'Dead? How?' His heart had leaped and then gone cold with fear. She had been sick, he knew that, sick for more than a year and very frightened, but nowhere near death.

'Is it murder?' God knows why the words had burst out from him. It was as if all the lies that others had spread had somehow clung to him too. He had seen the shocked surprise on Bowes' plain stolid face.

'My lord, I pray to God there is no question of foul play.'

3

'No, no, of course not. I'm so distracted I scarce know what I am saying.'

Then Bowes had told what he knew. How she had sent the servants to the fair at Abingdon so that she was alone except for her maid and a lady who lived in another wing of the great house at Cumnor.

'Yes, yes, I know,' he said impatiently. 'She is a sister of Mr Hyde and very close to my wife.'

'It was she who found her, my lord, she and Jennet . . . the serving girl was near out of her head with grief. She always loved your lady well . . .'

Jennet Pinto – who had been with Amy from the first and who had never liked him. What would she be saying? Concocting some tale no doubt of how when he was last with her, his wife had broken into weeping, falling on her knees, beseeching him to stay, until at last he had been forced to be brusque, knowing well Elizabeth's impatience if he delayed even a second beyond what was expected . . . Pray God someone had stopped the girl's mouth before she said anything damaging!

His thoughts had scattered all over the place. What best to do? Tom Blount had gone off to Cumnor on the day before, on Sunday at noon, carrying an answer to her letters. She had written twice in the last fortnight imploring him to go to her. He tried to remember the last scrawled note, so stained and blotted with tears that he could scarcely read it. Something about being frightened, something about her sickness. He had spoken to Dr Julio, who said the malady from which she suffered often made women hysterical. He had scribbled a reply saying she must not worry, he would come soon, and placating his conscience with gifts, a jewelled necklet, a roll of rich velvet; she always loved pretty things. Now he wondered . . . had there been desperation in that frantic note, real terror, real despair? Had it driven her to suicide? He cursed himself for tossing it carelessly into the fire, but how could he possibly know? Who would have thought such a thing could happen?

He gathered his wits together and penned a letter to Blount who must be at Cumnor by now, the quill racing over the paper, writing carelessly in his haste: 'Because I have no way to purge myself of the malicious talk, I pray you that you will use all the devises and means that you can possible for the learning of the truth . . .' He sent off the messenger, riding for his life with scarce time for food or rest. Another courier went to John Appleyard in Norfolk. That damned rogue, half brother to Amy, would make mischief if he could, he was sure of that. Invent some lying tale and then come whining to him, begging for money as usual. God knows how many times he'd got him out of debt already.

There still remained the most important thing of all. In his distraction he had left it too long already. He had to see Elizabeth, and quickly, before they reached her with their lies, blackening him before he had a chance to plead his cause. His apartments at Windsor were on the same floor as hers, but there was no communicating door. He had to go down the stairs and through the presence chamber. They were all there . . . friends, acquaintances, enemies: William Cecil's square plain face was grave, pitying; Norfolk, with his sheep-like look, flaunting his damned blue blood with conscious superiority; Rutland, Northampton, Mary, his sister, looking upset, she had always been fond of Amy. He felt their eyes following him, boring into him. How they hated him, Lord Robert Dudley, the upstart, son and grandson of executed traitors, whose looks and charm and ability had carried him straight into the heart of their Queen. How they envied him and how they would rejoice to see him in the dock, a man who had murdered his wife in the hope of marrying a woman who could make him king and his children princes. He strode through them with grace and elegance, arrogant head high. He was at the door of the privy chamber before Sussex stopped him, Thomas Ratcliffe, Earl of Sussex, who had long been his most bitter enemy.

'I think not, my lord. Her Grace is resting.'

He had never been denied before, never. He threw off Sussex's restraining hand.

'Let me pass.'

Then Mary was beside him, tears in her eyes, pleading with him. 'Robin, you should not, really you should not, not now . . .'

He was ready to hurl them all out of his path, but the door opened and she was there, her face white against the red of her hair, her eyes green and cold as Polar ice.

'I wonder at your effrontery, my lord, in daring to appear before us with your wife lying dead.'

The shock was so intense, it robbed him temporarily of speech.

5

He fell on his knees.

'Not by my hand, never by my hand.'

'There are more ways than one of ridding oneself of a burden,' her words hit him like the cruel lash of a whip.

He stretched out imploring hands. 'Listen to me, you must listen to me . . .'

'No, no,' she drew back, 'I have listened to you too long. Go, go now and quickly.' She raised her hand in command. 'Tom, see to it.'

In his madness he would have gone after her, but the door slammed in his face. It was Sussex, hateful Sussex, who helped him to his feet.

'You are commanded to your manor at Kew, my lord. There to await Her Grace's pleasure.'

He did not know what he had expected, the Tower perhaps. Maybe it was a sign of her affection that it was to his own manor at Kew. He had left at once with his escort, scarcely pausing for baggage to be packed, anger, grief, desperation surging inside him.

Why had she turned her back on him? Why now of all times, when he had such desperate need of her support? Without her he was nothing. He lived precariously by her whim, and sometimes it galled him or left him cold with fear. For two years she had tormented him, swaying this way and that, but since the summer he had been sure that she loved him; ever since August when they had been at Rycote on their way back from Oxford, alone, or almost alone, with only her waiting women and Sir Henry Norris and his wife, discreet hosts in the background. It was soon after they had returned to London that Dr Julio came with his report. The doctor had looked grave, pursing his lips, guarding his words, and they had looked at one another, he and Elizabeth, hardly daring to hope. God forgive them both for the unspoken wish. Can such a thing bring a person to death? Surely not. Only fools would believe such nonsense.

He brooded over it, staring into the fire, and the great lemon-coloured dog, which had been watching him from soft, brown eyes, lumbered over to lay a heavy head on his knee, thrusting a cold nose under the long fingers. He fondled the dark ears abstractedly. Cabal was a mastiff of the old Lyme breed and had been sent as a gift from the Legh kennels. From the first he had shown his preference openly, until Elizabeth had said laughing, 'He doesn't like petticoat rule. He is your subject, not mine. You had better take him, Robin.' They had named him Cabal, remembering from their childhood the ancient ballads of Arthur and his hunting dog that Blanche Parry used to sing to them in her soft lilting Welsh voice.

He roused himself. It was time to give up this fruitless brooding. He got up, stretching to his full height, long of leg, strongly built but slender still, though he was in his twenty-seventh year. He tugged impatiently at the emerald buttons on his close-fitting doublet and threw it aside. The room had grown warmer now, almost too warm on this early September night. He felt suddenly stifled. He crossed to the window and thrust the casement wide open. It was dark already and it had begun to rain; the soft air blew in, scented with late-flowering stock. The garden was overgrown, the hedges ragged. He would have to attend to it if he remained at Kew and was not banished for ever from the Court. He leaned against the window frame, breathing deep and feeling the drops on his face, cool and refreshing. Then he stiffened.

Below him someone was singing; low but clear in the silence of the night the sound stole up to him.

'The wind doth blow to-day, my love,
And a few small drops of rain;
I never had but one true love,
In cold grave she was lain.'

No, not that song, not those words! Was someone taunting him deliberately? Anger started up in him. He leaned from the window. He'd have him punished, he'd have the singer whipped for insolence . . .

'I'll do as much for my true-love
As any young man may;
I'll sit and mourn all at her grave
For a twelvemonth and a day.'

The song trailed away. There was a stir on the path, a murmur of voices, a smothered giggle, and he saw two dark figures come together and melt into one. His anger died. God curse all lovers

7

in their happiness! He slammed the window shut and leaned his forehead against the glass. All day he had not thought of his wife. He had been too much concerned with himself, with the danger in which he stood, with the frustrating, tormenting love that consumed him. Now, without any wish on his part, memories crowded in. How many times had he heard Amy sing that melancholy little ballad and had teased her about it, a song fit only for country pleasures, for bride ales and harvest suppers? Now it was as if her ghost were standing outside the window, the raindrops like softly tapping fingers, a pale frail ghost with bright hair begging him to remember. It was eleven years almost to the day when he had seen Amy first. Damn it, why did he have to think of it now? He would not let it torment him. It was over and finished with long ago.

He took up the velvet gown laid ready for him on the bed and huddled himself into it. He trimmed the candles and tossed more logs on the fire. They crackled and spat while he hunted for books and could find none. In his haste he had brought little baggage and he had no library here. Why the devil hadn't he thought to bring something with him? Now it would have to wait until he could send one of the servants to London.

He threw himself on the bed, but sleep was miles away. He was not a superstitious man. He did not believe in ghosts. Even the bleeding, headless bodies of his father and his brother had no power to haunt him after the first shock and grief were over. But now it was as if his wife lay curled up beside him like a soft brown-haired kitten, like the squirrel that was once his pet name for her, looking at him with fever-bright eyes, thin, hot fingers clutching at him, begging him to listen to her just this once . . .

I'll do as much for my true love
As any young man may . . .

Oh God! He moved restlessly and buried his face in the pillows, but the night hours stretched relentlessly and with them came the memories. He groaned and turned over, staring at the painted ceiling while the candles guttered, making strange shadows dance on the walls, and the voice went on whispering.

'You loved me once, Robert, we were so happy . . .'

That was true enough. He had been sixteen when he saw her

8

first, a boy hungry for love, dreaming of a golden future.

'When you were so often apart from me, I had so little . . .'

Hell and damnation! Did he have to remember her tears, her reproaches.

'It was raining that night too, soft September rain, when you came to my father's house, and I did not dream – how should I – that my death came to me that night in the lovely guise of love . . .'

Part One
1549-1553

'A marriage of desire begins in pleasure
and ends in sorrow.'

Sir William Cecil

One

Amy heard the cavalcade come thundering across the draw-bridge while she was sitting beside her mother's bed. She gave the grey, pinched face on the pillow a quick impatient glance and hurried to the window, pushing the casement wide and leaning out to watch the horsemen come clattering and splashing into the courtyard.

It had been raining heavily during the day, but now in the early evening a golden September sun had broken through the clouds. It struck a fiery gleam from the burnished steel corselets of the soldiers and touched to glory the jewelled caps, the gold-embroidered cloaks and glittering caparisons of the three splendid figures who rode ahead of the little troop.

Excitement went racing and tingling up her spine. She leaned out further, ignoring the shower of raindrops that sprinkled the bright brown hair with liquid diamonds. It was not often that the small moated manor of Stanfield had welcomed such illustrious visitors, and everyone in the house down to the smallest scullery boy had crowded to doors and windows to watch their arrival.

'Come away from there, child,' said the weary voice from the bed. 'Have you no sense of what is fitting? Do you want my lord of Warwick to see you gaping from the casement like some idle slut of a serving girl?'

Amy drew back a little, but she did not move away. Her fas-cinated eyes were watching the tall, dark-haired man swing him-self from his magnificent black horse and move gracefully to greet her father, who had come hurrying down the steps. Sir John Robsart of Syderstone, High Sheriff of Norfolk and Suffolk, for all his considerable lands and wealth, was no more than an obscure country squire beside John Dudley, Earl of Warwick, Lieutenant-General of the armed forces and high in favour with the twelve-year-old King Edward, who only two years ago had ridden to his crowning at Westminster Abbey.

'Did you hear what I said, Amy, or are you dreaming as usual?' urged the querulous voice behind her. 'I asked if your father was there, and your brother John. Is he wearing his new doublet, the one I stitched with gold thread?'

That was so like mother, always so concerned with her son, always pushing forward the children from her first marriage. Amy felt a sharp stab of resentment. It was she who should have been down there beside her father, not John Appleyard. Was she not her father's only true-born child and an heiress in her own right? Ever since she could remember there had been talk of her marriage, but Sir John had been indulgent. She had been born late in his life and for sixteen years she had been his darling.

'You shall choose where you like, my pet,' he had told her one day, fondling the bright hair when she sat close beside him after supper.

'And where do you think that will lead her?' asked her mother tartly. 'You'll have her picking on a ploughboy like as not.'

'Fie, wife, Amy's no fool, are you, my jewel, and I'm not anxious to lose you.'

She had turned up her pretty nose at all her suitors except for young Ned Flowerdew, son of their neighbour at Hethersett. He had been caught kissing her in the dairy when she was churning butter last summer, and had his ears boxed by her mother for his pains. Not that she really cared a rush for him, but she simply had to prove to herself that she could charm any young man if she put her mind to it.

'Are you sure everything is in good trim for supper?' went on her mother fretfully. 'Are the river trout fresh and the capons plump and tender? It's important for your father that he should stand well with Lord Warwick, and the good God only knows what they are doing down in the kitchens with me lying sick up here and unable to do a hand's turn. The meat could be burned to a cinder for all you'd care. You're as good as useless, Amy. What you will do when you have a home of your own, I don't like to think. Your servants will cheat you right and left.'

This was the old familiar chiding and she did not even listen. She had no intention of being like her mother. All she ever thought of was overseeing the dairy, darning the linen, watching over the ale brew as if it were the rarest of wines. How she hated it all, how she longed to escape from it.

14

I shall marry someone who will take me to Court, she had vowed to herself. There will be dancing, music and gaiety, with dresses of taffeta and wrought velvet and French satin shot with silver . . . on and on ran her thoughts in one of the glittering fantasies of her frequent day dreams until, suddenly, her eye had been caught by the two young men who had just dismounted and were following the Earl into the house.

The elder was Lord Ambrose, that she knew. He was the Earl's second son and already betrothed, but the other . . . At that moment he turned and looked up, directly at her it seemed. Involuntarily she drew back, afraid lest he should see her, and then she stood transfixed, unable to move, her heart in her mouth, a strange sensation running through her, frightening, like a sickness, like a fever which comes from you know not where and races all through your veins.

He was tall like his father and brother and moved with an easy grace. He stood for a moment, his hand on his sword hilt, his long scarlet riding cloak trailing carelessly in the slush of the courtyard, his black cap with its white plume at a jaunty angle on the thick curling hair, but it was his face that held her. The brilliant evening light showed her plainly the clear olive skin, the delicate arched brows, the short arrogant nose, the beautiful curling mouth. This must be Lord Robert. She stared and stared with a feeling of despair. He was the handsomest young man she had ever seen and he would never notice her, never even see her. Anguish cramped her heart. Last night, at supper, her father quite unaccountably had said, 'It is best you stay with your mother, daughter. Lord Warwick is only resting here for one night before he returns to London. With a company of soldiers in the house and your mother so sick, it is not fit for you to be seen. Stay close unless I send for you.'

She had pouted and begged and even tried the effect of tears, but Sir John had been firm and went on shaking his white head.

They treat me like a child and I'm not, she raged to herself. Other girls at my age are already married, and it's so dull here, so deadly dull. How can I ever meet anyone? Father never goes to Court, has never set foot outside Norfolk these ten years, and as for the Appleyards, she thought despairingly, they are even worse. All her half-sister Frances ever talked of was her husband, her babies and the everlasting dreary round of household duties.

It had been hard to swallow her bitter disappointment, and it had not been helped by her half-brother's malicious teasing.

'Don't think you can go setting your cap at a Dudley, sister. They're proud as Lucifer, the whole bunch of them. Lord Warwick looks for girls of better blood than yours to mate with his cubs.'

She had bridled and flung away from him. He had always resented her father's affection for her.

John Appleyard liked to pretend indifference, sneering at the Dudleys as vulgar upstarts, but how eagerly he had pressed forward just now, anything to win a word from the great Earl of Warwick. 'He's a toad,' she said to herself angrily, ' a sly, crafty, self-seeking toad!'

The Earl and his two sons had gone into the house by now and the bright glory of the evening seemed to have gone with them. Reluctantly she turned back into the room, gathering up the skeins of embroidery silk scattered in her haste. Her heart smote her because her mother looked so grievously sick. There was so little they could do to ease her. Pain and fever were burning her up. She took up a linen towel to wipe the sweat tenderly from her face and the hot hand, thin as a skeleton, closed round her wrist.

'I cannot rest easy not knowing what's going on downstairs. Run down to the kitchens, Amy, to make sure all is well. Don't stay too long, mind. No doubt the soldiers will be there and my lord's body servants. Tell cook to keep an eye on the maids, or we shall be having a fine crop of lyings-in next summer, and something else . . .' the hoarse voice halted her as she reached the door. 'Take care, child, you can be too free with strangers and my lord's sons are over young. Keep yourself away from them . . . haven't I told you often enough?'

All that fuss because of Ned Flowerdew . . . and he was no stranger. He might have been a brother, she had known him so long.

Glad to escape from the hot close smell of the sickroom even if only for a few minutes, Amy went down by way of the main staircase and into the great hall. To her disappointment, only the servants were there; putting up the trestle tables, setting out the giant salt cellar, the silver jugs, the fine drinking cups, all the treasures of the house only used on special occasions. The guests

16

must be closeted with her father in the summer parlour and she could think of no excuse for breaking in on them.

Lord Warwick had brought only a small company with him but all the same the kitchens seemed crowded with large men, unstrapping corselets and laying aside helmets, laughing, jesting, boasting, enjoying the gaping admiration of the serving girls. The talk ceased abruptly as she pushed open the door. She walked past them with a careful dignity, making a great pretence of examining the baking trays, the steaming cooking pots, chiding the maids for neglecting their work and ignoring their sly grins. Disdainfully she tasted the apple custard and defiantly pronounced it too sweet. She heard the derisive laughter as she closed the door behind her.

Back in her mother's room restlessness grew inside her so that it was hard to remain still. She fed her mother with the posset of curds and eggs beaten into goat's milk which the physician had recommended. Then there was the draught of hops distilled with camomile flowers to warm by the fire. But the room had grown shadowy before the herbs took effect. The sick woman at last drowsed into sleep and she was free to follow the plan which had been slowly maturing in her mind.

First of all she must find Jennet. She came upon her carrying extra goosedown bolsters into the room prepared for the guests' sleeping, and she told the maid to stay close beside her mother's bed in case she should wake and call for her.

'But what are you going to do, mistress?' the girl asked pertly.

'Never you mind.' Amy put her fingers on her lips, brown eyes sparkling. Jennet Pinto was the same age as her young mistress. They had shared already many a hidden confidence. Amy whispered in the girl's ear and they giggled together before she climbed the steep stair to her bedroom.

Tussie came tumbling out of his basket, eager for a walk after being shut up all day, but for once she had no time to spare for the little spaniel. She had flung open her clothes press. What could she wear? She had nothing fit to be seen. Lord Robert, they said, had been brought up at Court. He had shared the young King's lessons and princesses had been his playfellows. How could she possibly compete with them? Then some innate knowledge, some feminine intuition came to her aid.

She chose her simplest summer gown, a thin green silk with a

17

cream petticoat embroidered with tiny rosebuds. She shook out her bright brown hair from under the close cap, brushing it until it fell into shining ringlets on her shoulders. The gold net hid none of its beauty. She kissed Tussie, put him back in his basket, took up her lute with its bright scarlet ribbons and stole down the stairs, along the corridor and into the narrow passage of the tiny musician's gallery which overlooked the great hall.

Torches flared in the wall sconces and fine wax candles burned on the high table. My lord of Warwick leaned back in her father's great carved chair. She looked at him curiously. His proud pale face had a look of fatigue, but his voice, low, musical, cultured, was not at all what she had expected from so famous a soldier. He was speaking of the rebellion he had just crushed so triumphantly and so bloodily at Norwich.

'Robert Kett and his brother William will go in chains to London and in some ways I am sorry for it. They are men of ability, both of them, but they have led simple folk astray. Let them go free and we shall have all England clamouring for what it calls its rights.'

'They would have burned the roof over our heads if they had their will,' put in her father indignantly.

That was what everyone had said when the rioting began. She remembered the brothers Kett. When she rode through Wymondham on her pony, they would wave and call greetings to her. Robert owned a tannery and once, when she was still a child, he had made a crimson leather collar for her pet greyhound all hung with silver bells.

There had been arguments about lands, all mixed up with the new religion that was so confusing. There were disputes she did not understand. Her father had enclosed some of the common fields for his sheep and cows instead of letting the ground go to waste – and surely there was nothing wrong in that; but there had been fierce outcry against it. Men had stood up on the green, shouting that the villagers were being deprived of the grazing that had been their privilege since time began. Protest had turned into open rebellion and then into an army carrying ploughshares and billhooks, encamping itself on Mousehold Heath outside Norwich, tearing up palings, setting fire to ricks and holding up gentlemen for ransom. It could not be allowed to go on, all East Anglia would have been in flames. Now those two men who had been kind to her were like to be hanged for it.

'If the Privy Council heed my advice,' the Earl was saying, 'it is only the ringleaders who will be punished. Take away the head and the body will perish, and there has been enough bloodshed already. As I said to his late Majesty after we beat the Scots at Pinkie, it does not become the royal honour to make war on dead bodies, on widows and babes in arms. Besides,' he went on, his smile cynical, 'besides what are we to do, you and I, Sir John, without our tenant farmers and hired labourers? Are we to take the plough into our own hands and till the fields ourselves?'

But Amy was not listening any longer. Her eyes had strayed to Lord Ambrose who was peeling an apple, his square pleasant face intent on his father's words; but Robert sat carelessly on his stool, long legs stretched out, one fine brown hand idly pulling at the ears of one of her father's dogs. He had tossed aside his cap. The flaring candle flame lit copper gleams in the rich dark hair that fell across his forehead. His doublet of green velvet was slashed with gold.

She felt again that strange numbing sensation almost like a pain deep inside her. She picked up her lute, summoned all her courage, plucked at the strings a little uncertainly, and then began to sing, the small voice clear and sweet as a silver bell.

Robert Dudley was in one of his rare moods of pure content. The last few weeks had been momentous. He had thrilled to be riding beside his father in his first campaign. Even the Earl, who so rarely praised, had clapped him on the shoulder and told him he had acquitted himself admirably. That was something at nearly seventeen with two elder brothers who usually stole all the thunder. Not that he was on bad terms with Ambrose or Jack. The Dudleys were a closely united family.

It was true that the rebel army had not stood much chance against the trained German mercenaries, but there had been danger all the same. The Earl of Northampton had been scared out of his five wits until Warwick had come to the rescue and taken over command. And how brilliantly his father had acted. At the worst moment, with powder and shot almost run out and the soldiers whispering of retreat, he had called his young captains together, refusing to accept defeat, having them swear allegiance in true knightly fashion, kissing the cross of each other's swords, and then himself leading the cavalry charge that had broken the rebel army. After the fighting was done he had ridden alone into the enemy camp, chivalrously risking his life to offer pardon and restrain his fierce foreign soldiers from pillage and rape. Robert had an intense uncritical admiration for his brilliant father.

He looked around the dark panelled hall with a faint good-natured contempt. Compared with the royal palaces, or even with his father's fine house in Holborn, it was a humble place; and yet the Flemish tapestry that glowed on one wall must have cost a fortune. The food was good too and the wine even better. Not that Robert ever ate or drank too much. Young though he was, he had too much pride in his slim athletic figure and he had inherited a great deal of his father's high-strung fastidious taste. Not like Ambrose, who cheerfully stuffed himself to bursting and never put on an ounce of extra weight. Robert grinned at his brother who had now started on a pear and lazily reached out for his wine cup.

The music took him by surprise. For a moment he could not imagine where it had sprung from. It hung in the air, disembodied, not very expert and yet unexpectedly enchanting. His eyes roamed round the hall before they caught a glimpse of green, a flash of bright hair, someone moving behind the fretted screen. A girl . . . could it be? But who? And why had she not appeared at the supper table?

> 'Tomorrow shall be my dancing day,
> I would my true love did so chance
> To see the legend of my play
> To call my true love to my dance . . .'

It was an old carol and he wondered where on earth she had learned it in this remote country place.

> 'I shall dance in the morning when the world has begun
> And dance in the moon and the stars and the sun
> Sing, O my love, O my love, my only love,
> This have I done for my true love.'

The last note died away and there was a moment's silence before Warwick broke it.

'Charming, quite charming. Who is your nightingale, Sir John? One of your pages?'

'My daughter, my lord.' For some reason their host looked put out. 'You will wonder that I have not presented her to you, but my wife is sick and Amy has been tending her.'

The Earl smiled graciously. 'I am sorry for Lady Robsart's illness but so pretty a song deserves our grateful thanks. Won't you call your daughter down to us for a moment?'

Half elated, half scared at the success of her stratagem, Amy obeyed her father's reluctant gesture and came slowly down into the hall, avoiding John Appleyard's sly smile from where he lounged in the background.

With the charm that he knew so well how to exercise, Warwick rose to take her hand as she sank into a curtsey. Dazzled, she heard his graceful compliments on her singing.

'Though indeed I am but a soldier, Mistress Amy. For real appreciation you must talk with Robin here. He is the musician amongst my sons.'

She had succeeded beyond her wildest dreams. Lord Robert was bending over her hand. How tall he was. When he straightened himself, she scarcely reached his shoulder. He was murmuring something, and she was suddenly so shy she could hardly raise her head to meet those dark eyes looking down at her with a glow of admiration and interest . . . or was it? Passionately she wished she could be sure.

'You sing so sweetly,' he was saying, 'an angel sure, I thought, or a captured bird.'

She is exquisite, he was thinking, fresh as a garden rose and deliciously piquant with her tip-tilted nose and the tiny mole beside the tender mouth. Quite suddenly he desperately wanted to kiss it.

'I think you mock me, my lord. There are many birds, the rook, the crow, the jay, who sing sadly out of tune.'

Their eyes met and the words they spoke meant nothing beside the touch of hands. The same intoxicating wonder suffused them both.

'I think you know well what I mean. Where did you learn so rare a song?'

'My music master taught it to me.'

He still held her hand. He drew her to the stool from which he had risen and, as she sat down, his father broke in on them.

'Sing us something, Robin. What was it you and Mary were studying so hard all last winter?'

There was a note of command in the Earl's voice but Robert hesitated. His eyes questioned her.

'Shall I?'

Breathlessly she nodded and he took the lute from her, plucked the strings with an expert hand and then began to sing softly, for her ears alone it seemed.

> 'Take thou this rose, O rose,
> Since love's own flower it is,
> And by that rose
> Thy lover captive is.'

'How beautiful that is.'

'It's an old French song and Edward's musician set it to a new tune for us. They say Abelard wrote it centuries ago for his beloved Heloise.'

She knew no French and had never heard of the doomed lovers and their tragic story, but everything about Robert fascinated her. Beside her half-brother, beside the clumsy young sons of their country neighbours, he seemed like a being from another world, so elegant, graceful and accomplished.

'Do you often see the King?' she asked.

'Oh yes,' his answer was careless. 'Sometimes every day when we are at Court. This past year my father has been teaching him to ride and handle weapons. We have nought but tilts and jousts and tournaments.'

'And does the King win?'

'Only if I let him. He tries hard, but Edward is a bookish boy.'

He grinned with all the confidence of his newly discovered manhood and she smiled up at him. Her eyes are the clear brown of forest pools, he thought wonderingly. They are filled with light like Babette, my bitch, when she begs me to caress her. He wanted to take her into his arms, to fondle the bright hair, red-brown as a squirrel, and kiss the half-opened mouth.

He bent down to whisper into her ear. 'You are lovely, did

you know that? Lovely as your name. Do you know what it means . . . Aimée . . . beloved?'

He saw the carnation blood race up into her cheeks as he pressed her hand.

'You are too bold, my lord. You should not say such things to me.' But she let her hand lie in his and he could smell the sweet scent of the herbs with which she washed her hair.

Warwick had risen to his feet. He said, 'If you will pardon me, Sir John, I think we should get to our beds. We have a long day's ride before us tomorrow. We must make an early start.'

In all the bustle of servants bringing torches and lighting candles, there was no opportunity for more than a touch on the hand, a whispered goodnight. She had a courteous word from the Earl as she lighted him to the guest chamber.

Then she was free to run up the stairs, to stand for a moment outside her mother's door, pressing cool fingers to hot cheeks, heart beating, not sure of herself or of him. It was several minutes before she could smooth down her gown and go in quietly, demurely, as if nothing had happened, as if a pulsating excitement did not still go racing along her veins.

In the room he shared with Ambrose, Robert blew out the candles and crossed to the window, thrusting it wide open. The night air, sweet-scented with the rose that clambered up the wall, flowed all round him. The moonlight silvered the lithe naked body.

He looks like the young Apollo, thought Ambrose a little enviously as he lounged on the bed. His young brother was growing up. From the great age of twenty-one he viewed Robert with amusement. A week ago the boy had blooded his sword for the first time. Now it seemed he was waking up to the fascination of women. Well, it had taken long enough.

'No point in making sheep's eyes out of the casement, Robin. Mistress Robsart is safe in bed, and anyway she is not for you.'

The arrogant young face gave him a swift sideways glance. 'Why not, if I choose?'

'Why not? Don't be an ass, boy. Father would laugh his head off at the very idea!'

'Why should he? He has never been much concerned with me.'

'By God!' Ambrose sat bolt upright. 'You're not really serious. You couldn't be giving a second thought to that little nobody with no more brains than a pigeon.'

'How do you know? You didn't even speak with her.'

'I didn't need to.'

'And why should Father object anyway? Old John Robsart is rich enough.'

'You cynical young bastard!'

'Isn't that how his mind works? He's said so often enough.' The young voice held a note of rebellion.

For the first time it struck Ambrose how like Robin was to the father they both loved and feared. He was the very image of the portrait that hung in the hall of Ely Place, painted when John Dudley was nineteen and had won his first favour with old King Henry and married his guardian's daughter. Robin had the same devastating charm, the same silken sweetness of voice and manner, and the same sudden explosive rages when things did not go his way. Good-natured and easy-going, Ambrose had always been tolerant of his little brother's moody bursts of temper.

Robert yawned and came to sit on the edge of the bed. 'Ah well, marriage is for fools, not for me.'

'That's better.' Ambrose lay back with a certain relief. 'I thought for a moment you'd caught the infection.'

'She's pretty enough though, that you must admit.'

'Commonplace,' said Ambrose flatly.

'She might be rewarding in bed,' Robert's voice was dreamy.

'And what do you know about it?' mocked his brother genially. 'Don't try any tricks with her, Robin. Tumble a serving wench if you feel the need, not one of these rustic beauties. That half-brother of hers has the look of a damned rascal. I'd not care to tangle with him.'

Robert said nothing, but long after Ambrose was sleeping he lay awake. Not for a moment would he have revealed his true feelings. It had always amused Ambrose and Jack to tease him because he showed no interest in their amorous adventures. Even Guildford, who was a year younger, boasted of his successes though Robert was inclined to believe these no more than loud talk. But Mary would understand. Mary was in love with his friend Harry Sidney. He had always been close to his sister. They had all been inseparable when they were children, he, Mary and Harry . . . and Elizabeth.

He had not thought of Elizabeth for quite a time. He smiled, remembering their childhood lessons at Hampton Court under the guidance of Queen Katherine Parr when the old King was still alive. Elizabeth had been a spitfire even then. He and she had fought like cat and dog with Mary as peacemaker.

Suddenly Robert felt stifled. Lying within the narrow confines of the closely curtained bed was like being shut in a prison. He thrust aside the embroidered linen so that he could see the pale square of the window. All these last weeks he had been aware of an exciting feeling of freedom. He was poised on that step between boyhood and manhood with all the richness of life, all its infinite possibilities before him like an open book waiting to be read.

He had been strictly educated. Warwick was a careful father and, cultured himself, insisted on a high standard from all his children. He had given them the best teachers. Ambition had begun to stir, though as yet Robert hardly knew in what direction it might lead him, but Edward liked him and to have a king's favour meant everything.

Marriage would be yet another step to freedom from his father's authority, and why not choose Amy to share it with him? She had beauty and she was a considerable heiress – but there was more in it than that, far more. When his hand touched hers, it had felt like a river of fire running between them until her father and that ugly-faced half-brother of hers so obviously objected. It would be fun to outwit them, to show a Robsart that a Dudley was the equal if not the superior of any man.

'Aimée . . . beloved,' he murmured softly to himself in the darkness, and on that gentle note fell asleep.

The horses were saddled and the soldiers already mounted when the Earl of Warwick came down the steps with his two sons. It was still very early and a milky haze obscured the sun; it was going to be a lovely day, a day for flying a hawk or coursing a hare. Robert, sniffing the freshness of the air, wished he was riding into the forest or across the heath with his dogs at his heels and all round him the nutty autumn smell of beech mast and falling leaves. But his father never put pleasure before business: with the unrest throughout the country, and the slow march of the prisoners taken at Norwich going their painful way to London, it was very necessary to report his success personally to the Privy Council as soon as possible.

Amy had not appeared when they broke their fast on bread and meat, standing to eat in the great hall. Now the servants had come out with stirrup cups of hippocras. Robert waved away the silver goblet of hot spiced wine and swung himself into the saddle. His horse was fresh and he controlled it with difficulty. He circled the courtyard to Ambrose's laughter and, as he came up again beside them, caught a quick glimpse of bright hair at an upper window and a hand that waved and was quickly withdrawn, as if its owner feared to be too bold.

He mumbled something and leaped from his horse, throwing the reins to the astonished stable boy.

'What the devil has taken the lad?' exclaimed the Earl with exasperation. He had already bidden farewell to his host and was impatient to be gone. He was not a man who cared to be kept waiting.

'Forgotten his gloves,' murmured Ambrose and grinned. 'He might have thought of something more original,' and he leaned forward to take the gold-embroidered gauntlets from the stable boy who had picked them up from the flagstones as Robert dropped them in his haste.

'What's that?' His father looked at Ambrose and then followed his nod to the long window on the staircase where two figures could just be seen through the amber glass. He gave a short bark of laughter. 'So that's the way the wind lies. He could do worse. We'll ride on. He can come after us.'

As the cavalcade went clattering out of the courtyard, John Dudley dismissed his younger son from his thoughts. He had never set much store by Robin. There was Jack, his heir, and Ambrose, and Guildford, the beautiful gold-haired boy he loved above all and on whom his dearest hopes were pinned.

He was sincerely fond of his children but that had never prevented him from using them like counters to further the ravening ambition that had burned inside him for nearly forty years – ever since he had seen his father dragged to the Tower

26

and barbarously executed by Henry VIII simply for being too good a servant to his master.

Edmund Dudley had made himself the most hated man in England, and for what reason? He had been forced to bleed the country white with extortions and taxes to fill the first Tudor's empty money chests, and ignominious death had been his reward. It was a lesson seared into the sensitive mind of an eight-year-old boy too young to understand motives or to recognize that faults may lie on both sides. 'Put not your trust in princes' was scorched into his soul; learn to use them instead and discard them when you have sucked them dry.

John Dudley grew up, not in poverty, for his guardian, Lord Guildford, was a kindly man, but in the sour bitterness of a lost inheritance, a deprivation of all rank and privilege as the son of an executed traitor. He had clawed his way upward by sheer ability as seaman, soldier, statesman, and he had learned to deceive, to keep his thoughts to himself, winning battles for Henry and now for Edward, and holding his hand until the moment came to strike. And so subtle had he been that as yet there were few who guessed at the ruthless pursuit of power beneath the charming chivalrous manner that had captivated the admiration and affection of the young King, so that Edward was fast rebelling against the stern guardianship of his mother's brother.

'Edward Seymour, Duke of Somerset, Lord Protector!' thought Dudley to himself as he rode, contempt searing through him for the man who had once been his friend. But for his own swift action at Norwich, the whole of East Anglia would have been in flames by now. The Privy Council, that bunch of aristocratic blockheads, who sneered at the parvenu, the upstart, must be forced to realize in no uncertain terms that what England needed was a Dudley at its head.

While the Earl moved south, absorbed in ambitious dreams, the son he had dismissed so airily had gone bounding up the great staircase. He came up behind Amy on silent feet, putting two long slim hands over eyes. She gave a little cry as he turned her to face him.

'I looked for you earlier,' he said. 'I couldn't go without telling you I shall come back. That is,' and he hesitated, his youthful self confidence wavering a little before her steady gaze, 'that is, if it is your wish as it is mine.'

She did not answer because she could not, her breath seemed stopped in her throat.

'Do you wish it, Amy? Do you?'

'Oh yes,' it came out in a long sigh. 'Oh yes, yes, my lord.'

'Robin,' he corrected, 'between you and me, Robin and Aimée.'

And then he could not help himself. He took her hands and drew her towards him. He kissed the tiny bewitching mole and then found her lips. They were tender and yielding. For a second they clung together, swift young desire racing through them both. Then he broke away.

'I dare not stay longer. Father will be furious.'

Boyishly, clumsily, he pressed her hands to his mouth and then was gone, racing down the stairs two at a time.

She watched the tall figure from the window. He turned in the saddle to wave, and then spurred his horse to a gallop. The last glimpse she had of him was the flying crimson cloak and the flash of sun breaking through the clouds to catch the jewelled clasp in his cap. Then he was gone.

'You're a cunning little puss, aren't you? You flung your net and he tumbled right into it, a bigger fish than young Ned Flowerdew eh, my girl? Bring him safe to shore and you might benefit all of us.'

John Appleyard's insinuating voice close to her ear enraged and at the same time frightened her.

'What I do, I do to please myself, not you . . . or anyone,' she said fiercely, but his mocking laugh followed her as she escaped down the corridor.

Two

'Forward . . . back . . . take hands, twirl round, then curtsey. Gracefully now . . . you're not a goose laying an egg, you're a swan sinking to rest . . . Oh Lord, if only Jennet would keep better time, we might be able to step it out more elegantly. Now give me your hand, Amy, and we'll start all over again.'

Ned Flowerdew had spent his early youth as a page in a noble household and had been well instructed in all the graceful accomplishments of a young courtier. He was passing a very pleasurable afternoon teaching Amy one of the slow graceful dances which had been all the rage at Edward's Christmas Court last winter. He was an attractive fair-haired lad of nineteen and had known his pretty partner all her life. But it was only this summer, returning home after more than a year away, that he had realized with a sudden quickening of the heart that the child with whom he had run wild in the woods and who tore her long skirts clambering up trees after him when they went bird-nesting, the girl he had kissed in the dairy, had grown into a disturbingly lovely young woman, wilful, passionate and very desirable.

Jennet Pinto giggled, stuck her pert nose into the music book propped in front of her, and painstakingly began to strum out the melody on her mistress's virginals.

It was two months since Lady Robsart had died of the cruel cancer that had slowly consumed her for six long weary months, and after the funeral Sir John had returned to his own house at Syderstone since Stanfield Hall was John Appleyard's inheritance from his own father. Amy loved the great rambling inconvenient house with its warm red brick and mullioned windows where she had spent so many happy years of childhood. She mourned her mother sincerely but they had never been close. Elizabeth Robsart had always had far more in common with the daughters of her first marriage than with this unexpected last born and Sir John had always been far too dotingly fond of his little daughter, cossetting and spoiling her till there was nothing to be done with the child.

Amy would never have admitted such a shocking thing even in her most secret heart, but the truth was that the loss of her mother had given her a wonderful sense of freedom. There was no more scolding when she neglected her needlework, no more reproaches when she ran out into the park to play with Tussie instead of performing some dull household task. Father never noticed if there was dust on the polished oak, or if the servants neglected to sweep the scented rushes out of the hall each morning.

She should not have been here now. There was a great pile of goosedown waiting to be picked over and stuffed into pillows and cushions for the winter. Well, it could wait. She tossed up her head. This time she was following her partner's steps faultlessly, light and graceful as a bird, and when she sank into the final curtsey she looked up at him, her eyes sparkling.

'Did I do well, Ned?'

'Excellently well. The Lady Elizabeth herself could not have done better.'

'Now you're talking nonsense just to please me.'

Everyone knew that the Princess Elizabeth, daughter of that fascinatingly wicked Anne Boleyn who had streaked across their lives like a meteor when Amy was still a baby, was most exquisitely educated and danced like an angel. The thought raced across her mind that once upon a time, when they were children, Robert might have been her dancing partner. All the more reason why she must practise even harder.

'What else did you learn, Ned?'

'Well now, let me see. There's King Harry's jig, that's a tripping measure.'

He took one or two gay little steps and Amy, holding up her black velvet skirts to show slender ankles in the scarlet hose she should not have been wearing with her mourning, followed him gaily, kicking higher and ever higher while Jennet clapped her hands to a lively rhythm as they danced down the long gallery. They were enjoying themselves far too much to notice that a door had been flung open. A sharp voice cut across their laughter.

'So this is where you are, Amy. I've been calling you everywhere.' Frances, the elder of the two Appleyard girls had swept in, eyes flashing, outrage quivering in every line of her angular figure. 'Is this the way to behave, dancing, cutting capers with Mother scarce cold in her grave? Is this how you show your grief? And you too, Ned, you should be ashamed, both of you.'

They had stopped, hand in hand, abashed, like two scolded children. Amy was the first to recover her spirits.

'What harm are we doing?' she burst out. 'And don't put the blame on Ned. It was I who asked him to dance with me and why shouldn't we? Is it a crime?'

'How do you think Father would feel if he knew what was going on in a house of mourning? Have you no sense of what is fitting?'

'He needn't know unless *you* run and tell him.'

'How dare you speak to me like that? I would not give him so much pain.'

Oh, wouldn't you? thought Amy to herself unrepentantly. You would if you thought it might spite me. She only said, quietly, 'Father would understand.'

'You're an insolent ungrateful girl and he indulges you too much already.'

Frances was married to William, Ned's elder brother, and the young man had no love of her acid tongue. Now he stood up to her bravely. He gave a half-humorous glance towards the windows; outside the November rain and wind lashed at the trees of the park.

'It was cold in the house and we thought to warm ourselves with a little exercise. You're too hard on us, Frances.' He shrugged his shoulders with a tiny grimace at Amy. 'Maybe it's best if I go.'

'If you must, Ned, but I'll see you soon, shan't I?' Amy was still defiant.

'Surely.'

The young man smiled at her, nodding casually to Frances as he sauntered whistling through the door.

'Off with you too, Jennet,' went on Frances freezingly. 'I'm sure there are better things to be done than sharing in your mistress's idle ways.'

The girl scuttled away. Left alone, Amy stared at her half-sister. She had never in her life defied her mother and Frances, sixteen years older than herself, sometimes had a terrifying resemblance to the dead woman. Despite an inward quaver, she summoned all her courage to speak with determination.

'Now Mother is gone, I am mistress here, Frances. You are only a guest at Syderstone and I would beg you to remember it.'

The older woman gasped. This slip of a girl with her pretty wilful ways was daring to stand up to her. She should be taught a lesson and a sharp one. Resentment and jealousy edged her words with spite.

'Don't think I don't know what has bred this rebellious spirit in you. John told me of your shameless behaviour, prinking and pushing yourself forward when that young spark, Robert Dudley, was visiting Stanfield with my lord of Warwick. Did you think that young lordling would look twice at you, little fool, except to amuse himself as no doubt he has done with others? It takes more than soft glances and pretty speeches to make a marriage contract.'

The colour flooded into Amy's face. She bit her lip. He had not come back though he had promised. Only she knew he would. She was certain of it, but that was something she could not say aloud. They would laugh at her for a trusting idiot. It was something that had to be hidden deep in her own heart.

She raised her head to say haughtily, 'Your brother likes to make great things out of little. Lord Robert was a guest in my father's house. Should I not have welcomed him with courtesy?'

She swept past her half-sister with head held high, but outside her courage deserted her and she ran to her own room, a little frightened, a little disturbed at her first bid for freedom.

She did have one thing that no one knew about, not even Jennet. No young woman should accept gifts from a man she had only met once and yet . . . From under a layer of petticoats and freshly washed shifts in her clothes chest, she drew out the small package that had come just a few days after Robert had gone, sent back by one of his father's men who had bided his time to find her alone.

It was a rose exquisitely worked in gold and with it a line scrawled in haste as they rode on towards London. 'Take thou this rose, O rose.'

Where had he found so lovely a thing, and when would he come to claim his reward and to claim her?

*　　　*　　　*

32

Robert, riding towards Syderstone in late November only two weeks after Amy had kissed his gift and put it carefully back at the bottom of the chest, was wondering how he would be received, or even if he would be made welcome. It had taken considerable ingenuity to get himself back to Norfolk at all and had only been achieved by his volunteering to represent his father at the unpleasant business of seeing Robert Kett hanged at Norwich and his brother William strung up on the tower of Wymondham Church as dreadful examples to all those who might still be nursing rebellion in their hearts.

He had not relished either spectacle and was glad to be free of it so that he could pursue the aim on which he had set his heart. The last two months in London had been far too hectic for him to approach his father on what had quite suddenly become the most important thing in the world.

It had never been the Earl's custom to confide his plans to his family, or indeed to anyone, but it was impossible not to be aware that these were momentous times. Ever since their return to London, all the great nobles of the kingdom had been in and out of Ely Place conferring with his father. Every day members of the Privy Council had been meeting there behind closed doors. The Duke of Somerset had whisked his nephew off to Windsor Castle and under pretence of his safety was keeping him there virtually a prisoner.

Robert knew, as did anyone of intelligence, that the man who had the young King in his charge ruled the country, and he unhesitatingly backed his father to win; but even he, young as he was, realized that it would not be an easy victory.

John Dudley, taut, high-strung, overcoming opposition by sheer force of personality and the lust for power that thrust him always forward and upward, was not a comfortable man to live with these days. Only with his family could he relax, only in his own home could he be sure of an undivided loyalty and trust and sometimes even there the coiled tension would snap and he would break out in ferocious rage over some triviality that at other times would have mattered nothing. His children and his wife had long learned to avoid crossing him at such times.

His anger could be terrifying. Robert shivered still at the memory of his father's withering sarcasm when he had rashly pressed him too closely about marriage with Amy Robsart.

It was one evening after they had supped. The Earl sat staring broodingly into the fire, his gouty foot resting on the cushions Mary had piled under it, the long fine hands his son had inherited clenching and unclenching on the carved arms of his chair.

The dark eyes in brown hollows of sleeplessness turned slowly to Robert, standing respectfully before him.

'Marriage,' he repeated raspingly, 'marriage to that chit of a girl? You must be out of your mind.'

He dismissed him with a wave of his hand but Robert would not give up so easily. He saw Mary shake her head at him and Guildford, always sure of his father's favour, was grinning derisively. Opposition acted like a spur.

'What have you against it? Her family are as good as ours.'

'What's that?'

'After all our great-grandfather was only a farmer with a few holdings in Kent.' The Earl glowered at him but Robert went on, boldly ignoring the dangerous flash in his father's eyes. 'You yourself married for love. Mother has told us of it often enough.'

'Love, boy? You speak of love after five minutes in each other's company! You talk like a greensick fool,' said the Earl contemptuously. 'What is it you want to prove? Is it the itch of your manhood pricking in you? Well, that's easily satisfied. Marriage is another matter. It will be when I choose and to whom I choose.'

'Like Jack and Ambrose and Mary . . . is that it? Someone to help you up another rung of the ladder. Well, supposing I don't choose?'

All day the Earl had been fighting with greedy ambitious men, jostling one another and trying hard to oust him from his precariously held position of power. Dogged by pain he had still won. Somerset had been forced to bring the King back to Hampton Court and deliver him over to his charge. Now the Protector was on his way to the Tower. But supreme power is a lonely pinnacle surrounded by pitfalls and hard to maintain. He was not going to yield it to anyone and to be defied in his own home, by a slender stripling of his own breeding, was more than he could endure. All the exhausting day he had been outwardly calm, sweet-tempered and patient; now his control suddenly slipped. No one who encountered his rage ever forgot it. His voice could have a rasping sting.

'You saucy malapert, you insolent puppy! You'll do as I say or it will be the worse for you. God's blood! Must I listen to my own son teaching me what I should or should not do? You're not too old to feel the bite of a whipping or to live on bread and water for a week.'

'You can treat me like a child if you wish but it alters nothing.'

Robert and his father had stared at one another while Mary gasped and waited breathlessly for the blow to fall. Even hard-bitten soldiers like the foul-mouthed Earl of Pembroke, even that crafty time-serving customer, my lord of Arundel, had been known to quail before his father's unrelenting glance, but Robert did not move nor drop his eyes. With a wry twisted smile, Warwick recognized an obstinacy strong as his own.

'You've more spunk than some of our precious Council, Robin. You may go far one day, but not yet . . . not yet.' Wearily he thrust his son away from him. 'Get out of my sight before I forget myself.'

Surprisingly he had not punished him and in a few days his mood had changed. With Edward under his protection, he was virtual dictator of England; he was being besought for favours, foreign ambassadors craved audience, he could afford to relax and be gracious. They had all gone hunting the deer together in Richmond Forest and, riding beside the King, Robert had taken the opportunity to confide in him, telling the story laughingly, a lover thwarted in his passion.

Edward considered the problem gravely. He liked Robert and he took the responsibilities of his high office very seriously.

'I will speak to my lord of Warwick,' he said grandly, 'and if he is persuaded as I am sure he will be, I myself shall grace your wedding with my presence.'

His father would make up his own mind, King or no King, Robert was quite certain of that, but all the same there was no harm in having Edward on his side. In the meantime he had escaped and the Earl seemed to have forgotten how near Norwich was to Amy. He spurred his horse forward to cover the last few miles to Syderstone, his spirits rising. The knowledge that he was deliberately defying his father mingled with a delicious sense of anticipation.

He saw her long before she saw him. Outside the village the track crossed a common of heath and scrub. She was running,

35

her black cloak flying, the hood fallen back from her bright hair and a little spaniel racing beside her. She paused to throw a scarlet ball and the dog went tumbling after it, rolling head over heels in the rough grass. Her laughter, free and unrestrained, enchanted him. She was so unlike the girls he met daily at Court in their stiff bejewelled dresses with their painted eyelids and plucked eyebrows, their sly glances and malicious chatter.

He leaped from his horse, tossing the reins to the servant riding behind him. He had left his escort in Norwich. He ran to meet her across the frost-crisped grass.

Jennet, hurrying to keep up, could not take her eyes from him. Even in country riding clothes of russet and brown leather, Robert had a distinction, a grace and beauty of bearing that made him outstanding. No wonder her mistress had lost her heart to him at first glance . . . but what was in his mind? Jennet came of hard-headed peasant stock, practical, realistic, down-to-earth. Instinctively she distrusted gentlemen, all glamour, good looks and honeyed lies. Men were deceivers, even the best of them. That precept had been hammered into her ever since she was old enough to grasp it. She slowed to a standstill and watched them, a fear she did not understand clutching at her heart.

Heedlessly they had rushed into each other's arms. Amy was still not quite sure whether she could believe her eyes. She had been thinking of him and suddenly he was there. After a little she pulled away from him. He had drawn off his gloves to take her cold hands into his own warm grasp.

'I never thought to find you so far from home.'

'It is no distance across the fields. Jennet and I have been taking blankets and food to the poor folk in the village. My mother always took care of those who were old and sick before the winter. It is not right that they should suffer because she is gone.'

Of course, he remembered now, she was in mourning for Lady Robsart. The sombre black velvet was like a smothering pall. He wanted to strip it off her, dress her in gay light gowns. What was it that she had sung: 'I shall dance in the moon and the stars and the sun.' That was how he thought of her.

He said, 'I went to Stanfield and your brother directed me here. I was coming to call on your father.'

'No, don't . . . please don't,' she said quickly.

'Why ever not?'

'Because . . .' she looked away, confused and uncertain. How could she tell him of Frances pouring jealous poison into her father's ears, of John Appleyard who would be looking only for what he could get out of it for himself? 'Because . . .'

She was unable to say it and he guessed at her thought. 'Because if I do, Sir John may ask my intentions, is that what is troubling you?'

She nodded, blushing because it seemed so bold, like asking him for something when they had scarce realized what it was they wanted. But Robert only laughed, linking her arm in his and walking comfortably beside her.

'So long as I can see you, it matters little. You know, Amy, my father has been so preoccupied these last weeks, but I can persuade him, I'm sure of it, and then there is the King. Edward has promised to help.'

News had filtered through even up here in Norfolk. A sudden panic invaded her. The Earl of Warwick had risen to such dizzy heights. Everyone was saying that soon he would be the most powerful man in England. It was a world of which she knew so little. How should he be content with anyone as ordinary as herself for one of his sons?'

'You mean . . . ?'

'He will write to your father about our marriage.'

Even to hear him say it flooded her with joy, but still she could not quite believe. Troubled brown eyes sought his reassurance.

'Is it really possible, Robert, or are we mad? Is this all foolishness?'

He frowned in quick young pride. 'Is that the way to talk to me? Do you doubt my word?'

'How can I tell? We know so little of one another.'

'We have a lifetime to find out.' He looked round him impatiently. 'If I am not to come to Syderstone, is there somewhere we can walk and talk a little?'

'It is not easy and there's Jennet. We cannot leave her,' she sounded doubtful.

'She can follow with Dick Hunnicut.'

To send him away was more than she could bear. They strolled across the heath in the winter twilight. There was so much to talk of, so much joy in the unexpected meeting. It was so delightful to be alone, not overlooked by watchful eyes, that they did not notice the black cloud obscuring the red sun until the shower of sleet drove them into the half-ruined hut beside the reed-fringed waters of the dyke.

Outside Jennet and the groom huddled into their cloaks and eyed one another warily while the horses snorted and stamped their feet.

'Robert, I must go,' murmured Amy for the tenth time. 'They will be looking for me,' but she could not tear herself away any more than he could.

He had thrown his cloak around them both because she was shivering. He pushed back her hair and kissed her eyes and her little pink ears and the soft hollow at the base of her throat. He knew now the sweetness of which Jack and Ambrose and even Guildford had so often boasted.

Her trembling response awoke a craving in his young body which he had never known before. His kisses grew rougher. His hands explored further and his head began to swim. It was Tussie's frenzied barking that brought him back to his senses. Not here, not now, he thought dazedly, not in this dank cold place on a bundle of evil-smelling straw.

Then they were laughing together like children because the little spaniel, disappointed at losing his rat, was digging frantically in a corner, spraying up dirt and dust and dried leaves.

'We'd best go before he brings the whole place down on our heads,' said Robert, pulling the hood up over her head, hooking the silver clasp at her throat and kissing for the last time the mouth that parted so deliciously under his.

He walked back with her to the gates of the park, careless of the curious stares of the villagers gaping at the unexpected sight of the stranger in his rich dress and the servant leading the magnificent horses. They stopped just before they reached the lodge and he grasped her hands.

'When shall I see you again?' he said urgently. 'I need not return to London for a few days yet. I can stay on at Norwich and ride over. Shall it be tomorrow?'

Amy hesitated. She had acted unthinkingly in begging him not to come to Syderstone, but she wanted so passionately to keep him to herself, away from Frances's prying eyes and bitter tongue. It would be desperately difficult to slip out of the house unnoticed, but somehow it must be done. Once you begin to

38

deceive, you have to go on. She said recklessly, 'Yes, tomorrow at the same time.'

'I shall be there.' He kissed her fingers and she did not wait to see him turn to his horse, but flitted up the path to the house with Jennet panting behind her.

'You shouldn't have done that, mistress,' she said catching at Amy's hand as they ran. 'There'll be talk. Your father will be angry if it comes to his ears.'

'Why should it? Who is there to see us? None but you.' Amy's own anxiety made her speak sharply. 'You'll not say anything, Jennet, promise me you will not.'

'Never! What do you think of me?' Jennet would have been torn to pieces before she would breathe a word that might harm her young mistress, but to herself she was thinking, 'There's more than me that'll notice my Lord Robert so fine he is.'

Twice more that week Amy went running from the house with Jennet, pleading the excuse of sickness among the villagers until Frances said sourly, 'What's come over you, Amy? You've never cared a rap about the poor folk before.'

'I'm doing as Mother would have wished,' she retorted quickly. 'It ought to please you.'

It was Sir John who stopped her in the hall on the third day, looking at the baskets they were carrying. 'I don't like it,' he said, 'if there's sickness among our people, I don't want you to take it, my pet. Let Jennet go in your place.'

'It's not like that, Father,' she said almost frantically in case he should forbid her going. 'It's just that they're old. They are feeling the cold and the hunger. Mother always looked after them. I want to do as she did.'

'Well, well, go if you must. You're a good child, thinking so much of others.' He patted her cheek. 'Take care of yourself now. Jennet, make sure that your mistress comes to no harm.'

Amy had never lied to her father in her life and she felt the guilty blood race up into her cheeks. She had not meant it to be like this, but she was trapped in her own foolishness and now it had become so important to her, she could not draw back. She had to see Robert or she would surely die.

In the tumbledown shack he was waiting for her. He drew her impatiently into his arms, while outside Jennet kept watch, holding Tussie on his leash and slapping Dick Hunnicut's face when he sought to pass the time with a sly kiss or two.

For Amy the precious minutes went by only too quickly. Robert was all she had ever longed for, all she had ever dreamed. She listened entranced when he spoke of life at Court, the hunting parties, the jousts, the masques, the great people who thronged his father's fine house. He carried her into the magical world of her fantasies; this was her destiny, she had always known it.

It was hard to return to reality when Jennet knocked at the door. 'It will be dark soon, mistress, we must go back. They will be looking everywhere for us.'

Robert's cloak was tight around them, holding her close to him. 'It won't be long now, my darling, it can't be, I want you too much. I'll persuade my father, I swear, and then we'll be married.'

She shivered with joy under his tumultuous kisses. It was difficult to drag herself away, but Jennet was impatient and Amy knew only too well how right she was. She ran across the frozen grass, her heart singing even while the tears still sparkled on her lashes. She was quite unprepared for the storm that broke soon after she reached the house, though she might have guessed that curious eyes would have watched their meetings and carried a tale that grew in the telling.

She was hurrying across the great hall when a voice stopped her, a hateful voice that she knew only too well. She spun round to see her half-brother leaning in the doorway of the parlour, hat in hand, his boots mud-splashed from the hard riding.

'Aren't you pleased to see me, little sister?'

'What are you doing here?'

John Appleyard raised his eyebrows. 'Is that the way to greet me and is there any reason why I shouldn't visit my step-father?' He looked round him mockingly. 'Well, what have you done with him?'

Apprehension touched her because she realized why he had come. She tried to shrug it off.

'I don't know what you mean.'

'I expected to find my Lord Robert here. What have you done with him, Amy? It wasn't very clever to let him slip through your fingers now, was it?'

'So that's what you've been doing,' she exclaimed fiercely. 'Spying on me! I might have known.'

40

'Spying . . . now that's not a very pleasant word and I kept my distance, didn't I? Very careful I was. What have you been doing so long in that woodman's hut, eh? How many times have you met him? Your father won't be best pleased to hear about that.'

'You are not to worry him,' she said quickly. 'He has not been well.'

'Sick or well, Frances thinks he should be told. Young men who dally with his daughter and then ride away without a word can be brought to heel, you know. He may be my Lord Warwick's son but you are not a ploughman's daughter.'

She could see his mind. He would try to force a marriage and because of it the tenderness of love that had sprung between them could so easily be destroyed.

She said, 'It's not like that. You don't know what you're talking about.'

'I know very well,' he shot out an arm and his fingers closed round her wrist. 'Don't be a fool, Amy,' he whispered. 'Don't you want to capture your handsome Robert? Don't you want to be a Countess one day and queen it at Court? You have to work for your desires, you know.'

'Oh you . . . you're detestable, John Appleyard. You spoil everything.'

She tore herself away from him, running up the stairs in a storm of tears. She would not go down to supper. She stayed in her icy-cold bedroom, huddled in her cloak, defiant and miserable at the same time. If only she had thought, if only she had not acted so heedlessly. In the joy of seeing him all caution had flown straight out of her head. Now he would think she had set out to trap him.

It was dark by the time Jennet came in carrying a candle, her face grave and sympathetic.

'The master is asking for you, mistress. Shall I tell him you are gone to bed already?'

'No.' If it had to be faced, then best get it over with. She got up, pushing her tumbled hair under her cap, smoothing down her crumpled skirts. 'Give Tussie his supper, Jennet, he must be hungry. I shall go down to my father.'

Her heart sank when she entered the room and saw Frances standing erect and forbidding beside her father's chair. He looked so grieved she longed to run to him, put her arms round him and rub her face against his grizzled weatherbeaten cheek as she had done when she was a child. But it was too late for that now. She paused just inside the door.

'You wanted to see me.'

'Yes, Amy. Come closer, child. Your sister has just told me of something that has shocked me so deeply, I have refused to believe it is true unless I hear it from your own lips.'

'Of course it is true,' interrupted Frances. 'I have told you over and over. John saw them with his own eyes and he felt it only right that you should know. The villagers, the servants, everyone must be gossiping of it . . . a fine thing for our family!'

'I am asking Amy. Let her answer for herself.'

'If it is Lord Robert you speak of,' she replied, summoning all her dignity to face them calmly, 'yes, it is true. I did meet him — quite by chance, when I was walking Tussie on the heath.'

'By chance! A likely tale! No doubt it was planned, no doubt they have met before and who knows where,' broke in Frances, her voice rising. 'She was alone with him more than once, alone in a filthy peasant's hut like some village slut who's no better than she should be, while his man kept watch outside as I daresay he has done a dozen times already. You should be ashamed, ashamed!'

'Be silent, Frances!' Sir John's sharp tone checked her in full cry. 'Come here to me, Amy, and tell me the truth. Have you been alone with this young man as your sister says?'

'Only for a short time, Father, and at first only because the sleet drove us to take shelter, and we have done nothing wrong, only spoken together. Don't listen to her. She hates me, she is always attacking me for no reason. You must believe me, Father, you must, you must.'

She flung herself on her knees, beseeching him, seizing his hand and hugging it against her.

'But why did he meet you secretly in such an underhand manner? Why not come here openly, decently, like any honourable young man?'

'Because I asked him not to,' she said miserably.

'You asked him! Do you think us a pack of fools to believe such nonsense?' exclaimed Frances scornfully. 'Can't you see she's lying, Father? Can't you see she's let herself be betrayed by a young rake who has taken his pleasure and ridden away, laughing at us. What would my Lord of Warwick's son want with a silly girl foolish and wicked enough to let him have his will of her?'

'Hold your tongue, woman. I'll not have such things spoken in my presence.'

Outraged, Frances retorted, 'Mother would turn in her grave at such dishonour touching anyone of her family.'

'No doubt, no doubt,' said Sir John dryly. 'But in the meantime be good enough to leave us alone. My daughter and I have things to discuss that are not your concern.'

Frances opened her mouth to protest but thought better of it. With a spitefully triumphant glance at Amy, she swept from the room.

'Now,' said Sir John with a certain relief. 'Now we can talk to each other more easily. I want the truth, Amy, the whole truth if you please.'

It was not easy but she poured out the story, muddled, incoherent, trying to explain, half choked with tears. When she had fallen silent, her father sat for a moment, his face grave.

'It grieves me that you lied to me.'

'It was not all lies, Father. It was only that I could not tell you of Robert . . .'

'But why, why?' He took her hand in his. 'Do you think I would have let your sister or John influence me against you?'

'I didn't know,' she said wretchedly. 'I was not sure.'

'It was foolish of you, Amy. Why should you believe I would not open my house to Lord Robert even if he came against his father's wishes? All the same,' he went on, 'I fear Frances is right. Lord Warwick will look higher for his sons. Only this week I heard that his daughter Katherine will shortly be contracted to Huntingdon's eldest boy. Lord Henry Hastings has royal blood, Amy, Plantagenet blood. It is a great alliance.'

'But Robert is sure the Earl will consent,' she broke in eagerly. 'He says his father thinks more to his brothers than himself, and then there is Edward. The King is his friend. He is on his side.'

'The King is no more than a child,' said her father heavily. 'Warwick gives him lip service but goes his own way. All the same I shall write to him. He shall know of his son's indiscretion.'

'Oh no, no, please don't. He is a hard man. He will punish Robert . . .'

'As he rightly deserves,' her father cut her short sternly. 'He must learn that he cannot trifle with my child's affections. Your honour is dear to me and shall not be blown upon however innocent you may be. Lord Warwick may be riding high, but Robsarts have stood beside their King for the last hundred years. Our name is an honourable one. No one has ever been able to call us traitor as they did Edmund Dudley.'

She could not change his resolution, try as she would. He looked down at her fondly, touching her cheek with a gnarled finger.

'Why did you have to look so high, Amy? I would have been happy to give you to one of our neighbours, to have you settled quietly near me here in Norfolk.' He sighed. 'But there, the heart knows its own reasons. If you like him, you shall have him, child, if it is possible for me to get him for you.'

When she had left him and lay sleepless under the thick coverlet, Tussie curled up in a ball by her side, she did not know why her heart was so heavy when it should have been bounding with joy. It had been too sudden, too quick. She tried to stifle her anxiety by thinking of the afternoon, remembering the sweet things he had whispered in her ear, the touch of his hands, the feel of his lips on hers. Now there was nothing she could do, only wait.

John Dudley looked up with some impatience from the letter in his hand. 'Sir John Robsart writes in such a strange sort I can scarce make head or tail of it. Clandestine meetings with his daughter, her name dishonoured, her reputation lost . . . You had better have a good explanation, Robert. I thought I had knocked that crazy notion out of your head.'

Robert, hastily summoned from the parlour where he had been idly spending the evening playing chess with Mary, felt a quick stab of uneasiness. The Earl had been so unpredictable lately. You never knew how he would take anything. It had prevented him from going to his father immediately on his return from Norfolk.

He said carefully, 'What exactly does he say, sir?'

Warwick raised his eyebrows, regarding his son shrewdly. 'So there is truth in it. That was why you were so eager to undertake that unpleasant business in Norwich when I thought you were doing it simply to oblige your father.' He smiled ironically. 'I might have guessed if I had not been so occupied. You went running after your pretty mistress, is that it?'

Robert felt quite unreasonably angry. Why had she raced home to tell her father, and so put him in the wrong, when he had only acted as he did to please her?

'Well, answer me,' went on the Earl sharply. 'Don't stand there dumb as a booby. Did you have your pleasure of the girl so that now I have to pay the price for you? She is not a peasant's brat, you know.'

'No, I did not,' burst out Robert indignantly. 'If that's what he says, then it's a lie, a barefaced lie. We met and spoke with one another and that is all. I swear to God there was nothing else.'

'Softly, softly,' said his father dryly. 'There's no need to be so violent. Sir John does not say that. He writes that you acted with the rash and ill-considered behaviour of extreme youth and that I can well believe. Well, what do you say? Do you still want the girl?'

'You know I do . . . I've said so many times. I want her with all my heart.'

'More fool you. Very well, I'll write to the old man. No doubt he will settle something on his daughter, and she will have his lands when he dies, we will make sure of that. I have a little property up at Hemsby near Yarmouth. I'll give it to you as a marriage settlement. You'll not do so badly, Robin. I had other plans for you, but never mind. There's Guildford to be thought of, and young Hal will be out of the schoolroom soon. I'll not be sorry to get you off my hands.'

He should have felt elated. It was what he had thought about incessantly these past three months and suddenly it had all become so easy. His father dismissed him with a nod and he went back to Mary. She threw her arms round his neck and kissed him when he told her the news.

'I'm so glad for you, Robin, so very glad . . . and I do want to meet her so much.'

'You're such a comfort to me, Mary.'

She made a little face. 'That's what Harry says. It's such a dull thing to be when I want him to tell me I'm everything beautiful and fascinating in woman and that he would die for me on the instant!'

He laughed. 'You're the dearest, prettiest sister a man ever had.'

They sat down together to finish their game, only he couldn't concentrate. He kept wondering what it was his father had planned for him that was now to go to Guildford. Had he pressed too hard? Had he been too rash in opposing his father? Mingled with the exciting prospect of Amy and being his own master, the thought still nagged at him.

Three

Amy rode into London with her father in the middle of May. John Appleyard was with them, so was his sister Frances and her husband, with Ned Flowerdew and a company of thirty or more friends and neighbours, for tomorrow the marriage settlements would be signed and, God willing, on 4 June Robert and Amy were to be married.

The cavalcade clattered through the village of Shoreditch, past the muddy fields, the green of market gardens and the filthy ramshackle hovels that had sprung up beyond the city limits. Could this be London, thought Amy as they left Aldgate behind them, this noisy, crowded, vile-smelling place which a poet had once called the 'Flower of Cities'? The upper floors of the tall houses closed in like a prison above her head. There was a deafening uproar in the narrow streets, crammed with tradesmen's carts, clumsy coaches, troops of men-at-arms, royal couriers, private travellers like themselves. Pedlars screamed their wares at the tops of their voices while the beggars clutched at their bridles, their faces pocked with hideous sores, stained bandages slipping to show bleeding stumps, pleading for alms for the love of God. Frightened she shrank back, moving her horse closer to Sir John, and Ned Flowerdew rode up protectively to her other side. The air trembled with the sound of bells from the hundreds of churches, the tall spire of St Paul's towering above all.

They moved towards London Bridge and she quickly averted her eyes from the long poles stuck with the grinning heads of traitors, picked to white bone by the hordes of kites swooping down in black clouds to snatch at the rotting garbage piled in the gutters. It had happened to Robert Kett and his brother William. It could happen to anyone, and for an instant the bright day darkened and she shuddered. But soon they had reached the cleaner air of the Temple where the grass was green, roses bloomed already and gulls circled above the river with their raucous cry.

Here they were to stay with a lawyer friend of her father.

She was thankful to change out of her riding-dress and wash away the dust and weariness of the long days of travel. After a quiet supper she stood for a long time at the window, fascinated by the busy traffic of the Thames. After an early shower the evening was calm. On the steel-blue water the wherries were plying for hire; their cry of 'Eastward Ho' came up faintly on the evening breeze. Barges moved up and down, the rowers bending to their long oars. Some of the craft were painted in brilliant colours with awnings of purple velvet fringed with gold. The sweet sound of music floated on the air from the musicians playing to some great nobleman and his lady as they came from supper at one of the magnificent houses lying along the Strand between the Temple and the King's palace at Whitehall.

Was this to be her life from now on, she wondered, this idle life of pleasure shut into this great city? Unaccountably she felt suddenly homesick for the humble tasks she had so despised, for the country lanes, the open heaths where she had run free with Tussie, left behind at Syderstone. Ned had come up behind her, watching the delicate face for a moment before he spoke.

'What are you thinking of, Amy?'

She woke as if from a dream. 'Oh, I don't know . . . it all seems so new, so different. I can't believe it is really happening to me.'

'Are you happy?'

'Oh yes, wonderfully happy . . . only . . .'

'Only what?'

'It seems so long since I have seen Robert.'

Both the Earl and her father had decided that the two young people should not see each other until all was settled, and she had rebelled against their decree.

Ned said, smiling, 'One of my cousins did not meet her husband until they stood at the altar rails.'

'Oh I know that sometimes happens, but I've always thought it so barbarous and Father always promised . . .' she gave a little gurgle of laughter. 'Fancy being married to someone whose face fills you with disgust.'

'Well, at least that will not happen to you.'

'No,' she said, 'no, I am indeed fortunate.' She had his letters too, half a dozen of them, elegantly penned and more precious to her than diamonds. Each night she had read them, turning from one to the other. He had even written poems to her, stiff schoolboy verses, but to her it only proved how remarkable he was, how different from other young men.

Ned, leaning against the window frame, wished passionately not for the first time that he had not let the time slip by so carelessly. He had not yet set eyes on Robert, but already he disliked him, the young lordling who had stolen the flower that might have been his and most probably did not appreciate his good fortune. If he hurts her, he thought fiercely, I'll kill him . . . and then seeing her rapt face, knew how foolish he was. She would love him, as women do, whatever he did to her.

The great hall of Ely Place with its six pointed windows seemed grand as a cathedral when Amy entered it with her father. The walls were hung with fine tapestries glowing in the light of hundreds of wax candles. Gold and silver dishes in a lavish abundance were set out on the gleaming white tablecloths, embroidered with gold and semi-precious stones.

'Just a small family gathering,' the Earl had written, but it seemed to her dazzled eyes that the room was crowded with magnificent figures in silk and velvet and lace, and in the centre Lord Warwick himself, his black satin surcoat trimmed with sable, with his lady beside him and his tall sons at his back.

She trembled because her eyes were seeking frantically for Robert, and could not see him. Then the Earl was raising her from her curtsey, drawing her towards him, kissing her brow, calling her his new daughter, his voice a caress.

He passed her across to his wife while he greeted her father, and she felt the hard grey eyes of Robert's mother run over her, appraising her, summing her up and finding her wanting.

Warwick lived in royal state. Each new course was heralded by silver trumpets. Stewed carp was followed by roasted saddle of mutton, by beef, venison, a dish of larks, stuffed goose and a peacock brought to the table in all the glory of his feathers in a gilded fan.

Musicians played while they ate, and the family fool, a dwarfish creature with a humped back and short, twisted legs, went tumbling in and out of the tables, performing somersaults, turning cartwheels, twisting himself into knots, his pranks and antics smiled on indulgently.

Once he terrified Amy, plucking at her sleeve, his wizened, crumpled, ugly face painted into a grinning mask, appearing so suddenly at her elbow that she stifled a cry.

'Nay, nay, no offence, my lady, I ask only a riddle.' He cocked his head comically on one side.

'What nonsense is this, Rafe?' asked Robert.

'No nonsense, my lord, but wisdom, the wisdom of the fool,' and the little man capered out into the hall, facing Amy across the table. He struck an attitude. 'Why is a musician always in good health? Now answer me that.'

The high table had fallen silent. They waited for her answer; even the Earl was leaning back in his chair, smiling and nodding his head, and she could think of nothing. All her wits had deserted her. She gave Robert a quick despairing glance, but Hal, his schoolboy brother of barely fourteen, was bobbing up and down.

'I know, I know . . . may I answer, Father?' and went on before she could utter a word. 'Because he lives by a good air of course,' and all the table roared with laughter at the silly joke.

She felt desperately ashamed of her slow wits, but worse was to come; the wretched Rafe went dancing out into the centre of the hall, mopping and mowing before Warwick himself.

'By your gracious leave, my lord, by your leave, I have a new jest minted this very moment in your servant's wits.'

'Very well, say on, good fool.' Warwick good-humouredly waved his hand, summoning the page to fill his wine cup.

The little man looked from Amy to Robert, the sharp eyes glinting with malice.

'Listen then, my lords and ladies, answer me this. Why should a woman with the falling sickness never travel to the westward?' and when there was no reply, only a buzz of anticipation, he leaped into the air, lifted his eyes to heaven, put his hands together and intoned solemnly, 'Because she must avoid the Isle of Man.'

Before the tears of laughter had been wiped away, he was again holding up his hand for silence, speaking in the snuffling whine of a canting preacher, 'And for this evil, let her for a charm always keep her legs crossed when she is not walking.'

Amy saw her father frown. The bawdy jest brought a wave of colour into her cheeks, while the men around her bellowed with laughter and the women pretended to feel affronted, giggling behind their embroidered handkerchiefs. Only Warwick had a look of contempt.

He said with a touch of anger, 'Away with you, Rafe, before I have you whipped for impudence.'

Robert had laughed as heartily as his brothers, but now she did not mind so much. He pressed close beside her. Under the table his hand touched hers. Sometimes they ate from the same dish. He lifted the gold cup and she sipped the rich muscatel. Then he turned it so that his lips could touch where hers had rested, and his eyes pledged her over the rim.

After supper was done, the Earl withdrew with her father and the older guests, leaving the youngsters to amuse themselves in their own way. Led by Mary, they left the great hall to the servants clearing the tables and moved into a smaller room whose windows opened on to a cloister surrounding a small courtyard.

Outside a fountain went splashing and tinkling into a mossy stone basin, but within the air smelled sweetly of the logs burning on the wide hearth, for the evening was cool. Amy looked round at the family which would now be hers and tried to separate them in her mind.

Mary stood with her back to the fire. 'It's so early yet. There's hours before bedtime and Father has decided there shall be no dancing tonight. What shall we do to pass the time?'

Amy was a little in awe of Mary. She wanted to like her because Robert had spoken of his much-loved sister, but she was not like any of the girls she had known in Norfolk. Mary was a year younger than herself and not exactly pretty, but she had such elegance, she was so self-assured, so confident and, like the royal princesses, she had been as highly educated as her brothers.

'There's cards,' said Guildford eagerly. 'We could take a hand at Primero or cast the dice. I've a set of new ones, gold and ivory.'

'Loaded in your favour more than likely, eh Gil?' said Hal cheekily.

'Shut your mouth, insolent brat!' Guildford aimed a cuff at his young brother who dodged and stumbled over a stool with a noisy clatter.

Guildford was the only one of the brothers who had not inherited their father's dark colouring. He was golden-haired, excessively handsome, his girlish beauty only marred by a look of sulky petulance. Amy had noticed how close he had sat to his

51

mother at supper and how her every thought had seemed to be for him.

'No, not cards,' said Mary decisively. 'It must be something we can all play.'

'Speaking for myself,' put in Robert cheerfully, 'my pockets are flat. I haven't a stiver. Spent it all on a gift for my lovely bride.' He smiled up at her from the cushions he had spread on the floor by her stool.

The ring he had put on her finger glittered in the firelight. 'Dear Robin,' she put out a hand to touch his cheek and felt him drop a kiss on it. Just then she felt so happy, there seemed nothing more in the world she could possibly want.

'We could play the guessing game,' suggested Jack. Robert's eldest brother, Lord Lisle, was tall and elegant, as were they all, a grave young man without Robert's gaiety or Ambrose's lazy good humour or Guildford's aggressive temper.

'Jack is our scholar,' whispered Robert. 'He is translating Petrarch when he can find time.'

He was to be married to Anne, daughter of the Duke of Somerset on the day before their own wedding. The see-saw of politics had swung the Duke up again. For some inscrutable reason of his own Warwick had obtained his release from the Tower so that now he was back in favour once more.

'What is the guessing game?' she asked.

'Oh it's easy,' replied Mary lightly. 'One of us repeats lines of verse or prose, anything really, from any source and we each in turn have to guess where it comes from. You only have to the count of ten and if you fail, or are wrong, you must pay a forfeit. It's wonderfully amusing.'

Amy felt her heart sink. When they played games at home, it was always Kiss-in-the-Ring, or Rise Pig and Go, or Hoodman-Blind, but these clever young people would only despise such childish pastimes.

'Now who shall we choose for master of quotations? What about you, Robin?'

He shook his head. 'Too full of that roasted goose, dear sister.' 'Jack?'

'I will if you wish.'

The quiet voice took them by surprise. The small girl in the corner who had sat silent, her head bent over the book on her lap, seemed no more than a child. The pale face was powdered with golden freckles. The reddish hair, smooth under her velvet hood, hung straight to her waist. She wore no jewels, but her dress of pearl-grey velvet was slashed with silver and her eyes were large, clear and very beautiful.

'I'd forgotten you, Jane. You're like a little mouse in your corner. Are you sure you wouldn't rather read?'

'Oh no, I am sure she wouldn't,' said Robert dryly. 'The Lady Jane Grey is quite certain she can make fools out of all of us, isn't that so, my dear?'

'If you say so, Robert,' answered Jane composedly, pulling her stool into the centre of the company and folding her hands on the closed book. 'When do you want me to begin?'

In a curious way Amy sensed a reaction amongst the Dudleys, as if they closed their ranks against an outsider. She could have sworn there was dislike between them and the small pale girl. It had been said that her ambitious parents, the Duke and Duchess of Suffolk, had educated her to be the young King's bride and were angry that he was rejecting her in favour of a French princess. But Lady Jane was of the blood royal. Her grandmother had been old King Henry's sister.

Questions and answers flew between them with a speed that dazed Amy. How could that young girl know so much and how clever they all were. Even though Ambrose pretended to be at his wits' end, he still brought out the right answer, and Harry Sidney, who swore again and again that he was done, always got in his guess before the count was up.

Jane tested them in Latin, in French, in Italian, even in Greek. Here Robin scored so brilliantly they all cheered. They all knew everything, thought Amy in the depths of despair. The first round had passed her by, due to Mary's prompting.

'She's not played it before. Let her listen and get used to it.'

But eventually, as she knew it must, it came to her turn. Jane looked at her dispassionately, thought for a second and then began.

> 'Forget not! Oh forget not this,
> How long ago hath been, and is
> The mind that never meant amiss,
>   Forget not yet!'

They were all looking at her expectantly and she did not know, she just did not know. Why hadn't she listened to her tutor when he had tried to drum poetry into her head? She searched her memory painfully. Robert whispered something but she could not hear him for the frightened buzz in her ears. There was a poet once who had written a long, boring elegy about a sparrow. She had been forced to learn a dozen lines by heart. Boldly she ventured.

'Skelton,' she said in a rush, 'John Skelton.'

They stared at her and she knew it was wrong. Then Guildford let out a great guffaw. 'Lord God, I didn't think there could be anyone who wouldn't know Tom Wyatt's verses.'

Amy bit her lip and Robert said angrily, 'Shut up, you unmannerly cub!'

Guildford flushed red as fire. He would have given a sharp retort if Ambrose had not intervened.

'Mistress Amy has had something better to do than spend her time reading verses like you, lazybones,' he said peaceably in his quiet voice.

Hal was dancing up and down. 'A forfeit,' he said, 'a forfeit. She has to pay a forfeit.'

'No, she hasn't,' said Mary. 'It's different for her. She's a guest.'

'She's one of the family now,' put in Guildford spitefully. 'And she sings sweet as an angel, or so our brother tells us.'

'And so she does,' countered Robert with quick pride. 'That can be her forfeit. Sing to us, Amy.'

'A love song,' said Harry Sidney, gaily ignoring Mary's frown. 'That should be easy, especially on this day.'

'Oh no, I couldn't . . . I couldn't . . . please, Robert,' but she knew she must if she were to redeem herself in his eyes. What could she sing out of her pitifully small store? She said helplessly, 'I have no lute.'

'You can borrow mine,' said Mary gently, and went to fetch it from the chest against the wall.

They gathered round to listen. She was conscious of their glittering eyes, watching, criticizing, so secure in their strong family unity, so arrogant, so self-confident.

At home her father had always loved the old songs, the country ballads of his youth, not the new-fangled madrigals of the Court musicians, filled with trick and artifice and difficult rhythms.

There was one she had learned from an old servant that had always been his favourite.

It went wrong from the start. Her trembling fingers mishandled the strings. She saw Mary wince at the jangled chord.

> 'The wind doth blow to-day, my love,
> And a few small drops of rain;
> I never had but one true love,
> In cold grave she was lain.'

She saw Guildford give a quick look round, then shrug his shoulders with a smile of mockery.

> 'I'll do as much for my true love
> As any young man may;
> I'll sit and mourn all at her grave
> For a twelvemonth and a day.'

Hal began to giggle, stuffing his handkerchief into his mouth. She saw Jack lay a warning hand on his shoulder, shaking his head. She saw Robert's frown and Mary's studied gravity and suddenly she could not endure it a moment longer. The tension of the long exhausting evening caught up with her. She broke off, the string snapped under her clumsy fingers, the lute fell to the floor. A small sob broke from her and she ran from the room.

Outside in the passage she leaned against the stone wall, a storm of weeping gathering in her throat. Then the door opened and Mary appeared. She said, 'Don't take any notice of Guildford. He's never had any manners. It was a lovely song. Come back and finish it.'

'No, no, I couldn't . . .' She hated the pity in Mary's voice. If only she could run away. If only she need never see any of them again.

'Yes, you can.' Robert had somehow taken Mary's place. He turned her round to face him. 'Come back with me now.'

'No, I won't,' she sobbed, 'why should I? They're hateful, all of them. I'll not be made a laughing stock for their amusement.'

'As you like,' there was a touch of impatience in his voice. 'But it's I they will be laughing at, not you.'

'Oh, no.' With a flash of intuition she realized what she had done. She had made him look a fool in front of his clever family because he had chosen her against opposition, talked of her, boasted of her perhaps. All that and more she read in the proud handsome face and the curl of his lip. For one moment, in the extravagant despair of youth, she wanted to die, she was so unhappy. She whispered, 'Oh Robert, what have I done?'

'Shown up my loathesome brother for the spoiled pig he is,' said Robert, his mood changing. 'No more tears, my little squirrel.'

His arms were round her, his kiss on her wet cheek. No one even turned to look at her when they went back into the room. Guildford was at the card table with his two brothers and Harry Sidney. Jane was bent over her book again.

They sat by the fire and while Mary and Robert spoke of things mostly above her head, she leaned dreamily against him, her hand in his. Only now and then, like a tiny pricking barb, the thought ran through her that somehow, somewhere, she had failed him.

Four

There were a great many eyes to gaze enviously at Robert and Amy when they came from the chapel, the June sun blazing down on the bridegroom so tall and darkly handsome in his amber velvet slashed and embroidered with gold, and the bride lovely as a dream in her stiff, brocaded satin, a chaplet of white roses on the bright hair with the gauzy veil blowing out behind her and the bridesmaids scattering posies, clove-scented pinks and rosemary sprigs, before them as they walked.

John Dudley was not one to stint a public display of his wealth and power. Jack's marriage and that of Robert on the following day were celebrated with a royal magnificence at Edward's palace of Richmond with the King himself as chief guest. Crowds waited on the banks to watch the gilded barges come floating up the Thames to discharge their noble passengers, resplendent in silk and satin and cloth of silver, while bread, beef and ale were lavishly distributed to the poor, jostling and fighting one another at the gates for a share in the bounty.

Ned Flowerdew, from his humble place in the great hall, thought he had never seen Amy look so radiant and cursed his own fate while condemning Lord Robert to the lowest pit of hell if he did not appreciate his good fortune.

When Robert had led her before the young King and the boy raised her from her curtsey, kissing her cheek, it did not seem possible that it was only a few weeks since she had felt so wretchedly unhappy she had wanted only to run away.

Jack, from the lofty eminence of one day and night of marriage, nudged his brother in the ribs and grinned at them with a gesture that sent the blood flying up into her cheeks.

'Blessed is the bride the sun shines on,' said her father-in-law, tilting up her chin with one long finger. 'Come now, daughter, why so serious?'

She was still a little frightened of him, though he had treated her kindly and the pearl collar round her neck was his wedding gift. She might have been a favourite dog or a pet kitten, she thought, though he smiled so charmingly. She wondered sometimes if he really saw her, or even his family; the dark eyes beneath the delicate arched brows were always fixed on something else, something far away and beyond their reach.

And she was right. John Dudley sitting beside Edward at the marriage feast was concerned with other and far more important matters than Robin's marriage with his pretty nobody. He ate sparingly as always, listening courteously to the boy in the place of honour, answering his questions with the deference that always gave the lad such a delightful feeling of importance and self-confidence. But his astute mind reached out to a new idea that had leaped into it unbidden, an idea so daringly ambitious that even his bold spirit quailed a little before its presumption..

He glanced for a moment at Edward's thin, high-bred face. There was delicacy in his transparent pallor, in the feverish brilliance of his eyes. The boy was frail, there was no doubt at all about that; and, though he was in good health just now, sickness could strike at any time and if he should die . . . His eyes swept the company and rested speculatively on the Princess Mary. There would not be much hope for John Dudley if ever she reached the throne, a spinster of thirty-five, obstinately, fanatically Catholic, as stubborn as her Spanish mother, Catherine of Aragon. How much trouble she had caused with her refusal to accept divorce and retire decently, sensibly, from her husband's side. Mary would martyr him for his strict adherence to the reformed faith and his support of those whom men were just beginning to call Protestants. Not that he cared very much how God was worshipped. This life was good enough for him without worrying too much about the next.

But if Mary were to be set aside, there were others . . . that tall, pale girl, for instance, sitting just beyond Somerset. The Princess Elizabeth was barely seventeen. She was a girl after his own heart, high-tempered and clever as they come, too clever in fact; she would be as difficult to ride as a mettlesome, finely bred mare. The pluck of the devil lived in her as it had in her mother, Anne Boleyn. He'd not forget that white-faced, black-haired witch in a hurry. Perhaps if Elizabeth were married to one of his sons . . . Robin might have matched her, but the young fool had chosen to throw himself away on a nonentity; but there was still Guildford. Most girls would fall headlong for that golden beauty. His musing glance moved on and rested for a moment on Jane Grey, so quiet, gentle, demure as a dove, and so very near the throne . . . if Mary and Elizabeth were both set aside as the bastards old King Henry had once pronounced them to be . . . then he, John Dudley, Earl of Warwick, could make her Queen as another earlier Warwick had created a king out of Edward Plantagenet. The very thought was so audacious, so insanely ambitious, so beyond all reasonable possibility, that it both allured and terrified him. His hand jerked and the gold cup spilled, red wine running like blood across the white cloth.

A page sprang forward with a linen towel. He laughed and excused his clumsiness, but all the day at the back of his mind, as he spoke graciously and moved among his guests, the thought lay hidden, not entirely dismissed, but waiting for the moment when circumstances might bring it to maturity.

The Princess Elizabeth had not wanted to attend these days of festivity but it was only a month or two since her reconciliation with her brother after the disgrace that had so nearly wrecked her, and she wanted more than anything to please him.

The feasting was over at last and the guests had moved out into the courtyard to watch the tilting. Edward sat beneath a canopy of green boughs hung with flowers and gilded fruit, and the royal party settled themselves round him.

Elizabeth was very still, very erect, her hands loosely clasped in her lap, her white gown as plain and severe as any nun, the only note of colour the red-gold hair that flowed straight to her waist and the emerald glowing in green fire at her breast.

Her eyes were on the tiltyard but her thoughts were far away. What was it that my lord of Somerset had murmured to her as they sat at table?

'I have long wanted to tell you . . . if only my brother had come direct to me then I might have saved him, but he did not; he was ever too proud to beg and there were those who prevented him so that he went to his death.'

Why did he have to say such a thing now? Why? Was it merely to salve his conscience? Did it never occur to him that those few words could bring back the whole shattering misery of the months she had tried so desperately to forget?

Six young cavaliers with Robert at their head, resplendent in a cuirass of silver armour, had come into the courtyard and were riding against the opposing team with the clash of lance against lance. There was laughter as one of them, riding carelessly, went tumbling from his horse. An intense excitement had sprung up among the spectators, laying wagers on one side or the other. She did not even see them. She was reliving those six months of wild happiness, of mingled joy and torment, when she had gone to live at Chelsea with her father's widowed queen and had fallen desperately, agonizingly in love with Katherine Parr's new husband.

Lord Thomas Seymour, with his rakish charm, his gay swagger and his good looks, was fascinating enough to turn the head of any strictly brought up young girl of fourteen and a half. At first it had been a secret delight, a hidden trembling when he casually touched her hand, a shared jest, an exchange of looks in a crowded company. She had gone riding with him in the dawn of a spring morning when his wife's pregnancy kept her at home. Beneath the thrill of the chase there had been another emotion more intense, more enthralling. When his crossbow brought down the slender hart and he gave her the knife to deliver the *coup de grâce,* it might have been she herself, panting, defeated, lying at his feet.

But then it had changed. He took to coming into her bedroom in the early morning, barefoot, in his nightshirt, teasing her, chasing her round the room until she fled from him among her ladies, half terrified, half longing for the moment when she would be captured.

'Fie, my lord, you should not do such things and she so young!' exclaimed her governess, but she too was caught fast in his spell.

It was innocent fun maybe until the day she stumbled and he swung her up into his arms.

Oh, the exquisite rapture of that first kiss and the enchanted days that followed. The torment of knowing she was doing wrong only made it all the sweeter, until that terrible morning when Queen Katherine had come on them unexpectedly in the garden and found them locked in each other's arms. She had been sent away, not in disgrace, though she had known in her secret heart

60

she deserved it for the cruel blow she had delivered to the woman who had been kind to her. She suffered all the misery of loss, together with the bitter tears of remorse when Katherine died in bearing her child that autumn. But worst humiliation of all had been the realization that it had all been lies, that the love he had professed was nothing but a plot to further his own selfish ambition. It was not she, Elizabeth, he had desired, but the Princess, the girl who might one day ascend a throne and so make him king. He had tangled her in his reckless schemes to entice all the royal children into his power, Edward too as well as herself, so that when the accusation of traitor was hurled in his face, the stain of treason besmirched her too.

The slanders had grown; horrible, foul lies that made her flesh crawl with a furious disgust. She had lain with him night after night like any whore from the stews . . . he had raped her . . . she was already with child by him . . . there was nothing too vile to be whispered about them. Fiercely she repudiated them, but there were so many enemies, so many who hated the daughter of Anne Boleyn, so many who were glad to say with a sneer, 'Like mother, like daughter.'

Her beloved governess, her dear kind foolish Kat Ashley, had been questioned and questioned until she broke down, stumbling out truths and half-truths that could be twisted as they wished. The long slender white fingers clenched convulsively at the bitter recollection.

She shut her eyes, unwillingly remembering the days and days of torture when they had tried to trap her into confessing what she had not done. Days when her brain felt cold as ice while her forehead burned with fever as she fenced with men so much older, so much more experienced than herself in the wiles of intrigue and duplicity. Nights when she had lain sleepless, swallowing the useless tears until her head felt bound with bands of iron, her whole body throbbed and she could not eat or drink or lie still; and all the time the pain inside her, sharp as a knife, at his treachery.

She had escaped but he had not. On that frosty morning in March just over a year ago, when he had paid on the block for his presumption, she had nerved herself to face her attackers boldly.

'This day died a man of wit and very little judgment,' she had said coolly; and they thought her heartless, cruelly indifferent to the blood spilled on the scaffold, while something screamed inside her and for days, weeks afterwards, she neither slept nor walked without the memory of it staying ever in her mind.

Never again, she had vowed to herself, never again would she give any part of herself to another. It was a fool's trick, a snare that life prepared for you so that you were caught in it unaware, helpless as a rabbit in a trap.

'Is anything wrong, my lady Elizabeth?'

The gentle silky voice in her ear roused her so that she looked up with a start into Warwick's face and shuddered, though she hardly knew why. Some sixth sense warned her that he was another of the same breed, with the same charm and the same deadly, ruthless ambition that would sacrifice anyone and anything to obtain what he wanted.

'No, nothing wrong, my lord. Why should there be?'

'No reason, but you looked so pale I thought maybe the heat or fatigue had been too much for you.'

'Thank you, I am perfectly well.'

Deliberately she rejected his concern, turning her back on him and looking determinedly towards the lists. But now the tilting was all done with. They had slung a live goose on a long pole and one after another the young men came galloping past trying to lift the struggling bird on the tip of their lance. One of them came at a furious speed, lunging forward at so low an angle that when he missed his aim he flew over his horse's ears and went rolling over and over like a ball in the dust of the courtyard.

Unexpected laughter bubbled up in Elizabeth's throat. The more she tried to hold it back, the worse it was, peal after peal, half genuine amusement, half hysteria. And after a startled moment, the others joined in. They were all roaring with laughter, even Edward forgetting his royal dignity in boyish glee at another's absurd mishap.

Robert picked himself up. He was bruised and shaken but that meant little beside the smart of ridicule. He glared round at the grinning faces resentfully. Amy had cried out. She half rose and would have run to him, but he was not concerned with her, not just then. It was that tall girl who enraged him. She sat there, all white and gold, shaking with uncontrollable laughter like a jackass – Elizabeth, whose hair he had pulled, whose face he had once slapped when she had stuck out her tongue at him, who had gazed at him admiringly when he showed off his skill at swordplay in front of her. For an instant he forgot where he was and was back in the days of childhood.

His page had brought his horse. He seized the bridle and threw himself into the saddle. He turned back to the starting post and then came so fiercely that he lifted the pole out of the ground as well as the goose on his lance. He carried it straight to Elizabeth and tumbled it at her feet.

Her laughter had died now. She was quiet and still. She looked down at the goose and then at him.

'And what am I to do with it, my lord?'

'Goose for a goose, my lady. You can teach it to cackle at your pleasure.'

The insolence took her breath away. Robert found himself looking into eyes green as splinters of ice.

'I did not hear you, Lord Robert. Would you repeat what you said louder for us all to enjoy?'

She was taunting him deliberately, for though his impertinence could be spoken once and forgiven, to say it again would be deadly insult.

'No jest can be repeated, my lady, not without tedium.'

There was a touch of mockery in the sweeping bow, in the flourish of his cap, a hint of a swagger as he sauntered towards the King who had summoned him imperiously to his side.

She looked after him, amused, resentful and annoyed with herself because she had been betrayed into interest. There had been a faint crack in the armour with which she shielded herself against hurt.

The day's festivities were by no means done with. After supper the masquers came into the great hall, carrying garlands of flowers, winding in and out of the tables, singing as they wreathed the bride and bridegroom in their sweet-scented chains.

'Never have the hours seemed so long,' murmured Robert to Amy, pulling her towards him. 'I wish it were night. I want you all to myself.'

She blushed at the warm pressure of his hand and the kiss on the nape of her neck. Then a page appeared beside them, tugging at Robert's sleeve.

'My lord, your father wishes to speak with you.'

'And now what?' sighed Robert. He grinned lazily at John Appleyard sprawled at the end of the table. 'Look after my lovely bride for me, John, while I find out what my lord father wants with me.'

Amy's eyes followed him as he threaded his way through the guests. He had changed his clothes, dust-stained from his tumble in the courtyard. His doublet of white and green satin was barred with silver. He looked so splendid she had to keep reminding herself that this was her husband and tonight, when all was over, it would be to her bed that he would come. Her cheeks went hot and her heart beat thickly.

'They make a handsome pair, don't they?' whispered her half-brother, close beside her.

'I don't know what you mean.'

'My lord of Warwick is losing no chance to curry favour with royalty.'

'You are talking nonsense.'

'Maybe, but I say watch out for yourself, little sister.'

She gave him a look of scorn, but it did not still the sharp pang of disappointment. Robert, obedient to his father's command, had walked across to the Princess Elizabeth. He led her into the centre of the hall as the musicians began to play. It should have been she, Amy, beside him, leading the company in the dance. This was her day. She was the bride, the centre of all eyes, and it was being stolen from her. She resented that tall girl who danced with so much grace.

They spoke little as they moved away and together again in the slow formal steps of the pavane.

Elizabeth said, 'You have chosen to wear our colours, white and green, Tudor colours.'

'My father is Edward's most trusted councillor.'

'Maybe.'

They turned to face one another and he said quickly, 'Do you doubt it?'

She shrugged her shoulders, moving with a most exquisite precision and speaking over her shoulder. 'I have been hearing tales of you, my lord, more than once in the last few weeks.'

'What could be said of me that could possibly interest your royal highness?' Robert spoke with light irony.

'Did you not know that Master Ascham is reading Greek with me at Hatfield? He says regretfully that my Lord Robert would have been an excellent classical scholar if he had not wasted his time in the pursuit of science and mathematics.'

Robert laughed. 'He flatters me. I was never Roger Ascham's favourite pupil. That was always reserved for Jane.'

'I know that too well,' said Elizabeth dryly. 'He holds her up as a paragon of learning until I weary of it.'

They smiled at one another, back for an instant in the intimacy of shared lessons and the rivalry of the schoolroom. When the dance came to an end, he lingered beside her but she was cool again.

'Should you not return to your other guests, my lord?'

'Why so formal? It used to be Robin. "Bonnie sweet Robin is all my joy . . ." You sang that once, do you remember? How old were we – ten or eleven? We were at Hampton. I kissed you when we played hide and seek. Edward gave us away, the little sneak, and Kat Ashley boxed my ears for my presumption.'

He had run on unthinking and was astonished at her reaction. The colour ran up into the white face. She turned away from him, biting her lip.

'We were children,' she said stiffly. 'Those times are past.'

So she could still be stirred by him, she was not all marble statue, not all white and green fire like the snow maiden after all. Impulsively he stretched out a hand to take her icy-cold one and she shuddered at the touch of the long brown fingers. They were so like those others, those bold roving hands that had given her so much exquisite delight and were now festering in a dishonoured grave. She snatched away her hand.

'Go back to your bride, my lord,' she said freezingly. 'That is where you belong.'

She might have been queen when she drew herself erect and her eyes blazed at him. Dismissed so abruptly, Robert left her and Elizabeth took refuge in the one thought that was always with her, a certainty that had no basis in fact, for surely Edward would marry one day and have sons and there was Mary too . . . And yet it was there, had always been there, had sustained her during stormy days of childhood alternately caressed and neglected by her mighty father. From the moment the mother she scarcely remembered had gone to her death on Tower Green, she had been on a seesaw, now down, now up, but one day . . . one day, and in her worst moments she would repeat it over and over like a charm, an incantation, one day England would be hers.

It was long after midnight and all the rites and ceremonies of marriage were over and done with; the jests, the songs, the young men jostling for the knots of silver ribbon from her dress which she threw to them as bride's favours; the posset of wine, milk, sugar and spices, had been drunk, Robert's eyes sparkling at her over the rim of the silver cup. His brothers had carried him off to undress him and, alone at last in the bridal chamber, Jennet unhooked the stiff boned bodice and threw over her head the nightgown of lawn trimmed with lace fine as a cobweb.

Combing out the long hair and lightly braiding it, Jennet wondered what her mistress was thinking as she stared pensively into the hand mirror. Usually she chattered freely as a bird of the day's happenings, but this night she sat silent.

'That will do, Jennet,' she said impatiently when the girl would have lingered, putting away the jewels in their caskets and setting the untidy dressing-table to rights. 'Leave me now. My lord will be here soon.'

'Are you sure there is nothing more you need, my lady?'

'No, nothing.' Then with a touch of longing for familiar things of home, she said childishly, 'I wish Tussie were here.'

Jennet paused on her way to the door. More hard-headed, more experienced in the ways of men than her mistress, she felt a twinge of pity. She said, 'May Heaven bless you this night and for always, my lady.'

Robert was flushed when he came through the door, slamming it firmly on his brothers who had come crowding after him. She heard their laughter. She heard Jack call out jestingly, 'Do your work well, Robin,' and Guildford's voice, high-pitched, 'Sow the seed for the honour of Warwick, my brother.'

She lay in the great bed and waited for him, trembling a little at what she had determined to say to him before even he should take her in his arms.

He came across and stood looking down at her. He was not drunk but wine and excitement had made him a little unsteady.

He stripped off the brocaded dressing-gown and stood naked, the slender body glowing rosy red in the flare of the candles before he pinched them out and plunged the room into darkness.

'Aimée beloved,' he mumbled, his face buried in the scented cloud of her hair.

'No,' she said and struggled to hold him off while she nerved herself to speak. 'Wait, Robin.'

'Wait for what?'

'Robin, do you love me?'

'Do you need to ask, foolish one?'

'More than anyone else, more than anything in the world?'

'What is all this?' There was impatience in his voice.

'More than the Princess Elizabeth?'

'What! Are you out of your mind?' He sat up in the bed with a snort of laughter. 'That long stick of ice! That vestal virgin! What has been biting you to say such crazy things?'

'I thought . . . tonight . . .'

'This is no time for thinking.' He had her by the shoulders, shaking her playfully. 'It's you I love, little squirrel, now, always and for ever. Haven't I proved it?'

'Are you sure?'

'Great God Almightly, how many more times must I say it?'

He silenced her with kisses that left her breathless. His love-making was clumsy, inexperienced and painful, but she did not mind. In the mingled hurt and pleasure there was triumph and she gave herself to him completely and utterly, thinking herself happier and more fortunate than any other girl could ever be.

At some time in the night between love and sleep, Robert wondered idly whether Lord Thomas Seymour had ever succeeded in kindling that long stick of ice into flame.

Five

Amy looked down at her household account book with a feeling of despair. She checked through receipts and expenditure over and over again until her head was spinning, but still the long columns would not come right. Robert had said he had left ample funds to cover the debts he had asked her to settle for him but, however she counted it, there just wasn't enough gold and silver in the iron-bound box at her elbow to pay their creditors when it came to settling day, and Robert would be so angry. He took pride in the way he managed his estates and in the fact that he owed not a penny piece to anyone.

What could have happened to the money? Desperately she went through it again, running ink-stained fingers through her hair, indignation beginning to surge through her. It was Robert's fault. He knew she had no head for figures. She had told him so a hundred times. If they had been living at Syderstone with her father none of this would have happened. There John Flowerdew, father of Ned, acted as his agent and managed all these tiresome matters of business. But Robert hated being at Syderstone. It was not that he disliked Sir John, but he preferred to be independent, master in his own household, and that was why so often in the three years of their marriage he had carried her off to Hemsby Castle.

She pushed aside the papers on the table so impatiently that they scattered to the floor. She was so stiff and cramped, she simply had to stretch herself for a moment. From the high window of the small room in the turret she stared out resentfully at the flat Norfolk beaches all the way down to Great Yarmouth. The sharp gusts of March whipped the grey sea into white crests. The marsh grasses, even the few scrubby trees, were flattened and twisted by the wind. Overhead the gulls circled and wheeled around the old stone walls, their long moaning cries like the keening of souls in torment.

It was all very well for Robert. He had only been here for a few weeks before he was summoned to Norwich to attend the Lord Lieutenant on his official business in the county. It was two years since his father had been created Duke of Northumberland. He was virtual dictator of England and his son bathed in his reflected glory, while she was left here in this bleak spot with only the servants for company, bored, lonely, with no entertainment except for the occasional visitor or a travelling pedlar with his cheap goods . . . Her thoughts came to a halt with a sudden shock. Oh God, that was where the money had gone and it had slipped right out of her mind as so many things did.

It was all because of the tailor from Norwich. He had come out to cut and stitch at new doublets and cloaks, all the fine new liveries for the servants now that Robert had been made Master of the King's Buckhounds and Governor of Castle Rising, and cunningly the tradesman had brought with him a pack pony loaded with the most wonderful things. She had not been able to resist the rolls of silk interwoven with gold thread, the gleaming lustrous cloth of silver, as sold to the Princess Mary at Kenninghall, he boasted, who had sent it as a gift to the Lady Elizabeth. She had bought it all with a reckless extravagance, dipping deep into the iron-bound box, and he had made it up for her into gowns and petticoats . . . and all for what? To lie wrapped in clean linen in her oak chests waiting for a chance to be worn.

She would have to tell Robert of course and he would frown, saying that she was too lavish and would ruin them both. But then she would put them on for him and he would laugh, swinging her up in his arms and afterwards fumbling with the lacing, impatient because he wanted her so badly he could scarce wait for the gown to drop round her feet before carrying her off to the bed.

She came slowly back into the room to pick up the scattered papers. Robert used this room as a study and his books were piled up everywhere. Books in Latin, French and Italian, books on all kinds of subjects of which she knew nothing. In the first months of their married life he had tried to teach her and she had done her best, but it was useless. She listened and repeated the words, but the meaning just would not go into her head. Then he would smile, tossing aside the book and pulling her into his arms.

'You give me something better than book learning, little squirrel,' he would say.

But one thing she had not given him and it was a constant pain, a constant regret. In all their days and nights of passionate love-making she had never conceived a child, something she knew he wanted more than anything. She stood upright for a moment, pressing her hands against her flat stomach. How she had longed to feel it swell and quicken with the new life inside her. When Robert had left two months ago she had been almost certain. Twice she had missed the monthly bleeding, so surely this time . . . she had whispered to him and seen the glow in his eyes. But it had been a false hope and again as once before he would be disappointed.

She was putting the table to rights when Jennet came into the room. She had been bathing Tussie and her colour was high and her eyes bright. She put the little dog down and he scampered to Amy, still damp and smelling deliciously from the scented water as she picked him up. She glanced at Jennet standing just inside the door, the big towel still tied round her waist, her face flushed, her lips pursed tight.

'What is it? Is there something wrong with Tussie?'

'No, no, my lady, it is nothing only . . .'

'Only what?'

Jennet frowned. 'I shouldn't repeat it, only it made me so angry . . .'

'Angry? About what? Oh, for heaven's sake, Jennet, don't set me wondering and then say nothing. Is something wrong in the kitchens again?'

Amy sighed because servants had a way of defying their young mistress especially when Robert was away, and she had not yet learned how to be firm and yet kind at the same time.

'No, it's just that . . .' Jennet hesitated and then went on with a rush. 'It's Meg, the girl in the dairy, you know her, my lady, her father is a seaman from Yarmouth and, when her mother died, he came begging to Lord Robert and you took her into the household out of pity . . .'

'Yes, I remember . . . well, what of her? Is she sick?'

'Worse than that. She is with child.'

'Oh.' This was something that happened sometimes and Amy

found it hard to deal with. She said, 'Who is it? One of the stable boys?'

'No.'

'Who then?'

'At first she wouldn't say. Then I heard she is boasting to everyone that my lord gave her the child.'

'Oh no, no, I won't believe it. It's a lie, a vile lie. He would never do such a thing, never, never, do you hear?'

Her denial was quick and passionate because this slut of a girl could, she just could be bearing him the child that she could not.

Jennet looked at her with quick sympathy. 'That's what I said, my lady, and very firm I was too, but the girl is saucy and impudent and she loves to talk.'

'She must be dismissed. She shall be sent away.'

'But she is penniless. She has nowhere to go, no one to care for her.'

'I don't care.' Amy took a step away, turning her back, fighting with herself. She wanted to tear at the girl, hit her, banish her from her sight; but it could be all lies, it must be all lies. She said at last, 'Very well, let her stay, but I don't want to see her. I don't want to know. Do you understand?'

'Yes, my lady.'

'And Jennet . . . let her know that if she says it again, she will be beaten and sent away. I don't care if she starves and her child too. I will not have her slander my lord in his own house.'

'Don't be anxious, my lady. I will make very sure of that.'

When Jennet had gone, she told herself that she did not want even to see the girl. She would not believe it, she would banish it from her thoughts, but after a moment she went downstairs, found her thick cloak and hood and went out into the blowing wind.

She waved to the porter on the gate and then she was out on the rough tussocky path that led to the beach. The sound of the sea pounding on the shingle was in her ears and the wind tore madly at her hair, but still she went on.

It was along here when the tide was out that Robert loved to ride. He was crazy about his horses, was even talking of importing stallions from Spain to breed them with his mares for greater speed and lightness. She had learned to hide from him her own terror of anything but the mild elderly ponies she had

71

ridden at home, but she could not keep up with him, try as she would, and he would laugh at her sometimes as he waited for her to lumber along beside him.

One mad day in the great heat of last summer he had ridden a couple of miles at breakneck speed, then flung himself from the saddle, stripped off his clothes and gone plunging into the sea. When she came toiling up, she had seen him come out of the waves like some sea god, the early morning sun turning his body to gold. All naked and dripping wet as he was, he had lifted her from her horse, unhooked her heavy riding skirt and made love to her exultantly, joyously, there on the wet sands, smelling of the salt of the sea.

Afterwards, sitting up and pulling on his shirt, he had said thoughtfully, 'The Lady Elizabeth rides magnificently. I have promised her one of my horses.'

It was only a few weeks since he had returned from London. She said, 'Did you see her then? Was she at the Court?'

'We went hunting with Edward at Windsor. She has no fear, Amy, no fear at all. Isn't that strange in a woman?'

She remembered this now and her sharp pang of jealousy because he praised another woman. With a quick determined step she went back to the castle, going by way of the stables and through the stone dairy where the great shallow pans of milk were cooling for cream. She paused here and there to speak a word, her eyes searching and finding Meg at the butter churn. She was a big comely girl, clean and rosy. Already, Amy thought she could see the rounding belly beneath the brown fustian skirt.

With a sudden decision she crossed to the girl. 'Meg, I've been hearing a sad tale of you.'

'Yes, my lady?' The girl did not turn her head.

'Who is the father, Meg?'

The cream was just beginning to thicken and she bent forward to watch it, still turning the handle of the churn. The colour crept up her neck and went flooding into her face.

'I'd rather not say, my lady.'

Then the thought that he might have done the same to this slut of a girl as he did to her was more than she could bear. Before she could stop herself her hand shot out. She slapped the plump pretty face hard and then was aghast at what she had done. The girl cried out and the other servants stopped their work to stare. Amy pulled her cloak tightly around her and went swiftly out of the dairy and back to the house.

Robert returned just before dusk. He had ridden fast, outdistancing his men because the messenger from his father had caught him up soon after he left Norwich, and the news he brought had filled him with excitement. He flung the reins to the stable lad and went bounding up the stairs calling for Amy, forgetting his dignity, behaving for once like the boy of nineteen he still was. He burst into the small room where she sat by the fire with Tussie on her lap.

'Such news. You'll never believe!' He threw hat, gloves and cloak aside, coming across to her and pulling her up to kiss her. 'Guildford is to marry Jane. What do you think of that?'

Jane Grey, that mouse of a girl, and the petulant spoiled boy. It did not seem possible.

'But they never seemed even to like one another.'

Robert shrugged his shoulders. 'She would not be my fancy, nor Guildford's either if you ask me, but it's a great match all the same. She has royal blood, my pet, and it's all for my brother, that young puppy!'

'Do you envy him, Robert?'

'Envy him? God, no! I've no wish to spend my life being preached to death!' He threw another log on the fire and then kicked it with his boot, watching it spark into flame.

'What else does your father write, Robin?' she asked quietly.

'Very little, only that Edward is sick again. He is cautious. Letters can be intercepted and read, but I think there is more beneath what he says.'

'Do you mean that the King may die?'

'Possibly, and if he does . . .'

'Wouldn't the Princess Mary be Queen?'

'If she does, then it is goodbye to us, my dear. Mary will take England back to the old religion and the Pope.'

She watched him with troubled eyes. 'But I don't understand . . . how can it be different?'

'King Henry pronounced her bastard once.'

'But that was long ago. Who else could there be in her place?'

'There are one or two . . . the Lady Elizabeth for instance. She would be my choice.' Then he looked up, smiling. 'Oh to hell with it. It's not for us to say and it may never happen. We are bidden to the wedding, that's enough for the moment, and what's for supper? I've been riding all day without a bite of food and I'm hungry as a lion.'

It was not until after they had eaten and had come back to the fire that he said suddenly, 'I'd forgotten. Are you fit for so long a journey? Should you not stay quiet just at this time?'

It was hateful to admit it, to tell him the hope had vanished and see the eagerness die out of his face.

He leaned across to put a hand on hers. 'Never mind, pet. We've still time.'

Quite suddenly the bitterness welled up in her. She had brooded on it all day and now she could not keep it to herself. She lifted her head to look at him.

'I'm sorry I'm such a disappointment to you, Robert, but maybe there are others here to give you the son I have denied you.'

'What the devil are you talking about now?'

'Meg Tyson, for instance.'

'Meg . . . Meg . . . who is she?'

'As if you didn't know.'

Robert had risen. He stood looking down at her, his voice dangerously quiet. 'Would you mind telling me exactly what all this is about?'

'It's quite simple. Meg is with child.'

'Well, what if she is. It happens to girls sometimes.' Then he saw her face and he went on, his tone hardening. 'And I'm the father. Is that what she's saying, the little bitch? I'll have her whipped for insolence.'

'No, you won't, Robert, not if it is true.'

'True, by God! Of course it's not true. It's a damned lie. It's more than a year since . . .' and then he stopped, realizing what he had said.

'So it could have been true . . . you and her! And I would not believe it, I would not.'

'Oh Amy, don't cry over it, for God's sake. It meant nothing, nothing at all.'

'It sickens me even to think of it. When was it . . . when?'

He moved away restlessly, half ashamed and yet determined

74

to brazen it out. 'It was when your father was sick last year and you were three months away at Syderstone. The girl had just come here. I came across her one day. She was miserable, homesick for her dead mother and with her father gone . . . It was stupid, but it just happened.'

It was hard to accept, desperately hard, and yet she must. Once she would have cried herself sick and then ended up in his arms, but not now. She swallowed back the tears.

'I suppose I should be sorry for her, because to you it meant nothing and to her so much that even now she longs to boast of it. You are too easy to love, Robin.'

He looked at her for a moment, touched and regretful. He came to kneel beside her, putting his arms round her waist and leaning his dark head against her breast.

'Don't fret about it. Truly, love, it meant nothing to me beside you. Do you think I want some peasant's brat for my son?' He lifted his head to give her his charming heart-turning smile. 'We'll ride to London and you shall have some fine new gowns, something to outshine Jane, how about that, eh?'

He was trying to placate her with sweets like a child; once she would have accepted it, but now she had grown up a little.

'I have them already,' she said wryly through her tears. 'I've spent the money you left to pay our debts.'

'Have you, by Jupiter?' Then he laughed, too relieved at the way he had escaped to reproach her. 'To hell with our creditors. Let them wait. We'll away to the Court and enjoy ourselves.'

She put her arms round him and wished she did not love him so much and yet would not have him different from what he was.

When, a week later, they took the London road she was surprised to see how many of their men rode with them, and even more surprised that John Appleyard came to join them with half a dozen of his own retainers from Stanfield. There was something more in this surely than a mere wedding, but like his father Robert could keep his own counsel when he chose, and he evaded an explanation when she pressed him.

'We are not beggars,' he said gaily,' and I'm damned if I'm going to let that cub Guildford outshine us, royal bride or not!'

They were on the last lap of their journey, riding close together on a narrow neck of the road when the whole cavalcade jerked to a sudden standstill.

There were shouts and angry voices ahead. Robert frowned. 'What the devil is happening up there? Wait here, Amy.' He pushed his way forward and after a moment she followed after him.

John Appleyard was arguing with an elderly, handsomely dressed man with an escort of twenty or thirty men behind him in fine liveries of scarlet and black.

'It's a damned insolence,' exclaimed John over his shoulder as Robert came up beside him. 'They've taken the crown of the road and would force us into the mud of the gutters.'

'Nothing of the kind,' said the stranger with some asperity. 'But it is our right and we are in haste.'

'Do you then own the road . . . ?' began John aggressively.

'Let it be,' said Robert quickly. 'Don't act the fool.' He spurred his horse forward just as a clear, carrying voice said sharply, 'What is it, Parry? Why this delay? What is the trouble?'

'It is nothing, Your Royal Highness.'

'By God!' exclaimed Robert. 'I guessed as much. It is the Lady Elizabeth.'

He was riding his favourite white mare, a beautiful creature with soft dark eyes and a coat of satin of which he was inordinately proud. He swung her into a trot, the men parted to let him through, and he circled round, bringing her to an exact halt in front of the tall slender woman in the dark riding dress with the flaming red hair under the black velvet cap.

'I beg your pardon, my lady. My men didn't recognize the livery.'

'So it *is* you, my lord. I might have known. Do you always sweep everyone else out of your path?'

'If I had known it was you . . .'

Then they were smiling at one another with an easy familiarity that for some reason made Amy feel afraid. She edged nearer. Robert looked so handsome and managed his horse with such skill, she could not imagine any woman not looking at him with admiration; but Elizabeth was leaning forward and seemed to have eyes only for the white mare.

'Is this the one you told me of, the filly you bred yourself? She is a beauty. What do you call her?'

'Speedwell.'

'A pretty name, as pretty as she.'

76

Robert whispered something and Elizabeth laughed, a lovely bell-like sound, and Amy felt shut out, excluded from their private jest. A little worm of resentment curled inside her because Robert seemed to have forgotten her.

He said, 'Are you riding from London?'

Elizabeth's face clouded over. 'I heard that my brother was sick and I set out to visit him, but his messenger met me just outside the city. He refuses to receive me.'

'A sick boy's fancy. He will think better of it.'

'I wish I could think so.'

'Why should you doubt it?'

'These are strange times, Lord Robert.' She gave him a long look, then turned her horse away. 'Parry, do you hear? It is time we moved on.'

Robert commanded his party to stand back against the hedge and let the Princess and her retinue ride by. But when she had gone, he still stood staring after her.

Amy touched his arm. 'What is it, Robin? What did she mean?'

'I'm not sure,' he said, 'I'm beginning to wonder if . . .' Then he swung his horse round. 'Well, we shall find out soon enough. I daresay it is all nothing. We had better make haste if we are not to find ourselves without a bed by nightfall.'

Six

Amy disliked Syon House from the very first moment she stepped over the threshold – though the great mansion set squarely round its inner courtyard was magnificent – and Mary came running to greet them, kissing her warmly and hugging her brother. Perhaps it was because it had once been a great monastery where the monks prayed night and day for the murdered Richard Plantagenet. As they rode up through the water meadows along the banks of the Thames, they could see the gaunt ruined arches still standing among the lush green grass.

All the young Dudleys were there and Guildford was more objectionable than ever, blown up with self-importance because of the fuss that was being made over his wedding.

'Look out for ghosts,' he whispered in her ear when the page took the torch to light them to bed through the long dark passage on their very first night. 'They say the old friars still walk, or you might even see the Lord Protector himself with his bloody head under his arm.'

'Shut up, you fool!' said Robert fiercely, but Guildford only giggled and dodged the blow aimed at him.

'He's an idiot. Don't take any notice of him.'

Robert put his arm protectively around her shoulders, but Amy shuddered as the flame flickered over the portrait of the Duke of Somerset still hanging in the long gallery. It was barely a year since he had been tried for treason and lost his head on Tower Hill so that Syon House, which he had built with such loving care, had come to Robert's father. Rumour said that the great Duke had hounded his rival to his death, though Robert angrily denied it. Up in Norfolk he had once had a man flogged for daring to voice what everyone was thinking.

The house hummed with preparations for the grand occasion since not only was Jane to marry Guildford, but they would be celebrating the wedding of Catherine Dudley with Lord Henry

Hastings and Jane's younger sister with the Earl of Pembroke's heir. They should all have been as merry as larks, thought Amy the next afternoon, when Mary came to fetch her and they climbed up the narrow staircase to the cold room under the roof where the needlewomen were working night and day on the gowns for the triple wedding. But the only one of them who seemed truly happy was Catherine, who adored her good-looking bridegroom.

Jane stood in the middle of the room while the dressmakers bustled around her, taking in tucks and pinning up the skirts of gold brocade. The heavy gown, with its bodice encrusted with jewels and the under-kirtle of silver tissue embroidered with pearls, seemed to weigh the tiny figure to the ground. The freckles stood out plainly on the pale face and down one cheekbone lay a dark smear like a livid bruise.

The richness dimmed the lustre of the new dresses that had come from Norfolk strapped on the back of the sumpter mule. Amy said enviously, 'It's beautiful. The loveliest wedding dress I have ever seen.'

Jane looked at her with contempt. 'I don't like it,' she said flatly. 'It turns me into somebody I'm not, gaudy and vulgar as a peacock.'

'Oh no, my lady,' exclaimed one of the dressmakers in a shocked voice. 'How can you say such a thing? It's the finest French brocade I have ever handled. Not even the Princess Mary has worn anything so exquisite. It must have cost a fortune.'

Jane said nothing, but stood like a statue, her lips compressed as they stripped it off her. She quivered in her thin linen shift while they wrapped the plain velvet dressing-gown around her.

'You're cold,' said Mary sympathetically, 'and I don't wonder. This spring weather is treacherous, and having dresses fitted is always so exhausting. Come to my room. We'll get them to bring us something warm to drink and we'll be cosy together over the fire.'

Only there was never anything cosy about Jane. She sat silent, sipping the mulled wine while Mary chatted nervously to Amy asking about Hemsby and exchanging domestic gossip. It was two years since she had married Harry Sidney and like Amy she longed for a baby.

'These men,' she complained. 'Harry is just like Robert. He

wants a son but if God does not will it, then what can one do?'

Amy was tempted to tell her about Meg, but she would not betray Robert to his sister. She said instead, 'Has your father been ill? When I saw him at supper last night, he did not seem himself. Robin has told me nothing.'

'He is tired and overworked,' said Mary quickly. 'He would have been glad to stay in the country and rest, but Edward cannot do without him and he is still grieving for little Temperance. I sometimes think he was fonder of her than of any of us.'

Amy was silent. The dreaded sweating sickness had swept through London last summer, taking Ambrose's young wife and baby son and Robert's seven-year-old sister in its passing.

'Father grumbles sometimes,' went on Mary, smiling, 'four of us married and not one living grandchild yet. You will have to make up for us, Jane.'

The wide grey eyes turned to them, dark and troubled. 'I shall never have a child.'

'Oh Jane, don't say such things. It is unlucky.'

'It is true. I know it somehow, deep inside me.' The small hands in her lap clenched suddenly. 'I wish to God I didn't have to marry Guildford.'

'Oh Jane,' exclaimed Amy. 'Why!'

'Why, why? I don't like him, that's why. I know he is your brother, Mary, and I am sorry, but I detest him.'

'Mother spoils him,' said Mary hurriedly. 'He is young for his age, Jane. He says a lot of silly things, but he doesn't mean them. He will change when he is married. I am sure of it.'

'People don't change,' said the small remorseless voice, 'not in ways like that. He is cruel. He beat his dog this morning, beat it till it cried out, and only because the poor creature ran to me instead of him.'

Mary looked away uncomfortably. 'He has a quick temper. It means nothing.'

'I wish that were true.'

'Is there someone else?' whispered Amy sympathetically. 'Someone you care for?'

'No, no one,' said Jane stonily. She pushed back the heavy fair hair wearily. 'Oh, it's not just Guildford. I don't want to marry anyone.'

The girls were silent for a moment until Amy blurted out what they both thought. 'But everyone must marry sometime. You wouldn't want to be without a husband.'

'Why not? It would be wonderful ... to be alone ... to be able to do just as I wish. There are so many things, my books, my music, my studies.' Jane's lips trembled childishly for an instant. 'When I am married, I shall lose everything I love best.'

'No, you won't. It will be different, but you will begin to share ... it is part of marriage,' said Amy eagerly, but Jane turned on her, her eyes accusing.

'How easy it is for you. You love Robert, you don't have to live with someone you despise. Guildford cares for nothing that is dear to me.'

'But if you really feel like that, then why didn't you explain to your mother, make her understand? My father could be stern but he would never have forced me to marry someone I really disliked.'

Jane laughed, a harsh unhappy sound, and the colour flamed into her pale face. 'What do you know about it? You talk like a fool. What choice is ever given to girls like us?' Her scornful glance swept over Amy. 'It may be wicked to say so, but I hate my mother and father. When have they ever cared how I felt, when have they ever listened to me? Never, never once in my whole life. The only happiness I ever had was the few hours I spent with my tutor. John Aylmer is so kind, so gentle; with him the time flies by too quickly and now I must lose that too. I wish I were dead. I wish I could die tonight and then nothing would matter any more.'

One small hand touched the bruise on her cheek and in a flash of intuition Amy saw the hopeless struggle, the blows, the taunts, the complete lack of love, the burning ambition that considered a daughter's unhappiness as nothing in the struggle for power, and she was filled with a helpless pity. She would have liked to put her arms around the small shivering figure, staring white-faced into the fire, but when she touched the ice-cold hand, Jane drew it away and got to her feet.

'I must go back to Chelsea,' she said, 'or Mother will be angry.'

When she was ready, the two girls went down to the landing stage with her, their cloaks round them and the dogs racing beside them through the wet grass. They kissed the cold cheek before Jane stepped into the boat. Amy thought that she had

81

never seen anything more forlorn than the small figure wrapped in the costly fur mantle, surrounded by servants and yet utterly alone.

One morning a few days later a gaily painted barge went floating down the river towards Greenwich. Jane had never been easy company and, now she had gone back to her parents at Chelsea, they sighed with relief. Mary and Amy lay stretched on cushions under the purple velvet awning while the rowers dipped their oars and the water fell in glittering cascades in the May sunshine. They were all in the highest of spirits. Harry Sidney had told them that the young King had made a wonderful recovery from his sickness. He had invited them to Greenwich to watch Hugh Willoughby and Richard Chancellor set out on the first lap of their long voyage to the fabulous land of Muscovy. The holds of their ships were stuffed with fine English cloth to exchange for pearls and furs with the express purpose of obtaining trade concessions from the Tsar of Russia. How strange it sounded, a country as far away as the stars and almost as difficult to reach.

'Where is Russia?' Amy asked plaintively.

Robert smiled indulgently. 'Little ignoramus. I shall have to persuade Dr Dee to give you lessons in geography.'

'Will he be there today?' asked Mary eagerly.

'Father says so. He has been working with Chancellor for months. He has planned the navigation of the whole voyage.'

'Who is Dr Dee and what does he do?'

'It is rather what does he not do?' said Robert playfully. 'Dr John used to teach us mathematics. He is scholar, astrologer, philosopher, map-maker, spy, historian . . .'

'And magician, don't forget that,' added Ambrose. He leaned towards Amy. 'He has a magic glass and, if you ask him nicely, he might gaze into it and call up spirits to read your future for you.'

Amy looked from one laughing face to the other. She never knew whether the Dudleys were serious or making fun of her. 'You're teasing,' she said doubtfully.

'No, my pet, it's all true as gospel.' Robert was idly plucking at the strings of his lute. 'When he was up at Cambridge, the devils used to fly in and out of his rooms like a swarm of midges.'

'Beelzebub, Lord of the Flies,' whispered Guildford, grinning at her.

Amy shivered. There had been a girl at Wymondham whom they had called witch. She remembered the gloating faces of the villagers lined up on the bank when they threw her into the water. If she floated, then she was a witch proved; if she sank, then she was innocent. She had seen the swollen body, the white drowned face no longer beautiful, the bloody marks where the ropes had bitten cruelly into the wrists and ankles, when they had dragged her out of the pond.

'Sweetheart, you're shaking. Are you cold?'

She shook her head, but it was good to feel Robert's arm warm and comforting round her waist.

They saw the ships bobbing in the water as they came up the Greenwich steps, with the gay scarlet bunting spread along the bulwarks and the pennants flying in the wind.

Edward looked thin and he coughed frequently, but his eyes were bright and he welcomed them gaily. There were a great number of people and they all crowded to the windows, jostling one another for a good place. Amy felt very alone. Mary was caught up with some of her own friends and Robert had been immediately surrounded by a laughing group of young girls. One of them she recognized. It was Harry Sidney's sister, Frances; a child still, she defied her governess and clung to Robert's arm, looking up at him adoringly.

They were all so sure of themselves, chattering like magpies about things of which she knew nothing, making her feel shy and awkward beside their brilliance. There was one in particular. She could not have been more than thirteen or fourteen, the small breasts barely swelling the rich dress of gold and crimson, her white pointed face triangular like a little cat.

'You all talk and talk, but I want to see everything,' she suddenly cried out, breaking away from the others and running to the windows. She jumped on to the padded seat and leaned far out so that the wind tore at the long red-brown hair.

Someone shrieked, 'Come back, Lettice, you will fall.'

'No, I won't. It's wonderful. I feel as if I were flying.' She flung out her arms in a wild gesture, swaying forward.

In one stride Robert had reached her and lifted her down. She fought him and, as he put her firmly on her feet, she bent her head and bit the hand that held her, her wild ringing laugh reminding Amy of that lovely evil creature who had been drowned at Wymondham.

'Little wild cat!' exclaimed Robert, looking down at his hand ruefully.

'Who is she?' muttered someone near Amy.

'Lettice Knollys, cousin to the Princess Elizabeth and wild as a hawk. She'll lead some man a dance one day.'

Their pranks were interrupted by a shattering roar as the guns fired and the ships' cannons answered in a thunderous salute. The fifes and trumpets blared out and they waved to the crews standing along the decks. The sails opened out like huge white flowers as Amy gazed entranced. The ships moved slowly down the river on the tide.

'There is no land uninhabitable and no sea unnavigable,' said a voice close behind her. 'What wonders they will see on their voyage. Who would not wish to sail with them and discover a new world?'

'I for one,' answered Amy quickly. 'I don't like what I don't know. There is comfort and happiness in the dear familiar things of home.'

'Spoken like a true woman. You must be Lord Robert's wife. When I saw him some months ago, he spoke of you very tenderly.'

The man beside her was very tall. His hair hung to his shoulders, lank as yellow silk, matching the full soft beard. 'I am John Dee,' he said, smiling. 'Maybe he has told you of me.'

'Yes, yes, he has,' but she was confused. Surely one who commanded devils and read the stars could not look like this man with his rosy cheeks, or be so young still, scarcely more than thirty.

'You look alarmed. Have I startled you?'

'No, of course not,' she said bravely, but all the same she was frightened. Ambrose had been right. This was no ordinary man. The light blue eyes watched her face, gravely questioning, and she felt she had no secrets from him, every thought would be an open book for him to read.

Then they all crowded around him, taking him away from her, bombarding him with questions about his travels. Hungary he had visited, and Germany and the University of Louvain. He

84

answered, smiling. He was showing off a mechanical toy he had brought from Nuremberg. A giant raven four feet high, its black feathers sleeked, its voice harsh, croaking, like some monstrous parody of the real bird. She swept away her skirts in sudden fear as it jolted stiffly across the floor. It was then that she saw the thin dark man who followed his master like a shadow.

Afterwards she used to think that everything that happened started from that evening though, when she said it once to Robert, he only smiled and said she was dreaming. It was after they had supped and Edward had been spirited away to early bed by his doctors. All the young people had gathered round the stone hearth in a corner of the great hall, badgering John Dee to read their future for them, stretching out eager palms to him.

'How many children shall I have?'

'Shall I be rich? or happy? or successful?'

'Shall I be famous?'

'When shall I meet my future husband? Will he be dark or fair, prince or beggar?'

And so they went on and at first he laughed, but when they became insistent, he grew angry. 'No,' he thundered at them at last. 'You mock me. I'm not a fortune-teller at a fair. To peer into the unknown belongs to God alone. It is not a game for children,' and he walked away from them.

'Now you've offended him,' said Mary.

'Oh nonsense,' said Guildford pettishly. 'Why does he have to take himself so damned seriously? He's nothing but a charlatan after all, pretending to powers he doesn't possess.'

'You speak of what you do not know.' As if from nowhere the thin dark man was in their midst. There was something strange, something sinister about the pale face under the black hood that covered his head except for the pointed ears. 'I have some of my master's skill, only a little you understand, but if it will amuse you . . .'

Robert looked contemptuous. 'And if we pay you enough, is that it? Who are you? Is this something you've picked up among peddling magicians?'

'Only fools laugh at the secrets of the wise. I would have thought my Lord Robert, my master's favourite pupil, would have had more courtesy.' The stranger had a slight foreign accent. Now he drew himself up proudly. 'They call me Sirius. It is not my true

85

name but it will serve, and I was second to none in Nuremberg until Dr John came amongst us.'

'And now you follow at his heels, pecking at the crumbs of his knowledge.'

'Because I have true humility. I know, my lord, when I meet one wiser than myself,' he said rebukingly. 'But please yourselves. I thought to entertain the King's guests for an idle hour, but if you do not wish for it . . .' He looked round at the ring of expectant faces, a disdainful smile on his thin lips. One after another, half reluctantly, they tossed the gold into a glittering heap. He did not even look at it. Instead he clapped his hands and said commandingly, 'Bring me a bowl of ink.'

'Ink?' they stared at one another, tittering until Mary called one of the servants.

Twilight had crept into the room. The fire glowed on the pale face of the dark man, lighting up high cheekbones and deep hollows below the strange light eyes. The candlelight left pools of black shadows. They waited in silence and Amy plucked at Robert's sleeve.

'I don't like him,' she whispered. 'Must we listen? Can't we leave?'

'Not yet. Presently.' There was impatience in Robert's voice and his eyes were filled with eager expectancy. She thought, with sudden pain, he's not happy with me, he looks for something else, something I cannot give him.

The pewter bowl of ink was dark and mysterious. The white face bent over it and there was silence. Amy shut her eyes. She would not look. She heard the eager questions and the answers and thought scornfully it was no more than what happened every year at Wymondham Fair, when the black-haired Egyptian snatched the hard-earned coins from the horny hands of villagers and told them the hopeful lies they longed to hear.

Then something startled her. Robert had left her side. He was leaning forward. 'And now what do you see for me?'

The thin face bent over the bowl again and Amy, watching fearfully, could have sworn she saw the black liquid stir. Then he said slowly, almost as if the words were dragged out of him, 'It is confused. Blood first . . . a great deal of blood . . . then fire . . . but afterwards a crown, a crown of gold . . .'

'A crown for Robin!' crowed Guildford in derision. 'The crown is not for him, it's for me.'

'Be quiet, you fool,' hissed Ambrose.

Robert's face was intent, dreaming, as if he hadn't even heard the interruption. 'Look again.' he said insistently. 'What else do you see?'

'Nothing, my lord, it has gone.'

'There must be something more. Look again, I say.'

'No.'

'Look, damn you, or I'll have you flogged out of the palace for a lying trickster.'

'You would do so at your peril.'

For a moment two proud wills crossed and fought a battle, then the dark man shrugged, the pale eyes turned again to the bowl. It was then that it happened, or perhaps it was only overwrought imagination. Afterwards she could never be sure, but to her fascinated eyes it seemed that the ink began to quiver and in its ebony depths something formed, a picture, a steep cliff, a dizzying height or was it a flight of stairs, going down, down into nowhere. She felt an icy breath touch her cheek, then the face of the magician changed. He swept the bowl away with a violent gesture, the metal struck the floor and the ink ran across the stone.

'What is it? What has happened? What did you see?'

'Nothing, my lord. There was nothing. It was an accident. I caught the bowl with my sleeve. I apologize for my clumsiness.'

'Fetch another.'

'No, no, my lord. It is enough.'

He would have turned away, but Robert caught hold of him and swung him round.

'What did you see?'

'Must I say it again? I tell you there was nothing.'

'I believe you lie.'

'Believe what you wish. It makes no difference.' The long bony fingers clasped round Robert's wrist. 'Sometimes, my lord, it is better not to know what the future holds for you.'

Servants had come to mop up the ink. They were all talking now and laughing; only Robert stared after him, a dazed look on his face. It was all over. He swung round and smiled at her.

87

'The man is nothing but a liar and a cheat. I'll make sure Dr John hears of his exploits.'

'Leave him be, Robin. He meant no harm.'

'These fellows can be dangerous.'

Amy said no more, but she could not forget the look on the magician's face and the plain fact that the gold lay where it had been thrown. Something had sent him away in fear, leaving it untouched.

Seven

They returned to Durham House, a huge palace rambling along the Thames, which like Syon had come to Robert's father from the executed Duke of Somerset. Preparations began at once for the triple wedding. The state rooms were hung with gold and crimson tissue. There were costly Turkish carpets and embroidered tablecloths fringed with silver. There were to be three days of feasting with dancing, jousts and masques. The beggars who clustered at the gates went away with enough beef, ale and bread to last them for a week. If it had been a royal wedding, there could not have been a more lavish display. Those old enough to remember said darkly that London had not seen such pomp since King Henry crowned his witch-wife, Anne Boleyn, and look what came out of that. She was dead by the sword within three years.

And yet with all the rich show there was a sense of oppression coupled with a forced gaiety that struck Amy, the outsider, more strongly than the closely knit family.

She saw little of Robert. He was restless these days, spending a great deal of time with Jack and Ambrose. What sort of a wedding was it, she thought, running errands here, there and everywhere for her tireless mother-in-law, when the Duke came and went like a thundercloud, his temper so uncertain that the servants went in deadly fear of an explosion of anger at the least thing. When they dressed the bride in the gold and silver brocade, and knotted the strings of pearls in the pale hair flowing over her shoulders, her face was so chalk white that he commanded them abruptly to rub it with rouge.

Jane sat through the festivities still as a statue, eating nothing and speaking little, and when it came to the bedding, when the guests giggling and not a little drunk came crowding around them with nosegays and laughter and bawdy jests, she broke into wild hysterical weeping, pleading that she was too young to lie with a husband, that she wanted to go home. Home, thought Amy pityingly, home to a mother who had beaten her into submission to the marriage she hated with a young man she despised.

Surprisingly the Duke was kinder than anyone. He put an arm round the shivering girl's shoulders, rebuking his son for his petulant anger at his bride's inexplicable tears.

'She is wearied and no wonder. You shall do as you please, Jane. You shall lie alone tonight and tomorrow your mother shall carry you back with her to Chelsea. You shall have time to prepare yourself for your new life.'

The guests stared at one another, wondering at the Duke's indulgence towards a silly, frightened girl, but he remained firm with his wife who was angry that her favourite son should be so flouted, even with the Countess of Suffolk who had little sympathy with her daughter's distress. Guildford sulked but he was too afraid of his father to protest, and it was not until a month later that Amy realized what lay behind her father-in-law's gentleness.

It was one evening at the end of June. They had all gathered in Mary's room as they did so often to talk and play games, only there were no games or music that night. When Amy came in, she saw them all there, Mary, Jack, Ambrose and Robert, standing together while Guildford lounged on the window-seat. They were all looking at Harry Sidney and something in their faces frightened her. It was as if the feeling of tension that had hung over the household for so many weeks had suddenly come to a head. She went at once to Robert's side.

'What is it? What has happened?'

He put an arm round her comfortingly and Mary said quietly, 'It's the King. Tell them, Harry.'

She saw the look of strain on the young man's face. 'Edward is dying.'

'Oh no, it can't be true,' she exclaimed. 'He was getting better. Your father told us so, and he was so happy and in such good spirits that day we saw him at Greenwich.'

'The Duke tried to hide it. We all did. We hoped, but now there is no hope.'

There was silence before Jack broke it. 'That's not all, is it? Go on, Harry. You can tell them now. They will have to know soon.'

Harry Sidney raised his head. He was pale and tired from the sleepless nights he had spent beside the dying boy who was his friend.

He said heavily, 'Yesterday Edward signed a Declaration, putting aside his half-sisters, putting aside Mary and Elizabeth from the inheritance and naming the Lady Jane Grey as his heir. She will be Queen when he is dead.'

'Jane! That whey-faced ninny!' The words seemed to force themselves out of Robert. 'He must be mad. Sickness has crazed his brain.'

'Be quiet, Robin,' said Jack sternly. 'Go on. What else is there, Harry?'

'He is not mad, Robin, very far from it. His body is sick but his mind is absolutely clear. This is no new thing. As far back as January, Edward spoke of his intention and at that time the Duke, your father, was against it. He said that England would never accept it, nor the Privy Council, but Edward has not let it drop. He has clung to it more and more as his sickness has increased.'

'But why? For what reason?' exclaimed Robert. 'Old King Henry's will stated plainly that if Edward died without an heir, then the crown should go to Mary and afterwards, if she had no child, to Elizabeth.'

'Mary is Catholic,' said Harry Sidney sombrely. 'Edward believes that as Queen she will take England back to Rome even if it means going through blood and fire, and the very thought of what the country may suffer is driving Edward frantic. He talks of nothing else. He would not rest until your father had taken a solemn oath to carry out his will.'

Fire and blood . . . it was what that strange creature had said that evening at Greenwich, and what else had he seen and refused to speak of? For an instant in the darkening room Amy seemed to see the dying boy forcing his will upon the powerful Duke of Northumberland who had always seemed to dominate him and all around him so easily.

It was Robert who broke the silence. 'If it is Mary's religion that troubles him, then why not name Elizabeth as his heir?'

'Edward is fond of her but he has never forgotten that his father once declared Elizabeth bastard. Her mother was executed as an adulteress. How can he even be sure that the blood royal runs in her veins?'

'By God,' said Robert, 'you've only to look at her, the very image of her father. She is a cub of the old lion, no doubt of that.'

'So you like to think, Robin,' interrupted Guildford spitefully, 'but she has always been your fancy, hasn't she? I suppose you think that with her as queen, you'd stand a fine chance of winning her favour. Well, this time you are going to be unlucky. It will be Jane on the throne and she is my wife. You missed your chance there. It will be I to whom you'll be kneeling instead of that proud bitch.'

'Have some sense, Gil, for the Lord's sake,' said Ambrose disgustedly. 'You've a damned long way to go before you'll be king.'

Guildford turned on him viciously. 'Why? You're jealous, that's what it is, you're all jealous because Jane is married to me. Well, Father always intended her for me, and now I know why. You all like to crow over me, but now it will be my turn.'

'Shut up,' said Jack sternly, 'you talk like a fool.'

'Just because you're the eldest, you think you can say what you like to me . . .'

It was Harry Sidney who cut short the bickering. His words fell on them like a douche of cold water. 'Have you thought,' he said, 'it could mean civil war?'

'No,' said Jack decisively. 'Father will make sure of that. He has made his plans already.'

'Father has? How do you know?'

'He has spoken to me. Father has always looked ahead. Haven't you realized, any of you? It's not only Edward who fears Mary. She could be our ruin too.'

They drew together then, bombarding him with questions, even Mary, leaving Harry Sidney and Amy the only outsiders. She drew near to where he stood in front of the great chimney-piece. She whispered, 'Is it certain that Edward will die? After all he has been sick before and still made a good recovery.'

'Not this time, Amy. You have only to see him. He is in such pain he prays for death. It is only a matter of days.' He drew himself up wearily. 'And now I must go back. He doesn't like me to be away from him for long.'

He spoke to Mary and they went out together. The evening passed in eager discussion in which Amy did not join. She sat over her needlework listening to them talk with an inner trembling, a fear that somehow this was going to mean the end of her happy world.

A few days later there was a night of storm such as England had rarely experienced. Amy woke up to lightning so brilliant that the room was bright as day, followed by crashing thunder that shook the old palace to its very foundations. Robert leaped from the bed while the terrified Amy hid her head under the blankets. Outside she could hear excited voices. Dawn brought hailstorms crashing against the windows, tearing at the trees in the gardens. Jennet came running into the room without knocking, white as paper.

'They are saying that old King Harry has risen from his grave,' she gibbered in terror. 'It is raining blood and a thunderbolt has split the tower of the church . . . Oh my lady, what is going to happen to us? We shall all be killed.'

'Be quiet, girl,' said Robert angrily. 'You'll terrify your mistress with your foolery. We have had storms before.'

'Never such a one as this, my lord, when the dead come out of their tombs and monstrous things are born.'

'Go and comfort your mistress. I'll be back soon.' Robert flung his night-robe round him and went out of the room at a run.

The two girls clung together, their teeth chattering. 'Something terrible is going to happen,' moaned Jennet, her usual common sense drowned in the superstitious fears of her peasant childhood. Her terror had the effect of making Amy calm and collected. She sat up in the great bed.

'My lord is right. This is foolish talk, Jennet. Pull yourself together and bring me my dressing-gown.'

But before the girl could wrap her mistress in the fur-lined gown, Robert was back. One look at his face as he stood in the doorway was enough.

'What is it?'

'Father has sent a messenger,' he said, 'Edward is dead,' and while the girls stared at him, excitement mingled with a kind of awe flamed in his face. 'It has begun.'

After that, events moved so quickly that when Amy looked back on this time, it seemed as unbelievable and as frightful as a nightmare from which you wake sweating and thankful. Only from this evil dream there was no awakening. At one moment they were at the very top of the ladder, rich, powerful, the envy of lesser men, and at the next turn of fortune's wheel, they were ruined, their enemies laughing at the proud Duke of Northumberland, ruler of England, degraded, broken, a man who had recklessly ventured all on one desperate crazy throw of the dice and had lost.

That same day Robert rode out of London with five hundred men-at-arms behind him. Amy wept as she clung to him.

'Why do you have to go, Robin? Why you? Why?'

'Don't be foolish, love,' he said half impatiently. 'As soon as Jane is proclaimed Queen in London, then I shall do the same in Norfolk. It is essential that Mary should be captured before she hears of Edward's death.'

'But she is his sister. It is her right,' argued Amy obstinately.

'Not now,' said Robert sternly. 'It is treason now to say it or even think of it. Remember that, little squirrel,' but though he spoke boldly and kissed her lovingly, she sensed that he was not as confident as he appeared.

It was as if they were all under a spell, she thought, as if their father was a magician and, when he commanded, they obeyed instantly and without question. She saw the Duke calmly manipulating men's lives as if it were no more than playing a game of chess. Three days after Edward's death, he sent Mary to Chelsea to fetch Jane.

'Do not alarm her,' he said. 'Leave me to tell her of her great destiny.'

All the Privy Council had assembled at Durham House, all the great men, including Arundel with his crafty face, Pembroke with his rough manners, waiting uneasily.

'What will happen now?' Amy asked her mother-in-law nervously.

'You need have no fear, child. The Duke will see to all,' she answered confidently. 'He has waited for this moment all his life and now it is here. They are but mice obedient to his will.'

And neither of them realized with what mixed feelings John Dudley, Duke of Northumberland, waited for the young girl he intended to place on the English throne. For a long time now he had nursed a giddy ambitious dream. Like another earlier Warwick he would become a maker of kings. There is a subtle intoxication about power that blinds those who indulge in it. He whose father had been executed, he the first Duke not of royal blood, would henceforth stand at the right hand of the Queen of England and no one would be able to deny him the right. For two long years the dream had hovered at the back of his mind, but now that it had been placed in his hands by a sick boy fanatical in the cause of religion, it seemed as insubstantial as smoke that a passing breeze could blow into nothing. When Edward had turned his dream into reality, he had shrunk from it, had tried to dissuade him, but now he was committed, he drove forward with the same thrust that had carried him to supreme power.

It was evening when the barge brought Jane to Durham House. A light mist hung over the river when the Duke went down to the water steps to receive her. She looked bewildered as he bowed low over her hand and led her to the great hall where the Councillors waited. They fell upon their knees as she came in and she turned to him in distress.

'What is this? I don't understand.'

'You know already, Your Grace, that our late beloved King is dead. By Edward's will, witnessed and agreed by us all, you are today by the Grace of God proclaimed Queen of England.'

She snatched her hand away, staring at him, her face white as chalk. 'No, no, it cannot be. The crown is not mine. The Lady Mary is the rightful heir.'

She turned as if she would have run away but her strength gave way. She stumbled and sank to the floor.

The Duke lifted her up. What he said to her, Amy could not hear, but she knew well how persuasive he could be when he chose. Jane's mother, angry at her daughter's hesitation, was ready to attack. Her father said pressingly, 'You do yourself wrong, my daughter. Think of us, think of your family, think of what you owe to us all.'

She raised a distressed face, tears running down her cheeks, and the Duke thrust them aside.

'Let her speak for herself,' he said. 'She has the blood of kings. She will not fail us.'

Jane looked from him to her parents, to the husband she disliked and then to the greedy and ambitious men who surrounded her. She knew they cared nothing for her, the trembling girl, but only for the power and the riches that could come to them from the crown they placed on her head. Tiny though she was, thought Amy, she had grown in dignity and strength.

'If it is God's will that I be your Queen,' she said simply, 'then I pray that He will grant me spirit and grace so that I may govern to His glory and service and to the advantage of this kingdom.'

They came flocking to her then, kneeling and kissing her hand, swearing allegiance even to death.

The next morning Amy helped her mother-in-law dress her in the Tudor colours; her brocaded kirtle and long-sleeved gown were in white and green, embroidered with gold. The white coif set with emeralds, diamonds, rubies and pearls was placed on the long fair hair. She was so small, they strapped three-inch wooden clogs to her shoes so that she could be seen stepping into the barge. Guildford, magnificent in white and gold, sat close beside her as the boat floated down the river to the Tower. The banks were crowded, but they did not cheer. They stood silently staring. The storms had all gone. The sun shone brilliantly on the long procession, glinting on jewelled caps and swords, on gold and silver tissue, on furred hoods and velvets of red, purple, blue and lilac.

Amy longed for news of Robert but there was none. Of the next four days she could remember little, they were too strange, too bewildering and unreal. No one had time for her. When she spoke to Jane, she stared at her as if she were a stranger. Even Mary seemed different. She clung to Harry Sidney who looked pale and tense. 'He grieves for Edward,' thought Amy, 'and yet too he does not like what is happening.'

The Tower was dark and gloomy despite the rich hangings and fine furniture. Guildford fretted petulantly because Jane refused point-blank to proclaim him as King, and more and more frightening news crept in from outside. The Princess Mary had evaded Robert and had taken refuge in Framlingham Castle. Friends and supporters were flocking to her. The proclamation had been received coldly in the city. There had been many voices raised for Mary. Unpleasant rumours were rife that the Duke had poisoned Edward to gain his own ends. Traced to their roots, those found guilty were condemned to the pillory, bloodily whipped, their ears sliced from their heads, their tongues bored through with red-hot irons.

On 13 July, a day of breathless heat, the Duke was faced with a fearful decision. Troops must be raised and sent against Mary whose strength grew with every day that passed. Jane was adamant that he, the first soldier in her kingdom, must be the one to lead them.

The argument was long and bitter. He did not trust those whom he would leave behind him, and who had only been subdued by the force of his will, but the girl he had made Queen had to be obeyed. He yielded at last, and for the first time Amy saw his composure break down when he bade farewell to his wife and to Guildford, the boy he loved above all his sons. He smiled wearily when she curtseyed to him, taking her hand and kissing her cheek.

'Poor child, poor child,' he murmured. 'I will send Robin back to you if it is possible.'

She ran down to the courtyard to watch him ride out with Jack through the gate. His standard carried a gold-crowned lion on red damask, powdered with ragged silver staves, and it fluttered madly in the wind from the river. She pushed nearer the gate as he went through and saw how the crowd surged around him. Some of them were muttering. He threw them gold and they fought for it savagely even under the hooves of the horses, but none of them raised a cheer. She saw him turn to Jack with his bitter sardonic smile.

'The rabble press to us for what they can get, but not one of them wishes us Godspeed.'

It was ten days before she saw him again. Ten fearful days of waiting while the hours crept endlessly by, while the great lords kicking their heels in the Tower looked uneasily at one another and held whispered conferences behind closed doors. Then the desertions began. Like rats they abandoned the sinking ship. Arundel first, bowing low to Jane, saying that in such uncertain times he should reinforce the Duke who was their leader. Pembroke soon followed, then one by one the others. Amongst them was a small, quiet man who had once been Somerset's secretary and at his fall had discreetly attached himself to Northumberland. William Cecil's shrewd grey eyes had watched and said nothing. Then one day, unobtrusively, silently, he had disappeared.

Guildford came whimpering to his mother and for the first time Amy heard the Duchess speak harshly to him.

'Pull yourself together, be a man for once,' she said sharply. 'Try to be like your father and your brothers.'

Day after day Jane sat under the canopy of state in the White Tower and saw her tiny Court melt away, her mother angry and defiant, her father alternately blustering and cringing.

The July sun was still glorious. The roses were blooming in the Governor's garden. Standing on the high stone parapet, Amy felt the light breeze caress her hot cheeks and thought she could smell the strong salty tang of the sea. Gulls screamed, circling high above her head, and then came swooping down on the offal left outside the kitchen quarters. The sound of hooves on the cobbled causeway drew her eyes from the river. The messenger was white with dust, his horse flecked with foam. The news he brought was fearful. The nobility, the country folk had flocked to Mary. She was riding south in triumph.

'The Duke! What of the Duke?' cried his wife in anguish.

'His Grace rallied his men at first,' said the messenger sombrely, 'but it has been a losing battle. Every day there have been desertions.' He shrugged his shoulders hopelessly.

From a window high in the gatehouse, Amy watched the soldiers come marching down Tower Hill. The man who had ridden out ten days before in all his magnificence, virtual dictator of England, was returning, old, defeated, broken. He stared straight in front of him, arrogant still, though his red cloak was half torn from his back and the rabble screamed obscenities and pelted him with filth from the gutters. Beside him Arundel's face wore an ugly grin of triumph. Behind him Jack was crouched over the neck of his horse. Amy pushed open the casement and leaned far out in an agony of fear.

'Where is Robin?' she cried out to him. 'What have they done to Robin?'

Jack lifted his face, dirty and smudged with tears. He shook his head and the escort urged him on. Jennet put her arms around her mistress's waist and pulled her back, slamming the window shut.

98

'Be careful, my lady,' she scolded. 'Do you want to draw attention to yourself? Do you want them to thrust you into prison too?'

'I wouldn't mind. I wouldn't mind anything if I could be sure that Robert still lives,' she said wildly.

Everything was in confusion, but one thing was certain. The Duke with his sons and Jane were imprisoned. The Duchess was curtly informed that she was to be escorted back to Durham House and held there under house arrest until her husband's trial was over. Their clothes hastily bundled together, the boat carried them swiftly down the river to the great empty palace. Tight-lipped but courageous still, the Duchess said quietly, 'You had better return to your father, Amy. In Norfolk you will be safe in his care.'

'I will not go,' she said stubbornly. 'I will not go until I have seen Robert.'

She had not long to wait. They had captured him when he had been trying to join his father at Bury St Edmunds. He and Ambrose had attempted to escape and been seized as they fled alone with no followers. They were riding side by side along the Strand, but she had eyes only for Robert. This time the crowd did not hurl filth or curses. Amongst the women there were even murmurs of pity for the tall handsome boy glimpsed between the soldiers. Amy had escaped out of Durham House and was desperately trying to push her way through to him.

'Let the whore see her fancy man,' muttered a man coarsely, and was promptly slapped down by his wife.

'Shut your dirty mouth!' she snapped and elbowed him out of the way. 'God help you, my lady, and your lovely husband,' she said, and pushed Amy in front of her.

Like his father, Robert stared in front of him, dark head proudly erect. He was like a stranger, nothing left of the gay charming boy who had set out on this crazy venture.

'Robert,' she called to him, 'Robert, I am here.' But he did not see her and the soldiers thrust her back. Jennet drew her towards the gateway.

Her eyes blinded with tears, Amy did not see the dark man until she was face to face with him. She shrank back, but there was only pity in the strange eyes under the close-fitting black cap.

'He will not die,' he said. 'Do not be afraid.'

'How can you know? How can you be so sure?' she whispered half in fear, half hopeful.

'I know.'

'Thank God,' she breathed fervently. Then Jennet pulled her away so that she did not see him shake his head. She did not hear him murmur, 'For some there are things worse than death.'

Jennet, looking back fearfully over her shoulder, saw him staring after them, heedless of the jostling crowd. Then he turned and was gone so quickly he might not have been there at all.

Kew, Tuesday morning, 10 September 1560

It had been a disturbed night, a night of memories; even his brief snatches of sleep haunted by uneasy dreams. Outside in the elms across the lawn the birds were singing loud enough to arouse the dead. Wide awake and restless, Robert watched the dawn slowly creep in through the latticed windows and was glad of it. Things become less tortured, less complicated in the clear light of day. He stirred and Cabal stretched on the rug beside the bed, snorted noisily and thumped his great tail.

Robert was accustomed to waking early. Elizabeth always rose with the larks. He used to tease her about it. In the spring after he had complained that the cold and damp of his ground-floor apartments at Whitehall were affecting his health, she had given him the rooms next to her own. What a scandal that had provoked, he thought ruefully, Cecil looking disapprovingly down his thin nose and the other members of the Privy Council frowning heavily at him, the youngest and newest recruit amongst them and the most favoured. Sometimes he would go along the corridor to her bedchamber and share her light morning meal. She rarely had more than a cup of ale, a roll of fine wheaten bread and a bowl of thin broth.

'Go away or I shall have you arrested,' she would threaten. 'I am busy. I have work to do.'

'What work is more important than loving me?'

'The work of governing this kingdom.'

'It is a man's job.'

'It is mine and I'm giving it up to nobody,' she would say quickly and sternly, reaching up to box his ears when he bent to kiss the slim white neck above her bed gown.

There were days when she would respond to his teasing, laughing with him, and at other times she would be angry. It was part of her fascination that he was never certain of her. Once, when he leaned over her shoulder daring to question her decision on a matter of policy, she threw the inkpot at him, so that it spilled all down his shirt and ruined the silk rug at her feet. They had both been helpless with laughter while a shocked Kat Ashley mopped it up.

He wondered what kind of a night she had spent. Had she been sleepless too? Not Elizabeth, he thought bitterly, she would put him out of her mind as she could so easily, turning from woman to queen in a matter of seconds. She would sit down to her endless state papers with no more thought to him than to the pet greyhound which slept on the end of her bed.

The very notion of her indifference was enough to bring him to his feet. He had been away from her for only a few hours and already it seemed unbearable. Cabal had gone to the door, whining and asking to be let out. On impulse he shrugged himself into his doublet, pulled on the soft leather boots, threw a cloak round his shoulders and followed the dog out of the room.

Maidservants were already up, scurrying down the corridors, sweeping the rushes out of the great hall, and spreading new ones sprinkled with sweet-smelling herbs; rosemary, thyme, lavender and bay. They knew only too well their lord's fastidious nose. They dropped him startled curtsies as he strode through them. The sleepy-eyed porter leaped to attention, unchaining the massive door and swinging it wide. Outside the air was refreshingly cool and sweet after the stuffy room. A slight mist still hung above the rain-wet grass but it was going to be a lovely day. Fugitive rays of sun tinselled the spiders' webs to tangled nets of silver bespangling shrub and bush.

Cabal went bounding ahead and he idly followed, trying to thrust the dismal miasma of the night behind him. The path went past neglected flower-beds, through an orchard of ancient apple trees, and emerged close to the river. There were ramshackle cottages there, clinging to the bank beside a small jetty. He ran a keen practical eye over them and decided they must be removed. He would like to build a boathouse here. It was a magnificent stretch of the river on which to spend a lazy afternoon or hold a water party. Already in his mind's eye he could see the barges coming up from Richmond, the musicians playing under the gold-fringed awnings and Elizabeth leaning back on the cushions with him at her feet. His rosy vision was abruptly interrupted by a child's scream and Cabal's fierce growls.

A small boy of about five or six was hanging on to the dog's collar and pummelling him with his fist. Cabal was gentle enough but his dignity was badly hurt. Half amused, half irritated, Robert called him off and the small boy glared up at him, fair hair tousled, bare feet squarely planted in the mud, one grimy finger pointing to the overturned bucket and the squirming mass of sticklebacks, tadpoles and other small river fry scattered on the bank.

'Your dog did that,' he said accusingly.

Robert had always liked children. Long ago he had been kind to his own small brother and sisters, and something about the boy's fearless defiance pleased him. He smiled. 'You can pick them up,' he said gravely, 'if you're quick, they won't die.'

Emboldened by the charm, the child stretched out a hand and plucked at his cloak. 'Will you help me?'

He laughed and might even have done as the boy begged, but at that moment a woman came flying out of one of the cottages, scolding the child and looking up at Robert with terrified eyes.

'I am sorry, my lord, I am sorry, you mustn't mind the boy, he meant nothing . . . nothing at all . . .' She clutched the child against her, staring at him as if he were the devil himself, and it angered him.

'Leave him,' he said harshly, 'he was doing no harm.' He felt in the pouch at his belt and bent down, putting a coin in the muddy little hand. The boy's eyes widened in wonder at sight of the gold and the woman gasped. He cut short her cringing gratitude, called Cabal to heel and walked on.

It was a ridiculous sum to give, he knew that well enough. Someone would probably spread a story that he had slept with the woman and that the boy was his, especially if the fool babbled of his absurd generosity. But he would have liked a son like that, a sturdy handsome boy whom he would teach to ride and fly a hawk and use a sword. That was something that Amy had never given him. It had been a great grief to her in the beginning and to him too, though he had tried not to show his disappointment. Would it have made any difference if there had been a cluster of children growing up in Norfolk? Would she have been content then, fulfilled and happy at Syderstone . . . would he?

103

Perhaps, who knows? But it had not happened and now... now he was free. He quickened his steps. Now there was nothing to prevent him from fathering Elizabeth's son – a boy who would one day sit on England's throne, half Tudor, half Dudley. By God, that would bring them crawling to him ... all those proud blue-blooded non-entities who envied him so bitterly. They would have to kneel to him then, to the father of England's heir ... Then he stopped dead on the path, an echo from the past forcing itself into his mind.

That had been his father's ambition. He too had dreamed of being a maker of kings and what had it brought him – death by the axe, a dishonoured grave, disgrace to his wife and sons. And it could happen again. Wasn't he standing on the edge of an abyss at this very moment, just as he had done seven years ago, returning from his trial at Westminster Hall with the sharp gleaming edge of the axe turned towards him, the door of the Beauchamp Tower clanging shut on him and the ever-present fear that when it opened again, it would only be to bring the order of execution?

The radiance of the morning had dimmed. He turned his back on the river, that same river that he had watched with such helpless frustration from the battlements of the Tower all through that endless plague-ridden summer of his imprisonment. He whistled to Cabal and retraced his steps to the house. As he came up the elm-shaded avenue he saw a rider emerge from the copse. For an instant he thought it might have been a messenger from Tom Blount, and then knew it was impossible. There had scarcely been time for him to receive his letter, let alone make enquiries or send a report. There was something oddly furtive about the horseman's approach. Then Cabal raced up the path, barking madly, and the man swung his horse towards him. There was no mistaking the sandy hair under the jaunty feathered cap, the round shoulders, the half-ingratiating, half-flamboyant manner. Dress John Appleyard in the highest of fashion and he would still look the mean-minded grovelling knave that he was.

Robert stopped to face him, grim and unwelcoming. 'What the devil are you doing here? I sent you word. You should be at Cumnor with your sister.'

'My dead sister, eh Robert?' He slid from the saddle. 'Your messenger met me on the road but I had the news already. I thought it best to come to you first.'

'In God's name why?'

He came sidling up with his sly smile. 'To congratulate you, brother-in-law, what else? Isn't this what you've been hoping for all this past year?'

The very fact that it was true outraged him. 'What do you mean by that, you damned insinuating rogue? Do you think I am glad that Amy has come to her death so brutally? I never dreamed, never for a single moment . . .'

'Never, Robert, never? Oh come now, crocodile tears for those sour-faced enemies of yours at Court maybe, but not between us. We know one another too well, and that fine, red-haired light o' love of yours up at Whitehall who is still not too proud to show how hot she is for her handsome lover . . .'

A violent anger swept through him. If he had been wearing a sword, he might have drawn it and run him through. Instead he seized him by the throat, forcing him back against one of the trees, half strangling him, shaking him like a rat in one of the fierce rages that so rarely broke through his quiet reserve.

'You keep your filthy tongue off her and off Amy too, do you hear?'

'Devil take you, do you mean to choke me?' Gasping, fighting for breath, Appleyard leaned back against the trunk of the tree. 'All right, all right, I did but jest. You need not take it so badly.'

Robert released him, disgusted with his own anger against such a despicable victim.

The young man rubbed his neck tenderly. 'God damn it, did you have to half kill me? You've never been so sensitive before. I came here to do you some good and this is the thanks I get.'

'What good can you do me, in God's name?'

'More than you think. As soon as the news reached me in Oxford I rode south to you.'

'What were you doing in Oxford?'

'I had some business there,' he said evasively. 'I thought it better we should both tell the same story.'

'What story? I know no more than you. Amy was found dead at the foot of that staircase which I always thought dangerous. She could have become dizzy, faint, anything. She has been sick all this year, you know that as well as I. It was an unlucky accident . . .'

105

'Unlucky for whom . . . you or her? It could just as easily be suicide,' he gave Robert a quick look, 'it could be murder . . .'

'Why should you say that?' He spoke so fiercely that Appleyard backed away from him.

'Now don't attack me again. I'm only repeating what everyone will say.' He shuffled his feet. 'Can't we go into the house? It's cursed damp under these trees and I'm hungry. I've ridden all the night through.'

'No, we can't. Do you think I want the servants talking? You can eat in the first alehouse on the Oxford road as you ride to Cumnor. Say what you have to say and be on your way.'

'Very well, if that's what you want, but it's deuced unfriendly of you,' he said grumblingly. 'There are some very odd rumours circulating about you and Amy in Oxford.'

'There are always rumours,' said Robert bitterly. 'There's nothing new in that. A good many idle people have nothing better to do than invent lies about me and . . .'

'And Her Grace, the Queen of England,' said Appleyard with a faint sneer. 'Well, all pleasures have to be paid for. Only these are particularly damaging. Didn't you send Dr Julio to see Amy early this summer?'

'What if I did? He's a good doctor. The Queen has consulted him more than once.'

'He is also an expert on poisons.'

'He takes an interest. It is a fascinating study.'

'I can't make out whether you're just being naïve, Robert, or cunning as a nest of serpents. It's widely rumoured that Dr Julio has invented a poison so subtle that it leaves no trace in the body that any post-mortem can reveal.'

'That's sheer nonsense,' he said uneasily.

Appleyard shrugged. 'Of course you don't believe it and neither do I, but you know the rabble. They see a Borgia hidden behind every Italian face and, after all, he had been prescribing remedies for Amy.'

'What the devil are you implying? That I had Amy poisoned? It's a damnable lie. She died of a broken neck.'

'Ah, but did she? Are you sure? She could just as well have died in her bed and her body been neatly placed at the foot of those stairs. Have you thought of that? Anthony Forster who leases Cumnor Place was your treasurer, wasn't he, Robert?'

'What of it? He's a good fellow even if Amy never liked him. She had friends at Cumnor too. That sister of Will Hyde's . . . She has always hated to be alone.'

He paused, remembering her constant pleading that he should stay longer with her, her restless flitting from place to place seeking health and content and never finding it. It was not entirely his fault either. A couple of years ago he had been considering buying a suitable property, but she had not wanted the responsibility without him always at her side. Then the full realization of what Appleyard was saying struck him like a blow in the face. God Almighty, was there no villainy of which they were not ready to accuse him? He turned on his brother-in-law angrily.

'Is that what you're planning to say at the inquest? Have you got it all pat? The doctor as poisoner, Anthony Forster a murderer, acting on my instructions?'

'Now, now, you know me better than that, Robert? I'm only repeating what others may say. And Amy *was* terrified of the Italian. Surely you were aware of that?'

He knew it and had been irritated by it. 'Why should she be afraid? He is an excellent doctor and a kind man.' Then Robert swung round. He seized the other by the shoulders, his fingers biting painfully into the flesh. 'It has been you all along, hasn't it? You who have made sure she heard all these lies about me, you who made her afraid. When did you see her last?'

'Do you have to be so violent, Robert?' he complained. 'It was a few weeks ago and I simply felt she should know what was being said about you both. After all she was my sister.'

'Don't put on that virtuous face. All you cared about was what you could get out of her,' said Robert contemptuously. 'Do you think I don't know how much you wheedled out of her pocket? Is that why you have come here today? Are you threatening me?'

'Never. How can you say such a thing? When have I ever wanted to do you harm?'

'More than once I have no doubt, only I've been too useful so far, haven't I? What's gone wrong now? Haven't my enemies paid you enough to spread the false tales about me?' He saw by the quick shifting of his eyes that he had hit the mark, and anger welled up in him again that he should be entangled in a net of suspicion by this mean-minded knave who would bleed him white if he could. He said abruptly, 'You can say what you damned well please. I'll not give you another penny.'

'I'm not asking for money,' said Appleyard in a whining voice, 'merely for a helping hand when things work out for you. After all, with Her Grace, the Queen of England, practically in your pocket, you'd surely not grudge a little to Amy's brother.'

'I don't see why not. She never liked you,' he said sullenly.

'Amy was a silly goose. She never knew who were her true friends, but she worshipped you, Robert, you know that.' He paused before he looked up with his crafty smile. 'She might well have destroyed herself for your sake . . .'

The words struck him with the unwelcome force of truth and he shied away, unwilling to face up to it. What John Appleyard intended to do . . . that was the immediate problem. The cunning rascal had him in a cleft stick. Refuse him what he asked and like as not he would take a malicious pleasure in twisting the truth. There were plenty who would pay well for hints and innuendoes. Hadn't Norfolk said once, 'Is there no one to use a dagger on this man?' If the jury at the inquest brought in a verdict of wilful murder, there would be no need of a stab in the back . . .

He said reluctantly, 'If things go right, then you have my promise.'

'I knew you'd see it my way. And now, Robert, something else, the merest trifle. I left in haste and ready cash is hard to come by these days. I spent my last on post horses to reach you quickly.'

Already it was there, the outstretched hand. If he was the villain they all thought him, he told himself sourly, he would have this wretched fellow quietly disposed of before he got a mile on his road. He said irritably, 'Do you think I carry a pocketful of money about me at this hour in the morning? Wait at the Crown on the Oxford Road and Tamworth shall bring it to you.'

'You're a good fellow at heart.' Appleyard grinned maddeningly up at Robert. 'With Amy out of the way, the world's your oyster and Elizabeth Tudor the pearl in it. Good hunting, brother-in-law.'

He touched his cap in mock salute, swung himself into the saddle and went trotting down the avenue, leaving Robert staring after him, anger and frustration mingled with profound distrust.

Back in the house he was surprised to find it was already past eight o'clock and Dick Tamworth was anxiously looking for him. He knew well his master's tastes and he had harried the servants into unusual activity.

'I have prepared your bath, my lord, and breakfast is waiting. No one could tell me where you had gone.'

'I have been walking,' he said shortly. 'Dick, I want you to do an errand for me.'

'Yes, my lord, but what of your bath?'

'It can wait.'

He opened the money chest and gave him the small bag of gold with strict instructions to go quietly, telling no one of his destination.

'I will, my lord, have no fear.'

Robert watched him leave with relief. Tamworth was a quiet young man close in his confidence, utterly trustworthy and personally devoted.

He pulled a sheet of paper towards him and penned another letter to Bount, knowing it useless but filled with a restless desire to do something. He thought of writing personally to the Foreman of the Jury who would preside over the inquest and then rejected it, realising his folly. It would sound as though he were trying to coerce them in his favour and they would resent any threat to their independence of judgment. He had hoped against hope that there would have been a message from Elizabeth by now, a few words only, flying to him through the night, proving her love, her trust, but there was nothing.

He sat staring out of the window in the grip of a black depression, a failure of the will that occasionally engulfed him so that nothing had any purpose any longer, not love, nor desire, nor ambition. They all crumbled into dust at his touch. Seven years ago in the Tower it had held him in its grip, a time he did not want to remember except that out of it had sprung the first flame between him and Elizabeth. That spring when death had hovered above them both, together they had climbed out of the gulf of despair. The pen fell from his fingers and the bath with its herb-scented water cooled as he remembered.

Part Two
1553-1558

'When she was but Lady Elizabeth . . . in her trouble he
(Lord Robert) did sell away a good piece of his land to aid
her, which divers supposed to be the cause the Queen so
favoured him.'

Calendar of State Papers

One

Outside the stone-walled room in the Beauchamp Tower trees were budding, long green catkins hung from the spider-thin branches, while snowdrops and early daffodils bloomed in the Governor's garden despite the drenching rain. But to Robert, standing with his face pressed against the thick glass of the barred and latticed windows, there was no joy in the spring, no hope for the future, nothing.

Mary Tudor had been safely Queen now for over eight, painfully dragging months. Through the wet mist he could see the formidable bulk of the White Tower. It was there he had been led with his brothers one scorchingly hot day last August to bid his father farewell. He remembered how the Duke who had always been such a pillar of strength looked suddenly shrunken and old, though he was barely fifty. He had wept when he had embraced Guildford but Robert had stood aloof, the old love and admiration struggling with pity because his proud father had grovelled before the woman whom he had tried to push from the throne, begging for mercy, swearing he would turn Catholic, swearing anything to win her favour and trying to carry his sons with him. Jack, out of love and grief, had gone with his father, confessing to the priest and going to mass. Robert had stubbornly refused, not because he had any passionate loyalty to any religious belief, but out of a quick young pride. He was not yet twenty-one and would not deny the faith in which he had grown up even for his life.

'You'll learn, Robin,' said his father wearily, 'we all learn to compromise sooner or later. What is a prayer in Latin if it will keep you from the axe . . . better a living dog than a dead lion.'

It was a bitter lesson that he was only now beginning to understand.

Today was Palm Sunday and there was something going on in the Tower this morning. A company of the guard went by with a steady tramp, their halberds gleaming and water dripping from their helmets on to their steel corselets. Then he saw Sir John Gage emerge from his lodgings, resplendently attired despite the wretched day. They must be expecting a distinguished visitor . . . or was it yet another prisoner? His interest quickened and then died.

The Tower was packed to suffocation and had been ever since Tom Wyatt had raised his rebellion against Mary's intended marriage with Philip of Spain. They had heard the noise of battle even here, and for a few days there had been sheer panic, with messengers riding to and fro, weapons being gathered and pikemen drilling hastily before they marched out. He would have given what little he had to have been able to join them, sword in hand. He would have fought the devil himself just to be free. It was said half the citizens of London had rallied to Wyatt, screaming 'No Popery!' and pelting the Spanish envoys with filth, dead cats and anything else vile they could lay hands on. Wyatt had brought his troops to Southwark and the guns of the Tower had been trained on them across the bridge, though Mary would not let them be fired for fear of killing innocent folk going about their daily tasks. It had been maddening to be shut up with no real news, only disquieting rumours and false hopes of freedom. Then suddenly it was all over. Mary, with the courage of her great father, had gone to the Guildhall, making a challenging speech that had brought the fickle mob to her feet, forgetting their fear of the Spanish Inquisition and cheering themselves hoarse; so that afterwards it was only the stubborn who suffered imprisonment and torture, many of them poor men loyal to their honest beliefs, some of them innocent.

Through the window he could see the grass on Tower Green springing up young and rich and tender, watered by blood, he thought grimly. For the last month it had held a morbid fascination for him. Try as he would, Robert could not forget poor, petulant Guildford, his face all blubbered with tears as they dragged him down the stone stairs from the upper room he shared with Ambrose and Jack, until somehow at the last moment he had recovered his courage and gone bravely to his death on Tower Hill in the white satin he had worn at his wedding, the sun gilding his hair to a cap of gold. He was followed on that same morning by Jane, the young wife who had obstinately refused to see him even to say goodbye ... Jane, the little, freckled girl Robert had never particularly liked but with whom he had grown up, quarrelled with, danced with, the girl whom his father had made a nine-days' Queen and so signed her death warrant. He had watched the cart go past his window with the slight bleeding body and had felt the vomit rise in his throat.

He turned back into the room and began to pace up and down. It was the loneliness, the boredom, the frustration that was driving him crazy. Lately he had been allowed books and he read voraciously, but he had never been a scholar. He longed for his horses with passion. What had happened to Bay Bell, to Gentle, to Speedwell, the beautiful white mare whose velvet neck Elizabeth had caressed when they had met her on the road to London? To ride out even in this soaking rain, to feel the strong springing body between his legs, to smell the wet bracken, see his hawk soar up into the blue of the sky above the flat fields of Norfolk, to battle against the fierce sea wind on the Yarmouth sands ... would he ever be free again or would he rot here for ever?

He thought pityingly of Amy. The last time she had visited him he had tried hard, but it was as if a gulf had opened between them. He had grown suddenly from boy to man and she was still a child, a pretty, unhappy, bewildered child, begging him for the comfort he could not give. For a little there had been relief and solace to hold her in his arms, to feel the soft yielding body against his and forget for a few moments the catastrophe that had engulfed them all. But then they had quarrelled violently and stupidly over John Appleyard whom they both despised.

She had said unthinkingly, 'Everyone is not lost. I have heard from John. He has gone into hiding at Stanfield and they've left him untouched.'

Anger had flared up in him. 'He took damned good care to save his own skin at our expense.'

'That's unfair. How can you be sure?'

'How else did Arundel's troopers know exactly where to find us?'

It was foolish but he could not stop himself, and she had burst into tears. Afterwards he was sorry, told her over and over how much he loved her, and yet was glad to see her go. He felt happier about her now she had gone back to her father at Syderstone.

There was a clanking of chains outside, the turning of a key and the door creaked open. They were carrying in his dinner and Jem Saunders was with them. The younger of his two gaolers, not much older than himself, he was a friendly fellow who could sometimes be persuaded to disobey his orders of no communication with prisoners and stay talking for a little.

Robert said quickly, 'What is happening out there today? I saw the guard and Sir John Gage. Are we expecting Her Majesty to grace us with her presence?'

'No such luck, my lord.' The young man looked quickly around him and then lowered his voice to a conspiratorial whisper. 'Not a word's been breathed for sure but there's been talk . . . it is the Lady Elizabeth herself.'

'Elizabeth? A prisoner? But why? In God's name, why?'

'Ah, that would be telling. Now you sit down and eat up your food, my lord, before it grows cold.'

'In a moment. Why, Jem, why? Do you know?'

'They don't say much to the likes of us, my lord, but I know what I know.' He hustled the two serving men out and then turned back, speaking under his breath. 'There are some who're saying that Tom Wyatt was thick with her, that she wrote him a letter agreeing to the murder of her sister and half o' those lording it up at Whitehall.'

'I don't believe it. She'd not be such a fool.'

Jem shrugged. 'Who knows what any of those high-up ones will do if they're pushed, begging your pardon, my lord, and she's a deal younger than her sister . . . and prettier.' He winked at Robert, tapping his nose significantly. 'No love lost between sisters if you ask me, with one of them eighteen years older and plain with it and the other with men buzzing round her like wasps round a honey jar. Well, it'll all come out in the wash, I daresay, and like as not there'll be another execution out there on the green.' He misunderstood Robert's quick move of revulsion and gave him a friendly pat. 'You needn't worry, my lord, you'll have a fine view, free, gratis and for nothing. We're hard put to it finding room for all those they're bringing in, though there are gibbets strung along the roads from here to the Temple. Tarred the bodies are and hung up in iron cages with everyone gaping at them like some rare old peepshow,' he went on with gloomy relish. 'Don't seem right somehow when you come to think on it. Some of 'em were decent enough folk, one of 'em were my

116

mother's second cousin, a butcher in Cheapside he was and in a good way of business too. Many's the side of lamb he let us have at cost price . . .'

He suddenly seemed to recollect where he was. He broke off abruptly, 'You eat up now, my lord,' he said with rough sympathy. 'Can't have you falling sick like your brother upstairs, can we?'

'How is Lord Warwick?'

'Badly. Coughing blood so 'tis said.'

Poor Jack had taken their father's death and the whole sorry business of their imprisonment even worse than he and Ambrose.

He said urgently, 'Can't you let me see him just for a few minutes? It's only up the stairs. No one need know.'

'Now, now, my lord, you know better than that. Prisoners are not allowed to speak with one another, that's the order and it'd be more than my job's worth. Don't you fret now. 'Tain't you who'll be walking out there on to the green, not yet anyways.'

Robert watched the door clang shut with regret. Even the few words exchanged with this rough, not unfriendly fellow helped to break the monotony of the endless hours and today he had brought news, startling news.

For eight months he had lived in dread, every knock at the door, every sudden sound by night or day bringing the tremor of fear, the wildly beating heart, the breathless waiting and then the sick relief when it passed him by. Yet now, with danger coming a great deal closer, with prisoners being taken out every day to the gallows, for some inexplicable reason the black despair had vanished. He felt warmly, vibrantly alive, his blood surging in his veins, his manhood stirring inside him. For weeks now food had lost all savour, now he found himself attacking it hungrily. Shut up alone, separated from his brothers, there had been nothing to do but brood on the misfortune that had robbed him of love, wealth and ambition at one stroke. Now for the first time in months he was thinking of someone other than himself.

All that day and in the weeks that followed he speculated about Elizabeth, eagerly piecing together the scraps of information that reached him . . . how she had sunk to the cold wet stone of the causeway when the boat brought her to Traitor's Gate, despairingly refusing to move until one of her gentlemen attendants burst into tears at his mistress's plight and she had rounded on him sharply, finding her own courage in his misery. How day after day she had been questioned and bullied and how steadfastly she had denied any complicity in the plot against her sister. Now she was shut into the Bell Tower, separated from him only by a narrow walk along the leads of the roof, and he wondered if she too suffered the same frustrating boredom, the same nightmares of sheer blind terror.

He began to plan how they might meet. Of course the very idea was ridiculous, heavily guarded as they both were by day and night, and yet stranger things had happened here in the Tower. The idea took root and grew. It gave him something to think about, something to live for. Once or twice he wondered how it would have been if his father had picked on Elizabeth as his puppet instead of Jane. She might have been Queen by now and they would all have stood high in her favour; only she would have been no puppet, not if he knew her. Well, it was still not too late. Mary was betrothed to Philip but the bridegroom had not yet arrived and she was old to bear a child and sickly too. He did not let himself think beyond that and it was not entirely ambition that stirred him, not simply a desire to better himself, but something deeper, as if the very fact of Elizabeth coming here, a fellow prisoner, was part of his destiny. Once in the dark stillness of the night when queer thoughts rise unbidden, he remembered that odd creature who had come to Greenwich with Dr Dee. Sirius he had called himself, the dog star, and he had looked into the pool of ink, speaking of fire and blood and a crown. Of course the man was a liar and a charlatan and no one sensible really believed in such nonsense these days, and yet other and stranger prophecies had come true.

Luck came Robert's way but not until early in April, and then ironically enough through sickness. He developed a fever and for nearly a week alternately shivered and sweated in the damp cold room, unable to eat or sleep, until his gaolers became alarmed and called in John Brydges. No Lieutenant-Governor of the Tower cared for his prisoners to die unless it was suitably, legally, by axe or rope. There were a great many idle folk only too ready to spread rumours of poison and he had enough trouble on his hands already with the Lady Elizabeth, who went about with a face white as curds and beseeching him every time he paid his official visit for permission to walk outside the confinement of her few rooms. He called in the doctor who was brusque, and when Robert's temperature had steadied said forthrightly that it was madness to keep a lusty young man mewed up between four walls and expect him to remain healthy. And so one morning Robert's door was unlocked and, with Jem close behind him and two guards in front, he was permitted to take the air in the Governor's garden almost immediately beneath the barred and shuttered windows of the Tower where the Princess was imprisoned.

It was a mild day with the sun shining and he gulped in great mouthfuls of the clean sweet air. He was still feeling shaky and lightheaded so that after one or two turns he sat on a stone bench at one end of the garden and watched a little dark-haired boy, son of the Keeper of the Wardrobe, who raced up and down the paths playing with his ball. Once it bounced near him and he threw it back. The child giggled and tossed it to him again. Robert had a way with children. In no time at all they were fast friends, walking up the path hand in hand, the tall young man and the five-year-old boy. When he felt stronger, he let him ride on his shoulder, laughing when he jogged up and down, tugging at the thick red-brown hair, finding relief and pleasure even in this childish company. It was on his third walk in the garden that he had an idea. The boy ran to meet him, his hands filled with flowers, and he asked him if he had picked them for his mother.

The child shook his head and pointed up to the windows. 'They're for the lady,' he said importantly, 'I take them to her every day and sometimes,' he looked down shyly, 'sometimes she gives me a little cake or a piece of marchpane.'

It was impossible to write a message. It was bound to be discovered, and it could endanger her and himself however innocent. But there was a way if he had the courage to risk it.

He bent down to the child, whispering, 'Will you play a game with me? When you give the lady the flowers, will you say that if she looks from the window, she will see there is speedwell growing in the garden.'

The boy looked up at him. 'What is speedwell?'

'It is a little blue flower.'

'But there aren't any,' he said doubtfully.

'Never mind, there will be soon. Will you say it . . . quietly for

119

none to hear but you and the lady?'

The child's eyes sparkled gleefully. 'Is it a secret?'

'A very little secret between you and me.'

When the boy had run off he stood irresolute. It was a childish device. Was he acting the fool? She might not even remember the mare, she might not even be interested. He looked quickly around him. Jem was at the far end talking to the two soldiers who guarded the gate. He leaned against one of the stone pillars that supported a climbing rose, shading his eyes as if he were weary, not daring to watch too closely. One of the windows on the first floor of the Bell Tower was open. He waited breathlessly as if his very life depended on it and, when he had almost given up hope, suddenly he saw her. She was standing there, the flowers in her hands, wearing a dark gown that emphasized the creamy pallor of her face, the startling red-gold of her hair. Her eyes, quick and searching, ran around the garden and then met his. She made no move and neither did he. But for the space of a heartbeat it was as if their spirits leaped together. Then someone within jerked her back from the window, it was slammed shut and a heavy curtain drawn across it.

Elizabeth turned angrily on Mistress Brydges, the officious wife of the Lieutenant-Governor who had pulled her away from the window. With her back against the dusty-smelling stifling velvet curtain she said stormily, 'Are you my gaoler? Am I not even allowed to look at the sky or take a breath of air? Do they want me to die of suffocation in this vile place?'

'You know it is not that, my lady, but Sir John Gage said that you were not even to be seen . . .'

'By whom, for God's sake? Don't repeat to me what that wretched man said. Isn't it enough that I should have to endure his insults every time he visits me? Who is there to see me but the guards driving me crazy with their incessant tramp under my windows?'

'All the same, Your Royal Highness, he could order you to be shut in even more closely, every window shuttered, no light or air . . .'

It was only too true and her anger died, but not the indignant rebellion that she should be subjected to these restrictions. She sat down again at the tapestry frame, relieved that no one, not even the objectionable Mistress Brydges, appeared to have noticed the young man whose gaze had held her own with a strange riveting power.

Thankful that this time the storm had been only brief, one of her ladies began to arrange the flowers in a bowl of water while Elizabeth picked up her needle and sorted through the skeins of silk for the right colour.

If only there had been someone with whom she could talk freely, someone she could trust? She longed passionately for the friends of her childhood, dear Kat Ashley who had been forbidden to come to her again for some trifling reason, Blanche Parry who on so many nights had soothed her to sleep with her crooning Welsh voice. Did they want to rob her of everyone dear to her? All her life, it seemed, she had been forced to guard her tongue, to be eternally vigilant, to suspect everyone around her, even those near and dear who could be tortured into confessing lies and half-truths.

The nightmare of her first night in the Tower still hung around her. She shuddered, remembering the long black hours in which she had lain wakeful, hearing the heavy breathing of her sleeping attendants and seeing in horrible procession those who had gone before her in this terrifying place . . . her mother whom she scarcely remembered and only knew from the whispered gossip of servants . . . wild strange Anne Boleyn whom they had called adulteress and witch but whom she had loved with a passionate child's worship of a dream image. How extraordinary that it should be Tom Wyatt, whose poet father had loved Anne so desperately, who was now unwittingly bringing her daughter so near to death. She had thrust her fist into her mouth to stop herself crying out in terror.

There was Katherine Howard, her pretty cousin, her father's fifth wife, who had been kind to the motherless little girl. She had shivered in her bed in the nursery at Hampton Court while her attendants, believing her asleep, talked in hushed excited voices of the young Queen who had run screaming down the corridor, begging for mercy at the feet of her husband. There were some who said her ghost ran shrieking down that same passage even now.

'I shall never marry,' she had shouted defiantly when they had

121

told her about the pretty wanton stepmother whom her father had sent to the block after only a year of marriage. And, even more fearful, scarce a month ago with the blood hardly dry on the grass and the block still in position, there had been Jane with whom she had studied Latin at Chelsea, Jane of whom she had been jealous when her Greek exercises had been held up to her as a pattern by her tutor . . . Her hand trembled and the needle went astray, so that she had to unpick the stitches.

The little posy of flowers was placed on a small table beside her and she looked up at her young lady-in-waiting with the enchanting smile that could disconcert even her enemies. The primroses had a fresh earthy scent and for an instant she wished she had not been born a princess. How restful to be the daughter of some simple country gentleman with no other worries but her household duties, the fit of a new gown, the waywardness of a lover. Of course she had known that Robert Dudley and his brothers were imprisoned in the Tower but, beset by her own anxieties, she had not thought about him until now. When the child had lisped out that absurd message it was as if a hand had been stretched out to take hers, a warm friendly hand, part of her childhood. She was carried back to that morning in May on the Hatfield road, the magnificent white mare and the young man, tall, proud and confident, jesting with her, promising to send it to her. It had been their love of horses that had first drawn them together when they met at Edward's Court and had gone hunting with her brother in Windsor forest. The silk thread went busily to and fro and the Tudor rose grew and blossomed under her long fingers while she fell into an unaccustomed daydream, letting it sweep her away for a few minutes into a fantasy world where a girl could dream of a young man whose hair curled thick on his neck, who moved with grace and power, whose bold eyes caressed her. A tremor ran through her; the passionate feelings resolutely crushed down since Tom Seymour had once aroused them so disastrously burst into sudden clamorous life. The colour raced up into her pale face. The needle stabbed into her finger and she exclaimed, pushing the tapestry frame to one side so that skeins of silk, gold thimble, needle-case, went scattering over the floor.

'What is wrong, my lady? Are you faint? Are you sick?' They fluttered around her in concern.

'No, no, not sick, but dying from lack of air,' she cried out in desperation. 'I must be free of this room, I must I tell you, if it is only for an hour!'

There were still days to get through before she won even a brief respite from her strict confinement, days when minutes seemed like hours, and in the endless waiting for something to happen, her mind seized on almost anything to relieve the deadly tedium. On 11 April a week after she had seen Robert in the garden, Tom Wyatt was led out to execution on Tower Hill, declaring with his last breath that the Princess Elizabeth had never at any time involved herself in his plot. Beneath her regret for a gallant young man whose only crime had been a desire to put her on the throne in place of her sister, she began to breathe more easily. Not that the danger was past; she was still the focus of all those who were discontented, all those who feared Spain and who shouted, 'We'll have no foreigner as our king,' but at least she was spared more questioning for the time being and once or twice a week she was permitted to leave her prison rooms. While she walked in the garden or read or embroidered or listened to a madrigal sung by her youngest lady-in-waiting, she thought again and again of the young man who was only a stone's throw away from her and yet so effectively cut off by two heavy doors, bolted and barred with iron.

And then Fate – or maybe it was Sirius, the dog star, thought Robert wryly – again took a hand in their lives. At the end of April the Tower was attacked by one of its periodic epidemics arising from the crowded conditions and the overworked sanitation. One by one high-ranking officials, warders, soldiers and serving men went down like ninepins with the bloody flux; even the Lieutenant-Governor himself was stricken and his anxious wife abandoned her vigilant watch on their prisoner in order to nurse him. Carefully worked out turns of duty went by the board since men who were sound and well in the morning were desperately sick by afternoon.

One morning a new and very young recruit unlocked the door of Robert's room, his strict instructions sent flying out of his head by the charm of his noble prisoner, and quite unaware that at this hour all Tower inmates were kept to their cells while Her Royal Highness, the Lady Elizabeth, took her morning exercise.

When Robert came into the garden she was standing half

concealed by one of the stone buttresses, looking down the broad sweep of the river to the sea. He glanced quickly around him and, seeing that her usual guard had been reduced to one, he came quietly up behind her. The fur-lined mantle had slipped from her shoulders. He picked it up and put it gently around her.

'You will take cold, my lady, the wind is sharp.'

She turned swiftly, her eyes widening in surprise. He put his finger to his lips. She said breathlessly, 'Should you be here, my lord? Won't they see us? It is forbidden.'

'Don't be afraid. I will take all blame.'

'I wouldn't want that. Too many have suffered because of me.'

'You're thinking of Tom Wyatt?'

'Yes . . . and others, poor men who have lost everything.'

'They lose it gladly for you, just as I would.'

Green-gold eyes under the lion-coloured hair looked into his. 'They tell a different story of you, my lord. Your father would have put Jane on the throne.'

'Touché.' Against all reason it pleased her that he was not at all abashed by her accusation. He faced her boldly. 'What would you? He was my father. My choice would have fallen on you.'

'Can I believe that . . . traitor?'

'Traitor to your sister perhaps but not to you, never to you.'

And then she was smiling at him in spite of herself. 'Oh Robert, how long ago it all seems and what a plight we are in, you and I.' She touched the slim white neck with one long finger. 'Do you know there was a moment not so long ago when I made up my mind to implore my sister to send into France for an expert swordsman, anything rather than suffer the butchery of the axe.'

'I know,' he said gravely. 'I too have known despair. When I saw my brother die, I prayed they would come soon and take me too.'

'And yet we are both still alive.'

'And one day we will look back and smile at our fears.' He took her hand in his and she did not draw it away.

'Will we? How can you be so sure?'

'I don't know and yet I am sure. Whenever I think of you, I am certain of it.'

She looked searchingly into his face and found comfort and reassurance there. 'It is so strange. One can find the courage to face terror, it is the small things that are so exasperating, the petty pinpricks, the shameful indignities, even the lack of money. Sometimes I have been hard pushed to pay my servants.'

'I know that too. I have only two shirts to my back, one on and one off,' he said lightly. 'It is quite damnably inconvenient.'

And yet, despite the rigours of prison, there was a freshness, an elegance about him that pleased her fastidious taste. 'I think you jest.'

'Indeed I do not. My poor mother says my little brother goes barefoot and they eat off wooden trenchers since the silver has long since gone to pay my father's debts.'

'I have had difficulties over food too,' she sighed. 'I had a stand-up fight with Sir John Gage because he would not allow my people to provide my meals, though I must pay for them. I wore him down in the end.'

'Do you know why?'

She looked up at him questioningly.

'I had it from Jem who can be a talkative fellow at times. Sir John suddenly discovered that your cook was a great deal more skilful than his own, so now he eats from your table and saves his own pocket.'

'Oh no,' she exclaimed indignantly. 'How maddening. I shall tell him so next time he visits me.'

'I shouldn't if I were you, not if his good digestion keeps him sweet.'

'How can you laugh?'

'It helps,' he said gently. 'Laughter is a tonic in this wretched place. You watch him when he comes to you, his lips pursed and his chest stuck out, strutting like a pouter pigeon.'

'It's true.' She smiled at the absurd picture he had conjured up before she freed her hand, leaning on the stone parapet, looking down the river while above their heads a kestrel rose and dipped in soaring flight. 'How wonderful to be free as that bird. Shall I ever fly my hawk again or feel the wind in my face as I ride?'

She echoed his own longing and he came up close behind her. 'Yes, I promise you.'

'You are over-bold to promise what no one can foretell.' She stirred restlessly. 'Sometimes when I stand here, I think I can smell the sea.'

'And taste its salt on your lips.'

'You have felt it too.'

'Yes.'

She turned to look at him. 'Did you know they have forbidden the child to bring flowers in case he carries a message hidden among them?'

'The boy told me, weeping because he was not to see his lovely lady any longer.'

She smiled wryly. 'I think it is the sweetmeats he misses. What has happened to Speedwell?'

'Sold, so my mother tells me.'

'I am sorry . . .'

'So am I, but one day I'll have them search the whole of Spain for another Speedwell for you, even more beautiful.'

'Shall I ever be free, Robin?'

He looked at her speculatively. 'You could marry . . .'

'Whom?' she flashed at him proudly. 'Edward Courtney, Earl of Devon. He may be the last Plantagenet left alive but I'd not marry a man who thinks a princess of Tudor blood is beneath his unblemished lineage. Besides,' she went on naïvely, 'he is weak-minded as an idiot and chicken-hearted into the bargain.'

He smiled at her indignant rejection and was glad of it. 'There is still Emmanuel Philibert, Duke of Savoy.'

'You tease me. Savoy is Philip's friend and that is what Mary would like. If I am not to be murdered, then I am to be buried in some distant place, powerless, away from all my friends. I will never leave England willingly, never, never, it is part of me, it is my country.'

'And your people. Do you think we would ever let you go?'

He was so near she could feel his strength, his magnetism, and in her loneliness it had an irresistible appeal. It excited her and she was suddenly afraid of it. Then one of her ladies glided to her side, looking quickly at Robert.

'They are watching, Your Highness,' she whispered. 'It is not safe to stand here . . . it is better to walk.'

'She is right. We must not risk our good fortune.'

With a swift movement Robert took one of the slim hands, pressed his lips to the palm and closed her fingers over it. She looked down at the crisp brown hair, feeling the kiss burn into her flesh, then she snatched her hand away and walked quickly down the path with a lightness, a spring in her walk, that had not been there since she had come to the Tower.

They did not meet again though Robert tried everything he could think of, from pleading with Jem to outright bribery. After its lapse security was in full force again but, if anything, it only increased their awareness of each other. It gave even an exchange of looks an extraordinary significance. Sometimes, when she took a walk, she would see him standing at his window; sometimes they passed one another with their escorts and no guard in the world could prevent their eyes meeting. Once she glimpsed him in the garden with his brother Ambrose and dared to raise a hand in greeting. Someone sent her a gift of fine apples and she requested permission to send some of them to Lord Warwick whom she knew was sick. Gage had the messenger stripped to his shirt, but there was nothing to be found on him except the apples so they were reluctantly delivered. Once a little girl, child of one of the yeoman warders, ran up to her in the garden with a tiny bunch of keys and held them out to her, 'To open all the doors to your heart, my lady.'

She guessed from whom that daring message had come and treasured them, putting them in her needlecase with her gold scissors.

It was meagre enough and yet they fed on it, two lonely people grasping at straws to combat the deadly apathy of their days and to keep their spirit alive.

Then something happened. A newcomer came marching into the Tower followed by a hundred men all in splendid array of fine blue liveries. Robert watched them ride up the causeway and halt outside the Governor's lodgings. Later, when Jem brought his supper, he asked him what it meant.

'It's Sir Henry Bedingfield, my lord. He is to take over from the Constable and sour as a lemon Sir John is about it, I can tell you.' Jem grinned. 'The Lady Elizabeth has been in a rare taking so they say.'

'Why? What do you mean?'

'She thought it meant her head coming off right away, even asked if the block was still standing out there on the green, poor

127

soul. 'Tain't that at all. They'd rather have her room than her company if you ask me. Some of Sir Henry's men were talking down in the guardroom. Seems he has had his orders to escort her to Woodstock and he's none too pleased about it either. She'll be safe there while the Queen marries her Spanish Prince, I reckon. Can't have her sister catching the eye of the bridegroom now, can she? Stands to reason.'

He was right about Woodstock. On 19 May, shortly after noon, Robert saw the procession come out of the Bell Tower, the Princess in their midst, and walk down the causeway to where the boats waited for them, bobbing on the sunlit water. He rashly tore a budding branch from one of the roses and tossed it with accuracy to fall at her feet. Before she could stoop, Sir Henry Bedingfield had snatched it up and looked suspiciously around him. He was about to throw it aside when Elizabeth took it from him. Her voice, clear and distinct, reached Robert where he stood half hidden.

'A flower is surely harmless enough, sir. May I not even accept a gift from someone who wishes me well?'

Sir Henry grunted, but Robert had caught her swift glance and was amply rewarded. Then she was gone out of sight, the soldiers marching two by two swallowing her up.

He sighed. Now there was nothing but the dreary hell of waiting again, the sudden hopes and despairs. In a month he would be twenty-one. His life was passing with nothing accomplished, nothing done. How could he bear to go on as he had done before? He was as much boxed in as the great lions prowling in their cages, whose frustrated roaring kept him awake at nights. Oh God, if only he had the wings of the seagulls who screamed tauntingly above his head. But all the same a spark had been lit, a desire, an ambition, that never quite died all through the long dragging months that lay ahead.

Two

'It's no use, Jack, I haven't your skill,' said Robert sadly, stepping back and looking critically at the sprig of oak leaves, his own personal device, that he was laboriously chipping out of the stone wall and comparing it with the delicately carved roses, acorns, gillyflowers and honeysuckle with which his brother had entwined his name long ago when they were first imprisoned, before Guildford had been taken from them. 'You really carried that out remarkably well. You can take it up as a profession when we get out of here. God knows, we shall need an occupation of some sort if we're not to starve!'

'When we get out?' repeated his brother derisively, 'when, when? We've been saying that for months. I shall never leave this damnable place alive.'

'Oh come, take heart. I know you've been wretchedly sick during the summer but the doctor says you are improving.' Robert sat on the bed, speaking more cheerfully than he felt. Jack was painfully thin and despite the chill of the room there was sweat on his pale face.

'You know that's not true. He fobs us off with easy lies. Oh Christ, Robin, if you knew how I dream of home, of cool green grass, sweet air, the smell of flowers . . .'

'I do know, believe me.' There was no point in reminding Jack that they had no home. Everything they possessed, everything their father had possessed, had been sequestered by the State, even Hemsby up in Norfolk, even Amy's dowry, thought Robert savagely. Thank the Lord for his father-in-law. John Robsart still had enough. She was safe with him at least.

He had been shut up with his brothers shortly after Elizabeth had left the Tower, and though in one sense their company had helped to ease the loneliness and boredom, the long days of June, July and August had been stiflingly hot and very nearly unendurable. Now in September the rain beat down outside, the walls were clammy with damp and the air in the upstairs room was both chill and suffocating.

With the heat had come the dreaded sweating sickness that had once carried off Ambrose's wife and son and Robert's little sister. Many in the Tower sickened and died. Jack developed a low fever that no remedy seemed to alleviate and he coughed continually. The depression, the stench of sickness in the close confinement were hard to live with, even though affection had always been strong between the brothers. Young and healthy though he was, there were moments in the night watches when Robert wondered grimly how long, oh God, how long before it would be his turn. He got up and moved restlessly to the window. All this week with the incessant rain their daily walk in the gardens had been forbidden to them.

Ambrose looked up from the book he was reading. He had always been the most patient of the brothers, the most cheerful and determinedly optimistic, not like Robert tossed between wild hope and a wilder despair.

He said calmly, 'You forget. There's a good chance of pardon, better than there has ever been. Try and keep that in your thoughts. I know I do. Harry spoke of it again in his last letter. Ever since he went with the embassy to Spain in the spring, he has contrived to keep on excellent terms with Philip, and now that the Prince is here and safely married, the Queen will deny him nothing.'

'Harry Sidney is busy feathering his own nest,' said Jack bitterly. 'He took damned good care to keep out of trouble when they were hunting us down. Now he's sitting pretty at Penshurst while we are paying with our lives. He has even forbidden Mary to visit us.'

'That's unfair, Jack. He's done everything in his power to help and Mary is pregnant. You know how she has longed for this child, both of them have, it would be madness for her to come here and risk infection.'

'Ambrose is right,' said Robert, turning back from the window. 'Why shouldn't Mary think of herself? Harry too?' He looked from Jack to Ambrose, speaking with an angry vehemence. 'I'll tell you one thing. If ever I get out of here, I intend to make sure I stay out. Father was right. I'll compromise, I'll lick boots, I'll crawl to the devil himself rather than suffer this misery over again. There's no cause on earth worth dying for.'

'Isn't there? I wonder,' said Ambrose thoughtfully. 'Let's hope we never have to make a choice.'

He looked at Robert speculatively. His brother had been subject to all kinds of wild moods since the Princess Elizabeth had left the Tower and yet was remarkably silent on the subject, fiercely resenting even a few harmless jests. Too many had already died for her sake. They had escaped death by a miracle and he had no wish to see Robin endanger himself for her, even if she was their only hope for the future.

Unbelievably release did come at last. The Prince of Spain, married to a wife eight years older than himself who was almost embarrassingly in love with him, found that the nobility and commons of England gave him only bare courtesy and regarded him with grave distrust. He was having to step warily and saw no reason why he should not put as many men as possible under an obligation to himself, even if it were only attainted prisoners.

On a crisp October day with the wind piling up the falling leaves into great drifts and an early frost silvering the grass, a small procession rode out of the Tower with Robert at the head and took the road to Kent.

To be free with a good horse under him, to feel himself still strong and healthy, the blood pounding joyfully in his veins, went to his head. He wanted to shout and sing if that had not been childish and undignified. Once over London Bridge and out of the stews of Bankside, he could not stop himself galloping ahead, riding back a little shamefacedly to trot more soberly beside the litter that carried Jack.

'How is he?' he whispered to Ambrose.

'He has great courage but I fear the jolting and the fatigue.'

They had tried not to admit it even to each other, but deep inside they knew their brother was dying and the thought cast a shadow over the happiness of their release.

There was no doubt about their welcome at Penshurst. Harry Sidney came riding to meet them while Mary, heavy with child for she was only a month from her time, was waiting in the hall, throwing her arms around Robert, laughing and weeping at the same time, trying hard to hide her distress at the sight of her elder brother as he leaned heavily on Ambrose's arm. She came to his other side, reaching up to kiss his cheek.

'We'll take such good care of you, Jack. You'll soon be well again, never fear.'

He smiled but said nothing, taking her hand and pressing it. He would not go to bed as they urged but lay on a couch close beside them as they gathered round the table for supper. They were all together, thought Robert, for the first time since those wedding festivities nearly two years ago when it had seemed that nothing could destroy the brilliance of the future that lay before them. Now their father lay in a dishonoured grave, Guildford and Jane were brutally murdered, their mother a pale frail shadow of the vital figure that had dominated his childhood, Jack close to death. He smiled at Mary, complimenting her on the excellence of the food, and frowned at young Hal, nearly seventeen and far too boisterous and ill-behaved, lacking the discipline of father and elder brothers. He would have to take him in hand. The only one not there was Katherine. Henry Hastings, though he had sent a kind message, was not going to risk his position at Mary's Court by mixing too freely with such recently condemned prisoners. Where would they all be in the next few years, where would he be? Blood, that creature Sirius had foretold . . . well, they had seen enough of that! Then fire . . . and after that the crown . . . for whom? For Elizabeth? A queer sick feeling of excitement made his hands tremble, then he was aware that Harry was saying something, breaking in on his thoughts.

'Are you dreaming, Robin? I wanted to propose a toast.' He looked around the table, smiling. 'To the Dudleys and to us and my unborn son.' 'To us,' they echoed and got to their feet.

'To us and to the Princess Elizabeth.' Robert had surprised himself. He had not meant to say any such thing and he saw the quick exchange of glances before they drained the wine in their cups.

'To the Princess Elizabeth, Queen of Robert's heart and ours too,' said young Hal irrepressibly and received a light cuff from Ambrose.

'Don't be a fool, boy.'

132

Harry Sidney frowned at the schoolboy impertinence. Not that there was anyone here to betray them, but any unwary reference to her cause, if reported, could arouse her sister's jealous resentment.

Late that night when Robert went to bed, Mary came into his room to talk as she had done so often in the old days.

'Have you everything you want, Robin? I tried to make sure, but just now I'm not able to keep my eye on the household as much as I would like.'

He looked round the room, at the great bed with its rich coverlet, the tapestries on the walls, the manchet of fine white bread with the silver jug of ale on the table, in case he should feel hungry during the night. 'This is paradise after the Tower,' he said, smiling. 'Sheets smelling of lavender, apple logs on the fire, a bowl of mother's famous pot pourri on the window shelf . . .'

'Dear Robin, I've not forgotten how much you like everything to smell sweet and fresh. You were like Elizabeth in that. Remember what a fuss she used to make even when we were children. You'll stay, won't you, Robin, until after the baby is born?'

'I don't want to embarrass Harry. Hasn't the Prince promised to stand godfather?'

She grimaced. 'Yes, he has, and if it is a boy we are to name him Philip.'

'Why not? Harry would be foolish to let any chance slip if he wants preferment at Court.'

'Yes, and he does.' She sighed. 'I could find content in a quiet life. Suppose it is a girl.'

'Then it will have to be Philippa.'

Mary laughed and he sat down on the bed, pulling her down beside him.

'I'll stay if you really want me to.'

'I do, I do,' she leaned her head against his shoulder, 'though I know Amy will reproach me for keeping you away from her. She would have come here to meet you but her father is old and often sick, and she felt she should stay with him. Poor Amy, she will be counting the days. It is cruel of me to deprive her of you for another month perhaps. I don't know what I would have done if it had been Harry shut up in the Tower for so long.'

'You'd not have had this fine sprig kicking inside you for one

133

thing,' he said lightly, touching her swollen belly.

'Yes, that's true. What will you do, Robin, now you are free?'

'What can I do? Settle down at Syderstone, turn farmer, till my lands, sell cattle, breed horses perhaps.'

'Shall you like that?'

'The horses, yes, if I can persuade Sir John to let me experiment. I always got on well with him. He will probably be glad enough to shift some of the burden to me. It is only . . .'

'Only what?'

'I would prefer to be my own master, not dependent on him for every crust I eat.' He got up restlessly. 'Needs must when the devil drives. I'm lucky, I suppose, I shouldn't grumble.' He took her hand, pulling her to her feet. 'Now you must get some sleep. You have the young heir to think about.'

'Oh, I'm very well, you know.' She moved to the door and then turned back, looking up into his face. 'Why did you say what you did about Elizabeth, Robin?'

'God knows,' he said lightly. 'It was foolish really, and the boy made it worse. Harry was annoyed with me.'

'Robin, did you see her at all when you were both in the Tower?'

He laughed, pulling her close to him and tweaking her nose. 'My dearest sister, what are you dreaming up in that head of yours? We were prisoners, remember, with locked doors between us and armed guards going before and behind when we took the air. Go on, off with you. Harry will think we are plotting something behind his back.'

'I don't care if he does. You are my dearest sweetest brother.' She reached up to kiss him. 'And you won't do anything foolish, will you?'

'Of course I won't.'

He watched her go still with that same strange restlessness, then he shook it off. To hell with frets and anxieties, he was twenty-one and alive, exuberantly alive, not like poor Jack. He stretched himself exultantly. Life still held the promise of glittering awards if one could only learn to be patient.

Jack died three days later and though they had schooled themselves to accept it, it still grieved them deeply. Their mother wept inconsolably and Mary wore herself out in tending her. Perhaps it was as well that the baby's arrival at the end of November distracted her from her sorrow.

Philip Sidney was a fine bouncing boy with a cap of gold-brown hair and enormous blue eyes. Harry was overjoyed, but unexpectedly it was Robert who from the very first handled his new-born nephew as to the manner born.

'I never saw the like. You've an instinct for it, my lord,' said the midwife admiringly when the bawling baby hushed at once as his uncle rocked him in his arms.

Mary laughed at him, leaning back against her pillows, weary still after a painful labour, but very happy.

'I hope soon you will be fathering sons of your own, Robert.'

'Perhaps. I ought to go from here, Mary. I must not wear out Harry's patience.'

'I wish you would stay and spend Christmas with us but I really can't keep you from Amy any longer.'

'No.' He had delayed from day to day, unable to explain his reluctance to leave this comfortable home. He should by rights have been longing to ride back to Norfolk, to the arms of his loving wife, and yet . . . He turned to Mary with a smile. 'I thought of taking young Hal back with me if you consider it a good idea.'

'Oh yes, Robert, I wish you would. Mother spoils him. It's natural of course. He is all she has had to comfort her these last two years, but it's not good for him. He admires you so much. He'll listen to you.'

'I'll do my best. He'll be a companion for Amy.'

She thought it was an odd thing for him to say, but she did not comment on it. He was her dearly loved brother and she wanted him to be happy above all things, but prison had changed him. She wondered sometimes if his wife realized that he was no longer the gay carefree boy she had married nearly five years ago.

Amy was in the summer parlour at Syderstone when she saw her half-sister ride into the courtyard and dismount with a flurry of importance. A few minutes later she heard her sharp voice finding fault with everything as usual as she came through the hall. She waited until she had gone by and then guiltily fled up the back stairs and took refuge in her own room, hoping against hope that Frances would leave her alone for once. Tussie, who was growing fat with too much good living, wagged his tail ingratiatingly from his warm spot by the fire. She picked him up, hugging him against her.

'Do you think if we're very quiet she'll go away and forget us this time?' she whispered into his silky ear.

But she might have known it was a forlorn hope. She was sitting on the fur rug still cuddling Tussie when the door was flung open and Frances, sharp-featured and formidable, stood on the threshold.

'Is this the way you run your house, Amy? I've just been in to see Father. His room is a disgrace, dust inches thick and a tray of food left on the table since yesterday, I shouldn't wonder. I don't like the look of him at all. Have you sent into Norwich for the physician?'

'He doesn't like doctors,' said Amy sulkily. 'He says he has had the gout these twenty years and so far none of them have done him a scrap of good, only extorted a fortune from him.'

'Really, Amy, you've no sense of responsibility at all. Letting those maids of yours do just how they like while you sit here, playing with that ridiculous little dog. He ought to be put down. He's far too fat and he is beginning to smell.'

'That's not true,' said Amy indignantly. 'Jennet bathes him every week. He can't help it if he's growing old, poor darling.'

'Darling indeed. It is a pity you haven't a parcel of children to care for!'

'Is that my fault?'

'Maybe not.' Frances came into the room, holding out her hands to the cheerful blaze of the fire and looking disapprovingly at the cosy disorder around her. 'And when are we to have the pleasure of your dear husband's company?' she said dryly.

'I am not sure,' faltered Amy. 'The last message I had from him said he would be here very soon.'

'He's taking his time over it, isn't he? John said he was released in the middle of October and here we are in December already and he still hasn't troubled himself to return to his wife.'

'What's it got to do with John?' said Amy angrily. 'There has been the death of his brother. It was only right that he should wait until the funeral was over. Lord Warwick was the head of the family. Then there was Mary's baby . . .' Her voice died away miserably.

Frances gave her a sharp look. 'I should have thought a wife would have meant more to him than a sister's lying-in,' she remarked acidly, drawing on her gloves, 'but then it has been an unfortunate marriage from the start. I said so at the time and I say it again now. All that grand talk, such a fine match, all the splendid things he was going to do for John, for all of us, and where is he now? An attainted traitor, a beggar crawling back to live on our father's generosity.'

'That's not fair,' burst out Amy hotly. 'It was not Robert's fault and John can't talk. He got out of it safely enough by running away. He didn't suffer like Robert. You didn't see that dreadful prison in the Tower as I did.'

'Well, he is your husband, I suppose, so we shall have to put up with the disgrace. But I should take care if I were you, my dear. There's bad blood there. Once a traitor, always a traitor.'

'If you feel like that then you can stay away,' said Amy with spirit. 'Robert and I don't need your company, or John's either, come to that.'

'That's no way to talk to your own flesh and blood. You may be glad of it when you're cold-shouldered by everyone of importance in the county. Lord Robert Dudley he may be,' she said with infinite scorn, 'but Dudley is a name to be avoided nowadays. I shall come here as usual to enquire after Father's health. Goodbye for now, Amy, and for heaven's sake make sure those idle servants do their work properly. I noticed at once the moment I stepped inside the door. The rushes in the hall downstairs smell as musty as if they have not been changed for weeks.'

Amy watched her sweep out of the room with a strong desire to seize the nearest heavy object and hurl it after her. She was still standing there, her cheeks pink with indignation, when the door opened a crack and a merry face looked round it.

'You can throw it at me if you like and if it will relieve your feelings.'

'Oh Ned!' Amy relaxed and smiled. 'Do come in. Did you ride with her?'

'Yes, I did, but she doesn't need me to escort her home again. Was she very hateful?'

'Beastly, especially about Robert, and it's only because she is jealous. She's afraid Father might make a new will and cut her out of it.'

'Oh I don't think my dear sister-in-law is quite as mercenary as that.' The years had made a difference to Ned Flowerdew too. At twenty-three he was a solid dependable young man, still unmarried and a frequent visitor to Syderstone. He perched himself on the edge of the table. 'The trouble with Frances is that she thinks it is her Christian duty to make everyone feel as uncomfortable as possible.'

'Oh Ned, you're so good for me. You make me laugh. Can you stay for a little?'

'All the evening if it will please you.'

'Oh, it will. It is so lonely with Father confined to bed. We will sup in here and play a game of spillikins to pass the time.'

And it was thus that Robert came upon them, their heads very close together, laughing like children over the game, too engrossed to notice the bustle of his arrival. He stood in the doorway, chilled, wet and hungry, and was quite unjustifiably irritated at sight of the cosy domestic scene.

'Well,' he said at last. 'Here I am.'

For an instant Amy stared at him, unable to believe her eyes, then she was on her feet, the ivory counters spilling all over the floor, crying out his name as she ran to him.

'Careful, careful,' he said, 'I'm smothered with mud, it's snowing outside,' but all the same he swung her up in his arms, crushing her against him, kissing her, feeling her tears wet on his face. 'There, there, little squirrel, no need to weep.'

'Oh Robin, dear, dear Robin, it's been so long.'

He set her gently on her feet, keeping an arm round her waist. 'Well, I'm home now and I've brought someone with me. Come in, Hal.'

Shyly Amy held out her hand to her brother-in-law. 'Goodness, Hal, how you've grown.' She bent forward to kiss his cheek while Robert came to the fire, throwing his soaked riding cloak carelessly aside and looking down at the young man carefully picking up the scattered counters.

'How are you, Ned? I scarcely expected to see you here so late.'

Ned scrambled to his feet, glancing up at the handsome man, a full head taller than himself, with the small fashionably trimmed moustache and beard that he had grown in the Tower, elegant, very self-assured, and knew at once that there was an end to the happy hours he had spent with Amy at Syderstone during the past year. He said quietly, 'I am very glad to see you looking so well, my lord. Did you have an exhausting journey?'

'Only since Norwich when it began to snow. The roads are filthy. Hal wanted to stay overnight but I couldn't endure to wait another moment. I've been away too long, isn't that so, sweetheart?' He held out his hand to Amy and Ned saw joy on her face as she went to him.

Damn him, he thought, damn him to hell! He has kept her waiting on tenterhooks, crying her heart out for him for two months and more, and yet, the moment he appears, he carries all before him.

He said coolly, 'If it's as bad outside as you say, then I should leave or I'll never get home tonight.'

'Must you go, Ned?' said Amy, but her adoring eyes were on her husband.

'Yes, I must. Goodnight, my lord.'

'Goodnight. Remember me to your father. I'll be over at Hethersett to see him in the morning.'

'You need not trouble yourself. My father rides in to consult with Sir John most days in the week.'

John Flowerdew had acted as loyal steward, watching over all the Robsart interests for the past two years, and yet this noble sprig, just out of prison and owning nothing but his sword and his stained name, spoke with the same careless arrogance as if his father was still dictator of all England.

'Excellent,' he said, turning to the fire. 'I shall see him then.'

'Very well. Goodnight, my lady.' Ned bent formally over Amy's hand, nodded to Hal and went quickly from the room.

'Does young Flowerdew make a habit of spending his evenings here, Amy?' said Robert, kicking at the logs with one booted foot so that they crackled into flame and Tussie sprang back with a terrified yelp.

'No, of course not, but he has kept me company sometimes. It's been so very lonely. You don't mind, do you, Robert?'

'Who am I to mind or not mind?'

'Oh, it's so wonderful to have you here, all to myself now for ever and ever. I want to hear everything about Mary and the baby and poor Jack of course and . . .'

'And so you shall, my pet, but all in good time.' He captured her hands, giving her the heart-turning smile that she remembered so well. 'But now I'm starving and so is Hal. Do you think you could find some food for us?'

After they had supped and while Amy had a room prepared for Hal, Robert went to pay his respects to his father-in-law and noticed how sadly he had aged, lying propped up in bed, his gouty foot raised on a pillow.

'Well, my boy,' he said, stretching out a veined, knotted hand. 'It is good to have you back at last, safe and sound. My little Amy has been sick with anxiety for you these many months. I'm sorry your brother has not lived to benefit from his release. But your sister has a fine son, I hear; that should comfort your mother.'

'She wished to be remembered to you, sir.'

'Give her my greetings when next you write. Tomorrow we must talk about your future, Robert. We're simple country folk, you know. Life won't be the same for you up here. Have you made any plans?'

'They must depend on you, Sir John,' said Robert with difficulty. 'I have not been trained to any of the useful professions, but I do know something about horses . . .'

'Horses, eh?' The old man smiled. 'That's a far cry from a courtier.'

Robert returned the smile. 'Not so far. My father was once Master of the Horse in the old King's time. With your permission I should like to try breeding them.'

'Well, well, we shall have to see what John Flowerdew has to say. You'd a good head for business, I remember that from the old days. You'll not be troubled with me much longer and this place will be yours when I go.'

'Don't speak like that,' said Robert quickly. 'I hope you will have many more years yet.'

'That's as God wills,' he said dryly. 'Now go to your wife, boy. She's been dreaming of this moment for long enough, poor child.'

'Goodnight then, sir, and thank you.'

He paused outside the door for a moment, pitying the old man whose life was ending when his own was just beginning once again. If he got his way, and he had no doubt of his power to persuade, perhaps it would not be so bad living up here after all. He walked quickly down the corridor to their bedchamber. It was just as he remembered it; Tussie's basket in front of the hearth, a slopped food bowl beside it, shifts and petticoats tossed anywhere, a chest gaping open, a smell of spilled perfume, wood smoke, orris root and a faint acrid tang of sweat. He suppressed a spasm of irritation and began to strip off his doublet and hose. He had thrown his bedgown around his shoulders when Amy came in carrying Tussie in her arms, a thick shawl wrapped around her over her nightgown.

'He wanted to go out,' she said.

'Can't Jennet do that for you?'

'I don't like to ask her so late. Is Father settled down for the night?'

'Yes, I believe so. He has been very kind.'

He watched while she tucked the little dog in his basket. She was plumper than he remembered, the heart-shaped face innocent and empty as a kitten. God damn it, why did he have to keep on thinking of a tall slender body, fine-boned aquiline features, green-gold eyes that enticed and held him off at the same time?

Amy had begun to unbraid her hair and then to plait it for the night. He came up behind her. 'Leave it. I like it loose.' His arms slid around her, feeling the small firm breasts under the thin lawn. His blood began to pound.

It was so long since he had had a woman. He had always had a violent distaste for the brothels, the easy whores, the ever-present danger of disease. Now he was overwhelmed with a sudden flooding desire. He pulled her roughly to her feet and carried her to the bed. His kisses were violent and he took her with so fierce a passion that she cried out and then surrendered herself utterly and completely.

Long afterwards, with physical needs slaked, he lay wakeful with her head on his breast, the remembered scent of rosemary

141

from the bright brown hair all around him. Once she stirred sleepily, reaching up to kiss him.

'Are you happy to be home, Robin?'

'Yes, very happy. Go back to sleep.'

'I love you.'

His hand touched her hair and moved gently down the slender body but he did not answer and she nestled against him with a little sigh of content.

Three

The months crept by slowly enough but they did pass and now it was June, and a dismally wet one with squally winds that blew across the broads from the sea, driving the rain before them. After Robert had completed the business which had taken him into Great Yarmouth, he rode up to Hemsby, reining in his horse and looking across at the gaunt castle, angry that even this small property should still be withheld from him and its rents go to swell the coffers of the State instead of his own pocket. By God, he could do with the money, every penny of it. It was not that Sir John was ungenerous, but he felt his utter dependence on him keenly though he had enjoyed visiting the horse fairs, choosing carefully and proving himself a cool and shrewd bargainer to the reluctant admiration of the traders who had imagined the elegant young man with his pretty manners to be easy game.

He had always possessed an ability to apply himself to a subject in which he was interested. He had been an exceptionally skilled rider even as a boy at Edward's Court; now he studied every branch of the art, practising arduously every trick of the *manège* so that to Amy, watching him trotting and prancing from the windows, the horses seemed to dance under him and she would clap her hands with delight.

'He has a pretty enough style certainly,' muttered John Appleyard sourly, 'but where is it going to get him? He'd do better to buy a couple of stout Flemish mares and turn them to the plough.'

She turned on him like a flash. 'Robert is not like you. He'll be a great man one day, as far above you as . . . as . . .'

'As what, sister? His fancy ways won't get him far up here and he'll find no favour at Court. The stain of traitor still clings to him, you know. He could be knocked down and robbed but still have no redress in law.'

'You're jealous because Father likes him and trusts him. He

143

doesn't gamble his rents away like you do over at Stanfield. How much have you asked Father for this morning?'

'It's only a loan,' he muttered under his breath.

'A loan we shall never see again,' she retorted and turned her back on him.

There was no love lost between Robert and his brother-in-law. The latter's desertion at King's Lynn still rankled and, despite his interest in the horses, life had been full of petty frustrations, petty insults. There had been a cool reception from the town worthies when he visited Norwich; no courteous invitations were extended to him and Amy from Castle Rising where he had once been governor, or from any of the great families scattered through the county. To hell with them, he thought savagely. They had been lickspittle enough when his father had been Duke of Northumberland.

He took a last angry look at Hemsby before he turned his horse on to the homeward track. The wind from the sea was at his back now. He huddled into his cloak and rode slackly, his thoughts running back over the last few tedious months. Brought up in luxury in a brilliant intellectual circle, the slow wits and rustic conversation of their country neighbours had driven him to near distraction, and Hal had been no help at all. His young brother showed his contempt openly. His lively imitation of some of their more bovine acquaintances sent Amy into fits of giggles but distressed her father and forced Robert into angry reprimand.

'For God's sake, Hal, we eat their bread, the least we can do is to behave decently.'

The boy had looked up at him insolently. 'It's so cursed dull up here. I need to amuse myself somehow. After all you have Amy.' He had grinned infuriatingly and gone off whistling.

He was the other side of Norwich before the rain stopped and he roused himself from his abstraction. He threw back his wet cloak and looked around him. By the wayside an iron stake hung with rusting chains awoke disagreeable memories of a day in April when he and Amy had been riding along this same road. News of the burnings in London had reached them as long ago as February, but up till then there had been none in Norfolk. The crowd was surging all round them before he realized what was happening, a jostling pushing mass of men, women and children. At first he thought it must be some local festivity until he saw the stake, the chained victim and the piled faggots. There was the flame of a torch, the crackling as the brushwood caught alight and then the scream, ear-piercing, appalling. Amy clutched at his arm.

'I know her,' she whispered, 'oh God, I know her. It's Meg Tyson.'

'Who?'

'You must remember, Robert, Meg Tyson at Hemsby. She went away nearly two years ago. She was wed to one of the stable lads. What has she done? What *can* she have done to deserve this?'

'Denied the true presence, that's what, my lady,' said a man pressing up against her horse and looking up at her with sly relish. 'Swore to God the sacrament was nought but idolatry, only a bit of bread baked in an oven, no different from what we put in our mouths every day of our lives.'

Robert was staring at the long dark hair, the plump pretty face contorted with terror; Meg, the girl with whom he had enjoyed a few pleasurable hours. She had meant nothing to him, but she had come to him willingly enough and she had been a sweet armful, a simple country lass, smelling of milk and fresh-cut grass; not, he would have thought, the stuff of which martyrs are made.

Amy was white and trembling. 'They can't burn a girl like Meg just for that, Robert, can they?'

And he was suddenly angry because he could do nothing, because it could happen to any of them; the spiteful and the envious were only too ready to act the informer. 'They can and they will,' he said grimly. 'She has behaved like a fool. Put it out of your mind, Amy.'

He swung their horses around, curtly ordering his men to follow and forcing a way through the crowd, not caring whom he overturned. But he could not put it out of his own mind so easily. If you wanted to survive, you had to kneel and accept, go to mass and keep your beliefs to yourself. If the Princess Elizabeth could do it, so could he and a hundred others. You had to compromise. He was only now learning the bitter truth in his father's words.

He had thought of it more than once since that day. He remembered Mary from their childhood when she had sometimes acted the kind elder sister to Elizabeth. With her Spanish mother she

145

had always been passionately Catholic. But what had turned the timid bullied spinster into a monster who was rapidly earning the hatred of her people? Was it love, was she doing it to please her Spanish husband, or was it a salve to a tortured conscience, frightened zeal for the Roman Catholic faith that her father had once forced her to deny? Perhaps she was to be pitied after all. She had declared herself pregnant last November but the child that should have been born in May was long overdue. The bonfires were ready, the cannon loaded to fire a salute, all things prepared to proclaim the joyful tidings of a new heir, but still no news came from London. And if it should all be a sick fantasy or if she should die in labour as many women did, and she was after all approaching forty, then the seesaw would swing up again and it would be Elizabeth's turn.

Riding through the village, peaceful enough now on a wet June afternoon, the scene was still vivid in his mind and he came to a sudden decision. He must risk a visit to London. He could not endure to stay one moment longer mewed up in this backwater where news filtered through so desperately slowly. He would run mad if he did not escape from it, even if only for a few weeks.

When he reached the house he went straight to his wife's sitting-room, mud-splashed as he was, and was irritated to see Frances sitting there. He knew by Amy's heightened colour and the brightness of her eyes that she had been crying again. There were times when he could cheerfully have wrung his sister-in-law's scraggy neck. He greeted her with brief courtesy and took up his position in front of the fire, picking up the abjectly fawning Tussie. Dogs as well as horses always worshipped Robert.

'I've made up my mind, Amy,' he said abruptly. 'I shall leave for London tomorrow.'

'London?' she gasped faintly.

'London?' repeated Frances shrilly. 'Would that be wise, my lord? Surely you would be venturing into the lion's den.'

'Maybe,' he said, deliberately cheerful, 'but nothing ventured, nothing won, and there is my mother's will still to be settled and a legacy for Amy to be collected. As you know, the Duchess of Northumberland died in January.' No need to tell Frances that the legacy was no more than a gown of wrought velvet, rather worn, and the money left to him hardly worth mentioning. Since he had no civil rights, it was extremely unlikely that he could even claim it.

'And where will you stay?'

'There are inns and I still have friends,' he said airily. 'There is my lord of Pembroke at Baynard's Castle or Lord North at the Charterhouse.' He would not dream of embarrassing either of his old companions at Court but she would not know that.

She rose to her feet. 'Well, I only hope for all our sakes that you remain out of prison, my lord.'

'I think I can contrive that, Frances. John has taught me the art of vanishing at the crucial moment.'

He was rewarded with a look of pure hatred as he opened the door for her with a courtly flourish, and she swept past him with an indignant flurry of velvet skirts.

Amy was laughing now. 'Oh Robin, how could you say that? You made her look so foolish.'

'She had no right to make you cry. What has she been saying this time?'

'Oh nothing really, just finding fault as usual. Am I such a bad housekeeper, Robert?'

'Dreadful. Haven't I said so a hundred times?'

'I do try, really I do.'

'I know, little squirrel.'

The brown eyes were beginning to fill again, the soft mouth to tremble. He held back his impatience. Goodness knows, they had quarrelled over it enough already, quarrels that usually ended in floods of tears and a remorseful reconciliation in bed that settled nothing.

He said, 'Never mind that now. I must go out and speak with the servants if we are to make ready to leave tomorrow. I shall take Hal with me.'

She ran after him, clinging to his arm. 'May I go with you, Robert? Please, please . . .'

'No, my dear. I must ride fast and secretly.'

'Then Frances is right. It is dangerous.'

'Not if I am careful and I shall be, never fear. I shall be seeing Ambrose, Mary too, perhaps. If you have any message for her, you had better get it written now.'

The fires had died down on the day Robert rode through the wasteland of Smithfield, but he could see the blackened stakes and a greasy smoke still lingered in the air. The nauseating stench forced him to pull his handkerchief from his pocket and hold it to his nose.

'Turns the stomach, don't it, my lord?' said Martin Turnbull dryly when he turned into the horse-trader's yard. 'You're lucky today. It's worse when they're burning and the wind blows this way. Upsets the horses too. They don't like the smell of death no more than we do. London's a place for honest folk to keep away from these days.'

Robert was inclined to agree with him. Even in the brief time that he had spent there, the capital had seemed a dismal place. Everywhere a feeling of unrest prevailed, the people going about their daily tasks with grim faces. Only the churches were flourishing. It was strange to hear bells ringing for mass and see the streets filled with monks and priests, as they had not been since he was a child. He drew his horse aside as a small cavalcade went clattering arrogantly down the highway, guessing from their dress that they were Spanish, and as the mud splashed up, he saw the looks of hatred that followed them. Mary was trying to turn the clock back too suddenly, but all the same it was not wise to speak one's mind even here. There were spies everywhere. When he had called on his old tutor at Mortlake, it was only to be told that Dr Dee had been imprisoned simply for casting the Princess Elizabeth's horoscope. Involuntarily he had remembered that strange creature Sirius and then dismissed it from his mind. He turned to the business in hand.

'What have you to show me, Martin?'

'Ah, now you're talking,' said the dealer, rubbing his hands briskly. 'Business has been fair and I've one or two beasts that I think will please your lordship. Not like the old days of course when the Duke, your father, God rest his soul, was good enough to send for me. Many's the chat I had with him . . . but there, times change. Some of these Dons in the Prince's retinue have been sadly over-reaching themselves and are glad to part with their nags to pay their debts. I've a couple of Andalusian jennets, black as ebony, well-fed, healthy and with an Arab strain, I shouldn't wonder.'

Robert spent a pleasant hour in bargaining and bought the Spanish horses at an outrageous price, but still for less than he had expected. He arranged for them to be picked up by the two grooms he had brought with him and was preparing to leave when he caught sight of a flash of white in an inner stall, carefully hidden from the casual buyer, and was intrigued.

'What have you tucked away in there, you rogue? Something good you've been keeping from me?'

'She's a yearling,' said Turnbull reluctantly, 'not what you're looking for, my lord, pure white and finely bred.'

'Let me take a look at her.'

'She's not for sale, my lord, leastways I already have a prospective customer.'

'Oh? And who might that be?'

The trader looked around him and then lowered his voice. 'Well, since it's you asking, my lord . . . it's the Lady Elizabeth. Sir William Cecil was in here a short time ago. He saw her and thought the mare would please Her Highness.'

'Cecil, eh?' His father's secretary who had discreetly escaped involvement in the Duke's wrecked fortunes. Cecil had always had an uncanny flair for picking the winning side. Like a cat, whatever the upheaval, he always contrived to land on his feet. First the Protector Somerset, then his own father . . . Robert had always suspected that the message which had prevented him capturing Mary Tudor had been sent by Cecil, but that was old history . . . and now he was quietly cultivating Elizabeth. Interesting that and a useful pointer for any young man with his fortune to make. Will Cecil was a dull stick, but clever, no doubt about that. He would enjoy scoring off him just this once.

'All the same,' he said quietly but firmly, ' I should like to see the filly.'

The dealer hesitated, but he too had the future to think of and Robert, down on his luck now, might well be a valuable customer in times to come. You had to look out for yourself. It didn't do to neglect anything these days.

'As you wish, my lord,' he said and led the way inside.

The moment Robert set eyes on her, he knew he had to have her. The dark eyes turned to him reminded him of Speedwell. The narrow head, the quivering nostrils bespoke the quality of her ancestry. She was a gift worthy of a Princess and it would be he and not William Cecil who would make the gift in his own good time.

He ran his hand gently down the satin flank. The mare trembled and turned her head to nuzzle his hand. 'I'll take her,' he said.

'I fear the price is beyond your reach, my lord. More than the two you've bought already and, as I've said, she's promised.'

'I'll give you half as much again,' he said recklessly.

Turnbull hesitated and then grinned. 'Sir William will be annoyed but to tell the truth, my lord, he hasn't your touch. It's a pleasure to do business with a man who knows horseflesh as well as you do. She's mettlesome but she likes you, I can see that, only I must have the money,' he went on cautiously, 'no credit.'

'Is my word not good enough?'

'It's not that, my lord, believe me, but these are difficult times. You know that as well as I. There's no telling what will happen between one day and the next, and I've a wife and a growing family.'

Robert laughed. 'Don't break my heart with your tale of woe. You're a damned rascal but you shall have the cash, I promise you, only you'll have to wait a day or two. Hold her for me or I swear to God there'll be an end to business between us.'

He would have to see what Ambrose could do or what he could borrow on the strength of his mother's legacy. If the worst came to the worst, he could beg a loan from Harry Sidney. He swung himself into the saddle and turned his horse's head to St Paul's and the Cross Keys where he was meeting his brother before they rode down to Kent, fully aware that he had behaved with a crazy rashness and not caring a jot if he had.

'You've done what?' exclaimed Ambrose. 'You've paid out a fortune for a year-old filly that could get the staggers or the glanders or any of the other confounded diseases that horses are subject to before you get her back to Norfolk. Have you taken leave of your senses?'

'Nothing of the sort,' said Robert airily. 'It's an insurance against the future. It was Will Cecil who put the idea into my head. If he is hitching his waggon to the Princess Elizabeth's star, then we would be well advised to follow suit.'

'He has certainly kept himself out of trouble,' said Ambrose thoughtfully, 'and he is not doing too badly in a quiet way even now, but what the devil has Cecil to do with it? I don't ever remember him being a connoisseur of horseflesh.'

'I discovered he was intending to make a gift of her to Elizabeth and I beat him to it.'

'Oh Robin, for heaven's sake, what kind of dream world are you living in? When do you think you are going to find an opportunity to present any kind of gift to Her Royal Highness?'

'I hadn't thought as far as that,' confessed Robert, a little ashamed in face of Ambrose's common sense of the romantic impulse that had driven him to buy the mare. Yet he knew in some way he could not explain even to himself that it had been right even if it promised no immediate advantage.

'You certainly will not be allowed to come within miles of Hampton Court. Mary tells me that it is like a lying-in hospital just now, with doctors, midwives, nurses and cradle-rockers in attendance and Her Majesty bursting into tears and having hysterics because her husband, bored to distraction by all this female commotion, is indulging in a violent flirtation with his sister-in-law.'

'With Elizabeth?' Robert was immediately alert. 'Is she there at Court?'

'Indeed she is and has been ever since April. There's been a reconciliation with the Queen, at Philip's insistence. He is taking no chances, Robert. His wife is in precarious health and if she were to die, he'd back Elizabeth to win. Spain and England against France, that's his dream, and it's my belief he will pull us into his war sooner or later. The Church forbids marriage to your wife's sister, but I daresay he could get round the Pope to grant a dispensation.'

'Marriage? Elizabeth would never marry Philip, never!' said Robert with angry vehemence.

'You seem very sure,' said Ambrose, half smiling.

'The very notion is ridiculous.' Robert got up and moved away from his brother. Then he swung round to face him. 'Elizabeth is not like her sister. She'd not burn her own countrymen for the sake of religion. She believes as we do.'

'She's no fool,' said Ambrose dryly. 'Whatever Elizabeth believes, she would not let it interfere with what she wants and her heart is set on England. She will never put a foot wrong, Robin, you mark my words.'

The cool shrewd part of his brain acknowledged the truth of what Ambrose said; but there was another side, a wild irrational side that he only barely admitted, but that seethed with a sudden savage jealousy, a fierce anger that she could dally with the Spaniard, permit him to make love to her while he was forbidden even a glimpse of her.

They went on to discuss more mundane matters. Ambrose had been in consultation with the trustees of their mother's will. The money was still withheld from the brothers but he could borrow on the expectation. He heaved a sigh of relief. It meant that he could buy the mare without having to beg a loan from his brother-in-law.

There were guests at Penshurst when he and Ambrose rode in from London, most of them old friends who had been his companions in many a joust and tournament at Edward's Court, Lord Henry Herbert, heir to the Earl of Pembroke, and young Roger North among them. He smiled as he greeted them, remembering his boast to Frances and thought how Amy would laugh with delight when he told her about it. It was good to be in the company of his equals again and they made him welcome. There was only one who looked at him askance. Thomas Ratcliffe, whose father, the Earl of Sussex, had been one of those who condemned Robert to death at his trial, had recently taken as his second wife Harry Sidney's sister Frances, and he was not particularly pleased to find himself in the company of such recently attainted traitors. He was a solid, rather humourless, but immensely reliable young man some seven years older than Robert and already an experienced administrator. He had fought as a boy under his father in Scotland and was shortly to go as Lord Deputy to Ireland.

'Harry is to go with him as his second in command and he's so pleased,' whispered Mary. 'I do wish he wasn't. I shall miss him desperately.'

152

'Tom Ratcliffe will be at home in the bogs of County Dublin. He'll enjoy bullying the natives,' said Robert lightly, 'I wish him joy of it. He's a fine match, I suppose, but a grim one. Whatever made little Fanny marry him?'

There was an instant hostility between them, the instinctive distrust of the eminently respectable aristocrat of impeccable ancestry for the adventurer, the penniless upstart, whose father and grandfather were stained with treason and who possessed nothing to recommend him but his looks, his wit and his undoubted charm.

To Ratcliffe's annoyance it was Robert who shone at the supper table, who kept them roaring with laughter at the amusing mimicry of his rustic neighbours, and it was all the more maddening because his humour was not coarse or vulgar but spiced with wit and a lively intelligence. Too many damned Dudleys, he thought, looking around him, and all as clever as monkeys! He resented the way his girl-wife looked up admiringly at the young man, close friend to her brother, whom she had known as an adoring small child.

After supper, when the tables were cleared and the musicians began to play in the great hall, Robert strolled across to them, smiling down at Ratcliffe, the elegant simplicity of his brown velvet trimmed with gold contriving to make the Earl's handsomely slashed purple and silver look vastly overdressed.

'Will you permit me, my lord, to ask your bride to honour me? Fanny and I are old friends.'

She was on her feet at once, dimpling up at him. 'You've remembered! You once promised to dance with me when I was big enough.'

'So I did and here I am to claim my promise now you're as high as my shoulder.'

What could her husband do but smile graciously? Damn him, he thought, he talks the courtly nonsense that all women love and that's an end, and yet they're all devoted to him, his sister, his brothers, even Harry Sidney!

Robert danced, as he did so many things, with supreme grace. Ratcliffe watched them in the galliard, kicking higher and higher, Fanny's skirts flying up, revealing slim ankles in scarlet hose, a mere trifle and yet it irritated him. Presently she came running back, her cheeks pink, hand in hand with Robert.

'Did you see, Tom? Did you see how well I dance?' she exclaimed and then her face fell as she saw his frown. 'Have I displeased you?'

'Not at all, but you're over-exciting yourself, my dear. I think it best that you do not dance again.'

'Oh why, when I love it so?'

Robert smiled, touching her cheek with one long finger. 'And you do it divinely, but now you must obey your lord and master. He has had long experience with wilful little wives.'

He kissed the tips of her fingers, nodded carelessly to Ratcliffe and strolled away. Fanny plumped down beside her husband, pouting a little and pulling her hand away when he would have taken it in his own.

'Why don't you like Robert, Tom?'

'I don't like him or dislike him,' he said coldly. 'He is quite unimportant.' But to himself he thought, 'Arrogant bastard! He has nothing, he is nothing, he is no more than a gypsy with an eye to his own profit, yet he apes the manners of a prince!'

There was another guest who had been watching Robert closely that evening. Sir Henry Dudley was a man of forty-five or thereabouts, a man with raffish good looks who wore his shabby clothes with an air. Robert remembered him well from his boyhood. The Dudley children had called him uncle but he was only a distant cousin, turning up like a bad penny, asking their father for a loan and usually outstaying his welcome. The Duke had distrusted him but would put his hand in his pocket for old times' sake.

'What the devil is Uncle Henry doing here?' Robert asked Mary quietly. 'I thought he was safely abroad.'

'So he was, in Holland, I believe, and in France. He has only just come back. Harry wasn't too pleased when he turned up but what could I do? Father never refused him hospitality.' She put a hand on her brother's arm. 'I have an idea he is up to something. You won't let him tempt you into anything rash, Robin?'

He smiled, pinching her cheek. 'What kind of a fool do you take me for?'

It was late that evening when Dudley drew Robert aside into one of the wide embrasures of the great hall. It was a warm night, the windows stood open, and outside moonlight silvered the gardens and cast a greenish glow over the pale face and dark hair.

He dropped on the cushioned window-seat. 'It's a long time, Robin, must be nigh on five years and you've grown into a fine upstanding young man since I saw you last.'

'What is all this leading to, Uncle?' he asked bluntly. 'My pocket is flat as a winded bladder these days.'

'What a thing to say! I'm not asking for a loan, boy, though God knows it would be damned useful. We've all felt the pinch, you too these last few years.'

'I have indeed.' He was impatient. 'Well, what is it then? There is little enough I can do for anyone just now.'

Sir Henry studied him for a moment. 'Tell me, Robert, how well are you acquainted with the Princess Elizabeth?'

Startled he said, 'What do you mean by a question like that?'

'I hear things, you know, even in a hell-hole like Calais.'

'What is there to hear? I knew her as a child and have seen her perhaps half a dozen times since.'

'Is that all? I had other information.' He leaned forward, giving him a sly grin. 'And what happened in the Tower, eh? Now, now, don't jump down my throat. We'll say no more about it for the moment . . .'

'Nothing happened, nothing at all, no more than a few words. We were prisoners, and you ought to know what that means.'

'Only too well, still . . .' He eyed Robert up and down. 'They do say that she has an eye for a lusty young man with everything proper about him despite that cool "don't touch me" manner of hers. Her mother was Anne Boleyn after all and she . . . well, we all know what she was,' and he gave a little whistle.

Robert said stiffly, 'I've no idea what you're implying but I'd have you remember that I'm a married man.'

'Tcha!' His uncle snapped his fingers contemptuously. 'A little bread-and-butter miss whom you take good care to keep shut up in the country. That's no obstacle.'

'Obstacle to what?'

'Never mind. Just a thought.' He put a hand on Robert's arm, whispering, 'Can't speak too openly here. Harry Sidney's too damned careful, never saw a man so cautious. He has already hinted he'd rather have my room than my company. I don't want to upset Mary. I'm off early in the morning but I shall be in London for a few days at the Fountain in the Minories. Come and see me there before you go back to Norfolk.'

'Why? For what purpose?'

He lowered his voice still further. 'There are a great number of us here as well as abroad who would be glad of a change. Do I need to say more? We'd like to see you-know-who in place of her sister.'

'Wyatt tried to do that and lost his head.'

'Wyatt was a romantic fool. He'd have married her to Courtney who has never had the guts of a rabbit. We have other plans.'

'What plans?'

'Come and see me and you may hear of something to your advantage.'

He clapped Robert on the back and slid away, leaving him doubtful, full of distrust but at the same time intrigued. After all he had to stop off in London to pick up his horses. There would be no harm surely in going to the Fountain and finding out what was brewing.

In some ways he was sorry to leave Penshurst. The nine-months-old Philip was a sturdy boy, already trying to pull himself up by his uncle's knee and totter on unsteady legs, and Mary was pregnant again. No wonder Harry was pleased with himself, a growing family and an interesting post in front of him even if it was in Ireland. Mary loaded him with gifts for Amy and he left Ambrose and Hal behind him when he rode to London.

At the Cross Keys he found Dick Tamworth with the horses. He was a good lad, one of Sir John's men, steady and reliable. Robert went out to the stables to look at the mare. She was in fine fettle, as beautiful as he remembered her, and he christened her White Lady there and then. He would enjoy schooling her and wondered when, if ever, the opportunity would come to present her to Elizabeth.

After he had eaten, he walked down to the Minories. In East Chepe a crowd was baiting some unfortunate wretch in the pillory, a placard round his neck proclaiming him cheat who had short-changed his customers. Now they took their revenge with rotten eggs and stinking refuse. They parted respectfully to let him through and he looked up at the grim shadow of the Tower with a strong determination that he was not going to become involved in anything that might land him back there.

The Fountain was a large well-appointed inn. He wondered wryly where his needy uncle found the means to stay in so expensive a hostelry. The serving girl showed him up to a room on the upper floor. There were perhaps a dozen men gathered round the table; one or two he knew slightly, the others were strangers. Sir Henry greeted him boisterously and introduced him. He saw the way they looked up at the Dudley name. There was wine on the table. He noted the flushed faces and thought they had probably been indulging themselves for some time. He sat down quietly, saying little and forming his own judgment.

They talked of the discontent throughout the country, each one with some tale to relate that sounded impressive and meant very little. They don't understand the temper of the people at all, he thought after a while. They've lived abroad and listened to hearsay. They had not seen as he had how slow the country folk were to rebel. There had been enough bloodshed, enough hangings. Even the burnings wouldn't rouse them to risk their homes and their lives. Now they were bandying great names from one to the other – Percy, Pembroke, Arundel, Sussex . . .

'You forget, gentlemen,' said Robert quietly, 'some of these men betrayed my father in his greatest need. They are turncoats all if it is to their own advantage and, as for the Earl of Sussex and his son, the Ratcliffes have always been honest . . .'

'So are we all, but things are different now,' argued his uncle. 'None of them likes being crushed under the heel of Spain. They may pay him lip service but they would leap at any chance to pull King Philip off his high perch.'

'They hold great office, they are enjoying power and wealth. They can afford to wait," said Robert dryly.

'But we cannot. Where's your spirit, boy? Have you no desire to avenge your father? If we put Elizabeth on the throne, she will owe us everything. The name of Dudley will mean something again in England. Isn't that a worthwhile purpose?'

It was true that he wanted that more than anything in the world. He had nursed that secret ambition for the past year but, young though he was, Robert could also be cool and calculating. One part of him yearned to be in action, to break away from the

157

deadly boredom of his life, to win back his good name and all that went with it, high office, riches, power, but not like this. He looked around the ring of faces and distrusted every one of them. They were talking into the wind. Their plans would be blown away in the first storm and could drag her down with them. The Princess Elizabeth's worst enemies were the men who called themselves her friends.

He left early, pleading fatigue, and Sir Henry came out on to the landing with him.

'This is only a beginning, Robert. We've a long way to go but you could be useful to us.'

'In what way?'

In the dark his uncle's insinuating voice was close to his ear. 'She never cared a rush for Courtney, but she looks on you with favour, she likes you, Robert . . .'

'This is sheer madness . . .'

'Maybe, but madness has succeeded sometimes where women are concerned. Think on it.'

He escaped as quickly as he could. The whole plot, if it could ever be called that, was hopeless. It would never succeed. His father's soaring ambition had only brought him to ruin, and his uncle had not a tenth of the Duke's imagination and strength of character. Robert lay on his hard bed at the inn listening to Tamworth snoring on the palliasse in the corner and wondered how he could warn Elizabeth. If they were to entangle her in their wild schemes, it could endanger her, it could even send her to her death as Wyatt had so nearly done.

If he had needed any confirmation of his own opinion, it came the next morning in the person of Sir William Cecil. He was shown in just as Robert was finishing his midday meal. He paused in the doorway, soberly dressed as usual, a grave quiet man.

'I am sorry to disturb you, my lord.'

'No matter. I have finished eating already. Will you take wine with me?'

'Thank you, no.' Cecil was rigidly formal. It was the first time they had met since his father's execution and there was a great deal that must remain unspoken between them. 'I am a bearer of a message from the Privy Council.'

'You, Sir William?'

'They call upon my services from time to time and knowing

of my acquaintance with your family . . .'

Robert took the sealed letter. 'Do you know what is in it?'

Cecil hesitated. 'I understand it is a request that you should leave London as soon as possible.'

'Why?' He was indignant. 'Am I not a free man?'

'Only at Her Grace's pleasure.'

'What harm am I doing?'

'None, I am sure. Maybe it is not you, my lord, but the company you keep.'

So they knew something already. Was it possible? Had there been a spy amongst those he had met last night? He had been right to suspect them.

He broke the seal and read the curt order to leave the capital within twenty-four hours. It angered him but there was nothing he could do. He looked up to see Cecil regarding him gravely.

'You would be well advised to go at once, my lord.'

'Why should I?' he said rebelliously.

'It is hard to be patient when one is young, Lord Robert, but it affects us all. Our turn will come.' He said dryly, 'I should be angry with you.'

'Because of the mare?' Robert gave him his most charming smile. 'I am sorry, but she was the very embodiment of one I lost and dearly loved.'

Cecil shrugged his shoulders. 'I have not your passion for horses, my lord, nor your skill. I hope she brings you good fortune.' He held out his hand and Robert took it. 'Convey my good wishes to your lady.'

'Thank you, I will.'

They parted on amicable if guarded terms.

Robert left early the following morning. It had been a miserable summer with the endless rain bringing a murrain on the cattle and ruination to the farmers' crops, but at seven o'clock the sun was shining for once and the resolution he had pondered during the night hardened into action. He sent Tamworth ahead with the horses and with orders to wait for him at Ware, while he took himself alone to Hampton Court.

He had made no plan, had no idea of how he was going to approach Elizabeth. He had considered writing to her and dismissed it as useless. Letters could be intercepted and, however carefully worded, could be dangerous. He toyed with the notion of disguise and abandoned it. He was too well known to too many people. He dare not try and penetrate to the Princess's apartments. But she should be warned, he told himself, so that she could arm herself against those who would entrap her in their desperate plots. But there was another motive, one which nothing would have made him admit but which had always been there, too strong to be denied, a simple passionate desire to see her again.

That he did encounter her was the purest good luck, or perhaps part of the fatality that hung over them both and that sometimes he would believe in and sometimes dismiss with a shrug. He had ridden through Richmond and reached the deer park that stretched between Hampton and Twickenham, when he saw the cavalcade come trotting up the green glade and withdrew out of sight into the shelter of the trees.

He could see quite clearly the two who rode ahead of the others. Elizabeth wore a riding dress of deep green velvet, a high-crowned hat on the red hair, the white feathers drooping to her cheek, and on her gloved wrist she carried her favourite hawk. The man beside her, dressed all in black, must be the Spanish Prince. The sun sparkled on jewels, silks and velvets, on trappings of gold and silver. He saw Philip lean across and put his hand on hers. He saw the teasing familiarity of the look she gave him and burned with an entirely unjustifiable jealousy. Then, while he watched, he heard her say something and throw up her hand so that the hawk rose into the sky like an arrow, soaring up with a great spread of wings. She laughed, spurring her horse and galloping down the glade just as once long ago she had ridden beside him, far outstripping the Prince and his retinue.

He followed alongside her, still within the shade of the trees, risking a fall as he dodged the low branches until, at a bend in the glade out of sight of the others, he seized her bridle and whipped her far down a long path at an angle to the main drive. She was frightened but she did not scream, only struggled hard to free herself, bringing down her whip with a stinging blow across his bare hand. Then he pulled her into the shelter of a copse, released the bridle and swept off his cap.

'You!' she exclaimed. 'Lord Robert! In God's name, what are you doing here? Are you mad?'

'Don't be angry with me, I beg of you.'

'You've left me no breath to be angry.'

'I apologise for treating you so cavalierly, but I had to speak with you . . .'

'But you cannot. They will be coming after me at any moment and if they find you here . . .'

He knew what would happen to him if they did and so did she, and yet neither of them moved. They stared at one another. She was no longer the frightened girl of the Tower, but assured, confident and in her own way beautiful, everything of which he had dreamed.

She leaned forward, touching the weal the whip had left across his hand. 'What is it you have to say? Tell me quickly if it is so vital. Already I can hear them calling.'

The words came stumbling out. He gave no names but told her all that he knew. 'I don't know how far they have gone or any details or whether they have already approached some of your people, but I implore you with all my heart to have a care.'

'Who are they?'

'Some I know but not all, and I would not betray them.'

'God protect me from my friends,' she said fervently.

'But not from all.' He drew off her embroidered glove and kissed the long tapering fingers. 'Not from all.'

'No, you are right, and I am grateful to you. You have risked your freedom, maybe your life, to come to me.'

'I would risk more if I had it to give, only to see you for an instant.'

The voices were coming nearer. She said urgently, 'You must go now. Please go!'

'Yes,' but still he did not move. 'What is happening in the palace?'

She looked away. 'I believe there will be no child.'

'Thank God.'

'You should not say that. It is cruel. Poor Mary, she is sick with longing.'

'We do not want a Catholic heir. We want you.'

'Don't!' she said in a quick revulsion of feeling. 'Don't, it is like wishing for her death. It is horrible. It will bring ill-luck.'

'What of Philip?'

'It is because of his wish that I am here and I am grateful for

161

that, but now he grows impatient.'

'And while he waits, he courts you . . .'

She smiled tantalisingly. 'Sometimes. It passes the time.'

'Is he your lover?'

He had never meant to say it and she reacted swiftly and with outrage. The eyes flashed green fire. She raised the glove and slashed it across his face, the blow so fierce that the gold and jewels cut into his cheek. Then she swung her horse round and went back up the ride at a tearing gallop.

The whole party were in a state of distraction, preparing to separate and go in search of her.

Philip rode up in strong agitation. 'What happened? Were you attacked?'

Her laugh rang out clear as a bell. 'Nothing of the sort. What is all this fuss, simply because sometimes I like to ride fast. Where is my hawk?'

'But we saw a man come out from the trees,' persisted the Prince. 'Is that not so, gentlemen?'

He appealed to the others and they crowded up to her, all speaking at once. She drew away from them, assuming her haughtiest manner.

'Do not press upon me, I beg of you. You are mistaken, sirs, there was no one.' She raised her voice. 'And what has happened to my hawk? I would not lose Jezebel for all the world. My brother gave her to me.'

'She is here, my lady.' The falconer approached respectfully, the bird hooded again safely on his wrist, but the distraction had served her turn. Fortunately for Robert, they did not pursue further.

Elizabeth looked at the slight, fair Prince with the bulging blue eyes and the ugly Habsburg jaw. He had been responsible for her appearance at Court and for the measure of liberty granted to her; it had been good policy to play him along these last months, walking beside him in the gardens, hunting with him, letting him believe her fascinated by his wit and learning. It had been amusing too and flattering after the months, the years of isolation, to be conscious of his admiration, to use her powers to charm and tantalise, going so far and no farther, but now quite suddenly she disliked his attentions. He owed them to her sister, not to her. She smiled, but she withdrew the hand he would have taken

162

in his and called one of her ladies to come to her side.

Robert watched them ride on together. She was not so angry that she had set them on him and she could have done it so easily. He had not told her of the mare as he had intended, but that could wait another opportunity. He wiped the blood from his cheek and smiled down at the stained handkerchief. Then he turned his horse and rode quickly away.

Four

Robert sat in the room he had made particularly his own at Syderstone and went over the monthly accounts with Ned Flowerdew who occasionally substituted for his father. It was more than a year since he had been warned away from London and he had strong reason to thank the good sense that had kept him out of his uncle's schemes. News had filtered through slowly, often garbled and unreliable, but he had heard from Ambrose that murmurs and rumours of plots had simmered all during the hot summer months until the Privy Council pounced. There had been arrests, interrogations, rackings and the Dudley name had come up more than once, but nothing certain. Trust his uncle to keep out of trouble while others bore the brunt! The Princess's London residence, Somerset House, had been searched and some of her people implicated, ending up in prison for a spell, but thank God they could prove nothing against her. She must have heeded his warning.

Financially matters had improved for him, even if he had not yet been restored in blood and was still looked at askance by the powers-that-be at Court. His father-in-law, old now and very frail, had relinquished everything into his charge, much to the disgust of John Appleyard, and he had made good use of it. Hemsby Castle and other small properties granted to him by his father and sequestered by the State had been returned, officially to Amy, but it came to the same thing.

He ran his eye down the ledger and stopped at an item. 'One hundred pounds to my lady? What was that for, Ned?'

The young man shrugged his shoulders. 'No doubt Lady Dudley had need of it for household expenses.'

Robert frowned. He had never been ungenerous and he gave her everything it was in his power to give, but one hundred pounds in ready cash vanished into thin air and the household bills lying before him on the table still unpaid! He said ironically,

'It is a large sum to spend on fripperies. We have not been invited to Whitehall. Did she happen to mention what she wanted it for?'

'It was while you were away. You had better ask her yourself, my lord.'

There was a faint hostility in the reply that irritated Robert further. He prided himself on being popular with those who served him. He had the knack of being on familiar terms with them without losing their respect or undermining his authority, and it annoyed him that the only two at Syderstone who had never succumbed to his charm were Ned Flowerdew and Jennet Pinto.

He initialled the account and pushed the book across the table. 'One other thing, Ned . . . I asked your father to sell some land for me. Has it been done?'

'Yes, my lord. The money is here.' He put the leather bag on the table with a satisfactory chink. 'Is there anything more?'

'No. Give my regards to your father. Tell him I hope he will soon be recovered from his troublesome ague. He is fond of venison, I believe. I'll send Dick Tamworth over to Hethersett with a buck.'

'Thank you, my lord.'

Ned sketched a perfunctory salute, picked up the heavy books and went out of the room. Robert watched him go with a shrug of the shoulders. If he wanted to be sullen that was his own affair. He was well aware that Ned Flowerdew cherished a romantic affection for Amy and he was inclined to despise him for it. He had never had any doubt of her utter devotion to himself. He picked up the bag of money and weighed it in his hand. He knew exactly what he was going to do with it and the thought pleased him, but it would have to wait until he went to London next month. Then he remembered the missing one hundred pounds and felt irritated again.

He could let it go of course, but it was a large sum when they were often enough hard pressed for ready cash. No doubt she would cry and make a tremendous fuss over it, and there had been enough of that earlier this week. Now he thought of it, Ned Flowerdew had been there then. So that was why he had been in such a huff. Well, what business was it of his?

It had been the day before yesterday. He had come out of the house in the early morning, booted and spurred, on his way to join a hunting party over at Kimberley, to find Amy dressed for riding and the white mare standing ready saddled. She so rarely accompanied him that surprise and anger had caused him to speak with unusual sharpness.

'I thought I gave orders that no one was to ride White Lady except myself.'

Amy looked startled but it was Ned who had replied smoothly, 'But she is a lady's mount surely, my lord. I understood that you have been schooling her for your wife to ride.'

He bit his lip because that had been the ready excuse all this summer. Extravagant offers had been made for her and to the surprise of everyone, including Sir John, he had refused point-blank to sell.

'In matters like this you are hardly qualified to judge, Ned,' he said coldly. 'She is not yet ready for an inexperienced rider,' and he ordered the gaping stable boy to take her back to her stall.

'No, leave her,' said Amy, so quickly that the lad hesitated and glanced from one to the other. 'Why shouldn't I ride her, Robin? You are always telling me how important it is to make a good appearance. What will our neighbours think? That you deny me the best horse in your stable?'

Heaven knows she went into society rarely enough and now he had spoiled her pleasure; but he could not endure that anyone should ride White Lady except her for whom she was intended. He said more gently, 'Do you think I want to see you thrown, my dear, injured, perhaps even killed? Do be sensible. There are plenty of other horses, quiet and docile, far more suitable for you.'

'But none that look like her.'

He saw her mouth tremble and the look of dislike that Ned gave him, but he would not yield. White Lady was taken back to the stable.

'You will be happier on Brown Bess,' he said, smiling as he lifted her into the saddle, but she did not respond. Half way through the day he missed her and was told she had felt unwell and that Ned had taken her home. When he returned she had been strangely silent, instead of chattering gaily as she usually did after any expedition. He wondered what Ned had said to her on that long ride. There had been coolness between them for the past two days. He sighed. Well, maybe he had better go and make his peace with her and at the same time find out about the missing money.

He found Amy crouched on the floor with Tussie in her arms, cradling him like a baby, rocking backwards and forwards, with Jennet hovering protectively over her. As usual the little room was stiflingly hot and smelled overpoweringly of dog. He crossed to the window, swinging back the heavy curtain and pushing the casement wide.

'Don't,' she said, 'he will take a chill.'

He turned to her with some impatience. 'What on earth is the trouble this time?'

'It's Tussie,' she looked up at him, the tears running helplessly down her flushed face. 'Oh Robert, do something to help him, please, please . . .'

'It's probably a stomach cramp. You stuff him with cakes and sweetmeats and this is the result.' But he had always had a tenderness for all animals. He went on one knee. 'Let me see.'

She let the little dog go to him and he put a hand on the swollen stomach. Tussie was breathing in short hard pants. He looked up into Robert's face, the pale tongue licked his hand, the plume of a tail wagged feebly, then he gave a little whimper and died.

Robert laid him gently in his basket. 'I am sorry, my dear. There is nothing any of us can do for him now.'

'Oh, no, no, no,' she wailed. 'He is not dead. He can't be. I've had him so long. I can't bear it.'

She was sobbing wildly and he took both her hands and pulled her to her feet. 'It is sad but he was old and these things happen. Now pull yourself together. You'll make yourself ill. I'll buy you another dog to take his place.'

'How can you be so callous? No dog could take his place. I don't want any other. I loved Tussie more than anything in the world. How can I live without him?'

'Quite easily I should imagine,' he said dryly. 'After all you still have me.'

She collapsed against him and he put his arm round her, nodding to Jennet to take the basket out of sight.

'It is not the end of the world, Amy. There are more important matters than the death of one little dog.'

'Not to me there aren't,' she said in a fresh outburst of weeping. 'You don't understand, you've never understood. You have so much and I have so little.'

With a sigh he restrained his impatience and did his best to comfort her, succeeding in some measure. She became quieter after a time but it was certainly not the moment to enquire about the missing one hundred pounds. That would have to wait until later.

After they had supped together that evening he got up to go to his own room as he usually did if there was no guest, often reading far into the night and sometimes sleeping there. She looked up at him pleadingly.

'Please stay with me for a little, Robin. It's so lonely without Tussie.'

The childishness of the appeal momentarily touched him. 'Very well, if you wish it, my dear.' He bent to put more logs on the fire. Once or twice in the evenings he had tried reading to her, but she had become bored and restless so he gave it up, finding it only a source of irritation.

He stood with his back to the fire, looking down at her. 'By the way, Amy, while I think of it, there was something I have been meaning to ask you. What happened to the hundred pounds John Flowerdew gave you to settle the household accounts?'

'Hundred pounds?' she said vaguely. 'I don't remember.'

'You must remember. After all it was a large sum. It was at the beginning of the month. I thought the accounts settled and now they are all to be paid again.' She looked away without answering, and he was suddenly out of temper. 'For God's sake, Amy, I don't grudge you anything, you know that well enough. If you've spent it on silks and velvets and laces, then say so, though what the devil you want with chests and chests of fine clothes when we rarely entertain and are certainly not expecting to be invited to Court, heaven only knows!'

She was twisting her hands in her lap and then suddenly looked up at him with a kind of desperate courage. 'I didn't spend it like that at all.'

'How then?'

'I gave it to John.'

'You gave it to John and without telling me. In God's name, why?'

'I knew you would be angry.'

'Of course I'm angry. He's had enough out of me and out of your father. You should have sent him to me.'

'I couldn't.'

168

'Why not,'

'Because of what he said.'

'Amy, for heaven's sake speak plainly. You are talking in riddles.'

Then it was as if the floodgates were opened; it all poured out in one long muddled stream, the reproaches, the grievances, the accusations.

'John said you owed it to him now that Father has put all into your charge. He says you think nothing of the family, only of yourself. You spend everything you can lay hands on for your own purposes and care nought for me. What good are all the horses in the stables and the fine new stall you have had built for White Lady when no one else is permitted to ride her except yourself?'

'I've told you again and again . . . she is high-spirited, unreliable, and you dread even the mildest-mannered pony.'

'And you despise me for it as you do for everything. Nothing I do is right.'

'This is sheer nonsense . . .' he began, but she interrupted him passionately.

'Why did you have to shame me in front of Ned and the servants?'

'I did nothing of the kind.'

'You did, you know you did. I am not so stupid or so foolish that I cannot see it, and they are beginning to talk . . . the family, all our neighbours . . .'

The words were stumbling over one another while Robert stood absolutely still, his back to the blazing fire. When she paused for breath, he said coldly, 'What else do they say about me, John and Ned and Frances, all the precious Appleyards and their friends . . . what other crimes am I supposed to have committed?'

She was frightened but it was as if now she had started she could not stop.

'I know I've failed you,' she said despairingly, 'I know it, you make me feel it more and more every day.'

'When have I ever done such a thing?'

'Oh not in so many words, but it is there. Frances says the only reason you don't take me with you when you visit your important friends is that you are ashamed of me, and that when you are away you meet with others . . . others who please you more . . .'

169

'What others?' he said relentlessly. 'Women? Is that what you are trying to say? Other women whom I take to my bed?'

The colour ran up into her face. She said, stammering, 'Oh Robert, it is not I who say such things.'

'But you believe them, don't you? You believe all the lies they tell you, you swallow them all and hold them against me. Well, what do you expect me to do? Deny them? I wouldn't give them so much satisfaction. They can say what they please and much good may it do them.'

She stared at him, her cheeks flushed. 'Why do you hate me so?'

'Hate you? Are you mad?'

'I wish I were, then I wouldn't mind so much.'

'Mind what? Now what is it?'

She hesitated, looking away from him. 'It is something John told me . . .'

'Great God,' he exclaimed with anger. 'Is he an oracle that you must believe all he says?'

'I didn't want to. It was at the hunt supper when all you men ate together. There was talk of marriage and John said,' she swallowed and then went on quickly, 'he said you looked so angry . . .'

'And why should I look angry? What is all this nonsense?'

She turned to face him. 'Is it nonsense when you tell our friends that a wife who cannot give her husband a child is a useless burden no man should be asked to endure . . . ?'

Oh God, it was true! He remembered now. What in hell had made him say so cruel a thing? He had been drunk that night, something rare with him; they had all been flown with wine and a sneer from a fool who ought to have known better had riled him, touching his pride to the quick. Now he could have kicked himself for it, and John Appleyard too for repeating it. She was gazing at him pitifully and he knew she prayed that he would deny it, go down on his knees to her, swearing he never meant it; and he could not do it. Some inner honesty kept him firmly on his feet, forcing him to speak more harshly than he intended.

'If that is how you feel about me, you will be glad to know I'm going to London in a month from now and, if necessary, I can stay there. Then you will be rid of me. Ned Flowerdew will be delighted to look after your interests and dance attendance on you in my absence.'

He went out of the room with his long stride. She called after him, 'Robin, listen, please listen, I did not mean . . .' But he would not pause. He went up to his own room, slamming the door shut against her, against the whole crew of them with their spite and their envy.

He was bitterly, furiously angry, and all the more strongly because there was an element of truth in what she had said. There had been other women. His looks, his charm, his difference from others, made it easy for him. They came to him willingly, and once or twice he had availed himself of the opportunities that came his way. She ought to realize it meant nothing.

Long ago his father had been right. He had played the fool. At seventeen he had married a charming face, pretty kittenish ways, a yielding body, and now it was not enough. Many men would have been satisfied. They asked for nothing more in marriage. Maybe if Amy had given him sons, it would have satisfied him, but now it was too late. He craved for something more. He wanted the impossible, a wife who was his equal in mind and body, a proud fierce spirit with whom there would be constant battle, neither winning nor losing, but a constant joy in the play of intellects equally matched. He might as well admit now and for ever that the woman he wanted was Elizabeth, not just because of her royal blood and because one day she would be Queen, though that was part of it too, but because she was everything he wanted in a woman, spirited, wayward, cultivated to the finger tips, a woman who could meet and top him intellectually and whose fine-boned body held a fascination for him that was not wholly physical. To conquer her would be a never-ending triumph for she would not yield easily; he would have to fight every step of the way. She was a challenge, a desire, a passion, and as far out of his reach as the moon. But he was an opportunist as his father had been before him. His imagination soared beyond obstacles. Somehow, somewhere, there would be a way and he could wait.

His anger and agitation kept him walking about the room for a while until the tumult inside him subsided. Then he dropped into the chair and hunted through the books on his table. Years ago when he was a boy Roger Ascham had reproached him for not devoting more time to the classics and lately, in his leisure moments trying to combat the stifling boredom, he had been going back to his schooldays, re-reading the elegant civilized prose of Cicero and finding a kindred spirit in the bitter-sweet passion of Catullus. He had even tried his hand at translation :

I loathe and yet I love; wouldst thou the reason know?
I know not, but I burn and feel it so . . .

He took up a pen, crossed it out and began again.

Absorbed, he did not notice that the fire had died down. The candles were guttering when there came a gentle tap at the door. The house had long been quiet, everyone retired to bed, and he looked up in surprise. Then the door opened quietly and Amy stood there, a shawl over her long white nightgown, her hair loose on her shoulders.

For an instant he stared at her, then he got to his feet. 'What is it? Is it your father?'

'No.'

'What then? Are you sick?'

'I couldn't sleep. I was so alone.'

'For God's sake, my dear, you shouldn't be wandering about like this at this hour of night. You'll catch your death of cold.'

She caught her breath in a sob. 'I'm sorry, Robin, I'm sorry.' Then she came running across the room, throwing herself against him. 'I didn't mean all those things I said, I didn't mean any of them. Oh Robin, don't go away from me, please, please . . . don't leave me . . .'

She was trembling as she clung to him, weeping wildly. He put his arms round her. 'Hush now, don't cry like that. It's all over. Do you think I don't know who was responsible?'

He sat down again, drawing her on to his knees, petting and soothing her as if she were a child. After a while she quietened a little, leaning against him, her head on his shoulder. She had tight hold of his hand, playing with the long fingers, pulling off and on the heavy gold ring with the Dudley crest.

'Let me come with you when you go to London.'

'Now, Amy,' he began.

'Please, please. I shall die if you leave me here alone.'

'Well, in that case,' he said teasingly. 'But only if you stop crying this instant and smile at me.'

172

She looked up at him, the tears still sparkling on her lashes. 'Oh Robin, I love you, I love you so much.'

'I know, little squirrel.'

She pressed her face against his. He kissed the soft mouth and held her close for an instant. Then he got up. 'Come now, I'll take you back to bed.'

She laughed a little as he lifted her in his arms. She was small and light as a child, and he carried her into the hall and up the wide stairs to their room, depositing her gently on the bed.

She caught at his hand as he straightened himself. 'Stay with me, Robin.'

He smiled and pinched her cheek. 'You should sleep.'

'I will but only if you are with me.'

She was so easily pleased. He knew it all so well and it no longer had power to charm or excite him, but he could still feel pity and kindness. When he lay beside her, she was eager for him. It was not difficult to give her what she craved, the kisses, the caresses, the yielding body trembling under his, and then she lay back, the tears still staining her cheeks, but content. It was only the hunger inside himself that remained unsatisfied.

When she slept at last, he slipped out from under the covers, pulled them gently over her, threw the velvet bedgown round his shoulders and went down the stairs and back to his own room. The fire had died down and it was cold, but he preferred to be alone, free from clinging arms, free from nagging doubts of his own honesty, free to think and plan and dream.

On a foggy morning in late November Elizabeth came riding through Smithfield, past the Old Bailey and down Fleet Street towards Somerset House. Her popularity had grown stronger than ever. The crowds gathered to cheer her as she went by with her splendid escort in their livery of scarlet, handsomely trimmed and slashed with black velvet. She smiled graciously at them, raising her hand in greeting.

Robert pushed the casement wide open though it was raw and cold outside, leaning far out to catch a glimpse of the pale face under the plumed hat. The chill fog caught at Amy's throat so that she coughed and pulled the furred mantle closer round her. She saw one of the ladies riding behind the Princess lift her hand

and wave gaily to Robert. He smiled and blew her a kiss.

'Who is that?' she asked quickly.

'Didn't you recognize her?' he said carelessly. 'It is Frances Ratcliffe, Harry Sidney's sister.'

He knew that Fanny was now Countess of Sussex, her father-in-law having died earlier in the year, but he was not aware that she was in close attendance on Elizabeth while her husband was in Ireland. Fanny had always been his friend. It made it all the easier to carry out what he had in mind.

'Do you have to keep the window open? It's freezing,' said Amy pettishly.

'I'm sorry. I thought you wanted to see the procession.' He pulled it shut and turned to her. 'I've been thinking. Mary will be expecting us at Penshurst as soon as possible. It would be as well for you to ride on today, my dear, and tell her I shall be following very shortly.'

'Why, Robert? Why can't I stay here with you?'

'There would be no point. You will be far more comfortable with Mary than in this place. It is only for a day or so. I have one or two matters of business to attend to.'

'What business? I thought all was settled.'

'What are you afraid of? That I have some secret assignation? You should know me better. It is nothing so amusing, I'm afraid. I'll ride part of the way with you. You know how much you're longing to see Philip and the new baby.'

'I'd rather be with you.'

He smiled and touched her cheek. She realized with bitterness how little she knew of the secrets in Robert's heart, but she had learned not to argue with him when his mind was made up.

When Robert came back across London Bridge from seeing Amy on to the Kent Road with their servants in attendance, he wrote a hurried note and sent Tamworth with it to Somerset House.

He returned later that evening with a message that the Princess had been summoned to attend on Her Majesty so there was nothing to do but wait; and tedious he would have found it, if on the following day he had not had the good fortune to run into Lord Henry Herbert. He was glad to be back in London, to feel at the heart of affairs once more. Henry was bursting with momentous news. Earlier that year the Emperor Charles V had abdicated, giving over all his possessions to his son and retiring to spend his old age in the monastery of Yuste.

'Philip is King of Spain, Naples and Sicily, as well as Lord of the Netherlands, and as if that is not enough for any man he is still furious because the Queen has not been able to persuade the Privy Council to crown him in Westminster Abbey,' said Henry as they sat over their wine.

'He wants to hang England round his neck like another of his precious holy medals,' remarked Robert lazily, stretching out his long legs.

'If he ever comes back here, it will certainly not be on account of his poor love-sick wife,' said his friend cynically, 'but to drum up recruits for his war with France. At least that is what my father says and he keeps in close touch. There's a chance for us yet, Robert.'

The Earl of Pembroke was a turncoat who had deserted his father in his hour of need, but he was a good soldier and to fight under his banner would not disgrace any young man. Robert's spirits leaped at the thought of action, of escaping from the humdrum routine of his domestic life, of winning recognition, military glory, all that he had lost.

He sat up. 'For an opportunity like that I'd sell half of what I have and equip a band of volunteers.'

'Like that, is it? Wives can be the very devil!'

'You can't grumble.'

Henry shrugged his shoulders. He had been married to Catherine Grey on that momentous day that now seemed a century ago when her sister Jane had married Guildford. But his father had astutely made sure that the marriage was dissolved, wanting no link with either Dudleys or Greys, and had not yet found another heiress for his son. He poured more wine in his cup and winked at Robert across the rim.

'I shall not be sorry to get away myself. Life at Court just now is like living in a monkish penitentiary. Here's to war with France. May it come sooner than we think.'

It was a heartening prospect. They drank another bumper to it and Henry promised to mention Robert to his father when he returned from the Netherlands. That night, when he came back to his lodging, Robert found a note from Fanny waiting for him. It was very brief. 'I don't know what I can do, but I'll try.'

It was enough. He followed her directions, went unobtrusively to a side door of Somerset House and was admitted by Fanny herself.

'Will she receive me?'

'I don't know. I haven't spoken to her yet. She is distracted, Robert. Ever since she came from the palace. I don't know what happened but I've never seen her like this. She talks of fleeing out of the country. She sent me to the French Ambassador to ask if France would receive her, give her refuge.'

'She cannot be thinking seriously of such a step.'

'That's what the Ambassador said. The Bishop of Acqs was very forthright. He told me to tell my mistress to stay where she was whatever happened and that, if she ever hoped to succeed to the throne, she must not move out of England.'

'He is right, by God he is. What did she say?'

'She would not listen.'

'Let me see her.'

'What can you do?'

'I don't know,' but there in the dim anteroom where they were whispering together, he was possessed with urgency.

Frances said doubtfully, 'She will be angry.'

'With me, but not with you,' he said with a confidence he was far from feeling. But even if she stormed at him, she would see him, she would not forget him.

Fanny put a hand on his arm. 'Wait here and I will ask, but take care not to be seen. Mistress Ashley is very jealous of her privileges. She will half murder me for admitting you without her knowledge.'

Elizabeth was alone in the sanctuary of her own room. She had dismissed her ladies despite their protests because she could not endure their sympathy, their anxious twitterings, their trivial chatter. She was still shaken by the shattering interview with her sister. It had been so totally unexpected. All this year despite the murmurs of plots, the questionings and the torture, no breath of treason had touched her. She had grown more confident, more sure of her position as heir apparent if not yet acknowledged. At Hatfield, under the kindly guardianship of Sir Thomas Pope, a witty cultivated man, very different from the austere, unpleasant

176

Bedingfield, the summer had passed pleasantly enough. It had seemed when she came riding up to London that the end of the long dark tunnel of suspicion and distrust was in sight at last, and then suddenly, frighteningly, all was to do again.

She pressed the back of her hands against her hot cheeks and roamed restlessly up and down the room, the long velvet gown flowing out behind her, remembering every moment of the meeting that had begun so calmly.

When she came into the room, she had been shocked at the sight of her sister, so much had she altered in a few months. Mary's reddish-gold hair had faded; there were streaks of premature grey. The pink and white complexion had grown sallow with ill health. There were dark shadows under the eyes and heavy lines scored from nose to mouth. She had just passed her fortieth birthday but looked years older. If this was what the cares of a kingdom and marriage to a man you loved did to you, she thought with a faint shiver, perhaps she was a fool to keep the dream of it so steadily in front of her. She sank to the floor in a deep curtsey.

'You sent for me, Your Majesty?'

'Yes.' Mary was neither friendly nor unfriendly. She held out her hand with the black and gold betrothal ring of England for Elizabeth to kiss and then waved to a low stool. 'Be seated. I have something to say to you.'

But she had not immediately come to the point. They discussed trivial matters of health and mutual friends. Then Mary drew herself up in the carved chair, her hands clenching on the lion's paw arms.

'I have received a letter from the King . . .'

'The King?'

'Yes,' she said more strongly, 'from the King, my husband. He asks me to convey to you his command.'

'Does King Philip command me, Your Majesty?'

'It is his right. He is your brother-in-law and thus your guardian and he is deeply concerned that you should make a wise marriage.'

Immediately Elizabeth was aware of danger. 'I have always wished and wish still to remain unmarried,' she said steadily.

'The wishes of Princesses must bow to necessity,' said Mary coldly. 'He orders you to prepare yourself immediately for marriage with his friend and ally, Emmanuel Philibert, Duke of Savoy.'

'Oh no!' Taken by surprise Elizabeth got to her feet in consternation. She had thought this question done with once and for all, and now it seemed the battle must be fought again. 'I have said it before and I say it again; I shall never marry anyone outside this kingdom, never, never, and above all not the Duke of Savoy.'

'What have you against him?'

'It is not a personal matter.'

'In that case you will do as my husband wishes.'

'No, I will not. He may command me in other matters but not in this,' said Elizabeth in desperation.

Mary stared at her for an instant, then she said bitterly, 'When have people like us ever been allowed to follow our desires?'

'You married the man you loved,' said Elizabeth boldly, 'why would you let him force me into so cruel a fate as a loveless marriage far away from my native land?'

Mary looked at her, so tall and slim with flame-like hair and the creamy-white skin of her mother, and the hate she had felt for Anne Boleyn boiled up into a wild jealous anger.

'You were willing enough to listen to him at Hampton Court all last summer.'

The colour flooded into Elizabeth's face in spite of herself. There had been a secret triumph as well as disgust at Philip's pursuit of her. Then she flung herself on her knees, stretching out her hands in supplication.

'I never meant to hurt you.'

Mary drew herself away, the memory of her misery, her humiliation when the hoped-for child had proved a fantasy, choking her with wretchedness.

'Has your fancy fallen on some other young man among your followers,' she said with contempt, 'that you are so averse to this marriage?'

For an instant Elizabeth saw Robert's face, so boldly handsome. Had someone seen him that day in the forest? Had someone spoken? Was she never to be rid of spies and slanderers? Hysteria rose in her throat.

'Why should you say that? There has never been anyone. I am and shall always remain a virgin,' she said.

'Do you expect me to believe that? You are your mother's daughter, I've always known that. There was Sir Thomas

Seymour when you were hardly more than a child, there have been others . . .'

'Lies, all lies.' Frantically she pleaded. 'Think back to when we were children. Remember how fond you were then, how kind to Edward and myself, our dear elder sister.'

'Never, never!' exclaimed Mary with angry vehemence. She got up and walked away, leaving Elizabeth stretched on the floor. There had been plenty to tell her how the people had thronged the streets when Elizabeth rode through the city, how they cheered her. When she turned back to her, her voice was low and filled with venom. 'Your mother was not so careful of her honour, was she? Whose daughter are you? Who was your father? I've asked myself that a dozen times? Was it Sir Henry Norris, or Mark Smeaton the musician she picked out of the gutter, or was it Henry Rochford, her brother . . .'

Elizabeth shrank into herself, appalled at the savage bitterness she had provoked. Then she stumbled to her feet, hot fiery indignation burning inside her. 'Do not speak like that of my mother. I will not listen to you . . .'

'You will listen if I choose. That evil woman drove my mother to her death in misery.'

For an instant they glared at one another, hatred quivering between them, then with an effort Mary pulled herself together. She said with deliberation, 'If you do not obey the King's command, then you must be punished.'

'As you punish those unhappy men and women in Smithfield? Does it give you such joy to see them burn?'

Mary closed her eyes for a moment, flinching at the picture conjured up. She had never willed the death of anyone and shuddered when they brought her the warrants to sign, but it was for Holy Church, to save their souls from the fires of hell. Never, never must she forget that. If she did, then she was lost. She tried to speak calmly.

'You call yourself Catholic. You go to mass and receive the sacraments, though I do not doubt that in your secret heart you despise the beliefs you profess. I shall not have you burned, but I will have you declared illegitimate as our father did before he weakened in old age. If it is in my power to prevent it, England shall never be ruled by a bastard.'

With those cruel words beating into her mind Elizabeth hardly

179

knew how she got herself out of the room and back to Somerset House. She had suffered many bad moments in her twenty-three years but this was the worst because it had come when for a little it had seemed that the future was secure. High-strung nerves momentarily gave way to despair. It was then she had sent Fanny Ratcliffe to the French Ambassador with her desperate plea, only to have it refused.

She was jerked out of her thoughts by a tap at the door and she turned angrily on Fanny.

'What is it now?'

'There is someone here, someone who wishes to see you most particularly.'

The girl looked frightened, and with good reason. She had already suffered much from her that day.

She said more gently, 'I've already told you. I can see no one.'

'It is . . . Your Royal Highness . . . it is . . .'

Then she was firmly put aside and Robert stood in the doorway.

Elizabeth drew herself up haughtily. 'How dare you enter without my permission?'

He did not move. He leaned against the doorpost, tall, handsome, smiling. 'Do not blame Fanny for my insistence. She tried to be firm but I would have dared anything for a sight of my queen.'

Something about his boldness, his arrogant charm, his intense masculinity, pleased her even in the midst of her distress. 'I am not your queen yet, nor ever will be it seems.'

For an instant he let his eyes devour her. The glow of the firelight behind her lit the long unbound hair to a sheet of flame. She was like a lioness, he thought, in that tawny velvet gown; a lioness · supple, slender, fascinating and dangerous, with great troubled golden eyes. He said quietly, 'Why should you say that? What has happened?'

'It is none of your business,' she snapped. 'Go, please go, Lord Robert, before I call my servants and have you put out. You have no place here. You endanger me as well as yourself.'

He took a step forward, ignoring her command. 'It is my business. It is all England's business if you dare to speak of leaving her.'

She swung round on him. 'How do you know that?'

180

'Never mind. I do know. The Ambassador was right. The moment you leave these shores, all hope will be gone. Remember you are not the only one who can lay a claim to the throne,' he went on relentlessly. 'There is Mary Stuart, granddaughter of your father's sister, betrothed to the sickly Dauphin of France. Would you hand the kingdom to her?'

Then the coiled-up tension within her broke into a passion of tears. She sank on to a stool, burying her face in her hands. 'I don't care any longer. Let her have it. It is too great a burden. I've fought for too many years . . . now I'm weary of it. I have no courage left. If I do not do as my sister commands me through her husband, then she will have me declared illegitimate. She called my mother a whore . . . she said vile things, filthy things . . . and they are all lies, lies, lies!' She beat her fist on the cushion of the stool in a frenzy of frustration.

He watched her for an instant and then came quickly, kneeling beside her, taking her two hands in his own warm grasp. He spoke softly, the silky persuasive voice gentling her as he gentled his horses when they were restive, winning them to love and devotion, and almost in spite of herself, she responded, calmed and soothed by the magnetic quality which belonged to him alone, so that it hardly mattered what he said though that was sensible enough.

Presently, when she was quieter, he was gently reassuring. 'Mary will not be able to do that to you. She will not, I say. The people of England will not permit it. They will rise up and defend you against her.'

'How can you be so sure?'

'I am sure. I live amongst them, you do not. You cannot fail them now, you cannot refuse the challenge. You have been brave for so long.'

It was strange, but it was as if strength flowed back into her. She was shaken still but the crisis of nerves was over and some part of it at least was due to him. It was something she would never forget. She withdrew her hands, sitting up, pushing back the heavy hair.

'I will not fail. It was a foolishness but now it is over.' She smiled a little tremulously.

'And you, Robert, what will you do?'

'I?' He sat back on his heels looking up at her. 'What can I do?

Go on as before, and if our Spanish King sends us to war with France, I shall offer him my sword.'

'Oh no,' she was quick in protest. 'Not that. I pray God that England will not go to war. It is so useless, a waste of lives and money. When I am Queen, we shall have no wars if I can help it.'

'That is a woman's point of view,' he said indulgently.

'And a wise one,' she flashed at him,' and do not dare to smile like that.'

'I would not dream of such a thing.'

She moved impatiently. 'Women see far more clearly than men. What is it you all look for in this eternal fighting?'

'Many things... honour, reputation, glory.'

'A bubble,' she said disdainfully, ' a bubble that is nothing but vapour when it bursts. There are better ways.'

'You will teach them to us.'

'And I shall succeed. Be sure of that.' Then she stood up and he rose with her. 'You should not stay.'

'No, but I am in danger of forgetting the purpose that brought me here.' He felt in the pouch at his belt and put the heavy leather bag of money into her hands. 'It is not much, but it is given with my heart and my devotion.'

She looked at him wonderingly, 'But where have you obtained this?'

'I sold some of my land.'

She was touched, knowing well his straitened circumstances. 'I thank you with all my heart. So many people come to me asking for help and I have to turn them away.'

'It will serve for some,' he said lightly.

'And you? What do you ask in return?'

'Nothing, only that when the time comes, you will permit me to serve you.'

'I shall not forget.'

She was so near to him that he could not resist the mad impulse. He put his arms round her and drew her close, feeling the slender body under the velvet gown tremble and melt against him. For an instant only they were so close he could smell the faint perfume that clung to her, then she stiffened and he released her, falling on his knees and passionately kissing her hand. She let her fingers stray over the crisp curling hair.

'Have a care of yourself. I'd not have you killed.'

'There is no fear of that. I have other plans.'

Then he went quickly before he was tempted into further madness. Fanny, coming back from seeing him safely out of the side door, found her mistress in a strangely softened mood, no reprimand for her indiscretion, no box on the ear, not even a rap across the knuckles. Instead she said gaily, 'Tell them to start packing. We'll return to Hatfield. We'll spend Christmas there, and make it a right merry one.'

'So you'd not have me go back again to the French Ambassador?'

'A fig for France!' she snapped her fingers. 'England has always been good enough for me!'

At Penshurst Robert was idly watching Jennet Pinto hook his wife into a gown of carnation satin shot with gold. The gleaming folds gathered snugly into the slim waist.

'It suits you, my dear. You look very pretty.'

'Do you think so, Robin? It's the first time I've worn it.'

Jennet took a necklace from the open casket on the table. It was very elaborate, each small gold flower set with a pearl. Robert sat up, frowning a little.

'Have I seen that before? Is it one of your mother's jewels?'

'No,' said Amy composedly. 'I bought it when we were in London. The jeweller came to our lodging one morning when you were out.'

For an instant he was taken aback. It was so unlike her to show independence. 'Where did you get the money? Or did he give you credit?'

'No. The Dudley name was not surety enough,' she said with a touch of malice. 'Dick Tamworth paid him for me.'

'Tamworth did? But that money he was holding was intended to cover our expenses on this trip.'

'I did not see why I shouldn't buy something for myself when you have sold up my lands to waste on your own pleasures.'

Robert got to his feet. 'Who told you that? John?'

'No, it was Ned Flowerdew.'

'He had no right.'

'He had every right. Those lands were part of my dowry.'

'What has that to do with it?'

'You should have consulted me first.'

'When did you ever show the slightest interest?'

Their voices had risen and Jennet watched them, sharp eyes darting from one to the other.

Furiously he said, 'Leave us, girl.'

'Let her stay,' said Amy. 'I don't care who knows. Why should you grudge me a paltry necklace when you were eager enough to get me out of the way and waste my money on decking your mistress?'

He was so surprised at the unexpected attack that he could only stare at her. 'You must be out of your mind. I did nothing of the kind.'

'Don't lie. I saw the looks you exchanged with her.'

'But that was Fanny Ratcliffe . . .'

'So you said. Why did you go running to meet her at Somerset House?'

Who the devil had told her that? 'God's death!' he exclaimed. 'This is ridiculous. Ask Mary about her if you don't believe me.'

She swung round to face him. 'What did you do with the money then?'

'Hell!' he said, 'Hell and damnation! What does it matter what I did with it? You wouldn't believe me if I told you!' and he stormed out of the room, slamming the door against Amy's unhappy face.

In the passage he collided with Mary going in the opposite direction and muttered an apology. She touched his arm.

'What is it, Robin? You look ruffled.'

'Nothing,' he said abruptly.

'I'm just going to say goodnight to the children. Come with me.'

He turned and followed her. In the nursery there was a smell of milk and toasted bread. Mary bent over the cradle of the baby Ambrosina. Philip had just been undressed ready for bed. He wriggled out of his nurse's hands and ran mother-naked to his uncle, clutching his leg. Robert picked him up, tossing him into the air and catching him again, while the child shouted with laughter.

Mary watched them for a moment, smiling. 'Don't excite him too much,' she said, 'he'll never sleep.'

'There now, my hearty, that's enough.' He put the boy down

and slapped his plump bottom. The scandalized nurse picked him up, clucking disapproval of thoughtless young uncles.

'He's a fine lad, Mary. I envy you.'

'I know. I'm lucky.'

She linked her arm in his as they left the nursery. 'Now tell me what has upset you.'

'A stupid quarrel with Amy over money of all things,' he said disgustedly.

'I think she is unhappy, Robin.'

'Can I help that? She has everything she wants.'

'She feels she has lost your love.'

'Nonsense. It's that damned family of hers,' he said violently. 'They've never liked me and she listens to them. She believes I stayed behind in London to roister through the whorehouses.'

His indignation amused her. 'And did you?'

'God, no. I've got more sense.'

'Then what did you do with this money?'

'If you really want to know, I gave it to Elizabeth.'

'Elizabeth? But why? Did you see her? How?'

'Through Fanny Ratcliffe.' He gave a harsh bark of laughter. 'Amy even suspects me of sleeping with her.'

'Then why not tell her the truth?'

'She wouldn't understand.' Not even to Mary could he explain his secret feeling for Elizabeth. He looked away from her, speaking vehemently to justify himself. 'It's only common sense. I have to look to the future. No advancement is likely to come my way with the present Queen. She hates the very name of Dudley.'

'With some reason, Robert.'

'I know, I know,' he said impatiently. 'But the time passes. I am twenty-three, Mary. Am I to live like this till the tomb closes over my head?'

She smiled at his extravagance. 'Do you think you can buy Elizabeth's favour?'

'No, of course not, but she'll be grateful, she'll remember. I want her to know who are her true friends.'

'And is that the only reason?'

'What else can there be between Elizabeth Tudor and Robert Dudley?'

What else indeed? But Mary had loved her brother for a long

185

time and knew his power to charm and captivate. She knew too the restless ambition so like that of their father that would not let him live happily in obscurity. Whatever he did she knew she would support him, and yet she could still find it in her heart to be sorry for Amy.

Mary went downstairs and Robert returned to their room to find it locked against him. At his impatient knock Jennet opened the door a crack.

'My lady is lying down. She has a headache.'

'She was well enough a few minutes ago. Let me in.'

'Far better not, my lord. She was very upset, but she is quieter now.'

There was an unspoken reproach in her tone and he resented it angrily. He thought of thrusting her out of the way and then changed his mind. If Amy wanted to sulk, then she must.

'Very well. Tell her I'll come up later. I'll ask Lady Sidney to have food sent up.'

'I shall fetch anything my lady requires, my lord.'

She shut the door in his face. He stared at it for a moment and then shrugged his shoulders and went down to the great hall. Ambrose and Hal had ridden in earlier. There was news to be exchanged and a great deal to discuss. They were all three excited at the thought of the coming war, particularly Hal.

Later that night he shared his brothers' room while Amy lay wakeful, hoping against hope that he would come until she cried herself to sleep.

Five

❦

It was late but the August evening was still very hot, the air heavy with the smoke of battle and hideous with the groans of the wounded and dying. In the crude field hospital the surgeon shook his head. He said wearily, 'It is useless, my lords. To amputate will only cause him added agony. He will be dead within an hour.'

Robert looked down at the shattered body of his young brother. 'Is there nothing we can do?'

'Nothing,' said the surgeon flatly, wiping his bloodied hands on his stained apron. 'Believe me, I am sorry,' he went on more gently. 'He was a brave young man and, if it is any comfort to you, I doubt if he is conscious of pain. The shell has destroyed the nerve centre. Now if you will excuse me, my lords, there are others who need me more urgently.'

Ambrose touched Robert on the arm. 'It's already an hour since the soldier came with the message from the Commander. He is asking for your report.'

Robert shook him off. 'You go. I shall stay with Hal until . . . until . . .'

'It is you he will expect. You are the Master of the Ordnance.'

'To hell with that. Must I run at his bidding when my brother is dying?' he said violently.

'Hal can neither see nor hear any longer.'

'How do you know? He may regain consciousness,' Robert looked round wildly, 'and if he does even for an instant in this terrible place, he could believe himself in hell.'

'I'll go,' said Ambrose quietly. 'I'll tell him you are coming and then I'll return.'

Robert sat on the ground beside the palliasse on which Hal was lying, his back to the horrors around him, the sights, sounds and stenches of dying men. A monk from the nearby convent moved from one to the other with a murmur of prayer. It seemed

187

a century since the early morning when Hal had awakened him from an hour's snatched sleep, happy at the prospect of action, proud of the courage and ability that had already brought all three brothers to the notice of their Commander. And now . . . Robert shuddered at the blood spreading on the blanket that covered Hal.

Elizabeth was right. War was a filthy business and reputation a bubble that meant nothing, though they were already saying this battle at Saint-Quentin was a resounding victory. The French were routed, eight thousand dead or captured for the loss of a handful of Philip's men, but amongst them his own brother. And it could so easily have been himself. He had been going from gun to gun, inspecting each crew with the boy close beside him. Hal had sensed it first, had shouted a warning and given him a push. The shattering impact had flung him to the ground and when the dust and smoke had cleared, he was no more than bruised. It was the broken body of his brother that lay across his knees.

Hal gave a little moan and opened his eyes. Robert leaned over him.

'My legs,' he was muttering, 'my legs . . . I can't move . . .' His eyes questioned desperately.

'It's all right, Hal. You did bravely.'

'Did I?'

For an instant the old gaiety lit the white face, then a bubble of blood and froth broke from his lips. When Ambrose returned a few minutes later, he was dead.

'His Excellency is expecting you,' he said.

Robert left Ambrose to arrange for his brother's burial. Impossible to carry him back to England, but he should not be thrust into the common pit. He went back to his tent. He changed his blood-stained clothes and washed the smoke of battle from his face. The towel was still in his hand when the flap of the tent was thrust back and a man appeared in the opening. Robert stared at him for a moment before he realized it was the Commander-in-Chief himself.

It had given him a certain ironic amusement that he should be serving under the very man whom Elizabeth had so firmly refused to marry. Emmanuel Philibert, Duke of Savoy, was a spare man, brown of face, with certain rakish good looks and a reputation for hard drinking and gay living. He and Philip were boon companions and rumour said they were well acquainted with every notable brothel in Brussels as well as certain aristocratic bedchambers. He was a good soldier and had the habit of occasionally strolling informally amongst his officers.

He had discarded his armour and stood leaning against the tent post. 'Well,' he said in his heavily accented English, 'aren't you going to offer me something to drink?'

Robert had expected reprimand and braced himself against it. The request took him by surprise. 'I beg your pardon, Your Excellency.' He poured from the flagon on the table. 'It is rough, but it is the best we have.'

'It washes the taste of battle out of your throat if nothing else.'

He swallowed the wine at a gulp and held out the cup to be refilled. 'I understand your brother is dead.'

'Yes.'

'I am sorry for it.'

'I was just about to wait on Your Excellency with my report.'

'So I was informed.' said Savoy dryly. 'Bring it to me later, in writing if you please. His Majesty, King Philip, will be anxious to send news of our victory to his wife in England. I am going to recommend you to him as his messenger.'

Surprised and gratified, Robert said, 'You honour me, sir.'

Savoy studied him for a moment before he went on with a slight smile. 'To speak bluntly, when my lord of Pembroke first suggested that you should be put in charge of the ordnance, I was strongly against it, too young and too inexperienced, but you've proved me wrong, you and your brothers. You have a cool head, a talent for organization, you don't run for cover at the first touch of fire and you can count, a very valuable asset I can assure you.'

'I was not aware that Your Excellency had noticed so much about me.'

'It's the mark of a good commander to know the capabilities of his officers, young man. You have the makings of a soldier. Have you ever thought of taking it up professionally?'

'The life of a mercenary does not appeal to me, sir.'

'Pillage, loot and women,' he said and looked Robert up and down with a half smile. 'No, perhaps not. When His Majesty joins us tomorrow, there will be a mass of thanksgiving in the church and afterwards we shall turn to business. See that you are there in attendance with the others.'

'Yes, and thank you, Your Excellency.'

Savoy turned to go and then looked back over his shoulder. 'As a matter of interest, are you acquainted with the Lady Elizabeth?'

It seemed an odd question and Robert hesitated, wondering if someone had been talking. Then he said boldly, 'Yes, sir, since childhood.'

'Indeed!' The Duke came back. '*Mon Dieu*, but that is interesting. You can tell me then . . . what manner of young woman is she?'

'How does Your Excellency mean? In appearance?'

'Well, that also. I came to England in Philip's train at the time of his wedding but never a glimpse could I get of my intended bride . . . or indeed of almost anything,' he added wryly. 'Tell me, does it always rain so hard in England?'

'The sun shines occasionally, sir. As for the Princess, what can I say? She is tall, graceful, learned, red-haired . . .'

'With a temper to match, eh?'

'I have not found it so.'

'You speak as more than a mere acquaintance.' Robert shrugged his shoulders and Savoy looked at him curiously for an instant. Then he said, 'Learned too, a disadvantage in a woman; still I mean to try again.'

'The Princess has told me and others, Your Excellency, that she does not intend to marry.'

'*Quelle sottise*! What young woman of twenty-three doesn't yearn for a man, unless she is intending to shut herself into a convent and even then . . .' He made an expansive gesture. 'Perhaps we should not go into that. Are you married?'

'Yes, sir, these seven years.'

'*Sacrebleu*! and still so young! What induced you to put the halter round your neck? Have you sons?'

'Not yet.'

'Is she pretty, this wife of yours?'

'Very pretty.'

'*Diable*! What is the matter with you, man? Get to work, get to work,' he clapped Robert boisterously on the back, 'and convey my greetings to the Lady Elizabeth. Tell her I'm not such a bad fellow,' he laughed and spread his arms wide, 'and with plenty to please the most exacting lady, isn't that so?'

'I am sure Your Excellency has never encountered any difficulty.'

'You're right there. Ripe plums for the picking, most of them!' Savoy grinned and then was the soldier once more. 'Let me have that report as soon as possible.'

Robert bowed and held the tent flap back for his Commander to go out into the night. He returned to the table and poured some of the wine for himself and then stood staring down into it. It had been an odd little conversation, but it had made him very aware of something in himself he had only barely acknowledged. A fierce possessive instinct towards Elizabeth which was ridiculous, which could never be fulfilled. She would be Queen and he was what? . . . a commoner, a nobody, and married into the bargain. And yet . . . the dazzling vision of a crown danced before his eyes and was as quickly dismissed. He swallowed the wine, then pushed aside the flask and the cups and sat down at the table to write his report.

Spanish gratitude had done something for him at any rate, he thought wryly a month later, as he rode to Greenwich Palace, the despatches wrapped in oiled silk safely in his pocket with a covering letter from Philip to his wife.

When he knelt before the Queen, Mary gave him her hand to kiss and looked at the bold, handsome face with sharp dislike. The very name of Dudley was poison to her, traitors to the bone every one of them, heretics too, though they pretended to conform, and allying themselves unobtrusively yet undeniably with her sister's cause. But Philip had commanded her to be gracious and so she must needs obey him even though it was against her will.

She said through stiff lips, 'If you and your wife care to attend the Court, my lord, you will have our welcome.'

Robert bowed his thanks and was conscious of the open hostility, not only from the Queen but from most of those closest to her. Well, he had achieved something. Philip had been gracious with his promises; Parliament was to lift the attainder, the stain would be wiped from the Dudley name and the lands taken from him returned. He could afford to wait and, looking at Mary's ravaged face, it seemed to him that the waiting would not be too long. He backed his way out, head arrogantly tilted, aware of watchful eyes and caring not a pin for any of them.

It was good to be independent once again, freed from the hampering restrictions, with money in his purse. He could change his way of life and reorganize his household. He had no wish to go back to Norfolk and the stultifying existence he had endured there. He would let Syderstone and buy a new property nearer to London within easy reach of Whitehall; all kinds of fine plans went through his head in which his wife played little part. She had always done just as he wished.

On a lovely sunny day in early June Amy stood at the window of her bedroom at Syderstone and watched the servants strip the tapestry from the wall, tying it into a long sausage-shaped bundle and carrying it out with the clothes chests and the rolls of bedding. Outside they were being packed into the waiting carts. Ever since her father's death in the previous year, while Robert had been in France, the house had become a sad place for her. In one way she had been glad to leave and yet now, walking through the echoing empty rooms, she was besieged by memories of happy innocent days when she had run to her father in every childish trouble, or romped with Ned Flowerdew, knowing herself pretty in young men's eyes, by memories of those first joyful months of marriage when Robert had been so close. She sighed and turned away from the window, speaking unusually sharply to Jennet who was on her knees roping up a box of laces and ruffs.

'We mustn't be too long. My lord wishes to leave before noon.'

'I'm doing my best, my lady.'

'I know, I know,' Amy smiled repentantly at her, 'only there's still so much to be done.'

She went down the stairs to the great hall and Frances came bustling in, hot and dusty, with a large apron tied over her fine silk gown.

'Amy, there's that heavy oak chest that belonged to Mother and the Court cupboard with the carved doors. You'll surely not be taking those with you.'

'Why? Do you want them?'

'Well, left here they'll only go to ruin, eaten by worm more than likely.'

'Take them if you wish. I'm quite sure Robin won't mind.'

Frances paused to look at her curiously. 'It seems a peculiar notion to me, renting a house when you've a perfectly good property here.'

'It's old fashioned and Robert says it would take a fortune to renovate it. Besides he wants to be near to London.'

'I can't think why. It's not as if he had a post at Court.'

'He may have soon.'

'When Her Majesty dies, I suppose.' Frances snorted. 'Unlucky I call it, like waiting for dead men's shoes. It wouldn't suit me living in rented lodgings. I like my own place.'

'It's only temporary,' said Amy defensively. 'And Denchworth is a lovely place with a far larger park than this and fine stables for the horses.'

'Horses, horses, is that all he thinks about? He might consider his wife.'

'But he does,' said Amy quickly. 'He is very kind.'

Frances gave her a long look. 'That's as may be. No doubt it's just what you want, Amy, no household duties, nothing to do but amuse yourself all the day long.' She hurried off to bully the men who were carrying out the furniture she coveted.

Amy looked after her for an instant. At least in her new home she would not have to put up with her half-sister's carping criticism. Then she turned back and went up the steps to the minstrel's gallery. It was through the fretted screen that she had watched Robert with a wildly beating heart on the day he had first come to Syderstone and she had fallen so desperately in love with him.

I shall dance in the moon and the stars and the sun
Oh my love, my love, my only love . . .

The first few days after he had returned from France had been a very heaven. She was so happy to see him alive and unhurt, so guiltily thankful that it was Hal who had died and not Robert. They had all been so excited and pleased when he had returned from Greenwich and told them of what had been promised.

Just over a month ago he had taken her to Court. The Princess Elizabeth had come up from Hatfield for a short visit and there had been a grand reception. The flower-decked barges went floating down the Thames to the palace of Richmond. Mary Sidney was there with a wildly excited four-year-old Philip and a number of other guests. The young girls, brilliant as brightly coloured flowers in their new dresses, clustered round Robert like flies round a honey jar just as they had done five years ago at Greenwich, when they had watched the ships set out on their ill-fated voyage from which so few had ever returned. The gay banter, the wit and laughter flew from one to the other. She could not compete with them despite the new gown and the nosegay of spring flowers that Robert had bought for her.

Later that morning, as their boat drew alongside the royal barge, she saw the Princess Elizabeth in gleaming white satin, her hair shining like burnished copper in the sun, sitting under the green silk awning with its gold fringe all hung with garlands of flowers.

Robert was standing up and suddenly he leaned over, took the nosegay out of her hands and tossed it expertly to land at the Princess's feet. She looked up and smiled, then deliberately plucked a dark red bloom from the heart of it and tucked it into the bosom of her dress.

The look of pleasure and triumph on Robert's face was more than Amy could bear. 'The flowers were mine,' she said, unable to keep the hurt out of her voice.

He dropped down on the cushions beside her. 'I know, but it was a gesture. Did you see how she smiled? I have to think of the future.'

Only she knew there was more in it than that, far more . . .

'Amy, Amy, where the devil are you? I've been looking everywhere!' It was Robert's voice breaking in on her thoughts and she pulled herself together guiltily. He would be angry in a moment, reproaching her with dawdling the time away. He had come through the door of the hall with Anthony Forster whom he had recently appointed treasurer to the household. Forster was a good-looking, capable man, ambitious and very astute, always scrupulously courteous, and yet she knew he despised her and, try as she would, she could not like him. But it was he who had negotiated the renting of the new house. Denchworth belonged to Will Hyde who was his brother-in-law, whom she had liked at once.

As she came down the stairs, Robert said, 'What on earth are you doing up there, my dear? Is all done? Anthony will take care of the closing and locking of the house.'

'Certainly, my lord. Your lady can leave all to me. She need not trouble her head about anything.' Forster bowed and went out.

'He's a damned good fellow,' said Robert, 'worth every penny I pay him.' Then he raised the small basket he was carrying. 'Look, I've something for you.' He knelt down and lifted out a small puppy. It gave a little whimper and then waddled uncertainly towards her. It might have been Tussie's twin brother except that it was black.

'Like him?'

'Oh Robin!' She bent down to gather up the little dog. It nestled confidingly against her, licking her neck, and stupidly she began to cry.

'Now, now, little squirrel. I thought it would make you happy.'

It was so long since he had called her that. She drew a quick breath. 'Oh it does, it does. It was a sweet thought.'

'He comes from the same kennel that bred Tussie.'

That was so like Robert. Just when she felt most hurt or neglected, he would do something endearing like this, go to endless lengths to please her.

He put his arm around her. 'Are you sorry to be leaving Syderstone?'

'Not really if you want it, and it means that I can see more of you. I shall, shan't I?'

'Of course,' he said easily, 'we shall spend the summer together.'

Perhaps he had meant it but it did not work out like that. He was sometimes away for weeks and weeks and then would arrive for a night or two, bringing the house to life when he was there. Sometimes he would bring guests and they would gather round the card table with Will Hyde, while she sat with the other ladies, stitching at the Dudley coat of arms she was embroidering or nursing the little dog which Robert had laughingly called Fussy because she doted on it so much that nothing was too good for it.

For Robert the last months of that year could not pass quickly enough. He knew as did everyone close to the Court that Mary was grievously sick. The English success at Saint-Quentin had drawn French attack on the crumbling fortress of Calais, the last remnant of the conquests of Edward III and Henry V. It was of little value but the nation's bitter resentment at its loss centred itself on the Queen. Deserted by her husband and robbed of the last hope of a child, there was nothing left to Mary but devotion to her faith. All through that summer and autumn the persecution of heretics continued, sometimes seven burnings in one day; and more and more the road to Hatfield was clogged by ambitious men deserting the dying Queen, but not Robert. He would not be one among many. He would choose his moment.

At daybreak on 17 November Mary died. That day the church bells rang out all over the city of London. Bonfires were lighted and tables of food and drink set out in the streets for the citizens to make merry. The last martyrs had suffered on 11 November and the Registrar solemnly noted: 'Six days after these were burned to death, God sent us our Elizabeth.'

On the following day, in a mood of wild elation and careful calculation, Robert set out for Hatfield. Soberly but magnificently dressed in black and silver, he rode White Lady, groomed to a satin perfection, with only Dick Tamworth trotting behind him. The morning was cold but dry, no mud or fog. The moment had come as he had always known it would, and he was prepared to grasp it with both hands.

In the early afternoon of that same day Elizabeth was in the park at Hatfield. She had escaped for a little from all those who had come crowding around her, walking briskly as she loved to do with only Fanny Ratcliffe hurrying to keep up with her.

Yesterday, when the Lords of the Council had come upon her alone under the leafless trees with their momentous news, she had stood for an instant unable to believe and then fallen on her knees in a mood of thanksgiving, the words of the hundred and eighteenth psalm coming first to her mind.

'I called upon the Lord in distress and He answered me and set me in a large place . . .'

Nicholas Throckmorton had brought the black and gold ring

from Mary's dead finger. She was Queen at last. There were innumerable problems, but she was not afraid. She had been preparing herself for this moment for so long, and now she was free of the suspicion and distrust that had haunted her girlhood, free to love and hate as she wished, free to grant favours or withhold them. An enormous exultation surged through her and she walked faster and faster, taking in great gulps of the cold frosty air, happiness bubbling up irrepressibly inside her. Even in winter the park was beautiful and it was a prison no longer. She paused on a little hillock, looking at the great oaks, bare and leafless against the November sun like a fiery red ball, and it was then that she saw the rider who came up the long grassy stretch on the white horse, tall, handsome, gallant, with an irresistible appeal. He rode at a gallop, saw her, wheeled his horse round, reined in and leaped from the saddle, coming towards her with his graceful stride and kneeling at her feet.

'I am come, Your Majesty, to offer you my service. Command me at your will.'

He stretched out his hands and she enclosed them in her own long slim fingers in the traditional gesture of allegiance.

'I accept your loyalty in the spirit in which it is offered, my lord,' and then she laughed joyously because now for the first time she could indulge her fancy, she could show her feelings and pay no heed to what others might say or think.

She said teasingly, 'You are late, Robert. Others have been before you, all of them seeking favours from me.'

He stood up with a proud lift of his head. 'I did not come asking for gifts but to bring you one.' He beckoned and Tamworth led the white mare across the grass. 'I told you once I would find her for you. I called her White Lady and for three years I have trained and schooled her, letting no one ride her but myself.'

Everyone else had come to her as Queen, begging for the favours it was in her power to grant, but this was different. This was personal, a gift for Elizabeth the woman who loved horses. She clapped her hands with pleasure.

'She is beautiful. Can I try her now, this moment.'

'She is not saddled for a lady. Later perhaps.'

'God's blood,' she said roundly. 'I'll have it now and not later. Give me your hand, Robert.'

'You cannot, Your Grace, you cannot ride astride like a man. It would not be proper,' wailed Fanny in horror.

'Nonsense, girl, of course I can. I am Queen. I can do whatever I please,' she said imperiously. 'I command you, my lord.'

Robert grinned. He took her in his arms and lifted her to the saddle. She laughed as she bunched up her velvet skirts and took the reins from him. She urged White Lady forward and in another moment was gone swift as an arrow across the grass. Robert snatched the bridle of the black horse from Tamworth, flung himself into the saddle and galloped after her. It was a wild hectic ride across the park but any fear he might have had for her horsemanship was gone at once. She never hesitated, her hood fallen back and the long red-gold hair streaming out behind her. He reached her side and they rode together, exultant and wildly happy.

When they pulled up at last, the ball of the sun was just beginning to sink behind the rose-red roof of the old palace and the park was held in a frosty stillness. Robert slipped from the saddle and held out his arms to lift her to the ground. For an instant they stood very close.

'Do you approve of her?'

'Oh yes, yes, a thousand times. I shall ride her when I go to London.'

Fanny had come panting up to them. She said agitatedly, 'One of the servants has come looking for you, Your Majesty. The Spanish Ambassador is asking for an audience.'

'Bother de Feria!' said Elizabeth. 'That is the second time he has come bringing word from Philip. I don't need him or anyone to give me advice. He can wait.' She turned to Robert, a tiny teasing smile playing about her mouth. 'There is one office in my household unfilled for lack of a suitable candidate. I have still to appoint my Master of Horse.' Robert's heart leaped. Of all posts this, with its personal attendance on her at all times, had an irresistible attraction. 'Well,' she went on a little impatiently, 'doesn't it please your lordship? I thought it might have a special appeal for you.'

And he knew then with a joyous certainty that this was what she had reserved for him, knowing full well that he would come.

He said, 'Of all places in your Court, it is what I would most desire.'

198

'Good. Then come to me again very soon. In a few days we shall ride to London.'

She stretched out her hand and he knelt to kiss it, and then watched her walk swiftly across the grass. She had a long stride for a woman, nothing mincing or hesitant about her, and how she had blossomed. The creamy pallor of her skin, the brilliant gold-green eyes had a radiance about them, a magic that held him enchanted – and she liked him. He knew that, as any man does whom women find attractive. Now there was nothing, nothing at all to stand between him and a glorious future, and in that moment of ecstasy and exultation he never once spared a thought to his wife.

Kew, Thursday, 12 September 1560

The impatiently awaited report from Tom Blount arrived at noon just as Robert was being measured for his mourning clothes. Mr Whittle's assistant had been summoned by Tamworth and came down by boat from London in a considerable fluster. He had never waited on Robert before and the fact that the gentleman whose fine figure he was to take note of was reputed to be not only the Queen's lover but also more than likely the murderer of his wife, put him in such a state of agitation that his fingers shook and he kept dropping his tapes and his pencil, driving Robert to near distraction.

'How much longer have I to stand here like a dummy?' he exclaimed in exasperation. 'Get it over with, man, for the love of God!'

'Yes, my lord, of course. I am sorry, my lord.' Mr Jennings scribbled frantically on his tablets. 'Just the length of leg, my lord, and then I shall be done.'

Robert, desperately anxious to get at his letter, was already breaking the seal when he found samples of material were being anxiously pushed under his nose.

'Mr Whittle would like to know which your lordship would prefer, plain or cut velvet, or black figured satin with silver buttons and facings,' babbled the little man.

'What the hell does it matter? Do whatever you like.' Impatiently Robert thrust him aside. 'My man will settle all that with you. Dick, for heaven's sake, get this fool out of here. You know my tastes.'

'This way, Mr Jennings. My lord is distracted with grief, you understand,' said Tamworth smoothly, guiding the affronted tailor out of the room still protesting volubly that there were cloaks to be discussed as well as hats, and would pearls be considered suitable ornament for a widower and not too showy?

Robert, left alone at last, was already unfolding the thickly written sheets. At first sight they brought him little comfort. Blount had no doubt done his work well. He had questioned everyone closely, not only Amy's servants, but the other guests staying at the great house, and even the landlord of the inn at Abingdon where he had broken his journey, in a laudable attempt to sound out public opinion. But even now too many questions remained unanswered. Robert stared in front of him, certain of only one thing. The general public, the great mindless rabble, would look for a scapegoat and unless he could provide them with a murderer would without any doubt fix the blame on him. He had read the letter so quickly that he had not yet taken in all its implications. He turned back to it but had not got beyond the first sheet when Tamworth knocked at the door.

'Well, what is it now? Not that confounded tailor again?'

'No, my lord. I have sent him off quite satisfied. Sir William Cecil is asking if you will receive him.'

'Cecil?' He got to his feet and for an instant his spirits soared. Had he come from Elizabeth, a messenger of hope, bringing words to cheer him? He said, 'I'll come at once.'

Tamworth helped him into the long velvet gown over his shirt and trunk-hose and he gathered its folds around him and went down quickly to the great hall, stretching out an eager hand in greeting.

'I thank you with all my heart for coming to see me here.'

Cecil's hand was cool and dry but its pressure was warm. 'I hope I see you well, my lord. I have not roused you from bed, I trust, you are not sick?'

'No, no, I am well enough, as well as I can be in these wretched circumstances. The tailor has been here for the mourning and I would not keep you waiting while I dressed.'

'Her Majesty will be glad to know that your health has not suffered too much from this sad misfortune.'

He could not restrain his anxiety. 'She has not . . . she sends no message by you?'

Cecil shook his head. 'No, my lord. I told her I was coming to you but she only frowned and said nothing.'

'How did she look?'

'You know her, my lord, as well if not better than I. Her

202

moods are variable as April weather and more than ever just now. But I believe she is concerned for you.'

It was not what he wanted to hear but it was better than nothing. The servant brought wine and he poured it, offering the goblet to his guest. Cecil went on speaking in his quiet even voice.

'I had not visited Kew before. It is an attractive situation with a fine outlook over the river. With a few alterations and additions it should make a very pleasant summer residence for you, my lord.'

'Yes, I have been thinking of it while I have been here, but this is no time to make plans.' Then suddenly his feelings got the better of him. He put down the untasted wine and strode about the room in agitation. 'What am I to do, Sir William, what in God's name am I to do? I am forbidden to leave this place. I cannot investigate as I would. I cannot go myself to Cumnor.'

'Patience, my lord, patience. No doubt the truth will emerge soon enough.'

'But will it, will it? How can you be sure? Where is truth to be found in a matter of this kind? I have enemies, bitter enemies. A short time ago, as you know, there was a plot against my life. Is it not possible that some of those who wish me ill have murdered my wife in the hope that the infamy will come to rest on my shoulders?'

Cecil looked shocked. 'You are overwrought. You cannot surely believe that anyone could be so evil as to kill an innocent lady for such a reason. It will be for the jury to make a decision.'

'A jury from Oxford who do not know me, who are already prejudiced against me, listening to garbled lies and sly innuendoes, a jury who for some unknown reason have taken a dislike to Anthony Forster who leases Cumnor and has been in my service. How can I be sure that they will judge fairly? Supposing they bring in a verdict of murder by some person unknown, what then will be my fate? Won't every finger be pointed at me?'

'You must calm yourself, my lord. You are speaking wildly of what may never happen.' Cecil went on in his grave sensible voice, speaking soothingly, until he was ashamed of his outburst.

He said at last, 'And you yourself, Sir William, do you believe I am responsible for my wife's death?'

'I would not be here if I did,' said Cecil dryly. 'To have done such a deed would have been to destroy yourself and, though we have not always seen eye to eye, I have never believed you a fool.'

'You are right. I should never have asked such a question. I am more than grateful to you for your support.' Robert paused for a moment before he went on. 'I have a small gift that I had intended for Her Majesty's birthday, but the jeweller did not finish it in time and it has only just been delivered. Would you out of your kindness of heart take it to her for me?'

'If you wish, but I cannot promise she will accept it.'

'My thanks all the same.' He sent Tamworth to fetch the small velvet-lined casket. Inside there was the tiny figure of a horse, a costly trifle exquisitely wrought in silver, every hair, every sinew revealing the fine workmanship of the silversmith, the eyes of sapphire, the hooves inlaid with gold.

Robert put it into Cecil's hand. 'You will let me know if there is anything that you in your great wisdom think that I should do.'

'I will indeed, my lord. In the meantime I counsel quiet and patience. It is hard, I know, but you and I have had experience of such trials.'

When he had gone, Robert went back upstairs. In one way it was encouraging that Cecil with whom he had often been at odds should have taken the trouble to visit him. He took up Blount's letter and read it again, studying every detail, particularly the reported conversation with Jennet Pinto.

It seemed that Blount had asked her what she made of her mistress's death, was it chance or something else? 'Chance,' she had replied quickly, 'and not done by man or herself.' It was obvious that Jennet believed Amy had killed herself. Her words stared out at him in Blount's careful script. 'I myself have heard her pray to God to deliver her from desperation,' and then terrified at what she had said, she had tried to deny it. It was clear that Blount was of the same opinion. 'Truly the tales I have heard of her,' he wrote, 'make me think she had a strange mind in her.'

And if that was so, and if the jury brought in a verdict of suicide, that crime against God and the Church, then the blame would rest on him, the husband who by his neglect and infidelity had hounded his wife to her grave.

But who would think to kill themselves by falling down a

flight of stairs? And yet why had she sent the servants from the house? What was the explanation? He brought his fist down on the table angrily because he could not drive from his mind the memory of what John Appleyard had said. 'She loved you, Robert. She might well have destroyed herself for your sake.' Damnation! It could not be true. He had never intended to drive her to such desperate measures, never. It was just that events had piled up, one on another, and he could not help himself.

He wrote again to Blount hurriedly: 'Until I hear from you again, in truth I cannot be quiet.' Then his thoughts roved back to that November, nearly two years ago, when Elizabeth had made her entry into London riding White Lady in a dress of rich purple velvet, her face radiant, the aquiline nose and red hair reminding the crowds that thronged the streets of her mighty father and in some magical way enchanting them already, so that they shouted and cheered despite the raw east wind. As Master of the Horse he had ridden behind her, his dress as splendid as he could afford, and he knew that all eyes turned from her to him on his magnificent black horse.

That night when they had entered the Tower, after the greetings and the formal speeches she had given herself a thrilling indulgence and taken him with her. Together they had gone up to the Bell Tower where she had been imprisoned, standing at the very window where he had seen her first from the garden.

'There cannot be many,' she said, 'who have been as fortunate as I, a prisoner who has come back in triumph. You told me we would laugh at our fears . . .'

'And haven't I been proved right?'

'Yes, yes, a thousand times.' She spread her arms in an ecstasy of delight. 'Robert, I want you to do something for me, quietly, without making any show of it.'

'Anything. You have only to ask.'

'You are well acquainted with Dr Dee. Go to him. Ask him for the most propitious day for my coronation.'

He raised his eyebrows, looking at her quizzically. 'I had never suspected that you of all people would look to the stars for guidance.'

'Don't laugh at me.'

'I wouldn't dare.'

She gave him a sharp look and then smiled. 'Oh Robert, how good you are for me. With you I do not have to be all-wise, all-knowing. I believe and I don't believe, but Dr John is dear Blanche Parry's cousin and isn't it sensible to take all precautions?'

He knew then that she felt as he did, so giddily elated that she feared the malign touch of fate. He said thoughtfully, 'A strange man who was a disciple of Dr John once read my future in a bowl of ink . . .'

'Ink?' Now it was she who looked at him quizzically.

'It sounds absurd, I know, and it was only a game but . . .'

'What did he foretell?'

But he would not tell her all. 'Disaster . . . blood and fire . . . which certainly came true . . .'

'And afterwards?'

He remembered the breaking off, the queer look of fear in the light eyes and brushed it aside. 'And afterwards . . . this.'

For an instant their eyes had met but they had made no move towards each other. That would come inevitably and they both knew it, but there had been joy in the anticipation. The next day he had gone to Dr Dee as she had asked.

Part Three
1558-1560

'I have heard from a person who is accustomed to bring me veracious news that Lord Robert has sent to poison his wife. Certainly all that the Queen will do with us in the matter of marriage is only keeping the country engaged with words until this wicked deed is consummated . . . She is in a fair way to lie down one evening the Queen and wake next morning plain Madame Elizabeth, she and her paramour with her.'

The Spanish Ambassador writing to Philip II

One

It was a raw cold morning when Robert rode alone down to Mortlake. A thick white mist lay low over the river and shrouded the water meadows in a ghostly mantle. He shivered and was glad of his long riding cloak. The Doctor had always been a poor man and, when he dismounted at the neglected garden, he looked in vain for a boy to take his horse. He called to a passing villager, but the man gave him a scared look and took to his heels as if the devil were after him, frightened no doubt that the wizard might turn him into a toad or some other loathesome creature, thought Robert with impatient contempt. He tied the bridle to the gatepost and knocked at the door.

Dr John's study was as he remembered it, a mixture of scholar, astrologer, world traveller and magician; maps were pinned to the walls with navigational charts beside queer anatomical drawings; untidy piles of manuscript were held down, here by a human skull, and there by what looked like the mummified body of a small dragon. But Dr Dee himself, with his rosy face, light blue eyes and yellow hair straggling from under his black cap, was as genial and welcoming as always.

'I am delighted to see you, my lord. Do you come seeking assurances for the future like all the others?'

'Why?' asked Robert, intrigued. 'Have you had so many?'

'They have been lining up,' said the doctor a little wryly, 'including distinguished members of Her Majesty's Privy Council. After the late Queen's reign there are all too many anxious to know what the next few years are likely to hold for them.'

'And what do you tell them?'

Dr Dee spread his hands in a helpless gesture. 'What indeed? I send them away with hope. Most men are fools. They never realize the future lies in their own hands. The fault is not in their stars but in their own natures that makes them what they are.'

'I don't come for myself,' said Robert, 'but from Her Majesty.

She asks you to advise her as to the date of her coronation.'

Dr Dee smiled. 'When I cast her horoscope a few years back, Mary put me in prison. This time, I hope, I may be more fortunate. I will read the heavens for her and send her word.'

'Will it take long? There is a great deal of preparation to be made and she feels it should be soon.'

'Give me one day only.'

An ancient book was propped on the reading desk, its pages brown and curling, with an antique script that he could not understand. 'What is this?' he asked curiously.

'It is Persian, a book of magic that I picked up in Hungary; spells for sexual prowess, for riches, for disposing of an enemy or ridding oneself of an unwanted wife.'

Robert gave him a quick glance but the doctor's face was bland. 'Very useful,' he said dryly. 'Do you believe in such things?'

'No, but all knowledge is fascinating and there is always much to be learned. I believe magic comes from the effect on the victim's mind and not from a mere jumble of words. But there *are* inexplicable things. Do you see this?'

He held up the clay figure of a woman grotesquely fashioned with swollen belly and streaks of black human hair. Robert looked at it with distaste.

'What is it?'

'It was brought to me by a woman who found it on her doorstep and was convinced that someone was trying to murder her by witchcraft. I discovered that it had come from her lover's wife who was trying by this primitive means to rid herself of the woman who had taken her husband from her.'

'Did she succeed?'

'Yes, but not from the power of the little doll. The woman's sickness had a natural cause aided by her own sense of guilt and shame. She died, but not by magic.'

Almost without his volition, a vision of Amy swam across Robert's mind and he quickly brushed it away. He said, 'Do you remember years ago at Greenwich, when the ships sailed for Russia, there was a man with you who called himself Sirius?'

'Ah yes, a queer fellow right enough. That was not his real name. He was a man I met in Nuremberg but with Greek blood, I fancy. A very clever fellow. You see this?' He held up a black round object like a hand mirror; the dull obsidian reflected Robert's face smokily. 'He could look into this and see strange visions that were not revealed even to me. He was interested in you, my lord. He cast your horoscope and that of the Lady Elizabeth. He thought he had discovered a hidden conjunction of the stars at your birth and hers, what the Greek astrologers call *Synastria*, and he was very excited about it.'

Robert had a strictly practical mind, not given to fancy, and yet it touched some deep inner chord of feeling. 'Do you believe it is true?'

Dr Dee shrugged his shoulders. 'I would prefer to believe in a natural affinity of mind rather than in any influence from the stars. There was a man once, they say, of whom it was prophesied that he would be king, and he murdered his way ruthlessly to gain the crown. Did his destiny lie in his stars, do you think, or in the greedy ambition that inspired his crimes?'

Robert felt that Dr John who had known him since a boy was trying to warn him. He said abruptly, 'Does Sirius still work with you? I would like to meet him again.'

'No, my lord, he disappeared one day without trace not long after your imprisonment, and I have sometimes regretted it. He was a man of extraordinary powers.'

The day chosen by Dr Dee for the coronation was Sunday, 15 January, and on the morning before Elizabeth made her triumphant journey through the city of London from the Tower to Westminster. The snow and the slush kept no one off the streets and the procession moved at a snail's pace, pausing here and there so that she could receive loyal deputations, listen to children reciting tedious verses, smile when someone shouted, 'Remember old King Harry the Eighth!' and accept a branch of rosemary pushed into her hand by an old beggar woman, calling down blessings on her lovely face.

The seamstresses in the royal wardrobe had worked day and night on the gown and mantle of gold tissue sewn with jewels and worn with a cape of ermine, while Robert's tailor, harassed by Tamworth, cursed his apprentices and nearly went out of his mind turning the rich blue satin shot with gold into a dress of splendour for her Master of the Horse. Amy, watching the slow approach from a window high in Cheapside where the Governor and boys of Christ's Hospital, all in new gowns, waited to greet their Queen, had eyes only for her husband on his black horse, the caparison of purple velvet fringed with gold reaching to the ground. With a cold feeling at her heart she knew he would never belong to her again.

She had seen him only fleetingly since November and Mary had counselled her to be patient. 'You must understand, Amy, this is a great moment for him and he has waited for it so long. We all have. Afterwards things will settle down.' The whole Dudley family were overjoyed of course, already sunning themselves in his glory, and he would not fail them, she was sure of that. Her thoughts were bitter though she would not admit them even to Jennet.

When Robert saw the slight figure of his Queen walk up the purple carpet in the scarlet velvet gown high to the throat, he was surprised by the wave of protective feeling that surged through him. In the heat of the crowded Abbey, thick with the coiling smoke of incense, with its thousands of wax candles and the pipes and drummers already augmenting the organ, her pallor was so extreme, she looked so frail, he feared she would faint, and the crown of King Edward when the Bishop placed it on her head seemed too heavy for the slender neck. But he underestimated the steely courage that had sustained her in so many trials and would not desert her now in the hour of triumph. No one knew that her head ached intolerably from the start of a heavy cold, and that her throat was so hot and swollen it was an effort to swallow even a few mouthfuls of the coronation banquet.

There was no time for the most fleeting moment of privacy until the celebration ended at one in the morning, and for the first time she swayed a little as she rose. Robert was by her side in an instant, earning a black look from Tom Ratcliffe who as Earl of Sussex had stood at her right hand.

She let her fingers rest on Robert's arm for a second, answering the anxiety in his eyes with a hint of laughter.

'The oil in the Abbey smelled so rank, it almost turned me faint,' she whispered. 'Poor Robert, I fear there is no help for it. I shall have to miss your joust tomorrow after all.'

He was bitterly disappointed. It had been devilishly difficult to organize at such short notice and he had planned a brilliant entertainment, destined not only to amuse and delight but to show off his own supreme horsemanship.

'It is of no importance,' he murmured, 'It is only you who matter. There will be other occasions.'

He felt the pressure of her fingers and then she was gone, leaning on Lord Sussex's arm and smiling graciously through her exhaustion.

The first few weeks after the glories of the coronation were over were intensely busy ones for both of them. Elizabeth was faced with an empty treasury, a debased coinage, a war with France and a religious settlement that required the utmost tact if it were not to alienate the Catholics, or offend the Protestants, who flocked back from exile and had long looked upon her as their guiding star.

'I will have leniency and toleration in all cases,' she said fiercely in the teeth of argument as they moved slowly and painfully towards compromise.

Robert was plunged headlong into the work he loved. As Master of the Horse he was responsible for buying, stabling, physicking, training and breeding a large body of horses for the Queen and the royal household, as well as pack-horses and mules for baggage trains, and he threw himself into it with energy and intelligence. His talent for administration and for winning devotion from those who worked under him made itself immediately felt, and Martin Turnbull profited from his earlier foresight by finding himself attached to the royal service and packed off to Europe to hunt for riding horses of exceptional style and quality.

At the same time the question that obsessed Robert as well as everyone else, from Cecil as Secretary of State down to old Mother Robbins who sold hot pies at the corner of Gracechurch Street, was the Queen's marriage. She had already said very forthrightly to a Parliamentary delegation who waited on her in the Long Gallery at Whitehall that she would act as God directed her. She held up her finger with the black and gold coronation ring.

'I am bound already to a husband who is the kingdom of England.'

They bowed their gratitude but went away very unsatisfied. Suitors were beginning to queue up from all over Europe.

One morning late in February Robert came into the Presence Chamber at Whitehall and sensed at once that something had gone seriously wrong. Cecil stared out of the window, drumming his fingers agitatedly on the thick glass; Sussex looked black as thunder; Norfolk was biting his nails, and other members of the Privy Council stood silently together in uneasy groups. Robert glanced around him, caught sight of Harry Sidney and drew him aside.

'What the devil has happened? They look as if a thunderbolt had hit them.'

'It has,' said his brother-in-law ruefully. 'It seems Her Majesty has been in a right royal rage.'

'For what reason?'

'Can't you guess? They had a neat list of suitors nicely drawn up in order of preference, theirs not hers, and more or less demanded that she take her pick and name the wedding day.'

'My God, the fools! Have they learned nothing about her?'

'She swore that if they did not leave her alone, she would dismiss the lot of them and appoint a new Council.'

'She would never do that.'

'She might. She feels her power, but it could be disastrous. She has not been Queen three months yet.'

'I'll speak with her.'

'You? Don't be an ass, Robin. In her present mood she'll not brook anyone's interference. She sent Mary packing when she tried to reason with her. She could throw you over quick as that,' and Sidney snapped his fingers.

'Do you think so? We shall see.'

He did not know what he was going to say or whether it was wisdom or folly. But boldness, dash and brilliance were the qualities Elizabeth admired and he possessed them all as well as a talent for picking the right moment. He strode across the room watched by jealous and hating eyes. In the privy chamber her ladies-in-waiting were gathered, looking distracted.

'Where is she?' he whispered to Fanny Ratcliffe.

She indicated the bedchamber. 'You'll not go in, Robert.'

'Why not?'

Fearful eyes turned to look after him. He knocked at the door but did not wait for an answer. He opened it, went in and closed it behind him.

Elizabeth was at the far side of the room, standing by her toilet table. She said stormily, 'I said I did not wish to be disturbed.'

'I am sorry, Your Majesty, but you did ask me to let you know immediately when we could expect the horses from Italy. I have heard from Turnbull this morning. They should be here at the end of the week.'

She had swung round at the sound of the calm level voice. He stood leaning back against the door, superbly handsome in the amber and gold that suited him to perfection, and the very fact that already the sight of him had power to stir her, only made her all the more angry. She said furiously, 'How dare you come in here without permission? How dare you! God's blood, what do I care about your damned horses! Get out. Go back to your dealing and trading before I have you thrown out.'

Now was the moment. If he bowed and let himself be driven out like all the others, he would be lost. He must risk everything, win or lose on a single throw, and he had the gambler's instinct.

He said boldly, 'Not until you tell me why you are so angry. What have I done? What have those poor men on your Council done that you should be so harsh with them?'

'You have the insolence to question me, your Queen, as if I were a serving maid, a trollop, a nobody!' In a sudden burst of rage she picked up one of the gold-capped bottles of perfume and hurled it at him. He dodged and the alabaster vase smashed against the door and split. A deliciously fragrant scent of musk and damask rose pervaded the room.

'Not bad for a woman. With practice you might hit me next time,' he said approvingly, 'but very wasteful. That perfume is costly and you are always complaining of our empty treasury and the need for all of us to hoard our pennies.'

For a moment it was in the balance. She looked as if at any second she would fly at him with the angry claws of a cat and he braced himself, but then in an instant her mood had changed.

She let herself drop on the bed and began to laugh.

'Oh Robin, Robin, how absurd you make it sound . . . and what a fool I am to lose my temper over such a triviality.'

'That's better,' he said with relief and crossed the room to kneel before her.

The perfume had spilled on to his sleeve and she touched it with one delicate finger. 'I might have wounded you.'

'You already have,' he said, 'but without drawing blood.'

Her eyes met his and she looked away. 'I don't understand you.'

'I think you do,' but he did not pursue his thought. He reached out and took her hand. 'Now tell me what has happened.'

'They make me so angry,' she said. 'Presenting me with a list of names, demanding that I choose now this instant, commanding me to marry at their pleasure. Am I their Queen or am I not?'

'Most certainly you are, but there is some reason for their anxiety,' he said quietly. 'You know as well as I that now the Queen of Scotland is married to the French Dauphin, they have had the impertinence to quarter the arms of England with their own.'

'I know,' she said impatiently, 'I know.'

'You have no heir and they're desperately afraid of what may happen . . .'

'If I should die,' she flashed at him. 'Oh, I understand very well. It is their future they worry about, not mine. If they force me into marriage, I might well die in childbirth. Have they thought of that? No, they are men and therefore women must run at their bidding, and I will not. I will not be ordered to do this or that. I will take my own time.'

'Of course,' he said smoothly. 'So why be angry? Come, let us amuse ourselves by counting over your suitors, one by one. First, there is His Majesty, King Philip II of Spain . . .'

'I'll never take my sister's leavings.'

'His nephew the Archduke Charles, son of the Emperor Maximilian.'

She pursed her lips. 'A dull German.'

'Then the Duke of Savoy. He is not dull, believe me,' he said teasingly. 'I can bear witness to that.'

'A lecher and a drunkard.'

'But possessing all that pleases a woman.'

216

'A woman from the stews perhaps,' she said disdainfully, 'but not a Queen. Go on.'

'Prince Eric of Sweden.'

'He is half an idiot.'

'James Hamilton, Earl of Arran. After the Stuart he is heir to Scotland.'

She wrinkled her nose. 'A farouche Highlander.'

'So there we are, a sorry crew I must admit,' he said, smiling, 'Am I permitted to offer Your Grace advice? Pick on a different one of them every day and then begin to find fault . . .'

'Keep them guessing . . .'

'A woman's privilege . . .'

'Oh Robert, how wise you are. I'll be fickle and inconstant as the moon.'

'You'll have to marry one day,' he said seriously.

'No, I will not. I need no man to rule my life.'

'Are you sure?'

With a sudden swift movement he knelt upright, slipping his arms around her slim waist. 'Are you sure?' he said again. Taken by surprise, she looked at him with wide startled eyes and he kissed her full on the mouth.

She resisted at first but then the long, pent-up passion had its way. He felt her melt against him and his kisses became more tumultuous, her lips, her hair, her eyes, her throat, until panting and breathless, she pushed him away.

'No, Robin, no.'

The wild stirrings within her were making her afraid. She had once sworn to herself that no man should possess her body and soul and she knew she would have to fight herself as well as him to keep her independence.

He still had his arm round her, holding her very close. 'Shall I tell you something Dr Dee confided to me? An astrologer once discovered there was an affinity between our births, what the Greeks call *Synastria*.'

'But I was born in September and you in June you once told me . . .'

'My mother had eleven children. There's room for error.'

'Oh Robin, you have too smooth and silky a tongue,' she said laughing. 'You must go now.'

But there was invitation in her eyes and he knew he could come back.

She pushed away the disordered hair and drew herself upright. 'Send my ladies in to me as you go out.'

And so began the tormenting, frustrating but wildly happy relationship that by April had become an open scandal and the talk of the Court.

De Feria, the Spanish Ambassador, set his spies to work and wrote home to his master in Madrid that 'Lord Robert has come so much into favour that he does whatever he likes with affairs and it is even said that Her Majesty visits him in his chamber day and night.'

It was not strictly true. They were not yet lovers though she showered him with gifts and, like all women head over heels in love for the first time, she took delight in hearing him praised and in talking about him to his sister or anyone else who would listen. In June he knelt in St George's Chapel at Windsor to receive the garter with some of the greatest nobles in her kingdom, and afterwards the Duke of Norfolk, who to his chagrin had been forced to stand beside him at the altar, was heard to remark that if Lord Robert did not withdraw his present pretensions, he would personally make sure that he did not die in his bed.

During these halcyon weeks they did not care, either of them, what was said about them. Robert talked with her, walked with her and went in and out of her room as he liked. He shared her literary tastes, laughed at the same jokes, disliked cant and hypocrisy and yet could lie if necessary just as she did, and confess to it wryly afterwards. When they hunted together at Windsor, she was proud that he brought down the buck with a single shot from his crossbow. No one could stand up to him in the tournaments he staged for her amusement and no one else rode a spirited horse as magnificently as he did. In the evenings, when the musicians played in the great hall, it was his hand she took in the dancing she loved. When criticisms were voiced, she was angry. She worked hard at being Queen. Even Cecil, that tireless man, could not complain of her neglect in any matter of importance, but after the years of repression, she was determined to enjoy to the full all the pleasures she had been denied.

One exquisite evening in early summer they danced at Richmond until dawn. Sleepy-eyed, her ladies waited for her and when they had undressed her, she packed them off to bed. They curtsied and went yawning, leaving Kat Ashley still with her. Her elderly governess who had known and loved her since she was a four-year-old child was a privileged person, but even she hesitated to speak what was in her mind. She fidgeted around the room, tidying up where there was no need, picking things up and putting them down again until Elizabeth turned to her with affectionate impatience.

'Come along, out with it, Kat. I know you've something on your mind and it must be unpleasant since you're making such a fuss about it. Let's get it over and done with. I'm tired.'

Mistress Ashley came to a halt in front of her, twisting her hands together, still reluctant to criticize her darling. 'You shouldn't do it, Your Majesty,' she said at last. 'You really shouldn't.'

'Do what?'

'You know what I mean. To pick him out from all others as you do, to make such a pet of him in front of everyone, foreign ambassadors, great lords . . .'

'Are you speaking of Lord Robert?' she said with a touch of icy hauteur.

'Who else do you favour above all the world? It is not proper, Your Majesty, it is not right.'

'What is wrong about it? He was loyal to me when I needed friends badly, and many of those out there who now crawl before me were my bitter enemies. Isn't it only just that now he should be rewarded?'

'It's not that, lovey,' said the old woman, reverting desperately to the endearments of childhood. 'It's not what you give him, it's how you look and how he looks. I'm not the only one who sees it. They are saying terrible things, wicked things . . .'

'Let them,' she said defiantly. 'Why should I let the envy and lies of others trouble me?'

'But where is it all going to end? How far will it go?'

'As far as I wish and no farther,' she said with spirit. 'Why shouldn't I be fond of him? I like a man who is a man not one who sits at home and twiddles his thumbs like some of the fools they would force on me.'

'But he, your grace . . . he will not be content, don't think it, he will want more and more. A man like him . . . you remember what happened before with . . .' She wrung her hands in an agony of appeal, not daring to name the man who had once nearly brought them both to disaster.

'If you are thinking of Tom Seymour,' she retorted coolly, 'I was a child then. Now I am a woman and a Queen. If I choose to take a lover, I'd like to see who would dare to forbid me.' Then, seeing the shocked dismay on the kind old face, she put her arms around her and impulsively kissed her cheek. 'Don't worry, Kat. I'm doing nothing wrong, I swear to you. I've known so much sorrow, don't deny me a little happiness.'

'I want that for you more than anything,' she said fervently, 'but Lord Robert is . . . you cannot marry him.'

'Who is talking of marriage?' said Elizabeth lightly. 'Now I'm going to bed and so are you. It's late and we'll both be fit for nothing in the morning.'

But when Mistress Ashley had gone and she lay alone in the magnificent bed, with its carved canopy and coverlet of scarlet and gold thread, she did not sleep immediately. She lay listening to the first faint cry of bird song from the trees in the park outside. It was here at Richmond that she had seen him married to a girl she scarcely remembered. In a sense that very fact was a safeguard. She would not give herself entirely to him while he was pledged to another woman, but she could abandon herself to his passionate wooing and need make no decision about marriage or the future. And so long as she did not have to see his wife, it need not trouble her.

Two

'My dear Lady Dudley, I've been so much wanting to tell you, I saw your husband when I was in London,' said Alice, Will Hyde's widowed sister, a large fair gushing lady, meeting Amy in the garden of her brother's house in Berkshire on a fine morning in August. 'You knew of course that I was visiting my cousin. We were fortunate enough to receive an invitation to one of the entertainments at Court and I saw him riding in the tournament. My dear, what a handsome man! How fortunate you are! And so high in favour with Her Majesty too. Everyone is talking of it. No doubt we'll be losing you soon. She will be appointing you one of her ladies-in-waiting, I shouldn't wonder. How I envy you!'

'I have no wish to live at Court, but I am so glad you had such an enjoyable visit,' said Amy quietly. 'My lord writes that he is coming here soon, so you will have an opportunity of meeting him.'

'Oh, how wonderful! I've lived such a quiet life since my dear husband passed on. It will be quite an excitement for me. Will often speaks of when he was here last summer and dear Anthony Forster is devoted to him.'

'If you will excuse me I think I should go in now. Fussy has not been well and I think I have walked him far enough.'

'Oh yes, of course, your dear little doggie.' The large fair lady who had been looking forward to a cosy exchange of confidences looked disappointed.

Amy determinedly picked up the reluctant Fussy and escaped into the house. Alice Odingsell was pleasant enough but a great gossip, and she did not want to talk about Robert. Sooner or later everyone was bound to find out how things were between them. He had written so often saying that he was coming and then sent hurried excuses that important affairs kept him away. Even now she feared sickening disappointment, except that this

221

time Ned Flowerdew had arrived from Syderstone with a number of matters requiring his attention and Robert rarely neglected anything connected with his estates. •

As she neared the house she saw a strange horse being led into the stables and for a mad moment thought it was Robert arriving unexpectedly and unattended. It was no pleasure to find John Appleyard waiting for her in the summer parlour.

'So your dear husband has not yet taken you to Court,' he remarked after the first greeting.

'He has been so occupied,' she said quickly. 'You must have seen him yourself if you came through London.'

'Oh yes, I have seen him . . . from a distance,' he said sarcastically. 'He has become so important that the door to his lodging is besieged. I had to take my turn with the other petitioners and was graciously granted a few minutes of the great man's time.'

'I'm sure you're wrong. Robert is not like that,' she said indignantly. 'What were you asking from him this time?'

'You needn't speak like that. He's not given me that much . . . only a few loans from time to time and after all you are my sister.' He kicked at the rug on the floor discontentedly and then raised the light, shifting eyes to her. 'It's a small enough favour, God knows. The Sheriff of Norfolk is retiring soon. It would matter little to Robert to put in a word for me.'

'Did he refuse?'

'No, not exactly, but he frowned in that damned supercilious way he has and said he'd do what he could but he couldn't be begging favours from the Queen at every tiff and turn. It's different for his own family of course. He can ask the moon and the stars for the Dudleys. Mary Sidney is Her Majesty's closest companion and they say that soon she will be creating Ambrose Earl of Warwick.'

'And why shouldn't she? It's only what he deserves. He's the kindest of men,' said Amy loyally. 'It was his father's title after all and his elder brother's.'

'And what is she going to make Robert? That's the question, isn't it, sister? They're talking of Earl of Leicester. How will you like to be a Countess, eh?' He was strolling round the room. He picked up a pretty jewelled comfit box and peered into it. With his back to her, he said deliberately, 'You know the gossip of the Court, don't you, my dear? It must have reached you even here. They say he has the Queen of England in his pocket, that he means to marry her and make himself King.'

For an instant the room swam around her and she clutched at the back of the tall settle to keep herself from falling.

'But he can't. He is already married.'

He swung round. 'There's such a thing as divorce, you know. It's damnably expensive and troublesome but that wouldn't matter to him, not now.'

'Oh no, no, no. I'll never believe it. He'd not be so cruel.'

Her cry of anguish was so piteous that it penetrated even John's armour of selfishness. He said uneasily, 'Good God, Amy, are you all right? You've gone white as paper.'

She made a valiant attempt to pull herself together. 'It's nothing. I haven't been feeling very well lately.'

'Nothing serious, I hope.'

'No, no, just a summer fever.'

'You don't want to take it too much to heart,' he said with a touch of pity. 'It's only gossip after all. Probably doesn't mean a thing.'

'No, of course not. They are envious of him, they'd say anything out of spite. They don't know him as I do.' But secretly she felt its truth sharp as a sword piercing her heart.

He did not stay much longer but took himself off in the late afternoon with a sizeable loan in the pouch at his belt.

'I'll pay you back as soon as the rents come in,' he promised a little shame-facedly.

'It doesn't matter,' she said wearily. 'Robert gives me plenty and I have little to spend it on here.'

When he had gone, she lay down on the day bed. It was quite true what she had told him, she had not been feeling well these last few weeks. She shivered in the cool of the evening and told the servant to light a fire of sweet-smelling cedar logs on the hearth. Fussy had knocked the comfit box to the floor and was chasing something merrily round the room. She said, 'Jennet, look and see what he has in his mouth. He shouldn't have too many sweetmeats. He might choke.' She lay back and closed her eyes.

It was the silence that made her open them again. Jennet was standing rigid, looking down at what was in her hand while Fussy danced around her in excitement wanting his plaything.

Amy said sharply, 'What is it? Is it a wasp? Have you been stung?'

'No, my lady, it's worse than that, much worse.'

Amy sat up. 'Show me. Bring it here.'

Jennet came slowly towards her, hand outstretched; on the palm lay a little doll fashioned in a yellowish wax with bright brown hair and a long thorn that skewered cruelly through the flat breast.

'It's evil, my lady,' she whispered. 'It's witchcraft. Someone is trying to kill you.' Amy was staring at it, sickness rising in her throat. 'So it is true,' went on Jennet, lifting eyes dark with horror. 'I have heard what they say and wouldn't believe. It's my lord who wishes you out of his way.'

'No, no, never, don't dare to say such a thing to me!' She struck the girl's hand away so that the loathesome little object went spinning across the floor. Jennet fell on her knees weeping.

For an instant Amy stood shivering, then she bit back the hysteria. 'It's all right, Jennet, do you hear, but never, never repeat such a thing to me again and do not mention this to anyone, do you understand?'

'Yes, my lady.'

'Now take Fussy outside. It's time for his supper.' When Jennet hesitated, she said sharply, 'Go now please.'

Alone she nerved herself to pick up the little waxen doll. It is not true, she said to herself, *I will not believe it.* She was about to throw it into the fire and then stopped, some superstitious fear holding her back, a memory of servants whispering on winter nights. Didn't they say that life wasted as the wax melted? She felt cold despite the warm glow of the logs. Shuddering, she dropped it into the bag of embroidery silks that hung by her tapestry frame. Then she knelt down by the couch burying her face in her hands.

'Oh God,' she prayed, 'oh God, don't let it be Robert. Please, please don't let it be Robert.'

Two days later he came as he had promised, riding ahead of his escort with only Dick Tamworth in attendance, and in the first joy of seeing him, Amy forgot her fears, her anxieties, the past disappointments.

It was a hot still day and they were all in the garden, sitting under the sweet-scented lime trees. Fussy went flying across the camomile lawn barking hysterically and Robert laughed as he picked him up.

'Someone is happy to see me at all events,' he said jestingly.

He took his wife's hand, kissing her affectionately before he greeted the others with the charming courtesy that was so much part of him. His elegant dress, his air of distinction, brought excitement and the glamour of the Court into their quiet country lives. They plied him with questions and he answered them good-humouredly, speaking of the Queen with easy familiarity, relating amusing anecdotes, carrying them with him into the dazzling world of Whitehall. Alice Odingsell was gazing at him enraptured and for that afternoon at any rate Amy was happy and proud, stifling the misgivings aroused by John Appleyard's spiteful remarks. It was only later that she noticed how tired and fine-drawn he looked, how brittle was the gaiety and how the merest trifle irritated him.

For Robert these first quiet days were a relief and a relaxation. He had won Elizabeth's favour and it was a heady experience, but now at all costs he had to keep it and that, as he well knew, meant straining every nerve. She could be loving, exacting, tempestuous, wayward, tormenting all at once and life at Court could be dangerous. He needed to have eyes and ears all around him, and at every turn someone waited to trip him up and step into his shoes. One false step and he could be hurled back into the abyss with all to win again. Sometimes, he thought bitterly, she loved to humiliate him simply to prove that he was her creature, her slave, subject to her every whim.

It was she who had suggested he be created Earl of Leicester. He had not asked for it. The Privy Council had demurred but had been forced into agreement. Wasn't it only natural that he should be pleased and flattered? The result had been devastating. When the patent was prepared and brought for her signature, she had looked at it for a moment, then taken her gold scissors and cut it to shreds.

Involuntarily he had protested and she looked up at him with the regal manner she could assume so easily.

'It is not fit,' she said, 'for the son and grandson of executed traitors.'

The bitter humiliation was more than Robert could endure. He said angrily, 'Your Majesty dishonours me.'

'Not you, Robin,' she said, stretching up to pat his cheek. 'There is time enough for my Master of the Horse to prove his loyalty.'

He might have been her pet dog. He drew back, hurt and outraged, but he had been forced to swallow his fury, to bear with seeming indifference the sly grins, the undisguised glee of those who envied him.

That same day he had said, 'I would beg Your Majesty's permission to go into the country. There are private matters needing my attention.'

'So you want to leave me,' she said coldly. 'Go by all means. I shall not prevent you.'

Oh God! he thought, lying sleepless beside Amy in the great bed, it was like balancing on a tightrope. Fighting one's way to the top and staying there was not the life of ease and pleasure they all believed.

The week he spent at Denchworth might have passed peacefully enough if it had not been for Ned Flowerdew. He spent an evening with them, discussing the various matters that concerned Syderstone. When they had done, Robert asked him to sup with them. As they sat over their wine, the young man looked from Amy to Robert.

'I hear Her Majesty has granted you the manor of Kew, my lord,' he said.

'Yes, she has. What of it?'

'Nothing in particular, only I suppose that now Lady Dudley will live with you there.'

'Why on earth should you suppose that?'

'It seems only natural. It is within easy reach of London. It would surely be far more convenient for you than here.'

'It would not be at all suitable,' said Robert shortly. 'It is small and very run down. I have other plans.'

'What plans?' asked Amy, looking up from her needlework.

'Since Syderstone is out of the question, I have been thinking of buying another house or even building one to my taste, something larger, more fitting in every way. Would you like that, my dear?'

'If you could be there too.'

'My duties at Court keep me fully occupied, but I would come when I could.'

'I suppose we should feel ourselves honoured that you have spared us even these few days, my lord,' said Ned dryly.

Robert sensed the criticism and resented it but he did not want to provoke argument.

After Ned had said goodnight and left them, he poured himself more wine and remarked sarcastically, 'Young Flowerdew is still your "verray, parfit gentil knight" I see, ready to fly out at me at the slightest provocation.'

'You should not say that. He has been a true friend.'

'To you, I have no doubt.' He carried his wine over to the fire and stood looking down into it, dismissing Ned from his mind. He had hoped by now that there would have been a note from Elizabeth summoning him back to her. What was happening in his absence? Only a few days away from her and he was already consumed with a restless desire to be with her again. He realized that Amy was asking him something and brought his attention back to her with an effort.

'What did you say, my dear?'

'This house that Ned was speaking of at Kew. It sounds delightful. Couldn't we make our home there?'

'No, it would be quite impossible,' he said decisively, and then turned to her with a smile. 'Besides I thought you liked it here; pleasant company, no Frances to torment you, no household duties, no responsibilities.'

'That's not the real reason, is it? It is not I you are thinking of. Why don't you say what is in your mind?'

'And what do you suppose is in my mind? he asked banteringly.

Now she had begun she had to go on. 'Why not be honest with me? It's the same as it has always been. You're ashamed of me. You don't want me with you, do you?'

'Amy, for God's sake! I have explained already over and over again. The Queen is young and unmarried. No one in my position brings his wife to Court.'

'I don't believe you. Mary is there and there are others. Why should I not be one of the Queen's ladies?'

There was every reason and yet he could not say it to her. 'I have my way to win and it's not been easy. I can't always be asking favours. As it is I have to fight opposition every step of the way. Later perhaps . . .'

She had been walking round the room to still her agitation. Now she came to face him, everything she had heard about him boiling up inside her. 'Don't lie to me, Robert. I'm not so stupid that I do not hear what is said. I don't know what there is between you and Elizabeth, but you want her, don't you? You want her for what she can give you.'

Stung, he said, 'It's not like that. You don't understand.'

'I understand very well and I know too that you want me out of your path. What do you intend to do with me, Robert? Divorce or murder, or is it this?' With a quick movement she snatched the little wax image from the embroidery bag and threw it on the table between them.

He stared down at it, his mind flying back to that moment in Dr Dee's study when involuntarily the wish had taken root in his mind and never been entirely banished. Then his face changed. A wave of revulsion swept through him.

'Where did this filthy thing come from?'

'It was here in this room. Jennet found it.'

'Great God, you cannot believe that I am guilty of so vile a trick.'

'It's what others have done.'

'By Christ, it sickens me!' he said violently. He took it up and flung it into the heart of the fire. She watched the wax melt into shapelessness with an inner trembling.

He was saying urgently, 'You surely don't believe that of me, do you, Amy?'

'I don't know.'

'Some damned wretch has done this to frighten you and fix the blame on me.'

'Perhaps. But whoever did it knows what you desire.'

'You should not trust all that is said about me.'

'How can I help it? Sometimes it is all I have.' She brought her eyes back to his face. 'Do you truly love her, Robert, or is it just because of what she is?'

He could not meet her glance. He turned away, leaning one arm on the mantel, his face hidden.

She went on relentlessly. 'Does she love you?'

He hit his fist bruisingly against the carved wood. 'Christ, if only I could be sure!'

There was a pain in his voice which she recognized, and for a moment she felt older and wiser than he because she had already suffered it.

'Poor Robin.' She watched him for an instant and there was pity as well as anger. Then she picked up Fussy and trailed wearily from the room.

A long time afterwards he went up to the room they still shared for the sake of appearances. Sleep separately and every servant's tongue would be clacking of the quarrel between them. She looked very small lying in the big bed, her bright hair spread out on the pillow.

He stood looking down at her. 'I'm sorry, Amy. I never meant it to be like this.'

She did not answer directly, only reached out a hand and took his. 'Come to bed. It's late and you're shivering.'

He hesitated, then threw off his clothes. When he lay beside her, she put her arms round him. For an instant he did not move, then the familiarity, the scent of her hair, the touch of warm flesh, aroused response in him. All the torment he had suffered during these past weeks came to a head. With a groan he threw himself on her, assuaging his frustration, spending himself in a wild rush of passion. When it was over, he slept heavily, his arm still lying across her breasts. She did not stir, but lay wakeful until the dawn lightened the windows. She knew no triumph, only a painful certainty that Elizabeth had only to lift a finger and he would go without one thought, without one backward glance.

A day later, when the messenger came from London with the letter, she watched his face, saw how he frowned, how fiercely he crumpled the paper in his hand, and guessed what he would say before he turned to her.

'I'm sorry, my dear, I must leave sooner than I had intended. There are one or two matters still not settled at Syderstone. Don't leave it all to Ned. Write on my behalf to John Flowerdew, Amy. There is money owing and they are poor men. I would not have them suffer on my account.'

He gave her brief instructions, anxious to be gone. When he

had ridden away, she could drop the armour of pride that had sustained her and weep for what she had lost.

It was in September that she first felt the lump beneath her breast and knew how sick she was. For a little she was invaded by a superstitious terror, feeling strength and life ebb away from her as the wax image had melted in the heat of the fire. Then she thrust it away. The truth was worse, far worse. She had been sixteen when she had seen her mother die from this same malady of the breast, watched over her through months of sickness and fever with no remedy. If only she were not so desperately lonely, with no one to turn to but casual acquaintances, no friendly hand to sustain and comfort.

Jennet, coming in one morning early, found her mistress kneeling by the bed, her head buried in her hands. Alarmed, she went down beside her.

'What is it, my lady?'

'Nothing,' she said wearily. 'Help me up. I think perhaps you should send one of the servants to fetch Dr Bayley from Oxford.'

Three

❦

The letter Robert had received that sent him riding post-haste for London was not from Elizabeth calling him back to her, but a friendly note from his sister. It mentioned in passing that James Hamilton, Lord Arran, had arrived from France, had turned out to be a very personable young man and the Queen was much taken with him. Damn her! He had only to turn his back and she was smiling at another man, and Arran had the royal blood of Scotland in his veins to recommend him. He was possessed by a fury of jealousy. When he reached Whitehall he changed his travel-stained clothes and went at once to the great hall. The children of the Chapel Royal were entertaining the company that night. The boys' voices had a sweet and piercing clarity. Elizabeth was listening, absorbed. She had a passionate love of music. When he drew near and would have spoken, she silenced him with a gesture, and when it was over she turned at once to the slight, red-haired man who stood close beside her in the place that had always been his. It seemed to Robert that she was deliberately taunting him.

When she withdrew to her own room, he would have followed after her but was dismissed rebukingly by Mistress Ashley.

'You are too pressing, my lord. It is very late and Her Grace is weary. Any business you may have with her must wait till morning.'

He fretted all the night through and rose very early, determined not to let another hour go by without seeing her. Martin Turnbull was waiting to speak to him with all kinds of matters for his approval.

'Later, later,' he said and put him aside. The horse-dealer grinned and exchanged a significant look with Tamworth.

There was a nervous twittering among her ladies when he strode through the privy chamber, but this time he refused to be denied. He flung open the door and went in. The day was already warm and Elizabeth was at her writing-desk in a loose morning gown of sea-green silk, the long red hair hanging straight and shining to her waist. Fanny Ratcliffe was busy at the toilet table. She looked up startled, and would have protested but was silenced by her mistress's raised hand.

'It's all right, child. Lord Robert has an unfortunate habit of forgetting his manners. Go and call the others. It is time I was dressed.'

The girl gave him a pitying look as she passed him. Elizabeth went on writing. She signed her name with a flourish and looked up.

'I don't remember sending for you, Robert, but now you are here, I hope you enjoyed your little holiday. Did you find your wife well?'

'She was as usual, Your Grace.' So that was it. She was jealous too. His heart gave a sudden leap.

'I hope she was not too disappointed at not becoming Countess of Leicester.'

'She understands me better than that. The honour was not of my seeking. I am told that you have enjoyed pleasant company while I have been away.'

'Indeed I have,' she murmured thoughtfully, nibbling the end of the quill. 'Jamie is a charming young man, a little farouche but refreshingly different, and his suit is much favoured by Cecil. It seems our marriage would please everyone, not only uniting Scotland with England but preventing the French from using that country as a stepping-off ground for invasion . . . so many advantages.'

'Have you already put a date to the wedding?' he asked ironically.

'Not yet,' she replied airily. 'The truth is that his Scottish tongue is so thick I find it almost impossible to grasp what he says, and it would seem a pity to have to converse with one's husband in Latin, don't you think?'

'You could always study Gaelic.'

'Could you teach me?'

Then they were both laughing. He went across the room at a rush to fall on his knees beside her. 'Devil! Why must you torment me in this way?'

'I like to feel my power over you,' she said lightly, tickling his nose with the tip of the feathered quill.

'You know it only too well . . . *I shall forever burn Until dark death or time or fortune's turn Shall still my eye and heart, still fire and pain.*'

'Is that your own?' she asked with interest, 'or did you borrow it?'

'It's an Italian poet called Gaspara Stampa.' He slid an arm round her, feeling her body pliant and yielding under the thin silk robe. For an instant she responded to him, answering his kisses with her own, then she pushed him away.

'Enough of this nonsense. I have work to do and so have you. Come and read me your Italian poet this evening.'

All that autumn they were closer than ever and, by tacit consent, Amy's name was never mentioned between them. Politically Elizabeth had made a splendid beginning. The religious compromise was working well, the war with France had reached a satisfactory peace and she was still the matrimonial prize of Europe. Her Privy Council were worrying themselves into the grave because she stubbornly refused to marry and they were certain they knew why. They looked at Robert with renewed loathing. He himself was not so confident.

At the start of October she sent him to Colchester to meet Duke John of Finland, come on behalf of his brother, Prince Eric of Sweden, who was not only fabulously wealthy but would soon succeed his dying father as king.

'How do you fancy being Queen of Sweden as well as England?' he asked dryly when he had brought his charge safely to the palace.

'It has certain advantages.'

'Judging from his brother, Prince Eric is half an imbecile.'

'You are prejudiced. He has sent me a gift of the most exquisite furs. Look, Robin.' She peered at him from a mantle of creamy spotted lynx hooded with Siberian white fox.

'For a set of sables you'll be considering an offer from the Tsar of Muscovy,' he said ironically.

'There's safety in numbers. You taught me so yourself, Robert,' and with that he had to be content.

In November a storm blew up between them. He passionately wanted a seat on her Privy Council and a share in the government and she would not grant it to him. She had learned skill in dealing with men during the long troubled years of youth and had chosen wisely. She did not want to upset the balance, not yet.

'Your time will come, Robin,' she said, lightly patting his cheek.

'When I am crippled by the gout and my beard turns grey,' he said discontentedly. But occasionally he was invited to attend the meetings unofficially and he was present on the morning the question of Scotland was discussed.

A strong Protestant party in Edinburgh was opposing the Catholic Mary of Guise, Queen Regent for her daughter Mary now married to the Dauphin. They aimed to rid their country of the powerful French influence and they came to England for armed help. Elizabeth refused.

'We cannot afford it, gentlemen,' she said to her Council. 'I inherited a country bankrupted by a costly and useless war with France. By the grace of God and our own stringent economy we are pulling ourselves out of the slough of debt and I will not spare one man or one shilling. Let the Scots fight their own battles.'

Cecil was a careful man of his country's finances but he could see the advantages and urged them strongly. Scotland allied with France had been a running sore in England's back for centuries. Now was the chance to heal it under the guise of helping the reformers. The argument went back and forth without achieving anything and the Earl of Sussex took up the cudgels.

'Your Grace forgets that the Queen of Scots has had the temerity to call herself Queen of England. She is the next heir if . . .'

'I have no intention of dying, my lord,' interrupted Elizabeth tartly.

'Heaven forbid that any such thought should come into my head, but if Your Majesty had only consented to consider Lord Arran's suit, we might have had a ready answer.'

'What has Her Majesty's marriage to do with the present

question?' interposed Robert unwisely.

'Lord Robert's attitude to Her Grace's marriage is well known to all of us,' said the Earl scathingly, 'but I would beg him to remember that it carries no weight at this council table.'

There had never been any love lost between Robert and Tom Ratcliffe. He was on his feet in an instant, hand on sword. 'I think you insult me, my lord.'

'Take it how you please.'

'There is only one way to repay insult . . .'

'Gentlemen, gentlemen, I will not have quarrelling in my presence,' said Elizabeth sharply. 'Sit down, both of you.' They glared at one another but obeyed reluctantly. To Sussex she said mildly, 'Lord Robert is here at my request,' but she frowned at the angry young man beside her. 'Speak when you are asked and not before.'

He fumed all through the rest of the morning. The nerves of her councillors were worn to rags but she still would not yield.

Driven to his wits' end, Cecil said at last, 'If my advice is so useless and must go unheeded, then there is nothing left for me, Your Grace, but to resign. Command me to work for you in your kitchen or your garden or wherever you please and I will obey willingly, but as a minister I can serve no longer.'

She was taken aback. 'You are too hasty. I shall not accept any resignation made in the heat of the moment. Think again, Sir William, when you are cooler. We shall meet again tomorrow.'

She rose and swept from the room with an angry rustling of brocaded skirts. The great nobles seated round the long table looked at one another gloomily.

'I'd rather suffer five fits of ague than endure Her Majesty in this temper,' muttered Cecil, at the end of his patience.

The Duke of Norfolk gave Robert a covert look. 'Her Majesty disdains the advice given at the council table but may perhaps be persuaded in the bedchamber.'

Robert bit back the angry retort and Cecil sent him a look of appeal. They liked to scorn him but they were eager enough for his help if they thought it was to their advantage. He said nothing but turned on his heel and went in search of her.

He found her in the garden, walking briskly in the keen frosty air, wrapped in one of Prince Eric's magnificent fur mantles, her lady-in-waiting running breathlessly to keep up with her.

When he reached her side, she turned to him, her eyes still sparkling with anger.

'Men!' she exclaimed. 'The very word war is like a rallying cry to them. They care nothing for lives or what it costs. Isn't it ridiculous of Cecil to offer resignation over such an issue?'

'He would be a great loss. I don't always agree with Sir William but in this instance I think he is right.'

'Are you against me too?'

'I'm always on your side but sometimes the wisest policy is to be bold and show strength. The whole of Europe will be watching and they will judge you to be acting from weakness not from wisdom. Send Lord Winter with the fleet to destroy any French shipping that may dare to bring reinforcements to Leith. It will serve two purposes. It will please the Scots who favour us and enhance England's prestige after the shameful loss of Calais.'

'Perhaps. I will think about it.' With unerring instinct he had touched her on the right spot. More than anything she longed to increase the power and pride of her country, but still she would not grant his wish. He knew his ability and it angered him.

He said, 'Am I your kept man? Your lap dog whom you lead on a string? Am I to have no mind of my own?'

'Only if that is how you choose to regard yourself. It has never been my opinion.'

'I want to be by your side, sharing your burdens with you.'

'You do. Can't you understand that? Already they accuse me of listening to you far too much.'

'But that is in private,' he said obstinately. 'To be one of your Council would be public acknowledgement.'

'You ask too much,' she said coldly.

It was a relief to take himself off for a few days on a hunting expedition with his friend Henry Herbert, and it was unfortunate that, while he was still feeling sore and aggrieved, Sir Francis Knollys chose to bring his daughter to Court for the Christmas festivities. Lettice was the grand-daughter of Anne Boleyn's sister, Mary, and Elizabeth was gracious to her and her father as she was to all her mother's kin.

Robert on his return was bidden by his mistress to be charming to her. He eyed the young girl speculatively when the musicians played and the dancers took their places. There was nothing Elizabeth loved more than the lively galliard but, when he came to take her hand, she looked at him with her icy green stare and said she did not care to dance. Very well, he thought to himself recklessly, he would amuse himself elsewhere and to hell with all wayward women!

Lettice was tall and slender, red lights in the dark glossy hair, with a short arrogant nose and a mouth sullen and yet subtly enticing. She had been a provocative child of fourteen, and now at eighteen she had the look of a woman who is utterly sure of her power to captivate and has a searing contempt for others of her sex unable to compete with her. Ever since she had first seen Robert years ago, she had marked him for her own, and now she wanted him more than ever if only to spite Cousin Elizabeth whom she detested and secretly envied. The fact that all the world called him the Queen's lover and that she herself was already affianced to Walter Devereaux, Earl of Essex and Viscount Hereford, made not the smallest difference.

The moment Robert slid an arm round her waist in the dance he was conscious of her intense sexual magnetism. The galliard was followed by other dances. Lettice, he found, for all her youth had a barbed wit, spitefully apt but amusing. It was a long time since he had even looked at another woman. When they were dancing the volta, he caught Elizabeth's eye on him and it spurred him on. As he threw Lettice up and caught her again, she laughed with delight and pressed herself against him. He saw the curve of her breasts in the low-cut gown. Instead of offering her cheek decorously for the courtly kiss as the dance ended, she lifted her mouth to his. She was deliberately offering herself to him and it both amused and excited him. He brushed his lips lightly against hers and she gave him a little derisive smile.

'You are timid, my lord. I had not expected that of you. Your reputation belies you. Is that how you kiss my cousin Elizabeth?'

'That is none of your business if you will pardon me, my Lady Impertinence,' he said a little dryly. 'If I remember rightly, the last time we met, at Greenwich palace, you bit me. I believe I have the scar still.'

'I am a child no longer, Lord Robert.'

'No indeed.' Child she was not, he thought wryly. It was extraordinary but, in some indefinable way he could not lay his finger on, there was a subtle likeness between her and Elizabeth. Perhaps like her she too had a touch of the magic, the white witchery that had belonged to Anne Boleyn. It excited him in the same way but he recognized the danger. He made up his mind to avoid this alarming young woman and found it well nigh impossible. Wherever he went in their close circle, Lettice Knollys placed herself in his path. She brought her horse beside him when they rode out to hunt, she was watching when he competed at the tilt. Sometimes it seemed that Elizabeth was deliberately throwing her in his way, testing him perhaps. He could never quite fathom the subtleties of her mind.

On the Feast of the Three Kings, the last night of the Christmas revels, there was a masquerade that turned into a wild merry night of fun and gaiety. For a whim Elizabeth had dressed herself and all her ladies exactly the same, in gowns of white velvet sewn with pearls with close caps of silver hung with veils of gauze and fantastic jewelled masks. It was almost impossible to tell one from the other. There was a great deal of laughter and merriment with wild guesses that nearly always turned out to be wrong when someone was being kissed by someone else's sweetheart.

In the early part of the evening he had captured Elizabeth. He knew her, he told her, by the beauty of the long slender hands, for once without the betrothal ring of England. Maybe for that very reason she seemed more his than she had been all these past weeks.

He had drunk more than he usually did that evening, his senses aroused and vibrant from the flirtation with Lettice though it was not she he wanted. This night, he swore to himself, this night, come what may, he would make Elizabeth his own. She had tempted and then held him off too long. He was a man like other men. He could not go on like this for ever. They had moved from the stately court dances to the old country measures. When they were dancing Kiss-in-the-Ring he lost her, but the music was louder now, the fun faster and more furious. Very much later when they were playing Hoodman Blind and it came to his turn, the silk scarf was tied round his eyes. The girls ran shrieking and laughing around him, touching him and darting away. He caught one after the other and they twisted out of his hands. Then at last he was certain from the feel of the slender body, the musky perfume, that he had her again.

Daringly he drew her away into the shadows. He tore off the

scarf and her eyes glinted up at him through the jewelled mask. He kissed her and her lips opened sweetly under his.

'Tonight, beloved,' he murmured. 'It must be tonight.'

She did not answer, only pressed her mouth on his again. He felt the honey-sweet touch of tongue and a heady intoxication invaded him. Then she had slipped away from him again.

It was long past midnight before the revels were over and tired dancers limped their way to crowded bedrooms. He went swiftly through the hall, past overturned tables, spilled food, fallen goblets. His heart was singing as he made his way to his own apartments intending to strip off, wash away the sweat of the strenuous evening. He knew her tastes. He would go to her cool, refreshed, scented.

At the door of his bedroom Tamworth met him. 'There is someone waiting for you, my lord.'

'Who?'

'I'm not sure. She wore a mask.'

So she had come to him. His anticipation soared to a crescendo. He opened the door and went in. There was only one candle burning and in the dim light he saw the slim figure standing by the bed, wrapped in the heavy cloak.

'I did not dream you would come to me, my love.' He took a step towards her and then stood aghast. It was not Elizabeth who let the costly furs drop to the floor and stood swinging the mask by its silver ribbon, but Lettice, her eyes wide and dark, a triumphant smile hovering round her mouth.

'You've been so long,' she said, pouting a little. 'I've been waiting for hours.'

His disappointment was so acute that his reaction was savage. 'God damn you! What are you doing here?'

'You invited me. Don't you remember?'

Christ! What a fool he had been! For an instant he wondered if they had concocted this together, one of the tricks of women to befool and trap him.

'You thought I was Cousin Elizabeth,' she said, mocking him. 'Oh, how deliciously funny!' and went off into peals of laughter.

Anger tore through him. He said furiously, 'Do you want everyone in the palace to hear you?'

'I don't mind.'

'Well, I do.' He picked up the fur mantle. 'Please go, Mistress

Knollys. This is no place for you. Tamworth will conduct you back to your own apartments.'

'Suppose I say I'm not going?' She came close to him, putting her arms round his neck. She used a heady perfume. The red mouth, seductive and inviting, was only a few inches from his. His senses swam a little. 'What are you afraid of?' she whispered. 'You want me, you know you do.'

For a moment he was tempted. He had a savage desire to satisfy his rage and disappointment by throwing her on the bed and taking fiercely and without affection the body she was offering him so shamelessly.

She pressed her lips against his and then leaned back, looking into his face. 'Robin, dear Robin, does she give you anything like this?'

It was a mistake. It reminded him too keenly of what he would be losing. He put her firmly away from him.

'I think you forget yourself.'

She turned on him spitefully, a woman rejected. 'Supposing I scream for help? Supposing I say you enticed me here and then raped me against my will?'

'You will ruin me but you will also destroy yourself. I don't think you will like being banished from Court, will you? After all you will enjoy being Countess of Essex and Viscountess Hereford.'

'I hate you,' she said in sudden childish temper. 'I hate you.'

'No, you don't. You'll thank me for it. We'll probably laugh about it one day.' He was wrapping the cloak around her and now he held out the mask.

'You're frightened,' she said tauntingly. 'Frightened of what she might do to you if she was to find out. Lord Robert Dudley, Her Majesty's horsekeeper and her fancy man, so frightened he has to run at her bidding like a little dog.'

He slapped her cheek hard and her hand flew up to it in outrage. 'How dare you? My father shall hear of this.'

'Only if you tell him and Sir Francis is a hard man, I understand. He'll not be best pleased.' He saw by her face that he was right and felt a twinge of pity. She was after all very young. He said, 'Go now, Lettice. Forget this folly.'

'Oh, I'm going, don't worry. You think you are going to marry Elizabeth, don't you? You think only your wife prevents her from falling into your arms. You're a fool. Her mother kept King Henry waiting for six years. She'll keep you waiting for a lifetime.'

'Maybe, that's my concern.' He was shepherding her to the door but she still had one parting shot.

'There's one thing you don't know. Sirius cast my horoscope that day at Greenwich too. One day you will come crawling to me and then it will be my turn.'

Momentarily a curious dread touched him very close and then was dismissed. 'Life is what you make it, my dear, not what the stars foretell. You'd best remember that.'

Haughtily she went through the door and Tamworth, who was discretion itself, conducted the masked and cloaked lady back through the palace, delivered her safely to her own apartments and returned to his anxious master.

'Did you meet anyone?'

'No, my lord. I think all are sleeping.'

'Or drunk,' he said wryly.

But Robert felt far from laughing. There were not many hours left of the night and he spent them in a hopeless attempt to think up some plausible explanation in case the whole sorry episode reached Elizabeth's ears, only to find that by some miracle all his anxiety was for nothing.

She greeted him sunnily when she rose late after the fatigues of the night and kept him with her when Sir Francis Knollys, who had perceived something of his daughter's frolics with considerable concern, came to bid farewell. Lettice, pale and composed, walked straight past him as if he did not exist so that Elizabeth smiled as she touched his arm.

'What has happened to your famous charm, Robin?' she whispered.

He shrugged his shoulders, not sure how much she was teasing him and too relieved to make any comment.

The twelve days of Christmas were over. The Court returned to normal and Elizabeth as a New Year gift appointed him full member of her Council. The costly and unusual present he gave her in gratitude nearly beggared him. It was a loving-cup made of a coconut shell exquisitely mounted in gold. The bear and porcupine from his own crest formed the handles, and the whole was set with priceless gems. She was enchanted with it and they drank a toast to each other out of it.

Increasingly that spring those close to Elizabeth found their view of her blocked by Lord Robert Dudley. Protective and adoring, he was always at her side, and with extreme discontent certain among them began to look about them for some means of discrediting him.

Then something unexpected happened that would have delighted them if they had known, and that very nearly brought all his castles in the air crashing to the ground. One cold morning in late February after a hard game of tennis with Elizabeth herself and many of the Court watching, Robert came back to his own apartment in the palace and found his wife waiting for him.

Four

The fire had been lighted and Amy sat close beside it for the room was cold. Robert came in hurriedly, a cloak over his shirt and breeches, intending to change quickly and return to Elizabeth. At the end of the match he had suffered a fall on the court and hit his head on the post that held the net. There was a bruise on his temple and a trickle of blood.

She rose to her feet as he entered. 'You're hurt,' she exclaimed involuntarily, and would have gone to him but the look on his face held her back.

Shock and dismay combined to make him speak more harshly to her than he usually did.

'What the devil has brought you here?'

She found it almost impossible to answer. What was it that had brought her the long exhausting journey over muddy rut-filled roads knowing only too well the kind of welcome she would receive? Was it because it was five months since she had seen him and his letters had dwindled to a few scrawled lines? Because even at Christmas and the New Year he had not come, only salved his conscience by sending her expensive gifts – a fine hood trimmed with fur and sewn with pearls, a chain of gold studded with amethysts, presents you might send a discarded mistress of whom you had tired, not a loving wife? Mostly perhaps it was because of Frances who had come riding down the frosty roads from Norfolk with John Appleyard, had turned up her nose at Denchworth, and faced Amy forthrightly with a contemptuous glance around the prettily furnished rooms.

'You're a fool. He is your husband, isn't he? Then stand up to him, for God's sake. Insist on your rights.'

'What rights?' It was his love she wanted, not a great house and hosts of servants. She said lamely, 'Robert is very generous. I only have to ask and his steward gives me all I need.'

'His steward!' replied Frances wrathfully. 'What kind of a

marriage is that? He should set you up in a proper establishment, acknowledge you as his wife, entertain in a suitable style. There are his sisters, his brother, all in fine positions and well thought of, while you are hidden away in a corner as if he had married his serving wench. The Robsarts are as good a family as the Dudleys any day in the week and so you should tell him. You've no pride, Amy, that's always been your trouble.'

Perhaps it was. All she had wanted was to be proud of him and now even that was flawed and stained by what they said about him.

Frances came closer to her. 'You take warning from me, my girl. I've never trusted the Dudleys, never. Don't let him put you down. Go up there to Court, outface him.'

'How can I? she said faintly. 'There is the Queen and he would be so angry . . .'

'And what right has he to be angry, I'd like to know, or Her Majesty either if all we hear is true? Even if she takes him to her bed, what can she do to you? You are his lawful wedded wife, not a whore from the Bankside stews. And you tell him so!'

It was days before she nerved herself to it. Long nights when she lay wakeful, bitter resentment curdling inside her. Sick and unhappy, what had she to lose? Then came the final straw. A brief note from Robert arrived on a morning when Ned Flowerdew had called to see her, as he still did from time to time.

He found her reading it when he came in. It told her that Anthony Forster had leased a fine house at Cumnor and her husband had decided to rent half of it from him.

'You will like it better than Denchworth,' he wrote, 'and it will be more suitable in every way. I understand Will Hyde's sister will be living there, so you will not lack company.'

Why? Why had he decided this without consulting her? He knew how she disliked Anthony Forster. Was this a way of getting her away from her friends, isolated in a great house with a man who was devoted to his interests? For what purpose? All the spiteful slander and the cruel hurting gossip returned to her mind in a flood, though she tried to push it away. He could not really be intending to harm her, not Robert, not her own husband.

She made up her mind there and then. She said impulsively, 'Ned, will you escort me to London?'

He looked at her with surprise. 'With pleasure if you insist,

244

but are you sure it is wise? The roads are rough and the weather very cold. Are you well enough?'

She brushed his objections aside. Now she had decided she wanted to go at once. 'I am perfectly well. We will set out tomorrow.'

It was a long slow journey because she could not ride, and the coach with the six horses jolted slowly down the roads with an escort riding in front and behind. She travelled lavishly. Robert had never stinted her. Even Ned, riding beside the carriage, had to admit that. More than once she nearly turned back, daunted by bad weather and the discomfort of travel, except that having started on it, she was determined to carry it through to the bitter end.

But now, standing in his room in the palace, his possessions scattered around her, the great lemon-coloured dog that she had never seen before watching her from the hearth, she had the curious feeling that he was a stranger and she could not tell him any of these things.

Robert threw aside his cloak and came towards her frowning. 'How long have you been here?'

'An hour or so.'

'Did anyone see you?'

'Does it matter if they did?'

'No, no, of course not.' He took a restless turn about the room, trying to see his way around the problem. What in God's name was he to do with her?

She did not tell him that she and Ned had arrived overnight, that she had come early to Whitehall and been admitted to his apartment when she gave her name. Tamworth, taken by surprise, had told her his master was at the tennis court and she had insisted on him escorting her there.

Hidden at the back, she had watched the tall athletic figure in the silk shirt and trunk-hose, heard the applause when he scored a point, saw Elizabeth lean forward and wipe the sweat from his face with her own handkerchief in the pause between games, saw how they looked at one another and how he bent his head and kissed the fingers that held the kerchief. There was a buzz of comment around her, amused, spiteful, scandalized, scabrous. She did not heed it. She had seen for herself and did not wait until the end but returned to his rooms.

Robert was dabbing at his forehead with a towel. His temple had begun to throb. He must have hit it harder than he had thought. He said with some impatience, 'You still haven't told me why you've come.'

'You never visit me. Isn't it natural that I should want to see my husband sometimes.'

'I've told you often enough . . .'

'I know what you tell me.' Then she turned to face him. 'Why are you sending me to Cumnor Place?'

'I'm not sending you anywhere. It seemed a good idea when Forster told me of it. It's a fine place, larger than Denchworth. You can have a whole wing to yourself with rooms to entertain friends if you wish.'

'I don't like Anthony Forster.'

'For God's sake, Amy, what's wrong with him? Besides, he won't be there himself. I understand that Will Hyde's sister will be living there, and you like her, and another lady, a Mrs Owen. You'll not lack for company as I wrote you. It is altogether more suitable to your station. You are my wife after all.'

Was he really thinking of her or was he simply making excuses? She didn't know and a huge weariness swept over her. 'I suppose I might as well go there as anywhere.' She swayed a little with fatigue and wretchedness and let herself drop on to the stool by the fire.

He said, 'What is it? You look pale. Are you sick?'

'I haven't been well. I wrote you about it.'

She had and he had dismissed it as no more than women's vapours born of nothing to do but worry over trivialities.

'Have you seen a physician?'

'Yes. Dr Bayley of Oxford. It is a sickness here.' She touched her breast and raised haunted eyes to his. 'I saw my mother die of the same malady.'

It gave him a jolt. She looked small and helpless and unhappy and, because he had a natural compassion for all sick creatures, whether dogs, horses or now his wife, he drew up a chair and took her hand.

'You are distressing yourself unnecessarily I am sure, but you should have more skilled advice than this Oxford man. I will send Dr Julio to visit you.'

'Julio?'

'Yes, he's an Italian, but an excellent doctor. He has attended the Queen, and I myself consulted him last summer.'

'I don't like foreigners.'

'Oh Amy, for heaven's sake . . .'

'Especially Italians . . . They are liars, poisoners . . .' She drew her hand away.

'That is nothing more than a ridiculous prejudice,' he said with impatience. 'You don't know what you are talking about. He is worth the whole College of Physicians put together. Now, will you promise to see him if I persuade him to go to you?'

She felt she was in a trap. She looked at him helplessly. 'If it is what you wish, Robert.'

'It's not myself I am thinking of, but you.' He got up. The graze on his forehead had begun to bleed again.

She said, 'Are you in pain? Let me bathe that place for you.'

'It is nothing. I think perhaps you had better go. Where are you staying?'

'Can't I remain here with you?'

'My dear, I have only these few small rooms and I'm lucky to have them to myself. The palace is crowded to the doors. It would be hardly suitable.'

'Ned came with me. He and the horses are at the inn.'

'Ned again,' he said dryly. 'Was it his idea that you should come?'

'No, no, it was not.'

'Very good. Wait here while I dress and I will take you there myself.'

His hand was on the latch of the bedroom when he heard Tamworth's startled exclamation and saw the look on his face as he opened the door. Then Elizabeth was standing on the threshold.

'I came to make sure that your hurt was not serious,' she said and stopped short, staring at Amy. For an instant no one spoke or moved, then Robert took hold of himself.

'May I present my wife, Your Majesty?'

This was the woman who had stolen her husband. She had never been so close to her before. With one glance Amy took in the pale face, the red hair, the rich gown, the indefinable air of grace and distinction before she sank into a curtsey.

Elizabeth said smoothly, 'So this is Lady Dudley. I have long wanted to meet Lord Robert's wife. You are very welcome.'

'Thank you, Your Majesty.'

'My wife is here to see me on a matter of some urgency.' Robert was stumbling over the words, his eyes anxiously scanning Elizabeth's face, but she had learned to control her feelings and she gave nothing away.

She said quietly, 'No doubt you will wish to be free to be with your lady, Robert. You are excused all duties while she remains with you.'

She nodded to Amy and swept out of the door, Tamworth closing it behind her. Robert would have gone after her except that he knew it was useless. What could he say? He could not gauge her reactions. Everything he lived for hung upon the thread of her favour, and if he lost it he was finished. Now Amy had put it in jeopardy.

She was aware of what she had done and tasted triumph and yet, at the same time, she knew she might have ruined him.

She said, 'I am sorry, Robert.'

'Sorry for what?' he replied brusquely. 'Isn't this what you intended when you came?'

She could not stand up against him. Few could when Robert made up his mind. He did not bully, he did not command. He used sweet reason even with the indignant and hostile Ned, but he achieved what he wanted. Within a day he had seen her safely on her way back to Berkshire and went at once to Elizabeth, only to find all doors closed against him. Despair nearly overwhelmed him. By the next morning he had a raging pain in his head and the fever from which he had suffered in the Tower and which still occasionally attacked him, particularly in moments of stress, had him in its grip. Tamworth put him to bed and sent for the physician.

Without realizing it he had hit on the the one sure thing to bring Elizabeth back to him. She had an instinctive sympathy with the sickness of anyone dear to her. The sight of his wife had come as too much of a shock, too sharp a reminder of the barrier between them, and at first she had shut herself away from him until she had assimilated it. She had not allowed herself to think of it. It was there but they had never spoken of it, gone on recklessly from day to day, playing with fire. For a couple of days she tried to come to terms with it. She was not ruthless. She had some pity for the young woman who had lost him, but she had suffered too. She could not give him up, she could not. When Tamworth brought the message that his master was too sick to attend the meeting of the Privy Council, her defences crumbled.

Robert, opening his eyes after an uneasy night of pain and fever, saw her seated by his bed and thought he was still in the clouds of delirium. He struggled to sit up and she gently pushed him back against the pillows.

'You are to lie quietly. I have spoken with the doctor. He says your fall has given you a slight concussion and that has caused the fever and sickness.'

In a mist of pain and gratitude, he touched her hand. 'You should not have come to me here.'

'I go where I like,' she said. 'You must get well quickly, Robin. We set out on progress soon and what shall I do without my Master of the Horse? We shall go to Norfolk, then Oxford and afterwards to Rycote. I have long promised a visit to Henry Norris and his wife. They are dear friends. When I was a prisoner at Woodstock they helped to make my life bearable. It is quiet there. It will do us both good. We need a little holiday.'

She touched his cheek lightly and he moved his head so that he could press his lips to her fingers. 'I will be there.'

Cumnor Place had once been an abbey and the high vaulted ceilings on the ground floor still gave it a monastic appearance. The house was built around a stone courtyard, but Amy's wing looked out over the terrace and acres of fine parkland with a splendid view of trees and lake. With everything unpacked from the baggage carts and her own personal possessions scattered through the rooms, it was pleasant enough and she did not know why she still felt the slight sense of uneasiness. Mr Forster was away, but his wife was there and Mrs Owen, whose father-in-law had been the original owner of the property. She came to welcome Amy on her arrival and invited her and Alice Odingsell to sup with her that evening.

It was March before Dr Julio at Robert's request took a few days off from his professional engagements and rode up to Cumnor.

He was a small, brown-faced man, his receding hair close-cut and black as night, like his neatly trimmed beard and moustache. Since he moved in Court circles he was fully aware of the scandals rife about the Queen and her Master of the Horse and he had looked keenly at Robert when he asked him to attend his wife. At first he had hesitated, not willing to be mixed up in any doubtful matter. Already as a foreigner the College of Physicians, though accepting his high credentials, had been inclined to view him with suspicion. Then his interest was aroused and, sure of his own professional integrity, he agreed. His fees were high but Robert accepted them without comment; after all, if the young man wanted to know how long his wife was likely to live, he could give his opinion for what it was worth and do what he could to alleviate the symptoms of his patient.

Jennet admitted him and took him up to her mistress's bed-chamber. The staircase was one of the oldest parts of the house, built of the original stone, worn smooth and slippery from the sandalled feet of the monks and with an awkward turn at the landing on the first floor.

The moment Amy saw him come in, she was frightened of him. The dark face, the piercing black eyes, the soft slightly sibilant voice speaking good but heavily accented English, filled her with terror.

'Would you please lie on the bed, Lady Dudley, so that I can examine you?'

Dr Bayley had only asked her questions, he had not wanted to touch her. She shrank from the small brown hands that unlaced her morning gown and gently but skilfully kneaded her breasts.

'How long have you known about this?' he asked.

'Nearly a year.'

'So long.'

The cancerous tumours were already far advanced and she was still only in her twenties. Poor young woman! He made no comment, only asked a few other professional questions, then moved away to the window while with Jennet's help she gathered her dress around her and sat up.

'I would like to consult with Dr Bayley, my lady,' he said, turning back to her. 'Then I will send you remedies that I believe will help you greatly.'

'Am I going to die?' she asked bluntly.

'We are all going to die,' he said with a smile. 'Now you must not let yourself become upset or depressed. It will not help you. Your husband is very concerned about you.'

'I wish I could believe that was true.'

Her frankness somewhat disconcerted him. He took refuge in professional smoothness. 'I should like to see you again a little later. I will send my servant back with the remedies as soon as possible.'

On his way to the door he paused and turned back. 'There is one other thing. I would advise you not to take violent exercise. Do not ride or even walk too fast, and be careful to avoid falls.'

'Falls?' she said, 'I don't understand.'

'Your sickness may make you giddy and your staircase outside there, if you will pardon my saying so, is a little steep and inconvenient.'

For some reason this alarmed her more than anything else. In a flash of memory she saw that other dark man in the black, close-fitting cap, the look on his face and what she thought she had seen in the bowl of ink.

'You will remember?' said the doctor with some urgency.

'I will try.'

'Good.' He smiled. 'Now I'll bid you good-day, my lady.' He opened the door. Jennet was waiting to show him down the stairs.

She came back a few minutes later with a worried frown. 'That doctor's a queer one and no mistake, fretting over the staircase like that. He spoke of it again before his horse was brought round. Do you know what he reminded me of? He looked just like the devil in the mystery play at Abingdon Fair last summer.'

'Don't be silly.'

'It's true, my lady. He only wanted a forked tail. I don't know why my lord has to send a foreigner like that, as if there are not enough good English physicians.'

'He is said to be very clever. Help me to dress, Jennet, and don't go gossiping about his visit to the other ladies.'

Dr Julio was riding thoughtfully through the lanes to Oxford. He had seen many women with this same sickness and it saddened

251

him that so many of them were young and he could do so little to help them. If Lord Robert hoped for his wife's death, then he might not have long to wait, he thought grimly. Then he turned his thoughts to a professional problem that had long puzzled him. For years now he had noted a curious phenomenon that occurred with these particular patients. A number of them had died not from the sickness but from an unlucky fall; one from a horse which should have caused only bruising and instead broke her neck, another from a mere tumble down a couple of steep garden steps. Was it just possible that the disease caused a brittleness in the bones? He felt a familiar impatience with the limitations of medical research. He was not a surgeon; but sometimes he wished he could dissect the body of one of these young women, though he knew that was impossible. The relatives naturally enough would scream sacrilege at the very idea. The members of the College had raised their hands in horror when he had once suggested that the bodies of women prisoners condemned to death should be given over to dissection. They were always at war with the Company of Surgeons anyway. The English were a queer people, he thought. They would willingly watch some poor wretch hanged, drawn and quartered with the utmost brutality, and yet the very notion that the corpse of a criminal be cut up for scientific purposes aroused shrieks of protest. Four bodies a year were all that were permitted by royal decree and what could be done with so few? Sometimes he thought of returning to Italy where he had studied medicine. They arranged these matters better at the anatomic theatre in Padua. Still he would do his best for Lady Dudley. He would send her draughts that would calm her and help her to sleep and later, when she became worse, he would increase the dose a little.

Two days later when his servant returned to Cumnor with the sealed packet, Amy looked at the blue phials with the instructions written in a spidery, foreign hand with no intention of taking even one sip. She could not be sure they were poisoned, indeed there was no earthly reason why they should be, and yet she was afraid, terribly afraid. She put them away in a chest under her shifts and petticoats without saying a word to anyone. When Dr Julio came again in June and asked her if the medicines had helped her, she lied and said she was sleeping more easily. So he sent her more, slightly increasing the strength, and waited till Robert and the Queen should return to London before presenting his report.

Five

Elizabeth arrived at Rycote in August after a gruelling two months travelling from place to place, listening to long speeches, watching elaborate pageants, accepting splendid gifts and being entertained at a garden party in the drenching rain where mercifully she sat under a canopy. Her courtiers including Robert huddled into their cloaks with sodden feet and thought gloomily of heavy colds and limbs racked by rheumatism.

They came unofficially to Rycote with few attendants. Henry Norris's father had been unjustly executed for his loyalty towards Anne Boleyn and Elizabeth wanted to show her trust and appreciation.

'I am worn to skin and bone,' she said to Henry Norris when he greeted her. She kissed his dark-haired, dark-eyed wife, affectionately using her pet name. 'Dear Black Crow, don't dream of entertaining us. All Lord Robert and I long for is leisure to sit quietly and do absolutely nothing.'

The Norrises glanced at one another. They had heard all about her handsome favourite and accepted him with a certain reserve. They were very conscious of the honour bestowed on them and had a genuine loyalty and friendship towards their Queen.

Rycote in the peaceful valley of the River Thame was beautiful, far removed from the bustle and harrassments of courts and palaces. It was so rare to have more than an hour of privacy that these few days were bliss; as if for this short time they were in a world of their own, content with only themselves and their love.

The weather was perfect. They strolled on the lawns or sat in the shade of the giant beeches or talked with their hosts in the cool of the evening on the terrace, while the fireflies glowed like tiny stars in the lime trees and the moths hurled themselves to a fiery death in the fluttering flames of the candles.

If Henry Norris and his wife viewed their intimacy with some disquiet, they said nothing. Only once did Margery Norris dare to make even the slightest reference to it and Elizabeth put her finger against her lips.

'Dear Crow, I know what you would say, but there is no need, believe me. There is nothing dishonourable between us, I swear to you.'

'Do you love him, Your Grace?'

She would not answer directly. 'What is love? I have been alone so long. I enjoy his company.'

'Can you trust him?'

'Absolutely. He needs me as I need him.'

The last day of their stay was very still and hot. They were conscious of the passing of time and that tomorrow they must go back to the pressing urgencies of ordinary life, leaving behind them this brief idyll of happiness and peace in one another's company.

In the late afternoon the sun vanished and there was a hint of thunder in the heavy sky. Elizabeth retired to her room with a slight headache and it was later, when a shower of summer rain had cooled the air and the threat of storm had gone, that Robert knocked at her door and went in.

She was lying on the bed in a light silk gown for coolness, her hair unbound, and she looked up at him dreamily, her eyes still shadowed with sleep.

'Are you feeling better?' he asked.

'Yes. The pain has all gone.' She sat up against the high pillows. 'I must get up and dress. It is our last evening and it will be expected.'

'Not yet. There is plenty of time.' He sat beside her on the bed.

'What have you been doing this afternoon?'

'Norris and I had a shooting match.'

'In this heat? What energy!'

'It is cooler now.'

'Did you win?'

'We were fairly evenly matched.'

She put out a hand and touched him. 'Your sleeve is damp and your hair. You'll take a chill.'

'Nonsense.' He captured the hand. 'I've been walking in the rain.'

'Why?'

'I wanted to think.'

'What about?'

'You and how much I love you.'

'Would you care for me so much if I were not Queen, Robin?'

He bent his head and kissed each of the long slim fingers before he answered. 'I don't know. It is so much part of you I can't separate it in my mind.'

'That is honest at any rate.'

'Does it disappoint you?'

'No. It is what I expect from you.'

'I can lie to others, but not to you.'

'We are too much alike.'

He was bending over her. 'I only know one thing for sure. I can never be happy away from you.'

'Nor I from you.'

For a moment their eyes were locked together and then he began to kiss her. At first she lay passively and then, when he pushed aside the thin silk and began to kiss her breasts, she felt her body stir in a wild craving. His caresses became more urgent, more demanding, until at last she turned her head away.

'Robert, please please, no more.'

'Oh God,' he said, 'why, why? I love you in every possible way a man can love. Is that so evil a thing?'

'It isn't that.'

'Then what is it?'

But how could she explain? It was not a moral scruple, though perhaps that was part of it. How could she tell him of the fear, the instinctive terror that sprang from some dark source within her that she could not control or even understand, that black abyss where love and death were inextricably mingled. It had happened to her mother, to her pretty hapless cousin, Katherine Howard, even to her unhappy sister, Mary. To give herself in the act of love would only end in death. She could not yield, she could not, even though her whole being longed achingly to find fulfilment with him.

He felt her grow rigid, he saw the tears in her eyes and his passion faded. No other woman had ever found it possible to resist him, but she was different, unique. He would force nothing on her. She would come to him in her own time if only he were patient. He held her against him and stroked her hair until she had stopped trembling, then he kissed her gently.

'Time we dressed and went to supper.'

'Yes.' She caught at his hand as he got off the bed. 'You still love me?'

He looked down at her, smiling. 'You should know by now that I worship you,' he said quietly and went out of the room.

On that same day in August, not twenty miles away, Amy was enduring a visit from her half-brother. As usual John Appleyard had a grievance and was not backward in voicing it until she wearied of him.

'I don't know why you are grumbling,' she said at last. 'Robert did as you asked, didn't he? He had you appointed Sheriff of Norfolk and Suffolk.'

'Yes, he did,' he admitted grudgingly, 'but you don't understand these things, Amy. When Her Majesty came to Norwich on progress a month ago, I went to enormous expense to give her a fitting reception. The whole city was hung with garlands, the militia were fitted out with new clothes, white velvet trimmed with black, regardless of cost, the schoolchildren sang madrigals, the Recorder gave a Latin oration and there was a silver-gilt cup filled with forty pounds in gold.'

'Well, what of it?' she said, unimpressed. 'She was gracious enough, wasn't she?'

'Oh she smiled and took everything that was offered, but I did expect Robert to single me out after all that, bring me especially to her notice, acknowledge our relationship. These things make a difference. A word from him would have meant a great deal. But did he trouble himself? Not he. Just stood there, proud as God Almighty, and not a single sign. I might have been the dirt under his feet instead of his brother-in-law. It could have been the making of me. Anyone can see at a glance how besotted she is with him.'

Too late he remembered to whom he was speaking. He shifted his feet awkwardly. 'I'm sorry, Amy, but it's true enough, you must know it by now.'

'Yes, I know it.'

He had been too absorbed in his own grievance to take much

257

heed of her. Now he looked more closely and noticed how thin she had become these last months, that there were dark shadows under her eyes. He said uneasily, 'How are you feeling? Have you seen a physician since I was last here?'

'Yes. Robert sent Dr Julio to me.'

'Julio, eh? That must have cost him something. What did he say?'

'Not much. He has given me some medicines.'

'They're saying some queer things about him in Oxford.'

'What kind of things?'

He hesitated and then plunged in. It was not that he believed a word of it, but he was not unwilling to do Robert a bad turn. 'You know what people are. They say he is an expert on all kinds of poisons, and has made a close study of them.'

So it was true. All those phials upstairs, hidden in her chest . . . poison. And he had been sent to her by Robert who wanted to be rid of her. She caught her breath with a little gasp and he turned to her curiously.

'It's all nonsense I expect. He is Italian and there is always prejudice. You don't want to let it worry you too much.'

She could not help it. She felt the sweat break out all over her. She gripped her hands together. 'John, I'm frightened.'

'Frightened? Of what? Of Dr Julio?'

'No, not of him.'

'What then?'

'I think I'm being watched.'

'Watched?' he gaped at her in surprise. 'By whom?'

'I don't know. But there were two men walking in the grounds.'

'When?'

'A few days ago. Jennet saw them first and then I did. Fussy flew at them and one of them kicked him.'

'Probably new servants, gardeners perhaps or workers on the estate engaged by Anthony Forster.'

'No,' she said obstinately. 'They were strangers. I asked Mrs Owen. She keeps a record of all the servants at Cumnor. She knew nothing about them. They were spying on me, I'm certain of it.'

'Oh come, Amy, this is ridiculous. Why on earth should any-one be spying on you? It's all imagination. You're working your-self into a panic when you'll believe anything.'

Clumsily he tried to soothe her, while his devious mind busily explored the situation, wondering if there was anything to be gained for himself out of it. It was not until he was riding away that he remembered the two men he had met in the taproom of the inn at Oxford, and it struck him that they could be the two whom Amy was so sure she had seen. They had been quietly dressed individuals, superior servants he had thought them, hangers-on to some great lord. They had casually invited him to crack a bottle with them. Always short of money, he had readily agreed and they had spent a moderately convivial evening. He had been slightly fuddled with the wine they kept pouring into his cup, but he did remember how they had plied him with questions about Amy and Cumnor. He had thought it the usual avid curiosity about everything that concerned Robert. Now he was not so sure.

His brother-in-law had enemies, God knows – anyone in his position would. Enemies who would not scruple to stoop to anything that would pull him down. Was it just possible that one or other of those who detested him and wanted him out of the way could be plotting to injure Amy and then plant the blame on her husband? An accusation of murder could ruin him and ruin John Appleyard's future too, unless . . . No, damn it! He was not such a villain as to mix himself up in anything of that sort, and he wished his half-sister no harm. But it might be just as well to keep a watching brief, have a foot in both camps. Who knows, they might even be willing to pay . . . then he smiled to himself. If he played his cards carefully, he could probably persuade Robert to be even more forthcoming. It would give him great pleasure to have a hold over his high and mighty brother-in-law, something that would wipe that damned superior look off his face and make him shake in his expensive shoes. Should he warn Amy . . . or Robert? No, they might suspect him of having something to do with it. Better to wait and see which way the cat was going to jump . . . if it jumped at all.

When Robert returned to Windsor with Elizabeth he found two frantic letters from his wife waiting for him, so incoherent and badly written he could not make head or tail of them. She was terrified of something, that was obvious, but of what, for God's sake? Dr Julio called on him and was guarded in his report.

'Your wife is very sick, my lord, but this is a malady that kills slowly. It could be this year, or the next, or the year after.' He spread his hands. 'Only God can tell. I have done what I can but I fear she does not trust me. She would be much comforted if you were to visit her.'

But that he could not do, not just now at any rate. Elizabeth was tender and loving, their relationship had deepened. He did not want to do anything to damage it. Matters had gone swimmingly in Scotland after an initial setback: Cecil had negotiated most favourable terms in Edinburgh, the Queen of Scots was to relinquish the Royal Arms of England, France would withdraw her troops and acknowledge Elizabeth's title to the throne. England's prestige in Europe soared, and with it the reputation of Lord Robert Dudley. Everything was going so well. Surely it would make little difference if he waited a few more weeks before riding to Cumnor.

On a morning in September Amy made up her mind. All during that summer, during the tedious days and long sleepless nights, she had been beset by sick fancies, swaying this way and that. Sometimes she hated Robert and had a passionate desire to punish him, sometimes she wept grievously, mourning her lost love. There were days when she seemed to live in a dream – walking Fussy, reading a little, working on her embroidery that grew so slowly, talking to Alice and Mrs Owen, dining or supping with them, playing a game of cards, Gleek or Primero or Pope Joan – and she was not really there at all. She was seeing Robert with Elizabeth, kissing her or making love to her, and with a tearing at the heart she would remember moments of past tenderness when he had thought only of her.

She wrote to him, beseeching him to come to her, but there was no answer and she did not even know where he was or whether the letters had ever reached him.

One day she took out the untouched phials that Dr Julio had sent her and looked at them. What would happen if she swallowed them all? Would she die at once or would it take hours, even days? If it was poison as she firmly believed, then would they think that Robert had murdered her, or would she simply be giving him the freedom he craved, freedom to marry Elizabeth and make himself King. At one moment anger burned in her so that she wanted him to suffer, wanted to be revenged for all he had done to her. Then at other times she would fall on her knees, weeping and praying to God that the disease that devoured her would kill her quickly so that she need make no choice.

It was the Fair at Abingdon that finally decided her. Jennet had been full of it. There were to be plays, bear-baiting, cock-fighting, all kinds of rarities in addition to the usual booths and sideshows.

She said, 'You must go. You've scarcely left the house all this summer. All the servants can go.'

'But what about you, my lady? We can't leave you here alone.'

'It will only be for a few hours. I can look after myself for that short time.'

'But you're not well. I don't like to go.'

'Nonsense, Jennet. You must go, I insist.'

They argued about it until her insistence became feverish. She wanted by now to get them all out of the house. She wanted to be alone to carry out what she had determined on. The other servants were eager enough for a day's holiday. She gave them lavish gifts of money to buy fairings for themselves and their sweethearts, and tried to persuade Alice and Mrs Owen to go with them.

'Sunday is the day all the vulgar are there,' objected Alice. 'I don't care to mix with people of that kind.'

They could not understand why she kept pressing them and very nearly quarrelled over it. In the end the offended Alice stalked off to her own part of the house and Mrs Owen, who was a kindly woman and sympathetic towards Amy, put a hand on her arm.

'Don't worry about her. She'll get over it, Lady Dudley. If you find yourself lonely all on your own, come and sup with me this evening. I shall welcome your company.'

'Thank you. I will do that.'

The merry laughing company went off very early on the Sunday morning. Only Jennet lingered, looking at her anxiously.

'I still don't like it, my lady. Are you sure you will be all right. You won't overtire yourself.'

'Why should I? I'm going to have a quiet day with Fussy. Now you go and enjoy yourself.' Impulsively she gave the girl a kiss. 'You deserve it, Jennet. You've been so good to me.'

'Oh my lady, it's only what you deserve. I'll not stay late. I will be back early.'

'Now you're not to fret about me. Bring me back a ginger-bread baby. I remember so well how Father used to buy them for me at Wymondham Fair when I was a child.'

'I will, my lady. I'll bring two, one for you and one for Fussy.'

When it came to the actual moment, it was harder than she had imagined. It was a mellow September morning when she walked the little dog in the park. The grass had never seemed so green or the trees more lovely. She went back to the house at noon trembling, her resolution shaken. Then, as she climbed the steep stairs to her bedchamber, she thought of the last time Robert had come, a brief visit on his way to somewhere else. She had clung to him weeping, here on this landing, beseeching him to stay with her. He had been brusque, anxious only to be gone, to be rid of her.

She sat down at her dressing-table frightened at what she was going to do. She was deliberately destroying herself, the crime against God and the Church. That was what she had always been taught. She knelt down and asked for forgiveness and then comforted herself with a new thought. After all she didn't know for certain. 'I'm only doing what Robert wants me to do,' she said to herself. 'I believe he wants me to die and is using this means, but maybe I am wrong.'

She stared at herself in the mirror, at the pale thin cheeks, the eyes in dark hollows, the hair dry and lifeless that had once been so rich and luxuriant. His squirrel, he used to call her, his little red-brown squirrel. Tears of self-pity were rolling down her cheeks. She brushed them away and wondered if he would come and look down on her dead face. She would make herself beautiful for him. She put on her newest gown of rich satin with gold-embroidered gauze sleeves, and smoothed her hair under the jewelled hood he had sent her in the New Year. She put the amethyst chain round her neck and caught sight of something else in her trinket box, buried beneath the many gifts he had showered on her. She took it out, a golden rose, worth little compared with the rest but rich in memory of the love that had come with it . . . 'Take thou this rose, O rose . . .'

With trembling fingers she unstoppered the phials and swallowed them one after the other. She had expected something vile-tasting, burning, corrosive, but strangely it was not, only faintly bitter with an aromatic flavour, almost pleasant. She lay down on the bed with the golden rose clutched in her hand and waited to die.

A long time afterwards she thought she heard someone calling her. The opiates Dr Julio had distilled so carefully were beginning to take effect. She struggled to sit up and her head swam as if she were lost in mists of sleep. She felt heavy, each limb weighted with lead. It was an enormous effort to move, like a nightmare when you are paralysed. Fussy was barking furiously and scratching at the door. She heard someone call her name again and her drugged mind thought it was Robert. He had come in answer to her pleading, so she must go down to meet him. She dragged herself off the bed and moved inch by inch to the door. Half falling, stumbling, she opened it and, still clinging to the latch, moved out on to the landing. She wanted to answer but her tongue was thick and heavy in her mouth. Dimly she saw a tall figure in the hall below. She tried to say, 'I'm coming, Robert, I'm coming.' She swayed forward, her foot slipped on the worn stone. Giddily she put out a groping hand but there was nothing to grip. Her fingers slid helplessly along the wall. She could not keep her balance. The floor seemed to rise up to meet her and she pitched head first down the steep stone stairs into darkness.

In the hall the two men looked at one another, then one of them knelt down and bent over her. A golden rose lay by her outstretched hand. He looked at it curiously but he touched nothing for he was a man experienced in death. He shook his head significantly at his companion and got up. Fussy had nosed his way through the bedroom door and came running down the steps. Growling fiercely he hurled himself at the two men and the tall one gave him a vicious kick. He fell back whimpering, then crawled to his mistress's side. The two men left as silently and unobtrusively as they had entered. Their work had been done for them.

Kew, Saturday, 14 September 1560

Confinement and anxiety were fretting unbearably at Robert's
nerves. The brief hope aroused by Cecil's visit had faded. All
night his restless mind had roved back over the last two years so
that when he had woken on Friday morning he had a fierce
headache, and by midday his old enemy had taken possession of
him. His body ached unendurably as he sweated and shivered
with fever. It made him short and irritable with Tom Blount
when he arrived in the early afternoon, having ridden at breakneck speed the forty-odd miles from Cumnor. Later he apologized
for his brusqueness.

'Don't mention it, my lord,' said Blount sympathetically. 'I
understand what you must be going through.'

There had been little to add to what he already knew,
only that Bowes had been wrong about one thing. Amy had not
even kept Jennet with her on that fatal Sunday. According to
Alice Odingsell she had been insistent that the reluctant girl should
go to the Fair. Jennet had returned early before the other servants because she was anxious about her mistress.

'Incidentally she is taking care of the little dog, my lord.'

Robert nodded absently. There was one other matter which
his mind had seized upon hopefully. He took a turn or two
about the room. 'Tell me again about those two men seen in the
grounds.'

'There is nothing more to add, my lord. I questioned the other
ladies. It seems that Jennet saw them and then Lady Dudley. It
appears to have disturbed her, but neither Mrs Owen nor Mrs
Odingsell paid much heed to it. The park is large and there is a
path used by villagers on the outskirts. Strangers might well have
strayed accidentally from it.'

'Do you believe there is anything in it, Tom?'

Blount shrugged his shoulders. In his opinion his master was clutching at straws, hoping to shift the blame somewhere else and avoid the moral responsibility for his wife's suicide. It was natural enough in the circumstances. No man wants to bear the weight of another's death.

He said bluntly, 'They were never seen again and we have no knowledge of who they were or if they even existed. I fear that to mention it to the Coroner would seem like a distraction intended to confuse his judgment.'

'You are probably right.'

'There is one other thing, my lord.'

'What is it?'

'This.' Blount held out the golden rose. 'Jennet found it lying beside your lady as if she had been holding it in her hand. I thought it as well to bring it to you.'

'You did quite right.' He took it with a certain reluctance. His first gift. He had bought it . . . where for God's sake? It must have been at Bury St Edmunds on their journey to London . . . a boy in the grip of his first passion, routing out a jeweller and borrowing the money from Ambrose to pay for it. It brought Amy uncomfortably close. He put it on the table. 'Thank you, Tom. It was thoughtful of you.'

There was still much to be settled before Blount returned to Cumnor that same evening.

'When is the inquest to be held?'

'On Monday, my lord.'

'When it is over, see to her burial for me, Tom. Everything in order and in good state as befits my wife. You understand? Spare no expense.'

'I will see to it, my lord.' He hoped to God the verdict would not be suicide, otherwise there might be grave trouble with the church authorities, but he would not worry his master with that now.

After he had gone Robert sent Tamworth to London to fetch a certain remedy prescribed for him by Dr Julio. It was bitter as gall but it had proved effective in the past. When the young man returned he brought with him a pile of correspondence that had accumulated in his absence.

He felt too ill to open it until noon on Saturday when the medicine had begun its work and the fever had abated a little. He did not dress but huddled himself into his velvet gown and

266

turned to his letters. There was much connected with his work as Master of the Horse. He put it aside to be dealt with later. The rest was not calculated to aid his recovery. Many were politely phrased notes of condolence, some of them sympathetic from those who knew him well, others merely formal. But by far the greater number were unsigned, vile, indecent, abusive, calling him murderer, lecher, whoremonger, spattering him and Elizabeth with filth until he was sickened.

'Take this trash away and burn it,' he said to Tamworth when he came to let Cabal out for his exercise. But try as he would he could not completely thrust them out of his mind.

Tamworth had brought also a parcel of recently ordered books. He chose one that had been sent from Italy, a difficult text that would require all his attention. Somehow he must try to keep his mind occupied.

It grew very late. He lay on the day bed; Cabal stretched beside him on the hearth was dreaming with little snorts and whimpers. The fire lit against the chill of the evening was dying and the candles guttered. He trimmed them and went on reading, knowing well enough that sleep was impossible.

When he heard the door open, he did not turn his head. He said, 'I don't need you any more, Dick. You can go to bed.'

There was no answer and, surprised, he looked up. The book went crashing to the floor as he rose to his feet. She must have borrowed one of her maid's plain riding dresses. The hood of the long cloak partly concealed her face but he knew her instantly and was speechless, his throat choked with mingled wonder and joy, only half believing what he saw.

She said, 'They told me you were sick.'

'I am better today.'

'Have you proper remedies?'

'Yes. Dick fetched them for me.'

The words mattered nothing. They were devouring one another with their eyes but they made no move.

Elizabeth pushed back the hood and he saw how pale she was. She said with only the faintest trace of feeling in her tone, 'Did you kill her, Robert?'

'No.'

'Can I believe that?'

'It is the truth.'

267

She stared at him for a long moment. If she could not trust this man to whom she had given her love, then it seemed to her that she would never trust anyone again. It was a bleak and frightening prospect.

She said at last in a whisper, 'I had to know,' and swayed a little, putting out a hand to support herself against the door. He was by her side in an instant.

'I should not have come,' she murmured, leaning on him.

'But you have and I shall thank you for it as long as I live. Did anyone recognize you?'

'I don't think so.' She smiled faintly. 'These clothes are not mine and Fanny came with me. She is with Dick Tamworth downstairs.'

'You have ridden here alone?'

'Only from Richmond. It is not far.'

She let him guide her to the day bed and he knelt to replenish the fire, building it carefully log by log until it began to flare, before he turned to her.

'Why have you come?' Then he saw she was holding the golden rose in her hand.

She said, 'What is this?'

He was tempted to lie but, with her eyes fixed on him, he knew it was impossible. He said with difficulty, 'It was found in her hand when she fell.'

'Your gift?'

'For God's sake!' he burst out. 'I was a boy then.'

'In love for the first time.' She looked at it for a moment before she put it down again on the table. 'Do you know what happened?'

'Something of it.' He began to tell her what Blount had reported to him and she listened in silence until he had done.

'And that is all you know?'

'Yes.'

'And what do you think?'

He looked away from her. 'I don't know. There is so much that is difficult to explain.'

'Is there? It seems clear to me. I believe we killed her between us, you and I, Robin.'

'No, not you. You have nothing to blame yourself for.'

'Oh yes, I have. I share the guilt with you. I took you from her and so she destroyed herself.'

'No,' he said, denying it because he wished still to deceive himself. 'You don't understand. There were other reasons. She was sick. Dr Julio told me.'

'But not mortally. What do you know about a woman's heart? You are too easy to love, Robin.'

Amy had said that to him once and he did not want to remember it. 'She was not like that.'

'Women are not so very different from one another. How she must have hated me and loved you!'

He knelt upright beside her. 'Must it always come between us?'

She smiled a little and touched his face. 'You are fevered still. Now let us think practically. From what you have told me, I don't think the Coroner's verdict can be anything but accidental death.'

'I wish I was as sure. I wrote a note today to the Foreman of the Jury.'

'That was foolish. He will think you are using your high position to coerce him.'

'I know,' he said half ashamed. 'I should not have done it, but it has been agony to sit here and feel myself condemned for what I have not done. They will call me murderer.'

'Not to me they won't,' she said with a touch of hauteur. 'And I am Queen. If I show my trust and confidence, who will dare to raise his voice against you?'

'Oh God! I longed to be free for you, but not like this!' He buried his head in her lap.

'Do you grieve for her?'

'She was dear to me once.' His voice was muffled.

'We cannot escape its consequences, either of us.'

She let her hand stray amongst the thick brown hair and wondered if he realized yet how serious they were. For now, whether she wished it or not, she would be faced with a choice. If she married him, and it had crossed her mind more than once, it would be in the teeth of bitter opposition, not only from her Councillors but from her people. She knew what was being said about them, but it was not open, not to her face, and she could ignore it. Now all Europe would be free to speculate and deride the marriage of the Queen of England to a subject sprung from a family tainted with treason and who had murdered his wife for her sake. She had no illusions about it. It could cost her the throne. She had not been Queen for two years yet and she was still feeling her way. It had happened to others who let passion sway reason. She shivered and drew a deep breath, but it was a problem that somehow she would have to solve alone. She could expect no help from him.

She stirred uneasily. 'Robin, I should go.'

He raised his head. 'Not yet, please not yet. Stay a little longer. I have been so desperately alone.'

She knew something of loneliness and, because she loved him, she yielded. 'Not too long. I must not be missed.' He was still on his knees beside her and she smiled at him.

'Cecil brought me your gift. I think he expected me to send it back.'

'I had it made for you as a token, to remind you always . . .'

'And it will. It stands on my desk.'

Cabal got to his feet, stretching noisily and padding away from the heat of the fire so that she saw the book, lying where it had fallen on the floor.

'Tell me. What have you been reading?'

He picked up the heavy folio and gave it to her.

'*De Revolutionibus*,' she said and grimaced. 'Why something so indigestible?'

'It forced me to concentrate; besides I find the theories of this Nicolaus Copernicus fascinating. Do you know that he would have us believe that Ptolemy was wrong and that the earth revolves in orbit round the sun?'

She smiled at his momentary enthusiasm. 'That is too difficult for me. I am content to leave the planets where they have always been.'

'And yet you too consult the stars,' he said, with a hint of the old loving teasing.

She had an idea that they were talking merely to stave off what they both desired. They had, in different ways, been through an emotional ordeal and here, in this small homely indifferently furnished room, the Court and palaces seemed part of some other existence. For these few hours it was no longer queen and adoring subject but a woman and a man who loved and needed one another. When he reached up to kiss her, she did not resist. There was no violence in his caresses, only an infinite tenderness.

The dark fear that had haunted her for so long became unimportant. It had no place in this quiet room and there was peace and gentleness in their love-making. When his kisses grew more urgent she did not protest or cry out. She felt his hands touch her breasts and trembled, but this time the terror was purged and there was only a surging longing to know his strength, to feel herself one with him. It was not agony or tragedy or death, but a sweet and utter fulfilment of their love as natural and inevitable as night following day.

When she lay back against the cushions, there were tears in her eyes and he kissed them away.

'Why weep, dear heart?'

'For joy,' she murmured, and lay content and happy in his arms.

She drowsed for what seemed only a few minutes and woke to see a thin bar of light across the floor. Outside a faint murmur of birds told her that dawn was near. She must go now and quickly.

He had fallen into an exhausted sleep, his arm still around her, the dark head very close to hers. She looked at the handsome face, unguarded in repose, more vulnerable than he thought despite the strongly marked lines of pride and strength, traits she loved in him and would not have otherwise. She knew then that for months, years maybe, she would have to fight him as well as herself. This night in this room was separate, apart from their ordinary lives. Here she had not been Queen, here she had known the simple joy of a woman who loves and is loved, and it must be forgotten. It could never come again. If she let him conquer, then she would be lost. For as long as she could remember she had known one overpowering desire, to be Queen of England, and that she could not deny not even for him. She must be Queen first and woman afterwards, but would he be content with that? She knew him so well, ambitious, self-willed, passionate. He too had a dream and he would not give it up easily. She would have to be wise and clever beyond anything she had ever imagined if she was to keep him beside her as she must. He was hers now and for ever. She could not let him go.

Very gently she slid from under his arm but he was awake at once and caught at her hand.

'Is it time?'

'Yes.'

'One more kiss, beloved.'

'Only one.'

He held her by the shoulders, his eyes looking deep into hers. 'The future. It is all ours now.'

She knew what he was thinking but she gave him no promise, and when he would have kept her longer, she was firm with him.

'It is another day and we must face it. Don't come with me even to the door. Stay here, Robin. I shall tell Fanny and Dick Tamworth that I found you very sick and stayed to watch over you.'

'Would you lie for me?'

'It is not all lies.' She touched his cheek lightly. 'You must take care of yourself. You look wearied to death.'

'*Lassa, ch'io sola vinco l'infinito . . .*' he murmured.

Tired and alone I have conquered infinity. She smiled at him. 'Your Italian poet again.'

'My love, oh my love . . .' He caught her to him, kissing her passionately, eyes, cheeks, mouth, until she thrust him away from her.

'No, Robin, no. You must be sensible. If I do not leave now, if I am discovered, it will be the end for me as well as for you.'

She was hooking the high neck of her riding dress. He picked up the cloak and wrapped it around her, holding her close as if he could not bear to let her go from him.

Face to face, her breath on his cheek, she whispered, 'When it is all done with, then come back to me. I shall be waiting.'

Then she pulled the hood over her face and went swiftly without looking back.

He watched her go, love and exultation running through him like a fire. She loved him, she had come to him as he had hoped so desperately and thought impossible. He was dizzy with joy and triumph. Now surely there was nothing, nothing that could come between them.

Part Four
1558

'The bruits be so brim and maliciously reported here I know not where to turn . . . one laugheth at us, another revileth us, another threateneth the Queen. Some let not to say "What religion is this, that a subject shall kill his wife and the Prince not only bear withal but marry him."

Sir Nicholas Throckmorton, Ambassador in Paris,
to Sir William Cecil

Epilogue

❦

'Weak, frail, impatient, feeble and foolish,' that was what that damned Puritan John Knox had the impudence to write of women who ruled, only she had not been like that. She had been strong and resolute and never counted the cost until now . . .

For two days, ever since the news had reached her, Elizabeth had sat alone in her bedchamber at Whitehall, the door locked against everyone. She had not wept. Once she was so filled with rage that she could have willingly smashed everything within reach of her hand because it was so unfair, so unjust that he should die suddenly, unexpectedly, for no reason, when she was far away from him. But mostly she had sat quietly with the dreadful feeling that her heart was being torn out of her breast, that she was utterly bereft, that half of her life had gone with him and she could not go on living the rest of it alone.

They were hammering on the door, calling out to her, asking if she was sick, begging her to let them in, but all she said again and again was 'Go away'.

She sat motionless, remembering with an anguish that pierced too deep for tears. It was nearly thirty years since that day in his room at Kew and she had won. There had been other women . . . that she-wolf Lettice Knollys had trapped him into marriage, but what else could she expect? He was not a saint or a monk sworn to chastity. She had raged at him but always it had been there, the trust, the companionship, the sharing of laughter, the one man who knew her through and through, with whom she never needed to pretend, who was her relaxation, her joy, her rest.

They were growing positively frantic in the corridor outside. By the sound of it they were preparing to break the door down. Let them . . . they would feel the lash of her tongue when they did. It angered her that a Queen could not be allowed to mourn, to weep for what has gone.

She got up and went to the gold casket that she kept close beside her bed. She took out his portrait, painted in the first flush of youth, handsome and bold, as she always thought of him though he had aged and changed as she had.

She looked at it for a moment and then picked up the note he had sent her from Rycote, that dear place where they had loved and been so happy. She took a pen and wrote on it 'His last letter', then put it with his portrait. There, with the things she valued above all, it would lie until her own death.

She closed the casket and raised her head. Tired and alone I have conquered infinity. Let them come now when they will.

AUTHOR'S NOTE

This is the personal story of three famous people: one of them Queen Elizabeth the First, the second Robert Dudley, and the third Amy Robsart, who was in a sense their victim. It seemed obvious to me in studying their lives that Elizabeth and the man whom she loved until his death and afterwards must already have been well acquainted before their relationship emerged into the limelight and shocked Europe. The period between Robert Dudley's early marriage and Elizabeth's accession is one of the least documented so far as he is concerned, and therefore, within the framework of the known facts, much can only be conjecture. The theory of Amy's death is my own, based partly on the unproven allegations made against Robert Dudley in the infamous *Leyester's Commonwealth*, on an unsubstantiated accusation levelled against him by Amy's half-brother, John Appleyard, seven years after her death, and on recent medical investigation.